To Steve,

In early 1980, you saved me from the horro[r] that this book represents. I'll always remember that.

Thank you for being you, & for being such a good friend.

Bob Mari[...]

BORN TOO SOON

BORN TOO SOON

Robert Marion, M.D.

DOUBLEDAY & CO., INC.
GARDEN CITY, NEW YORK
1985

All of the characters in this book are fictitious,
and any resemblance to actual persons,
living or dead,
is purely coincidental.

Library of Congress Cataloging in Publication Data

Marion, Robert.
Born too soon.

I. Title.
PS3563.A659B6 1985 813'.54
ISBN 0-385-19833-7
Library of Congress Catalog Card Number 84-28682

PRINTED IN THE UNITED STATES OF AMERICA
FIRST EDITION

To Beth,
Who survived the writing of this book
And the living of it.

All this was a long time ago, I remember,
And I would do it again, but set down
This set down
This: were we led all that way for
Birth or Death? There was a Birth, certainly,
We had evidence and no doubt. I had seen birth and death,
But had thought they were different; this Birth was
Hard and bitter agony for us, like Death, our death.
We returned to our places, these Kingdoms,
But no longer at ease here, in the old dispensation,
With an alien people clutching their gods.
I should be glad of another death.

T. S. Eliot
"Journey of the Magi"

"I have always said that it is a mistake to start new interns at St. Anne's. It does something to their brains that seems irreversible. . . ."

Dr. Harold Channin
Pediatric Cardiologist
Boston Medical Center

PROLOGUE

Friday, June 15, 1984

The invitation arrived in the mail sometime in the middle of May. I was being invited to attend a symposium on neonatal medicine which was being held to celebrate the fifteenth anniversary of the opening of the Perinatal Intensive Care Center at St. Anne's Hospital in Cambridge, Massachusetts.

At first I didn't pay much attention to the invitation. I regularly received come-ons to attend symposia on a whole list of topics from an even longer list of places. But then it really hit home that this event was being held in honor of the Pit's fifteenth anniversary, for if the Pit were really fifteen years old, then it must be eight years since my internship there. I did some rapid calculations in my head and realized that this fact was indeed true. It had been nearly eight years since I, fresh out of medical school with absolutely no previous experience taking care of babies of any kind, first walked into that stainless steel, high-tech nightmare that had been dubbed "the snake pit" by the interns and residents who had preceded me. It had been eight years since I, not knowing the difference between an endotracheal tube and an umbilical artery catheter, had been expected to hold together a premature nursery filled with desperately ill newborns, with very little guidance and for up to thirty-six hours at a stretch without relief. And it had been nearly eight years since I, during my one-month rotation in the Pit, learned how to do some of the things necessary to hold that nursery together, how to make decisions even when I didn't have enough knowledge, and how to work with other interns so that things could get done for the patients and the unit could function like a well-oiled machine.

But the price I had to pay for learning all of these things nearly eight years ago was an expensive one. In order to succeed as an intern in the Pit, it was necessary for me to make a transition; a transition from the idealistic, sensitive observer I had been in medical school to the hardened, slightly jaded physician I had to become. The realization that this transition had occurred so quickly during that first month at St. A's would alter the rest of my internship year.

I was somewhat surprised that the invitation had been sent to me. The two other interns and I hadn't been exactly the kind of interns you'd want to invite back for a celebration. I reasoned that in making up the guest list they had just invited everyone who had ever worked at St. A's, and in fact that was exactly the case. It appeared that St. A's, its administration exuberant over having survived intact throughout a decade and a half in spite of having been associated with Dr. John Sullivan for a good deal of that period, had decided to reach out to and forgive all of those who had been led off the path of righteousness.

At first I had no interest in going. Sure, I loved to have the opportunity to get together with Ray and Terry and even Dan Berkowitz, but going to St. A's for an all-day symposium just didn't sound like the best way to do that.

But as I read the invitation more carefully, something caught my eye, something that did interest me a great deal. In addition to the all-day symposium to be held on Saturday, June 16, there was to be on Sunday the fourteenth annual "Premie Picnic." As always, all "graduates" of the neonatal intensive care unit were being invited to attend. And this fact intrigued me. All those creatures who had weighed less than the tubing and the hardware we had stuck on them and in them to monitor their every breath, their every heartbeat, and whose warming tables we stood over every day on rounds and lost sleep over every night we were on call, trying to prevent them from going to heaven, those creatures would now be eight-year-old boys and girls. It was a staggering thought. And I wanted to see what had become of them all.

But I didn't want to be the only one of us there. So I called Ray in Ann Arbor, who said he was just getting ready to call me to see if I wanted to go. And then I called Terry in Seattle, and she, too, wanted to attend. This would justify the trip; Terry, Ray, and I had not had a chance to all be together since we left Boston at the end of our internship year.

So with a lot of anticipation and a little excitement, I left my office in Jonas Bronck Hospital at a little after 5 P.M. on the weekend that had been specified on the invitation. I threw my overnight bag into the backseat of my Volvo and aimed the car for the Connecticut Turnpike.

BOOK I

I

Monday, June 28
Morning Rounds

It was amazing to me, that first morning, that those creatures were alive. That row of babies, none of whom had weighed more than two and a half pounds at birth, were lying on their warming-table beds, each with a tube through the nose, another tube in the mouth, cardiac monitor leads stuck to the chest and intravenous lines coming out of just about every arm and leg. My eyes fixed on one in particular; with every breath her little ribs clearly visible through the skin of her chest, her chest laboring at a rate of about eighty breaths a minute. Her hand was so small that someone, perhaps the child's mother or a nurse, had slipped a tiny hoop earring like a bracelet onto her wrist.

My musing was interrupted by the senior resident. "Please pay attention, Dr. Sharon. This is a busy place and we don't have time to screw around. We've only got enough time to go over these babies once and I'm not going to answer any questions later on information I'm covering now." I snapped to attention. The senior resident continued. "This is your patient," he said, pointing to the baby at whom I had been staring. "Baby Girl Summlitz." In a monotone he read a short history of this baby which he had written out on a piece of paper attached to the clipboard he clutched tightly in his left hand, using words I could barely understand and medical terms I had never heard before.

"She is the seven-hundred-gram product of a twenty-six-and-a-half-week gestation born ten days ago by C section for premature labor and fetal distress. She's had a rough course so far and Dr. Sullivan says the next two weeks aren't going to be easy for her. She's got bad respiratory distress syndrome requiring high pressure from the ventilator; we've been able to cut her F_iO_2 down from 100 percent to 70, but when we go lower she crumps. She has an umbilical artery line in as you can see." He pointed with the index and middle fingers of his right hand, which he had been rubbing against his thumb repetitively trying to establish some rhythm to his presentation, to some tubing coming out of her belly button. "And we're giving her hyperalimentation through it. Dr. Sullivan thinks that sometime last week she had an intracranial hemorrhage because she suddenly stopped moving around as much as she used to. As soon as we get her respiratory problems a little more stabilized, we'd better make plans to send her over to the Medical Center to get a CT scan, so we can see what we're left with, above the shoulders. But for now, we have to concentrate on the cardiorespiratory problems. Okay?"

Even though I had just about no idea what this resident, whose name was Frohman, was talking about, I answered, "Okay." In my four years of medical school, nothing had prepared me for anything like this. I had never even come this close to a premature baby. The premie nursery was strictly off-limits to medical students. There were two basic reasons for this: first, the neonatologists who ran the premie nursery didn't want inexperienced people, like medical students, anywhere near their sick patients; second, the directors of the pediatric teaching program didn't want to scare the students away from their specialty at so tender an age. And so here I was on the first day of my internship, a veritable babe in the woods, charged with the responsibility of caring for a tiny infant whom I couldn't even believe was human, and having to worry about manipulating the ventilator, figuring out what hyperalimentation was, and worrying about an intracranial hemorrhage while communicating with a resident who seemed to speak in a foreign language. But I said okay just the same.

Our morning work rounds that first day seemed to go on forever. Frohman had divided most of the thirty-odd patients who inhabited the Pit among us three new interns. He told us at the beginning of rounds, snapping his fingers for emphasis, that he had tried to divide the patients up fairly so that each of us would start off with the same number of "sickies," his term for relatively fresh or recently born premies, like Baby Girl Summlitz, who had multiple problems and truly required intensive care; "growers," babies who had successfully passed through the early stages of prematurity and now were hanging around the unit, trying to get themselves up to five pounds, the magic weight necessary for discharge; and "chronics," babies who had either experienced some complication of being born too soon, like a hemorrhage into the brain that could cause permanent brain damage (Baby Girl Summlitz was already destined to become a chronic after she graduated from sickie) or who were born with a birth defect that required surgical repair and a postoperative recovery period for survival.

The intensive care nursery at St. Anne's Hospital was an expansive, low-ceilinged room with babies arranged on either side of four rows like a baby parking lot. The sickest babies were placed in the first row, closest to the left wall. There were setups for four ventilators on either side of the first row. Therefore, the nursery could accommodate eight critically ill, ventilator-dependent babies at any given time. As the sick babies improved, they were moved toward the right. The second row was filled with sickies who had improved enough so that they could breathe without the use of the ventilator but who still required intensive care and close monitoring. The third row was home to most of the chronics, and the growers occupied the fourth row, closest to the large picture windows that looked out onto the southeast and the Boston skyline. Because of this arrangement, it was never necessary for a visitor to ask a nurse or a physician about the condition of a particular baby. All one had to do was check in which row that baby's warming table was situated.

The nursery, which was brightly lit both day and night by banks of fluorescent lights overhead, was kept at a constant temperature of seventy-two degrees, regardless of the season. There was an enormous amount of background noise, loudest in the first row, caused by the oxygen compressors and the "siss-pump, siss-pump" sound made as each ventilator took a breath, making it necessary to yell to be heard; but all this faded to just a murmur in the peaceful, healthy fourth row. The smell of hospital disinfectant permeated the unit, the nurses' station at the front of it, and the hallway through which one entered it. To this day, I gag when I smell the particular hand soap we were forced to wash with before and after any contact with patients.

The two other interns starting that day in the unit seemed as astonished as I by these creatures and by the activities going on in the first row. While Frohman was telling us the tale of Baby Boy Argos, a premie assigned to the female intern whose name was Terry Costa, the other intern, a man named Ray Brewster, leaned over to me and whispered, "Have you ever in your life seen anything like this?"

"No," I whispered back. "This is like 'Star Trek.' "

"I don't feel safe even touching these little guys. And they're going to expect me to take care of these fellas when I'm on call?"

"Pay attention!" Frohman shouted, looking up from his clipboard and snapping his fingers at us. "I've already told you we don't have a lot of time. We have to be finished by attending rounds. Sullivan gets angry if we're not at attending rounds on time. And one thing we're not going to do this month is make Sullivan angry. Now you guys pay attention. Even though Argos is Terry's patient, you're all going to have to take care of him at night. So you'd better listen now!"

Work rounds continued that morning as they would almost every other morning, except that they lasted much longer this first day. The longer rounds lasted, the more patients we met, and the more patients we met, the more and more depressed I became. The whole event that first morning took slightly over three hours. Half of that time had been spent covering the problems of the patients in the first row. I had tried very hard to listen, at least for a while, but had tuned out Frohman's monotone after the introduction of my second chronic. Terry and Ray had each apparently stopped listening earlier. All told, we wound up with eleven patients each. Ray got the sickest baby in the house, an unfortunate premie named Baby Girl Torres. A few babies were left unassigned to an intern. Frohman explained that these patients were being cared for by a nurse practitioner who was also the head nurse in the Pit.

When it was finally over Frohman said, "Okay, that's all of them. Attending rounds will start in Dr. Sullivan's office in exactly . . ." he looked at the wristwatch on his left wrist, "twenty minutes. You better get moving. There's a lot of scut work to do, and you don't have a lot of time to do it. And don't forget, you'd better not be late for rounds."

Ray, Terry, and I walked slowly back to the first row. "Nice guy!" Terry commented after Frohman had gone. "He has real fascist potential."

Back at the first row I picked up Summlitz's bedside chart. I tried to decipher the rows of numbers that represented the results of all the blood gases, tests that measure the amount of oxygen and carbon dioxide in the blood; the daily "inputs," or the amount of fluid infused each day through the umbilical artery line, a plastic catheter placed into the umbilical artery—the artery that travelled in fetal life from the placenta through the umbilical cord and into the fetus's circulation—and the "outputs," or the total amount of urine passed in a day; the calculations of total calories taken in; the daily blood electrolytes; and the transfusion record. I couldn't make out any rhyme or reason for what had been done and, I suspected, for what I was expected to continue doing. My depression intensified. I wanted to do a good job in my internship, I had worked hard and long, beating my brains out through college and medical school, in order to reach this day. And now it seemed clear to me that I was so unprepared for working in this nursery that I couldn't possibly do even a fair job, let alone a good one. I also was developing a loud banging in my head, as if there was a ventilator inside there going "siss-pump, siss-pump" against my brain. I looked up toward Terry who, just as bewildered as I, was trying to make some sense out of Baby Argos's bedside chart. Our eyes met and we both smiled. "This place has given me the biggest headache in the history of the world," she said.

I told her that I had a similar complaint and suggested we get the hell out of there. We picked up Ray who was struggling with the numbers in Baby Torres's chart and headed for the nurses' lounge where we had been told a coffee urn was situated. Here we were, only a few hours into our internships, and our problems seemed so insurmountable that we each were considering alternative careers in nonmedical fields. And we hadn't even met Dr. Sullivan yet.

II
Attending Rounds

After picking up cups of coffee in the nurses' lounge across the hall from the entrance to the nursery's nurses' station, we headed out to find the intern's on-call room which would be our home away from home for the next month. We entered it and found a room that was more like a closet. It was about seven feet long and five feet wide. The walls, painted that delightful, restful shade of institutional green so popular with hospital decorators, were of cinder block and bare. The room was windowless and furnished with a folding cot, a folding chair, and a nightstand on which was placed the room's most important item, a telephone. The place didn't look like much, but I knew there would be nights when getting between the sheets on that cot would be almost heaven.

We sat in the room, Ray and I on the bed, Terry on the chair, and silently sipped the coffee. Terry broke the ice. "Is it just that I'm stupid, or did you both have trouble figuring out what Frohman was talking about out there?"

"No," Ray answered. "I have to admit, I don't know what the hell he was talking about either."

"This is terrible," I said, sounding more depressed than either Ray or Terry. "It's only eleven-fifteen and we already seem to have more problems than we can deal with!"

"Look," Ray said, trying to cheer me up, "it's not so bad. At least we all understood the part about not being late to attending rounds or else the attending will go berserk."

I didn't laugh but Terry looked at her watch and said, "It's getting to be that time. We'd better go and find Sullivan's office."

Just then Ray's beeper went off. It screeched, "Dr. Brewster, call 3434, 3434 please." He dialed the number and was told that an intern was needed in the delivery room to attend a cesarean section. The intern who was on call at night got all the delivery room calls during the day. So Ray ran off to find the DR somewhere on the fourth floor of the hospital while Terry and I set off to find Dr. Sullivan's office.

It wasn't hard to find and, there, behind the desk on a swivel chair that allowed him to face the people seated on the couches arranged around the office, or to turn away from them and peer off through a picture window to downtown Boston, sat Dr. John Sullivan himself. Dr. Sullivan was looking directly at us. He rose to greet us but did not approach us or offer us his hand. Sullivan, who appeared to be in his early forties, had once had red hair, but it was thinning and there was a lot of gray now mixed with the red. He had a plain, pudgy face and did not look particularly unfriendly. He was sloppily overweight—not fat, but with enough of a beer belly to make his clothes look wrinkled and unkempt. As a greeting he said, "Please come in and take a seat. It's getting a little late. Isn't there supposed to be a third one of you? Or is Jennings trying to tell me that he thinks you two can do the job of three?" This seemed to amuse him.

"Ray Brewster is the third intern," Terry answered. "He just got a call to the delivery room."

"He went to the DR alone?" Sullivan asked.

"Yes, sir," Terry answered.

"Well, I guess we'll hear from him when he needs help. He is smart enough to know when he needs help, isn't he?"

"I think so," Terry answered.

"Good. Please take a seat." We sat on the couch directly opposite the door. "Is anyone else missing?"

There were two people already in Dr. Sullivan's office when we entered. The first was Frohman. He had seated himself upon the hard-backed chair next to the couch on which we sat, closest to Dr. Sullivan's desk. Frohman always seemed to be in motion. The finger clicking that he had used to punctuate and emphasize his remarks during work rounds continued now as he sat in Dr. Sullivan's office. In addition, his feet slid up and down the sides of the chair legs. I found myself beginning to itch just looking at him, and I couldn't get comfortable with him fidgeting. Of less than average height, he had a mass of kinky brown hair that seemed to stick straight up from the top of his head. His most outstanding feature, his eyes, were small, deep-set, and a little too close together.

The second person in the office was a woman who appeared to be about the same age as Sullivan. She was tall and thin and very plain in appearance, wore no makeup and a shapeless, unflattering surgical scrub dress. She was sitting in the second straight-backed chair directly opposite Dr. Sullivan's desk.

To Sullivan's question, Frohman, who would prove to be ever-helpful when it came to putting down one of his colleagues, answered, "Dan Berkowitz isn't here yet."

Sullivan's face contorted when he heard this name. "Berkowitz is supposed to be here this month?" he asked in an icy voice. "You must be mistaken, Dr. Frohman. Dr. Jennings has assured me that Dr. Berkowitz would not be assigned to St. Anne's this year."

"That's what's listed on the schedule, Dr. Sullivan," Frohman said, snapping his fingers at a more rapid pace now. He dug a copy of the house staff master schedule out of his ever-present clipboard and brought it over to Sullivan. "See?" he said, pointing to something on the page. "July, Dr. Berkowitz is assigned to the well-baby nursery."

"Dr. Frohman, it is already eleven-thirty. Since Dr. Berkowitz has not shown himself yet, I think we can assume that the schedule is incorrect." Frohman returned to his seat, and his fidgeting started up again. "So let's begin. I am Dr. Sullivan. I want to first tell all of you some things about me and about this unit." He made a sweeping gesture in the direction of the intensive care unit. "I have been in charge of the nursery here at St. Anne's since the unit opened in nineteen sixty-eight. Before that I was the assistant director of the nursery at the Massachusetts General Hospital. I have been a neonatologist for over ten years now.

"Right from the beginning, it is important for each of you to understand that I am the boss here. Whatever I say goes. Neonatal intensive care is a complicated business. If everyone working here does what he or she wants, no one knows exactly what's happening with the babies.

My way, I know everything that's happening to each baby; I make all the decisions and nobody makes any mistakes. Got it?"

Terry and I were twitching uncomfortably during this speech but we both nodded our heads at the end of it. He seemed to be speaking entirely for our benefit. Neither Frohman nor the woman reacted.

"Right. Next piece of business: as Dr. Frohman may have told you, you are to have your morning work rounds with him completed by ten sharp. You'll have attending rounds with me starting here every day from ten to eleven, except Friday. On Fridays, I'll be coming with you on your work rounds. I want to know all the details, the numbers, and any other information on all the sick patients. When the babies are all squared away, I'll teach you some things about neonatology. But there will be teaching only if time permits. Therefore it is in your best interest to get here promptly at ten. In my unit, patient care comes first; teaching comes last."

Just then the office door opened and a resident walked in. He was tall and thin, had dark, wavy hair and a thick, black mustache. He wore a sardonic smile on his lips and it had clearly been a few days since his face had last seen a razor. His clothes looked as if he and at least one other person had slept in them. I knew from the pained look on Dr. Sullivan's face that this had to be Berkowitz.

"Sorry I'm late, Dr. Sullivan," he said, still with that smile on his face. "I got caught in some fierce traffic coming over on Mass. Ave." Terry and I smiled at his audacity. Sullivan, Frohman, and the woman did not.

"Dr. Berkowitz, you are nearly four hours late!" Sullivan enunciated. "You know how I feel about people being late to work here. And also, if you are going to work here, you'd better make sure to do something about your appearance. I will not tolerate sloppiness!"

Berkowitz's grin broadened during this little tongue-lashing. He seemed calm and sure of himself. "I'm happy to see you again too, Dr. Sullivan," he said. "I'm late because I was on call last night in the cardiac surgery ICU at the Medical Center. I was up all night with a sick baby. I was only able to leave a half hour ago. Is that okay?"

"No it is not okay!" Sullivan answered. "When you are assigned to work in my unit, it is your responsibility to be here, not in the cardiac ICU. As I recall, tardiness was also one of your problems the last time too, wasn't it, Dr. Berkowitz? You seem to have a problem handling your responsibilities."

Berkowitz laughed at this. "I have trouble with responsibilities?"

"Sit down, Dr. Berkowitz," Sullivan ordered. "Sit down and shut your mouth! You've already wasted enough of our time." Continuing to smile, Berkowitz took a seat on the unoccupied couch opposite Sullivan's desk. I didn't know exactly what had happened between these two in the past, but I was dying to find out.

Sullivan tried to continue. "Now then where was I?"

Berkowitz interrupted him. "Did you give the new interns the 'I'm the boss here and what I say goes' speech yet? I always liked that one!" Terry and I laughed but Sullivan stared us down. I already loved Berkowitz.

Sullivan continued, ignoring Berkowitz. "I'd like to get to know something about each of you. Dr. Frohman, why don't you start? Tell us something about yourself."

Frohman's face turned red. His hair seemed to stand up a little straighter from his head than it usually did. The rhythm of his fidgeting became more rapid. He was momentarily speechless. When he began talking, it was in an embarrassed whisper. "My name is Simon Frohman. I went to Boston University both as an undergraduate and for medical school. I hope to do a fellowship in Allergy and Immunology when I finish my residency. Anything else you want?"

"No," Sullivan answered. "That was fine, Dr. Frohman. Kathy, why don't you go next?"

Without hesitation, the woman in the green scrub dress began. "Okay, John. I am Kathy O'Connell. I come from Burlington, Vermont, and went to nursing school at St. Mary's College for Women there. I started working as a neonatal nurse at Mass General, just after Dr. Sullivan came to be assistant director there. I came over to St. Anne's with Dr. Sullivan when this unit opened. Dr. Sullivan and I have worked together closely for over ten years now. In addition to being the nursing supervisor of this unit, I am also the primary caretaker for a few of the patients. I can do this because I received my pediatric nurse practitioner degree from Boston University four years ago.

"I want to tell you all that my nurses and I are here to carry out Dr. Sullivan's orders. He is the man in charge and, as such, he's my boss, and the boss of all of my nurses. If you interns work well with Dr. Sullivan, you will find that the nurses will cooperate with you fully. But if you take it upon yourselves to make decisions, or to get out of line, we'll all give you such a hard time that you won't get finished with your scut work until midnight. So I'd suggest you stay in line."

"Okay," Dr. Sullivan said. "Thank you, Kathy. Now one of you," he said, nodding toward Terry and me. When neither of us began, he pointed a finger toward me and said, "How about you?"

I pulled at the hairs of my mustache and tried to get my thoughts together. "I'm Bob Sharon," I finally said. "I was born in New York, went to Yale as an undergraduate, and did medical school at Einstein in the Bronx." I felt like a jerk. I hadn't done anything like this since grade school. "Do you want me to give my vital statistics or can I stop now?"

"You can stop now," Sullivan said in an unfriendly tone. "That's really . . ."

"Dr. Sullivan, can I ask a question?" Berkowitz asked, interrupting Dr. Sullivan.

"What is it?" Sullivan asked, sighing.

"I want to ask Bob when he graduated from Yale and Einstein. I also went to Yale and Einstein. And I was also born in New York. It's just like he was my little brother."

"God forbid," Sullivan muttered under his breath. Then out loud he said, "Dr. Berkowitz, I think you can hold questions like that until after attending rounds are over." Sullivan next pointed to Terry and said, "You're on."

"I'm Terry Costa," Terry began with a little smile. She was an attractive woman with shoulder length dark, curly hair. She had pleasant features and deep blue eyes. She wore jeans and a blue shirt. "I was born in New Jersey, went to Cornell as an undergraduate and then to the University of Washington in Seattle for medical school. My hobbies include sewing and baking, and if I were Miss America I'd try to end wars and poverty throughout the world." Her facial expression never changed during this little speech. Berkowitz and I began to laugh, but Sullivan didn't seem to get it, although he laughed along with us slightly before going right on with business. "Okay, Dr. Frohman. Tell me who's sick."

Frohman looked down at his clipboard which was always either in his lap or clutched tightly under his arm. "I guess the sickest baby we have is still Baby Torres. Should I review his history?"

"Please do," Sullivan answered.

"Okay. He is the 690-gram product of a twenty-six-week gestation born by C section for fetal distress to a twenty-nine-year-old woman. He is now about forty-eight hours old and has severe RDS. He is currently on high ventilator settings and continues to have poor oxygenation. . . ." Frohman droned on and on in his monotone, as he had done during rounds, speaking in words that I didn't understand, reciting numbers that may have had some meaning to Sullivan but were certainly meaningless to me. When Frohman had finished his presentation, Sullivan, who now looked sleepy, arose from his swivel chair and said, "Let's go see him."

We followed our leader into the nursery. When we arrived at the warming table we found Mr. Torres, the baby's father, standing near the bedside, looking frightened. He also looked as if he wanted to ask a question. Kathy took the nurse aside who was caring for the baby, a red-haired woman, and told her, in a whisper, to get rid of the father. This nurse led Mr. Torres away. Sullivan didn't say a word to this man and, in fact, seemed uninterested in Baby Torres until the nurse and Mr. Torres were out of the nursery. But as soon as they were out of sight we approached the infant who was lying on her back. Her skin, where it wasn't covered with tape or other paraphernalia, was thin, translucent. I could see the tiny blood vessels through it. Her eyes were covered with gauze pads to protect them from damage from the harsh, bright, blue fluorescent "bili-lights," which lower the level of the chemical bilirubin in the blood. Bilirubin, the principal breakdown product of red blood cells, is the cause of jaundice. Most babies get a little jaundiced because their liver, the organ responsible for clearing bilirubin from the blood, is often not mature enough during the first three days of life to perform this function. Although this slight elevation of bilirubin usually causes no long-lasting adverse effects, babies who are born very prematurely or babies with certain rare pathologic conditions may develop severe brain damage. So infants like Baby Torres were kept under these harsh lights as a prophylactic measure from the time of their birth and were thus fitted with these special gauze pad goggles.

There was a tube in the baby's mouth that led down the trachea and was attached outside the mouth to coiled tubing that led to the ventilator, the breathing machine that was pushing oxygen into the baby's lungs. There was a tube in her nose that led to her stomach and that allowed drainage of excess air that had escaped from the ventilator. Both of these tubes were taped to her upper lip and nose with so much tape that most of the baby's midface was obscured. She had three cardiac monitor probes glued to her chest, a heat sensor probe stuck under the skin of her right shoulder, and an intravenous line in her right arm. In the place where her belly button should have been was an umbilical artery line. This creature was more plastic tubing than she was baby.

Sullivan began to examine the infant. From out of a green plastic pouch that was attached to his belt, he pulled his wallet, a toothbrush, a collapsible cup, and finally a stethoscope. Replacing everything else in the pouch, he put the stethoscope over the infant's heart. Although it was a special "premie" scope, a miniature of the regular adult model, it still covered a large part of the baby's chest. After listening and watching the baby's chest movements for a while, Sullivan turned to the ventilator and began altering the settings. As he worked, he said matter-of-factly, "This baby has very poor lung compliance. His only chance for survival is for us to be very vigorous with his respiratory therapy. If we're not, he'll simply die a slow, bad death." Although he had just examined the entire infant, including her genitalia, Sullivan still referred to the child as if it were male. This was standard procedure. We were to find that Sullivan referred to all babies as "him." No one ever corrected him.

Sullivan continued fiddling with the ventilator settings. He would change the dials, take another look at the baby's chest, then fiddle some more. "What are you aiming to do with these adjustments, Dr. Sullivan?" I asked.

He didn't answer but kept right on fiddling. The only person to have any response to my question was Kathy, and all she did was shoot me a look that suggested I had broken one of the Ten Commandments. I thought Sullivan simply hadn't heard me, so I repeated the question a little louder, "What are you aiming for?"

Sullivan then looked at me angrily and said, "Look, I thought I told you, teaching is done after the babies are all taken care of. I'm trying to concentrate here. Don't ask any more questions!"

I had never heard a response like that and was truly astounded. Terry also seemed surprised but Kathy and Frohman both seemed to share Sullivan's contempt for a lowly intern who interrupted rounds with a question. Berkowitz walked over to me after Sullivan had gone back to the ventilator and placed his hand on my shoulder. "Welcome to the Snake Pit, Bob," he whispered in my ear.

The rest of rounds passed unremarkably. Sullivan never did answer my question. After rounds had finished, Terry and I set off to find the cafeteria. While waiting for the elevator, we ran into Ray, who appeared to have survived his first trip to the delivery room.

"What happened down there?" I asked.

"A scheduled C section. They always have to have a pediatrician at the sections in case anything sort of goes wrong."

"Did anything go wrong?" Terry asked.

"No, everything went fine. And that's pretty lucky too, because if anything had gone wrong that baby would have been screwed. I mean, I don't exactly know what I'm supposed to do!"

This was a fact that had occurred to me too. I had never resuscitated a dying baby, or put an umbilical artery catheter in, or even started an IV on anything as small as a full-term baby, let alone something the size of Baby Torres! Yet here I was, expected to go down to the delivery room to use my "expertise" to save dying babies. And it appeared that prospects for learning anything useful were slim, at best.

The elevator arrived and we got in. "How were attending rounds?" Ray asked.

"Great, if you're a fan of fascism," Terry said.

"What do you mean?" Ray asked.

"Well, between Sullivan, Kathy, who's the head nurse, and Frohman," Terry said, "it was like we were on a visit to the Hitler family." Terry filled Ray in on all the policies and attitudes of Dr. Sullivan. We had gotten out of the elevator on the first floor and had followed the crowd into the cafeteria.

"I don't understand why you guys are so upset. He sounds like a real sweetheart to me!" Ray said, and cracked up almost immediately.

"Well, there seems to be at least one good person here," I said. "That Berkowitz seems nice."

"Who's Berkowitz?" Ray asked.

"He's a senior resident. I think I heard Frohman say he's supposed to be working in the well-baby nursery, wherever that is," Terry said.

"Sullivan seems to hate him a lot," I said. "It was pretty funny when he came in four hours late and said he hit some traffic."

"Well, so maybe the month here won't be all so bad," Ray said. "All you need is one good person. And besides, the food smells sort of good."

We got our trays, picked up our meat loaf, and sat at an empty table. "I hope things back at the Medical Center are better than this!" Terry said when we were settled. "I forced my husband to leave Seattle so we could get a taste of this superior Boston medicine. If the place turns out to be filled with schmucks like Sullivan, I'll die or my husband'll kill me. I don't need to be overworked and mentally abused too!"

"I don't even need to be overworked," Ray added. "I've got enough problems." He didn't elaborate on this.

We stumbled through the rest of that first day, not doing anything that could harm the patients but, likewise, not doing anything helpful either. We soon realized that the nurses had the place under control and ran their patients like well-oiled machines. It also became apparent that the nurses looked upon us as people who were present only to interrupt their precise routines and to interfere with their care of the premies. I wasn't sure if this was due to the fact that we were inexperienced interns or whether we were just doctors in general.

At around six o'clock, I tried to sign out my patients to Ray, who was not exactly thrilled with the idea of being on call the first night of the rotation. He seemed to cheer up a little when the resident with whom he'd be sharing night call for the month showed up. She was an unbelievably beautiful senior resident named Lauren Feinman, with long, flowing honey-blond hair, a beautiful tan on a flawless complexion, and a terrific body. When she first entered the nurses' station while I was signing out, Ray's eyes nearly popped out of his head. "I think I'm in love" was all he could say.

By six-thirty I was turning my car onto Memorial Drive, heading west for the short trip back to my apartment in Watertown. By six-forty, the headache I had been working on all day had faded away to a memory.

III

St. A's

St. Anne's Hospital for Women had been constructed by the Catholic Archdiocese of Boston in the late 1930s. St. Anne's was not the first maternity hospital in Boston and, in fact, the Boston metropolitan area really had no need at that time for another hospital built specifically for the care of pregnant women and their babies. However, St. Anne's did fill a niche: it was and, to this day still is, the only maternity hospital in New England to have been built and run entirely by the Catholic church. In the early days, St. A's was an institution filled to the brim with happiness; healthy women came here to deliver healthy babies in a cheerful Christian environment. Soon after the hospital opened, Church officials, seeing that a need existed, began a well-baby clinic to ensure that none of the babies born in St. A's would ever fail to get regular pediatric care because their parents could not afford the cost of a private doctor's services. A home for unwed mothers was also constructed on a tract of land adjacent to the hospital building. Both of these were designed to complement the hospital's services. St. A's seemed like a low-pressure community hospital in a small, friendly town.

But a change began to occur in pediatrics and obstetrics in the mid-1960s, and this change revolutionized the way these two specialties were approached and practiced. Through technical advances it became clear that very premature babies who had previously been left to die, gasping for air until their hearts stopped beating, could be saved and go on to lead more or less normal lives. This revolution became known as perinatology, a branch of medicine that spanned the gap between obstetrics, the specialty concerned with the care of pregnant women, and pediatrics, the specialty dealing with diseases of infants and children. The perinatologist became the physician whose main concern was the welfare of the fetus and newborn.

Caring for premature babies required expensive equipment, lots of space, and a large staff. With proof that the premature infant could survive if given a chance, the administration of the hospital decided to allocate funds to alter St. A's so that these infants could be offered that chance. In 1968 the rebuilding began. The top two floors of the hospital, the fourth and fifth, were completely gutted, the fourth transformed into an ultramodern prenatal intensive care center and the fifth the intensive care nursery. By the time patients began to arrive in the spring of 1969, the perinatal center of St. Anne's Hospital was the most modern and efficient facility in all of New England.

The hospital became the main referral center for the greater Boston and mid-New England region. All women whose pregnancies had become complicated were sent to the new perinatal unit. Women in labor thirteen weeks before the baby was due to arrive were rushed in from the North Shore by ambulance. Women whose amniotic membrane, the sac that holds the fluid that protects the baby from injury and infection, had broken three days before and who were developing fever, a sure sign that the fetus was becoming infected, were transferred to St. A's for emergency cesarean sections. The fourth and fifth floors became a high-powered, ulcer-producing academic center, where there was far less happiness and where the staff turned over almost completely every year due to burnout caused by watching too many critically ill patients suffer and die.

With the opening of the perinatal center the hospital board, the governing body of St. A's, found itself facing an entirely new agenda of problems. There was the question of staffing. Since critically ill mothers and infants were now inhabiting the center, it became necessary to provide round-the-clock medical manpower. This meant only one thing: house staff, interns and residents who would be available twenty-four hours a day, had to be hired. Only a house officer would be crazy enough to work those kinds of hours.

It's not that interns and residents are actually crazy; it's just that, as the lowest people on the totem pole, they are the ones who are forced to take these jobs. "Someday," the house officer is told by the physicians in charge, "you will be an attending just like me and there will be interns and residents to cover your patients so that you can sleep comfortably at home in your own bed at night." In other words, working like a dog day and night are the dues, the price that must be paid for admission to the medical fraternity.

And so, the hospital board contracted with the New England School of Medicine and its main teaching arm, the Boston Medical Center, to provide house officers in pediatrics to care for the babies, and in obstetrics to care for the high-risk mothers. In return St. A's promised to provide teaching in critical care perinatology and pay some of the money for house staff salaries.

In addition to round-the-clock doctors, the hospital board also had to hire round-the-clock nurses. And the nurses had to have special training in the problems of the critically ill newborn and mother. They managed to find enough nurses, but only for two shifts a day initially, and each nurse had to work twelve hours a day rather than the usual eight hours most nurses worked. Interestingly, the nurses seemed to like this schedule and so, when a larger pool of nurses became available, the nurses continued working twelve-hour shifts, but only four days a week. Although this was more convenient for the nurses (they got three days a week off and still worked over forty hours), the long hours caring for those sick and dying patients rapidly took their toll. The nurses seemed to be the staff members most prone to burn out and occasionally they tended to lose their perspective on what was good for their patients and what was not so good.

Another problem facing the hospital board was that the institution seemed to have developed a split personality. All the time that the top two floors were moving ahead to become the best perinatal center in New England, the bottom three floors continued to function as they had since St. A's had been founded. It was still a place where healthy women could come to deliver healthy babies. The hospital board had decided, unofficially, that St. A's had to be run as if it were two separate facilities with one staff for the "new" St. A's (the perinatologists and pediatric and obstetric house staffs) and another for the "old" St. A's (the neighborhood obstetricians and pediatricians, all of whom were in private practice). As time passed it became clear that each group of physicians harbored, for a large number of reasons, deep-seated resentment and distrust for the other. A generation gap existed between the old and the new. This problem became exacerbated when the two centers had direct dealings with each other. For instance, when a private obstetrician's patient became critically ill and needed to be referred to the perinatal center for treatment, or when a formerly well baby became sick and was transferred to the intensive care nursery, the referring physician would resent, and the patient's family would not understand, the fact that their doctor was excluded from participating in the patient's further management.

Another problem with which the hospital board then had to grapple was the question of which patients should be saved and which should be allowed to die. And once the decision to save the patient was made, the question of what responsibilities the hospital had for caring for that patient in the future had to be addressed. In the days before the perinatal center, those questions were rarely raised: babies either were able to survive on their own or they died; if they survived, they either went home with their mothers or they were put up for adoption. But with the coming of the perinatal center, those ethical issues became extremely important. The hospital board answered the first question without difficulty; since many of the hospital board members believed that life was sacred, they decided that everything should be done to preserve life. The answer to the second question was not so easy. Although perinatal intensive care usually resulted in saving the life of a baby who would be able to lead a full, healthy, and productive life, it also created a disturbing minority of children who were left physically damaged. The damage ranged from mild, such as residual lung impairment manifesting as occasional bouts of childhood asthma, all the way to severe, so severe that the child would require full-time custodial care for the rest of his or her life. Most children still went home from the hospital with their parents whereas others were placed for adoption, but some of the severely damaged babies, babies who had been kept alive by the new technology, were totally abandoned. Their parents did not want them and foster homes would not accept them.

And so in addition to the perinatal center, it became necessary to establish some additional care centers. Pediatric nursing homes were needed. Full-time custodial care was an extremely expensive proposition and the hospital board found that it could not afford such an expense. But St. A's was lucky. Graduates of the Pit were welcomed at the Waltham Home. The Waltham Home, established in the late 1950s by Dr. Edward E. Jennings, a world-renowned pediatrician, chairman of the Department of Pediatrics at the New England School of Medicine and our boss during our internship, was generally considered the finest pediatric custodial care facility in all of New England.

When Ray, Terry, and I came to St. A's that early summer, the perinatal center was already seven years old. But these problems that the hospital was facing were still far from being resolved. It was in this environment that the three of us had to begin our pediatric training and learn all we could about neonatology.

IV

Tuesday, June 29

On Call

I didn't get much sleep the night following my first day as an intern; I was tense, and it was hot in my bedroom. But I still remember the little sleep I did get because it was during that night that I had, for the first time, a nightmare that recurred over and over again throughout my training. In the dream I am called to the delivery room to attend a routine cesarean section. I am handed a perfectly normal, apparently healthy baby by the obstetrician. And then, right in front of my eyes, in my hands, the baby dies. Nothing I do can make that baby breathe, or make that baby's heart beat. I am totally paralyzed.

I got out of bed early on Tuesday and jumped into the shower. I felt the start of the queasiness in my stomach and the slow, steady return of the headache I had lost the night before on Memorial Drive. These bad feelings intensified as I finished dressing and made the short car ride back to St. A's.

Ray was sitting in the nurses' station, slouching over a Styrofoam cup of coffee. "How was it?" I asked.

"Well, Bob, all things considered, it could have been worse." I was to find over that month that Ray was a cockeyed optimist, always seeming to find good in the most horrendous situation. Ray's appearance that morning betrayed his words; his dirty blond hair was sticking up all over the place, he needed a shave, his eyes were half closed, and his clothes were crumpled. But in fact that first night on call hadn't been so bad.

"I got a couple of DR calls but no keepers," he said, meaning no admissions to the Pit. "And everyone up here sure behaved themselves."

"How was it being on call with that resident?" I asked.

"Lauren?" he asked back with a smile. "Well, she's sort of disappointing. I went up and introduced myself and told her that it was nice to be working with her, and she took one look at me and said, 'It's nice meeting you, too, but I've got a headache now, so I'm going to my on-call room to take a nap.' And that was the last I heard from her for the rest of the night."

"She left you here all alone?" I asked, amazed. "All night?"

"Yep," Ray answered. "But it wasn't so bad. After all, I knew where she was in case of emergency. And the nurses told me what to do. They're real nice if you level with them and tell them you don't know shit. But they do have one problem."

"What's that?" I asked.

"Well, they seem to send blood gases off on every baby about every fifteen minutes. And even though I told them I didn't know what any of the numbers meant, they insisted that I hear the results at least. So one of them'd call, I'd answer the phone, she'd tell me the result on one baby and what she wanted to do about it. I'd say, 'That sounds fine,' and I'd hang up and try to fall asleep. But by the time I fell asleep, the phone would ring again."

"Did you get any sleep?" I asked.

"Nope. But I did learn a few things about how to change the ventilator settings when the carbon dioxide rises or the oxygen falls. So it wasn't so bad. That stuff's pretty important."

In fact, the monitoring of arterial blood gases was probably the most important part of the management of the premie sick with the lung disease called "respiratory distress syndrome" or "RDS." Because the premature baby's lungs are too immature to make the exchange of carbon dioxide and oxygen with the blood, an exchange that is necessary for life outside of the womb, the child must be ventilated by machine. So it is of maximum import that the people caring for the baby are sure that just enough oxygen gets into the baby's blood. Too much, and the baby may develop "retrolental fibroplasia," a disorder of the eyes that causes blindness. Too little, and brain damage may occur. By frequently sampling the blood, usually obtained through an umbilical artery catheter, the caretaker can be sure that the ventilator is doing its job. Fine tuning of the ventilator settings, that is, changing the oxygen concentration, or the pressure with which the oxygen is being delivered into the lungs, or the rate at which the ventilator is "breathing," has to be done very often. The ultimate goal is to slowly, but steadily, wean the baby off the supplemental oxygen and the ventilator.

During our month at St. A's, we were to learn that the nurses had been taught to watch the blood gases very closely. Ray's estimation that they sent blood on every baby every fifteen minutes was an exaggeration, but only a slight one. The nurses tried to send blood to the lab for evaluation at least once an hour on any baby who was being ventilated. Since, as Ray had said, the intern on call was required to be informed of every result so that the appropriate ventilator changes could be made, it was about impossible to do any sleeping, even on a relatively quiet night on call in the Pit.

And so Ray, who in fact had had a quiet night on call, went through that Tuesday unable to keep his eyes open.

My beeper went off about twenty minutes after Frohman had started work rounds. "Dr. Sharon, call 3434, 3434 please," it ordered. Rather than calling, I left rounds and ran off to find the delivery room.

I found the delivery suite, as it was called, behind a set of electric eye-operated double doors on the fourth floor. At the far end of the lobby which was situated behind those doors was a desk, behind which sat a clerk. I walked immediately to the desk and said, "I'm Bob Sharon."

The clerk, an obese woman of about forty-five with a bouffant hairdo, looked up from the copy of *People* magazine she was reading and said, "So what?"

"I'm from Peds," I answered, a little nonplussed. "I was paged."

"Oh yeah," she said, totally unmoved, her eyes darting back immediately to the pages of the magazine. "Elective section in three. You can change in there." She raised a pudgy, red-nailed index finger and pointed it in the direction of a door located next to the electric eye double doors, which was marked "Locker Room."

I ran into the locker room which resembled the inside of a shower; changed into a green scrub suit which would have fit someone who was six and a half feet tall and weighed over three hundred pounds, but not me; put on a mask that covered my nose, mustache, and mouth, a paper surgical hat under which I could barely fit my hair, which was pretty long in those days, and a pair of blue shoe covers; and ran into the delivery area. I found the obstetric attending, a Dr. Parris, and the resident who would assist him, scrubbing at the sink outside DR 3. I introduced myself. "I'm Bob Sharon," I said.

Parris looked me over. He said, "So what?"

"I'm the pediatric intern."

"Oh," he answered, looking me over again, "you a new one?"

"Yes. Started yesterday."

"Okay," he said in a friendly tone. "Would you do me one favor, Doctor?"

"I'll try," I said. "What is it?"

"Stay as far away from the baby as you can. Don't screw anything up!" With that, Parris turned off the water with his elbows and went into DR 3 to get gowned.

As I took his place at the sink and leisurely scrubbed with Fredericks, the resident, we looked into DR 3 as Dr. Parris, a short, squat man with a large nose and an olive green complexion, tried to flirt with the nurses who were trying to get him gowned and gloved for the operation. Fredericks filled me in on Parris's life story. He was an "old" St. A's private practitioner, and he didn't approve of the way modern obstetrics was practiced. He disliked anything that had come into use following the completion of his training; that had been in the early 1950s.

Early in his career, Parris had figured out that the reason that obstetricians tended to get old before their time was that they always spent their nights in some labor or delivery room rather than home in bed where they should have been. They then had to spend their days seeing patients in their offices or making rounds at the hospital. Therefore, his reasoning continued, if he could find a way to deliver all his patients' babies during the day and then spend the nights sleeping at home, then he would stay young forever.

The elective cesarean section became the answer to his prayers. He embraced the concept of an elective section for all as if he were Ponce de León discovering Florida. At first it was difficult to convince all his patients of the need for a section. It was, after all, a major operation with a significant risk of morbidity and required an extensive postoperative recovery period. But gradually, over a year or two, his practice changed over, with many patients leaving to seek obstetric care elsewhere and others, hearing that they would not have to endure the "agony" of labor and that they would know well in advance the exact hour their babies would be coming into the world, flocking to Dr. Parris's outer office. The hospital board offered no opposition to Parris's scheme. They were his patients to manage as he liked and, besides, a post-op patient brought in more revenue than a patient who delivered vaginally.

Soon Parris was sleeping at home almost every night. The only times he was ever seen in the hospital after 5 P.M. were on those nights on which one of his patients had had the nerve to go into labor prematurely. At those times, Parris would appear in the delivery suite, angry and abusive, and would deliver the baby. In retribution Parris would refuse to accept the woman as a patient during subsequent pregnancies. "If your uterus is unreliable in one pregnancy," he would tell them, "it's going to be unreliable in the next."

Considering that Parris did one or two cesarean sections almost every weekday morning, one would think that in the twenty years that this had been going on he would have become damned good and efficient at doing this one operation. But he hadn't; his surgical technique was slow and sloppy. The longer it took him to get the fetus out, the more anesthesia the fetus received and the more neurologically depressed that fetus would be after birth. Also, although it was a relatively easy task to determine the day on which a woman was supposed to deliver a baby and then to subtract a week or two from that day in order to decide on which day the section should be scheduled, some women had erratic menstrual cycles. There were tests, like sonography and amniocentesis, available to tell exactly how old a fetus was, but since these tests had been developed in the late 1960s, Parris simply didn't trust them. As a result, on more than one occasion Parris had delivered a premature baby. Most of the time premies have some advance warning that they are going to be born early, some stressful incident like the onset of premature labor. These stressful occurrences serve to mature the premie's lungs a bit. But Parris's premies were totally taken by surprise; one minute they're lying peacefully in the womb, sucking down some amniotic fluid and sloshing around in the stuff, and the next minute there's Parris's big paw reaching in through the darkness and dragging them out into the light. As a result of this surprise, these babies never did as well as the premies with advanced warning.

Because of these dangerous, medically unacceptable practices, Fredericks told me, all the staff of the "new" St. A's had been trying for years to have Parris thrown out. It hadn't worked though, because in addition to the fact that the hospital was gaining monetarily by the way Parris practiced medicine, he was being supported uniformly by the staff of the "old" St. A's who, although they didn't necessarily agree with Parris's ideas, did agree that they didn't want their lives and work interfered with by the perinatologists.

We saw Parris gesturing furiously through the window. He had tired of flirting with the nurses and wanted to get on with the operation. We stopped our scrubbing and entered the DR. I took my place by the baby warmer. I figured out how to turn on the warming element and also how to work the oxygen. Outside of these two things I didn't know what else to do. As the woman was being gassed by the anesthesiologist, I looked at my watch. It was nine thirty-five.

Parris and Fredericks cut skin at nine thirty-seven. They argued for a minute about the site of the incision. Parris finally won, insisting that they perform a "bikini" incision. "One thing you residents are going to have to learn is that you've got to leave the patient with a good cosmetic appearance. Otherwise, they won't come back to you for their next delivery," Parris said as he cut skin. Fredericks knew better than to make a sarcastic response.

I left the warming table and went over to where the action was, looking over Fredericks's shoulder at the operative field. They were dissecting through the fat and muscle of the lower abdominal wall. Parris was having trouble getting the suture material over Fredericks's outstretched clamp, which was compressing a small, cut blood vessel. Parris would drop the suture, have trouble picking it up, then tear the material while trying to tie the knot. Fredericks just looked skyward during all this, not saying a word.

By the time they cut through the lower portion of the uterus and ruptured the amniotic membranes it was nine-fifty. Parris placed his gloved hand through the incision, tried to grab the fetus, had trouble getting a grip and, after three attempts, decided they had to extend the incision they had made in the uterus a little farther to accommodate the fetal head. "Big head!" was all Parris said. He reached in again, after the flap had been extended farther, at nine fifty-five. He finally got a hold of the fetus, got the head out above the incision, but then it slipped out of his grasp and fell back in the uterus. Fredericks, who was holding the retractors that were keeping the incision open while Parris rummaged around in the womb, started to get uneasy. "Get the kid out!" he screamed at Parris.

Parris gave him a disgusted look and again delivered the head through the incision. With a little more tugging he got the baby out and clamped off the still-pulsating umbilical cord. By the time the cord was cut and the baby was handed to me it was two minutes after ten. The baby had been anesthetized for twenty-seven minutes.

The baby didn't breathe. The heart rate was less than a hundred, a sure sign that the baby was in distress. The baby was limp and turning blue. I gave some oxygen through a tube held in front of the baby's face and jiggled the baby around a little, hoping that this stimulation would make him breathe. By one minute after birth the baby was truly blue. He still hadn't taken a breath and I saw my nightmare of the night before actually coming true on my first trip to the delivery room. I panicked.

I tried suctioning some fluid from the baby's nose using an instrument called a deLee suction catheter. The baby gasped once in response to this but still didn't start breathing regularly. His heart rate was now down to fifty beats per minute. He was going fast. I didn't know what to do. I panicked some more.

"How's the baby?" Parris asked, his hands back in the uterus trying to tear the placenta from its site of attachment on the uterine wall.

"Not breathing," I said softly.

"What?" Parris shouted. "What have you done? I handed you a healthy baby! How did you screw this up?"

I was at this point joined by the anesthesiologist who left the mother's side just in the nick of time. By this point, my legs were shaking and I felt I was going to faint. But I didn't. Without saying a word, the anesthesiologist placed a face mask over the baby's blue face. He attached the oxygen hose to it and began rapidly pushing oxygen through a bag under some pressure into the baby's mouth and nose. "This is an ambu bag," he said. "It works on the same principle as a ventilator, but it's manual." The baby's heart rate rapidly came up to a hundred beats a minute while he was saying this, and the baby's color was getting slightly less blue. He continued bagging. "No harm done. These babies have to be without oxygen for at least five minutes before you start to

ordered to refer any questions from the child's parents to the intern on the case. I can't order you three but I suggest that you then refer the parents to Dr. Sullivan. He is the boss here and he has the most experience."

"I still don't understand," Ray said. "Doesn't the child's father have the right to know what the child will be like? And doesn't he have the right to help in making decisions that are going to affect the future of his child and of his whole family?"

Sullivan now became furious. "Absolutely not!" he roared. "That is our major problem around here! I am an expert in neonatology. I have spent years in training and have been running nurseries for ten years. I have at my fingertips the technology to save anything with a heart and lungs, and I also have the power to say, 'That's it.' What does this Mr. Torres or any other parent know? They're all scared because these babies are so small and frail. They've never seen a baby this small. They just can't understand that something that small could ever grow up into anything that's human and normal. So how can they add anything at all helpful to our decision-making process?"

"But this guy's got to take home and live with and be responsible for what's left after this child leaves the nursery," answered Terry. "You work hard and you do a good job just keeping these babies going, but your job ends when they reach that five-pound limit, regardless of whether there's a brain somewhere in those five pounds or not. This guy wants to know if he's going to be left with a kid he can take to a ball game after all this is over, or with a vegetable he's going to have to feed a puréed diet through a tube. And I, for one, think he's got a right to know!"

It was obvious that Sullivan was losing patience with us. "It looks like it's going to be a long month!" he said to Kathy. She nodded her head in agreement. "Look," he began patronizingly, "you're all new at this. I've been doing these things for years. I know it must be upsetting to you interns at first, too. You look at all these goings-on and you're not able to comprehend why these things are happening. But please just trust me; I promise you that if you do, this will be a good learning experience for all of you. If you don't though, you'll find that this month is going to be hell. Dr. Frohman will tell you it'll work if you let it. He had a wonderful time here as an intern." As if on cue, Frohman nodded his head. "So please, just give it a chance."

That afternoon the three of us had a chance to quiz Berkowitz over lunch in the cafeteria. "Which of you lucky three is on call tonight?" he asked us.

"I am," I said. "Why?"

"Because you have the ultimate honor of taking night call with me. How lucky can you get?"

I laughed. "What is it you actually do around here, Berkowitz?" I asked.

"You guys should call me Dan," he said. "The only person in the world who calls me 'Berkowitz' is Sullivan. And he only does it to irritate me."

"Okay, Dan," I said. "Well, what is it you do?"

"No one ever knows because Sullivan never let me talk at that 'let's get acquainted and be friendly' rounds he had at the beginning of the month. I'm the resident this month in the well-baby nursery downstairs. My main function, as I see it, is to protect those babies from being abused by both Sullivan and by their own private pediatricians, most of whom are incompetent."

"It doesn't sound like you get along so well with Dr. Sullivan," Ray said.

"When he heard you were supposed to be here this month, he just about stroked out," Terry added.

"Dr. Sullivan and I aren't what you'd exactly call close friends. In fact, he tried to get Dr. Jennings to promise him that I wouldn't be assigned to cover anything anywhere near the Pit this year. But Dr. Jennings had no choice. Nobody wanted to work here. Three senior residents threatened to quit if the master schedule came out with their names assigned to cover St. A's. So he had to assign me. I was the only person to request to work here."

"You requested to work here?" I asked.

"I don't understand," Terry said. "If you and Sullivan hate each other as much as you say you do, why would you actually want to work here?"

"There are a lot of thing about neonatology I need to learn," Dan answered. "And I'd rather pay the price of having Sullivan aggravate me for a month so that I can learn them, rather than staying away from here and not learning the stuff at all."

"I guess that makes sense," I said after thinking this over. "Why is it you and Sullivan dislike each other as much as you do?"

"Dislike is putting it a little mildly, Bob. We hate each other's guts, plain and simple. I hate him because he's a schmuck and a two-faced liar who cares less about his patients' families than almost any other pediatrician I've ever heard of. I guess he hates me because I figured all this out and because I also know a secret about him."

"Secret?" Terry asked, smiling. "This is starting to get interesting. What's the secret?"

"I'm not allowed to tell you," Dan answered with a sheepish grin on his face.

"Oh come on," Terry shouted. "Why not?"

"I've been sworn to secrecy," Dan answered, still grinning.

"Have I just become a character in a murder mystery?" Ray asked smiling.

"You're joking!" Terry yelled. "You can't do this to us, Dan! You can't set us up like this and then not tell us."

"Sorry," he said. "I can't tell. You can try to guess though."

"Can you tell us who it was who swore you to secrecy?" I asked.

"I guess so," Dan answered. "It was Dr. Jennings. He didn't want you guys destroyed in the first week of your rotation here. He wants you to pay as little attention to me as possible, and to make judgments about things for yourselves. It's really not such hot stuff."

"He's gay!" Ray guessed. "Sullivan's gay and Jennings doesn't want us to know."

Dan laughed. "He may be gay. I don't know about that. But that's not the secret. Honestly, it's nothing to get this excited about."

"He's a fetishist," Ray guessed again. "He performs weird sexual acts on premature babies. Is that it?"

"I don't know about that either. No, that's not it."

"Will you ever be allowed to tell us?" I asked, not as curious about this as Ray was.

"Probably, after a couple of weeks. But it really isn't that much of a secret. If you guys are smart, you'll figure it out all by yourselves."

We went back to eating lunch. After a while I asked, "Did I miss much when I went down to the DR?"

"Not much," answered Ray. "You got most of it. But you were sure down there a long time. Anything happen?"

I told them all the story of Parris and of the delivery I had recently attended. Terry was astounded. "You mean he actually delivers all his babies by section?" she asked in disbelief. "How does he get away with that?"

"Parris is quite a piece of work," Dan said. "He's a big political problem. Everybody knows that what he does is malpractice. But he's got the total support of the other privates. They'd tear the hospital apart if the hospital board tried to throw him out."

"I can't believe a guy like that can still practice medicine in the nineteen seventies!" Ray said. "Doesn't he ever get sued?"

"He's getting sued all the time," Dan answered. "He's just about got a lawyer on his full-time office payroll. But that still doesn't stop him. Every time he loses a case and his insurance premiums go up, he just raises his fees. So he's still making the big bucks and, for some reason, the patients keep coming to him. It just proves, there's a sucker born every minute."

Just then my beeper went off again, another page to the DR. When I got to the fourth floor the clerk, sitting in exactly the same position as she had been a few hours earlier, but now reading a copy of the *Ladies' Home Journal*, said, "Elective section in three," without looking up.

I changed into another enormous green scrub suit in the locker room and went back into the delivery area. I again saw Parris and Fredericks but they hadn't begun to scrub yet. Instead, they were involved in a heated argument and were standing at a distance far enough away from DR 3 to be out of the patient's earshot.

"You can't mean you're going to deliver this one by elective section!" Fredericks shouted incredulously.

"Of course I am," Parris answered. "Why shouldn't I?"

"You know damned well why! She's carrying an abnormal fetus! You can't justify doing an operation that in the best hands has a two- to three-percent risk of morbidity and in your hands has a significantly higher one electively in a woman who's over thirty-seven years old and who's probably carrying a mongoloid fetus!"

Hearing the slur about his surgical technique, Parris lost it. His face got bright red and I thought steam was going to come out of his ears. "Look, you asshole," he shouted, "don't you smear my record! I'm a damned good surgeon and you'll be lucky to be damned near as good as

I am when you're done! And I'm the attending here and I make the decisions! I can do whatever the fuck I want with my own patients!"

I went back out into the lobby area, figuring that the middle of a fight was not the best place for a pediatric intern to be on his first day on call. I went over to the delivery suite's nurses' station and looked for Parris's patient's hospital chart. I wanted to try to understand the story a little better.

The patient's name was O'Hara. She was, as Fredericks had mentioned, thirty-seven years old. She had not had an amniocentesis, a test performed routinely on women who are over thirty-five to detect chromosomal abnormalities, such as Down syndrome, or mongolism, in the fetus. I was not surprised that Mrs. O'Hara had not had the test; amniocentesis hadn't been developed when Parris had been a resident. But although the risk of bearing a child with a chromosomal defect is increased in women over thirty-five, the vast majority of these women still bear totally normal babies. Why then did Fredericks believe that this woman's fetus was affected with Down syndrome?

Looking further through the chart, I found the answer. About four weeks before the date of her scheduled C section, Mrs. O'Hara had come to Parris's office for her routine visit. Parris had been out sick that day and one of the other local obstetricians was seeing his patients for him. This obstetrician, a Dr. Krumholtz, was either of a later vintage than Parris or had been keeping up a little better because he had detected an abnormality in Mrs. O'Hara and had performed the appropriate diagnostic test to evaluate that abnormality. He noticed that Mrs. O'Hara's uterus had grown at far too fast a rate over the past few weeks and was, by measurement, well above what it should have been for the fetus's gestational age. Because of this discrepancy he had ordered an ultrasound exam of Mrs. O'Hara's uterine contents. Ultrasound, developed in the 1960s, uses sound waves to get an image of an internal structure such as a fetus. That sonogram, according to the report in the chart, had revealed polyhydramnios, an excess of amniotic fluid, and the "double-bubble" sign in the fetal abdomen, consistent with a condition called duodenal atresia.

Amniotic fluid is the magical liquid in which the fetus grows. It is made up, unmagically, largely of fetal urine. The fetus urinates the stuff out, then drinks it down again, only to pass it once more through the kidneys and out again as urine. If the fetus can't drink the amniotic fluid because of some intestinal blockage, as occurs in duodenal atresia, which is actually the absence of one portion of the intestine, then the amount of amniotic fluid in the uterus increases and, clinically, polyhydramnios results.

To jump from duodenal atresia to Down syndrome as Fredericks had done is not unreasonable. This intestinal malformation is found much more commonly in children with Down syndrome than it is in children who don't have it. Considering Mrs. O'Hara's relatively advanced age, the chance that this fetus had Down syndrome was a good one.

I looked up from Mrs. O'Hara's chart when I heard Fredericks, cursing, come through the doors from the delivery area. He walked through a door into a room next to the nurses' station, directly opposite the locker room. In a few seconds I heard loud shouts coming from the room. In another few seconds the shouts ceased and another man, dressed in surgical scrubs, came through the door and walked toward the delivery area. When he saw me, he mumbled, "You from Peds?" in my direction.

"Yeah," I answered.

"Well come on. You ever see a mongol delivered by elective section before?"

I didn't answer but followed him into the delivery area. I was later to learn that this was Andy Schwartz, the chief obstetric resident at St. A's. Schwartz looked like a bear. He was short, heavyset but solidly built, and had very curly brown hair and a very curly beard. He was wearing a scrub suit that was covered with the blood and gore of at least one or two previous deliveries.

He began scrubbing at the sink next to Parris. I scrubbed at a sink outside DR 2. In a few minutes I followed them into the delivery room.

Other than the technical instructions given to Schwartz by Parris, not a word passed between the two during the entire operation. Looking over Schwartz's shoulder, I could see that the movements of his instruments were simply beautiful. All moves, performed with the least amount of wasted motion, looked like part of a ballet compared with the clumsy, inept movements of Parris's pudgy hands. Yet, although he was a superior surgeon, Schwartz listened to the attending's orders and carried them out without a whimper. The baby's head was out in less than fifteen minutes. With just the face showing above the surgical incision, it was clear to all of us that Fredericks's prediction had been correct. The baby had the upward slant of the eyes, the flattened facial profile characteristic of children with Down syndrome.

The rest of the features, the floppy posture, the redundant folds of loose skin, the short fingers and toes, and the simian lines on the palms of the hands, were apparent after delivery. I was handed a baby who was breathing, had a good heart rate, but who almost surely had Down syndrome. Parris and Schwartz finished the operation in silence. I went out of the room to call the nursery to inform the nurses up there that we had a "keeper." Although it was not necessary to admit all babies with Down syndrome to the Pit, it was necessary, because of their requirements of intravenous feeding and intestinal surgery, to admit all babies with duodenal atresia.

I put the baby in the transport incubator which was always kept warm, in case of emergency, and started to leave the DR.

"Well, Doctor," Parris said sarcastically as I was nearing the door of the delivery room, "did you do anything to this one? Is he blue or pink?"

"She's pink," I answered. "And I think she's got Down syndrome."

"Well, that's not my problem" was Parris's response to this. "I did my job. The baby's your responsibility."

It was here that I began to realize for the first time that doctors, at least some doctors, could actually treat patient care as if it were a job they had to do in order to make a living. I had been so damned idealistic; this idea had never occurred to me before, but it hit home now and it made me angry.

I pushed the baby out of the delivery suite into an elevator which had been called for, reluctantly, by the clerk and out again when it reached the fifth floor. I angrily kicked the door leading to the Pit open and carried the baby over to a vacant warming table in the chronics row that had been set up in anticipation of her arrival. Gloria Higgins, the nurse who had been assigned to care for this baby, immediately began to perform the procedures necessary for admission to the Pit. She washed the baby's hair and called the priest.

While Gloria was admitting the baby, I found Frohman, who was sitting alone in a corner of the Pit reading, and I told him about the admission.

"Interesting case," he said after he had written all the information down on a piece of paper which instantly became a permanent part of his clipboard collection. "It's like Dr. Sullivan says, 'Common things are common.' "

I was to learn as the month progressed that Frohman could always be called upon to illuminate all cases as well as he had just illuminated this one. "Can you help me put an IV into this baby now?" I asked. "I've never done it before."

Frohman hesitated. "Uhhh, have you talked to Dr. Sullivan or Kathy about this baby yet?" he asked, snapping his fingers again.

"No," I answered. "I just got back from the DR." I was still steaming from my encounter with Parris. Frohman's stalling wasn't calming me any.

"You'd better talk to them first," he said, the finger snapping reaching a climax. "You know they're the ones who make the decisions around here. Once they've cleared it, I'll be happy to help you."

"Look, Simon, I'm not asking you to decide whether this baby should be resuscitated or not if she codes!" I shouted angrily. "I'm just asking you to help me put in a damned IV! Certainly Dr. Sullivan isn't going to object to this baby having an IV!"

"Calm down," he said soothingly. "You better just ask them first. We'll put the IV in together after they clear it."

This was his last word. Realizing that pursuing this any further would get me nowhere, I calmed myself and went off to look for Kathy or Dr. Sullivan.

As luck would have it, Kathy was standing at Baby Girl O'Hara's warming table. She had obviously had her radar out and picked up a new bleep coming from the Pit. And she had come running to find out about it.

"Dr. Sharon," she said as she saw me approach, "is this your patient?"

"Yes," I answered calmly.

"Did you just bring her up from the DR?"

"Yes," I answered again.

"Weren't you planning on presenting her to either me or Dr. Sullivan?" she asked.

"I was just coming to talk with you about her."

"Good. That should be the first thing you do after bringing a baby into the nursery. Dr. Sullivan doesn't like surprises. Now why don't you tell me this baby's story?"

I told Kathy the story as she examined the baby. After I was finished, she said, "It appears as if your diagnosis of Down syndrome is correct, at least on clinical grounds. But how certain are you of the duodenal atresia?"

"I only have the report from the mother's chart of the ultrasound exam," I said. "I haven't done anything to prove it in the baby."

"Well, that should be the first thing you do for this child. No telling what those sonographers saw. You can't trust anything around here unless you've done it yourself. You'd better remember that. This baby needs a barium swallow stat! And in the meantime, don't give her anything to eat. When you get the results of the X rays, come and talk to me again." She left the baby's bedside and went to play with another baby, her patient, whose name was Freddie Endicott and who occupied the warming table next to Baby Girl O'Hara.

One thing I'll say for St. A's: the ancillary services sure worked well. I called the radiology department. I told them I needed to have a barium swallow done immediately on a newborn. The secretary told me to bring Baby Girl O'Hara down right away. When I reached the radiology suite in the basement of the hospital, I was met by the radiology attending. He took the transport incubator in which I had brought the baby (the same incubator I had used to transport the baby from the DR to the Pit) and pushed it into an X-ray room. I followed and watched him take the baby from the incubator, put her on the X-ray table, center her, put a very thin tube down her nose and into her stomach, pass some barium, a white, soupy liquid that "lights up" on X ray, through the tube, and take films of what happened next. What happened was that the barium didn't go anywhere. It stayed in the stomach and in the first part of the duodenum, both of which were greatly enlarged. The radiologist then removed the barium by sucking it back through the tube. "This baby's got duodenal atresia," he said when he saw the developed X rays.

I pushed the baby's transport incubator back into the Pit and transferred Baby Girl O'Hara back to her warming table. Kathy was still playing with Freddie Endicott. I went over and, without interrupting her, watched the baby for a while.

Freddie Endicott was a very, very unfortunate baby in a nursery full of unfortunate babies. Baby Boy Endicott had been born a normal, full-term infant and had been transferred to the well-baby nursery in the beginning of April. He had become slightly jaundiced on the first night of life and the intern who had been on call that night hadn't thought much of it. By the second day of life, when the bilirubin level was checked by the lab, the jaundice had become worse. Baby Endicott also was not as active as he had been the night before. The lab called the resident working in the well-baby nursery that morning and told her that the bilirubin level was eighteen. When the bilirubin reaches twenty, a serious problem may occur. The bilirubin may cross into the brain and cause permanent brain damage.

Baby Endicott was immediately transferred to the Pit. He was placed under the ultraintense bili lights, called the "death ray" by the nurses, which lowered the bilirubin level to fourteen. This improvement, however, was just temporary; whatever it was within Baby Endicott's system that was causing an excessive production of bilirubin was not deterred, and the bilirubin level rose again. When it had reached nineteen on the morning of the third day of the baby's life, Dr. Sullivan ordered that an exchange transfusion be performed.

Exchange transfusions are horrendous procedures. The principle is the same as leaching in that bad blood is removed, but with a twist. In an exchange transfusion all the bad blood is slowly removed by hand while new blood is slowly injected as replacement. The whole procedure takes a few hours, is very boring, very messy, and more than just slightly dangerous.

As the procedure was being set up for Baby Endicott, the infant had had a cardiorespiratory arrest. He was vigorously resuscitated by Dr. Sullivan and the senior resident working in the Pit that month. Blood samples were sent to the lab for just about every test imaginable, but the only one to come back positive was the blood culture. Baby Endicott had been found to have an infection in his blood with a bacterium called *E. coli. E. coli* only rarely infects the blood of the newborn and, when it does, the infant often has some underlying medical disorder. This should have been a further tip-off that Baby Boy Endicott was not as normal as he had appeared to be.

The baby was treated vigorously with antibiotics, taken off all oral feedings, given an exchange transfusion, then another one, and over the next few days began to show a marked improvement. Three days later, on the sixth day of life, feedings were begun again. And within two days, Baby Endicott was again critically ill.

He again was found to be growing *E. coli* in his blood. He again was taken off all oral feedings. The antibiotics he was ordered to receive were switched to more potent and more toxic ones. And again he began to improve.

Like clockwork, on the ninth day of life Baby Endicott was again put on oral feedings. And again, on the eleventh day, he was critically ill. This time, in addition to the infection in his blood, he was found to have meningitis. The bacteria had invaded his cerebrospinal fluid, the fluid that envelopes and bathes the brain and the spinal column. Again his antibiotics were changed to more potent ones; this time the drug he was started on had been approved only for experimental trials. This drug didn't even have a name; it was known only by a serial number.

It was only at this point that the senior resident working in the Pit figured out what was wrong with Baby Endicott. He reread the history as it had occurred since the child had been born. He reasoned that the baby had only become sick when he had been fed a cow's-milk-based formula. This had rung a bell in the resident's brain: galactosemia.

That resident next examined the baby to try to confirm his diagnosis. He found that the baby had an enlarged liver. Next he took a specimen of the baby's urine and performed a test on it to detect the presence of substances called reducing sugars. The urine gave a four-plus positive response. The resident had been correct: Baby Boy Endicott had galactosemia.

Galactosemia, a rare disease, is caused by the total absence of an enzyme necessary for the breakdown of one of the two main components of lactose, the sugar found in milk. If this component, called galactose, is not properly utilized, it builds up in the blood and causes damage to organs throughout the body. All of Baby Endicott's symptoms were manifestations of galactosemia. No one had taken the time in the period before the child was eleven days old to put all the pieces together. And when the diagnosis had finally been made, it was already too late.

It wasn't certain exactly which event caused the neurologic catastrophe that Baby Endicott had suffered during his first eleven days of life. It might have been the galactosemia itself; it might have been the cardiorespiratory arrest he suffered on day three; and the meningitis certainly didn't help the situation any. But, because of the neurologic problem, Baby Endicott had been left a vegetable. After the diagnosis had been made, he was started on a soy-bean-based formula that contained no galactose. On this formula the baby thrived. He gained weight and suffered no further infections. But he never improved neurologically.

If all this hadn't been enough, Baby Endicott had other problems as well, problems not directly related to his medical condition. His mother had abandoned him the day after his birth. She was sixteen years old and unmarried. The day after the baby had been delivered, she simply had gotten dressed and walked off the floor. She had never returned and had no idea that her son had become critically ill less than twenty-four hours after she had left him.

The original plan had been to place Baby Endicott in a foster home but, as he became sicker and sicker, that plan was abandoned. After the diagnosis had been made and he had stabilized, it became clear that he would require full-time custodial care. So plans were made to have the child placed in the Waltham Home. He was presently on the waiting list. The home was full and he would have to wait until a bed became available.

Kathy's heart had gone out to Baby Endicott. Dr. Sullivan asked her, for the sake of continuity, to accept the child as her own personal patient, and Kathy happily consented. The baby's plight had brought out her maternal instincts and she felt the need to protect him from harm. She named him Freddie on the day that he became three months old because she felt that it was unconscionable for a child of that age to be known by no first name other than "Baby Boy"; she and the other nurses bought Freddie clothes and toys and tried at all times to stimulate him by talking to him, playing with him, reading him stories. But through this all, Freddie just lay there, seemingly oblivious to all the attention, doing about nothing to let his caretakers know that he was responding.

But Freddie played an important role in our nursery. He taught me, Terry, Ray, Frohman, Berkowitz, and all the other interns and residents who had passed through the Pit in the four months he had been a patient there an important lesson. He taught us to think, not to just accept things as natural events that were fixed in time and would not progress, but to delve deeper into the etiology of the problems, and to carefully observe as changes occurred. And he taught us about galactosemia. Kathy drove these lessons home. I'm sure that none of us who worked in the Pit during that period will ever miss another child with galactosemia. The memory of Freddie Endicott stays with me to this day and served a critical role during the final week of my rotation in the Pit. But Freddie was an expensive way to learn these lessons.

And so when I returned from the X-ray department with Baby Girl O'Hara, clutching in my hands the films that confirmed that the child had duodenal atresia, I found Kathy tickling Freddie's abdomen. She was saying "cootchie cootchie coo" to him. The baby just stared off into space.

"Here are the X rays," I said, finally interrupting her. "They confirm that the baby has duodenal atresia."

"Did you see them take these films yourself?" she asked. I didn't know what she was thinking.

"Yep," I answered. "I watched the whole fluoroscopy."

"Good," she said. "See as much as you can while you're here. Don't take anything for granted. So what do you want to do for this baby now?"

I outlined my plan of management cautiously. "Put in an IV. Don't give any feedings by mouth," I said.

"That's it?" she answered after a pause. "Just IV feedings and nothing by mouth? How long do you think she'll survive like that?"

"Oh," I said. "And of course get a surgeon to come and see the baby. That goes without saying."

"If you don't say it, it won't get done," she answered snappily. "And while you're at it, you'd better get a Genetics consult. I don't think there's any question that the baby has Down syndrome, but they ought to do chromosome studies to confirm the diagnosis. Okay?"

"Okay," I answered, and turned away to leave.

"One other thing," she said, pulling me back to attention. "I'll tell Dr. Sullivan about the admission, but you'd better be prepared to present this case on rounds tomorrow. You'd better get consent for the surgery from the parents." And with that, she went back to playing with Freddie.

So after nearly an hour, I was left in the same position I had been in when I had first tried to get Frohman to help me start an IV. But now Frohman seemed to be gone. I couldn't find him anywhere around the Pit, so I decided to try to start the IV on my own.

Although I had never started an IV on a newborn before, I had, while in medical school, started a number of lines on young children. I figured the principle was the same. And so I started to stick Baby O'Hara.

The first attempt ended unsuccessfully; I never hit a vein. On the second attempt, I hit a vein but as soon as I started to push fluid in, the vein blew up like a balloon. The third attempt failed because I hadn't carefully secured the baby's arm and she wiggled out of the restraint. With discarded needles spread around, the warming table began to resemble the set of a snuff film.

While working on the fourth attempt, Kathy approached. She looked over my shoulder. "What the hell are you doing?" she asked loudly. A few nurses who were working in the area turned to hear what the shouting was about.

"I'm starting an IV on this baby," I answered with some remorse.

"No you're not," she answered angrily. "What you're doing is sticking needles into this baby. Haven't you ever done this before?"

"No," I answered.

"How many times have you stuck her so far?"

I counted the dirty used needles. "Four," I said.

"When were you planning on calling for help?" she asked. One of the nurses listening giggled.

"Well, I had looked for Frohman before I started. But he wasn't . . ."

"Let me in," she interrupted, pushing me away from the warming table. She retaped the baby's arm on the restraint and, with one needle, got the IV running. "That's what you call starting an IV," she said. "Next time, you'd better get help after you've missed twice. But better yet, why don't you just learn how to start a damned IV!" By now all the nurses were chuckling.

By six o'clock Ray and Terry had signed out to me. My ego, which had been sagging through the first full day and a half of my internship, was now severely damaged. The only comfort I was feeling was due to the fact that I would be on call with Dan. He was the only one around who seemed to be a mensch.

Dan Berkowitz always looked as if he were about to fall asleep. He slept at attending rounds, when he was present for them; he yawned during work rounds; he was about the most laid-back house officer I had ever met. But he always seemed to wake up just at the moment that help was needed. Unlike Frohman, who was afraid to perform his own bodily functions if they hadn't first been cleared with Dr. Sullivan, Dan did things his own way, regardless of the political consequences. Because of this, although he was probably the best doctor among the pediatric house staff at the Medical Center, he was hated by just about every attending.

After everyone else had gone home and the nursery had calmed down a little, Dan sat me down in the nurses' station and started what he called "your pediatric education according to Berkowitz."

"Bob, there are times when you're working in this, or any other nursery, when you need to do things and there's nobody around to help you. Because of this, there are a certain number of facts you need to know. In most nurseries you'd learn this stuff from the attending. But if you wait for Sullivan to teach you, you'd probably wind up spending your entire life here. So I'll teach it to you. And we'll start right now. Follow me." He led me into the Pit to a large, red portable cart that had about six drawers of different sizes. This was the code cart, and it was filled with the equipment necessary to resuscitate a baby.

From one of the drawers Dan pulled a two-foot-long piece of plastic tubing which was in a long sterile bag. "This," he said, pointing to the tubing, "is an umbilical artery catheter. It is the nursery intern's best friend. This little piece of plastic, when inserted through the belly button of the premature baby, assures the intern of days, or even weeks if necessary, of bliss. There are lots of things you can do with a UA catheter. You can give fluids and medications through it. You can draw blood from it. You can give blood transfusions through it. UA lines, unlike IVs, rarely fall out accidentally. They rarely become infected. With a UA line in place the intern never has to actually touch the premie, which is a very desirable feature because the fewer times you actually lay hands on one of these babies, the fewer times you can actually do something that will hurt the child. Because of all these features, it is in the intern's best interest to care for and preserve the UA line. *Never* pull a UA line for any reason, unless you are prepared to spend three hours every night starting a new IV or doing the stabbing that's necessary in order to get all the damned blood for the worthless tests Sullivan's always ordering. If it does become necessary to change the UA line, like in the case where the old one has become clotted, this

can easily be done. But never, ever, remove it until the baby is better and is ready to go home. There may even be some argument in favor of sending the child home with the UA line in place. No, only kidding. Do you understand all that?"

"Yes," I answered.

"Good. Now let's move on to another good friend of the intern." He reached into another drawer of the code cart and pulled out what looked like a straw with a paper clip through the middle of it. This, too, was in a sterile plastic bag. "This," he said, pointing to this thing, "is not only a good friend of the intern, but also is a good friend of the premie. This is an endotracheal tube. When this tube is passed through the baby's vocal cords and down into the trachea, it assures that the baby, when hooked up to a ventilator, will get oxygen pushed into his lungs all day, every day. A well-oxygenated premie is a happy premie. And a happy premie generally makes for a happy intern. Therefore, like the UA line, caring for and preserving the endotracheal tube is also in the intern's best interest.

"The little endotracheal tube requires a lot more care than the UA line does. That's because the endotracheal tube has a lot of enemies: it can get clogged with the dreaded mucous; it can accidentally work its way out through the vocal cords and wind up in the back of the baby's throat; or it can be tugged out accidentally by the nurse when she's repositioning the baby or just trying to behead him." I laughed at this. "You always must remember, Bob," Dan continued, "that if a baby who is being ventilated suddenly crumps, you know, starts going down the tubes, no pun intended, you have to first think that something's gone wrong with the ET tube. The first thing to do is to try to suction gunk from it. If that doesn't help you should remove the tube completely and try to pass another one. If that doesn't work, think collapsed lung. That's an emergency. You know how to diagnose a collapsed lung in one of these premies?"

"No," I answered.

"You use one of these." He picked up an instrument from the top of the code cart that looked like a ray gun. "I'll show you how this thing works later. Any problems with the endotracheal tube?"

"Only one," I answered. "I don't know how to put one of those things in!"

"Oh, that's not a big problem," Dan answered. "Nobody knows that when they first get here. I can't tell you how to do it, though. You've got to do it for yourself. And once you've done it, it's like riding a bicycle, you'll never forget how. So don't worry about it. I'm sure I'll have the opportunity to let you try it in the next few days. Okay?"

"Okay," I answered.

"Right. So those are your two lessons for tonight. If you're a good intern and you do your work and, most importantly, if you don't wake me up in the middle of the night to tell me there's a full moon, I'll give you two or three of these pearls a night. Over the month that we're here, that'll add up to a pretty good course in neonatology. Okay?"

"Okay," I answered.

"Is something wrong?" he asked, studying me carefully. "Did your cat die or something?"

"What are you talking about?"

"You seem kind of sad. Did you have a fight with someone or are you just generally depressed about working here?"

I was surprised he had picked up on my sadness which I thought I was hiding. "I guess I got into a fight," I said.

"With whom?" Dan asked. "Sullivan or his *gruppen-führer,* Kathy?"

"Kathy," I said, smiling a little.

"Oh that's not so bad. What did she do?"

"It was nothing really. I was trying to start an IV on that new baby with Down syndrome. I missed a few times and she made me feel like I was needlessly torturing the baby."

"Great!" Dan said calmly. "Just what you'd expect from her. After all, it is your second day here. You should be an expert at starting IVs by this point, right? Don't worry about it, Bob. It's not anything to get upset about. You've got to learn how to do these things and, unfortunately, the only way to learn them is by practicing on babies. You're going to have to miss a few times in order to get good. That's all there is to it. End of discussion."

I felt a little better. Dan was right. It was unfortunate, but this was the way it was. "I get the feeling Kathy doesn't like me."

"Well, they can't say you're an insensitive dummy," Dan said. "You're right. Kathy doesn't like you. But don't take it personally. She doesn't like any of us house staff."

"That's crazy," I said. "She doesn't even know me. How can she hate me just because I'm a member of the house staff?"

"Well, she thinks that all we do is take, take, take from the babies, and that we don't give anything back. If it was up to her, the Pit would be staffed only by Dr. Sullivan, giving all the orders on every baby, and by her and her nurses, carrying out those orders."

"That doesn't make any sense," I answered. "Sullivan can't be here twenty-four hours a day. Sure, he might be able to make all the decisions between nine and five, but what happens if there's an emergency at night?"

"I didn't say it made any sense," Dan answered. "I'm just telling you how she feels. In fact, by the time you've been here two weeks, you'll be questioning whether it makes sense that Sullivan makes any decisions at any time of day."

"It's crazy," I said, thinking a little more about Dan's interpretation of Kathy's thinking. "Kathy sounds like she's crazy."

"Are you surprised, after working here for two days, that someone working here is crazy?"

"No," I answered. "Everybody working here seems crazy."

"Bob, there's hope for you yet. Well, since everything seems to be quiet around here, I'm going off to my luxurious on-call room. Call me if you need me, Bob. I'm just at the end of my beeper."

After Dan had left, I went down to the recovery area in the delivery suite to talk with Mrs. O'Hara. The recovery area was across the lobby from the delivery area. I found Mrs. O'Hara awake, lying in bed, and sobbing quietly.

"Mrs. O'Hara," I said solemnly, "I'm Dr. Sharon. I'll be taking care of your daughter in the nursery upstairs."

At the mention of the word "daughter," her sobs crescendoed into full-fledged crying. "I don't want to know anything," she cried.

"Well I just came to tell you that everything is fine with. . . ."

"Didn't you hear me?" she screamed. "I don't want to have anything to do with her! And I don't want to know anything!"

"But it's your daughter," I said quietly, unsure of the ground on which I was treading. I had never talked with a mother who had just given birth to an abnormal baby before and I sure didn't feel comfortable doing it now.

"I didn't ask for her!" she said through the tears. "I don't need another baby. I've got my family. She's a mistake and I don't want her!"

Finally realizing that I was probably the next-to-last human she wanted to see at this moment (the last, of course being Baby Girl O'Hara herself), I turned and left the recovery area. The nurse taking care of Mrs. O'Hara had been standing at the door listening to our conversation. As I was leaving the room, she stopped me.

"You from Peds?" she asked.

"Yeah," I answered.

"I wouldn't push Mrs. O'Hara on this right now. Her mind's pretty set."

"Pretty set on what?" I asked.

"On not wanting this baby to live."

"What?" I asked. "She didn't say that!"

"Yes she did. She said it to me. She didn't tell you because she doesn't want to have anything to do with anybody from Pediatrics. She's been prepared for this for a couple of weeks. She pretty much knew that she was going to have a mongoloid. She told me she didn't want to get pregnant in the first place and then, when she did, she couldn't bring herself to have an abortion. Then she was told the baby would have an intestinal problem and probably be a mongoloid and that if the baby didn't have surgery, the intestinal problem would kill it. So in the weeks since she was told all this, she decided, okay, it's God's will, let me have this mongoloid baby with an intestinal problem and then let it die. She didn't want to even know the sex, but Parris blurted out that she had a girl as soon as she came out of the anesthesia."

"She told you all this?" I asked.

"Doc, she's been telling this to anyone who'll listen. We're afraid to bring any other patients back here, for fear that Mrs. O'Hara will tell them that she wants her baby to die."

I couldn't believe what I was hearing. I figured that when Mrs. O'Hara realized what she was doing, she'd recant and want to see the baby. "Well, I was supposed to get her to sign a consent form so we could do the surgery. I guess it'll have to wait."

"It may have to wait a long time," the nurse answered. And with that I returned to the Pit.

The rest of the evening passed without event. I sat through the evening in the nurses' station outside the Pit, reading Berenson's *Textbook of Neonatology.* Every few minutes one of the nurses would bring me the results of a blood gas, and she'd tell me what she wanted to do to the ventilator, and why. I always approved. It was through this method that I eventually figured out what to do when there wasn't a nurse around to tell me. I was learning something.

At a little after eleven o'clock, I went back down to the delivery suite to find out if they were expecting any problems during the rest of the night.

The lobby of the delivery area was totally empty except for the evening DR clerk sitting behind the desk. She looked amazingly similar to the day clerk and was even reading the same issue of the *Ladies' Home Journal.* I approached her and asked where I could find Dr. Fredericks. This clerk, who seemed just as friendly as her daytime counterpart, directed me to the on-call room. This turned out to be the room into which Fredericks had vanished just prior to the cesarean section that led to the birth of Baby Girl O'Hara.

Fredericks was sitting in an easy chair with his feet up on an operating room stool watching a rerun of "M*A*S*H" on a color TV. The obstetric resident's on-call room was about three times the size of ours. There was a set of bunk beds, not folding cots, two easy chairs, and the color TV. The walls were painted a nice light tan, and there was a window that looked out onto the hospital's parking lot.

When he saw me at the door, Fredericks summoned me in and motioned for me to sit down and be quiet. I sat on the lower bunk bed and waited for the show to end.

When the episode was over, Fredericks sighed. "That Hawkeye! What a doc!"

I asked if anything was up.

"Not really, not really. We got a thirty weeker on the ward but she's okay. She was in real active labor earlier today but we slowed her down with about a ton of mag sulfate. Great drug that mag sulfate, great drug! I think that stuff could stop a bull from charging." He pulled at a dark hair in his mustache.

"Not a bull," I said. "Maybe a cow, but not a bull." I at least knew what mag sulfate was.

"Oh yeah," Fredericks said. "I get it, I get it. A cow, not a bull! That's pretty good. Your name is Sharon, right?"

"Yeah," I said. "I'm Bob Sharon."

"And I'm Tom Fredericks, Bob. So how do you like our little hospital so far?"

I hesitated. I didn't want to tell him how miserable, scared, helpless, and angry I was. "I haven't really settled in yet," I finally said. "Things are still pretty . . . new to me."

"Yeah, Bob, I know what you mean, I know how that can be. But you'll find after you've been here for a while that things are . . . interesting here."

"Yes. I gather that. That was a pretty interesting scene between you and Parris outside the DR this afternoon," I said, trying to change the subject away from my problems. "You two always get along that well?"

"That fart!" he replied. "That incompetent asshole! It's still hard for me to believe, truly hard to believe that he's allowed to practice medicine, let alone have admitting privileges to a perinatal center like this! He's a money-hungry bloodsucker! What he did today was malpractice, straight and simple! You just don't do an elective section when the fetus is malformed unless the mother's life is in danger. Every medical student knows that!"

"Did you leave or did he throw you out?"

"A little of each, Bob, a little of each. He says he's gonna bring me up on charges in front of the hospital board. Let him do it! I'll file a class action suit against him, charging him with malpractice. The man's really dangerous, Bob, really dangerous."

With that Fredericks turned his attention back to the TV. "The Tonight Show" had started and Johnny was getting into his monologue. I was exhausted and decided to go back to the Pit to try to get some sleep. I checked in with Angela Meroni, the head nurse on nights. She told me that things were pretty quiet, that everyone was stable, and that I looked a little sleepy.

"I thought I'd stay up and read for a while," I said.

"Dr. Sharon, let me give you a little advice. When it gets quiet up here, you shouldn't read, you should sleep. It usually doesn't stay quiet for long." I decided to take her advice, headed for the on-call room, turned off the light, and lay down on the cot. I was almost asleep in the dead-quiet room when the air was shattered by the sound of the phone ringing. It was Angela with the results of a blood gas on Baby Summlitz. The gas results sounded pretty good and Angela said she wanted to lower the ventilator pressure a little. I told her that that sounded like a good idea and hung up. I was on the verge of sleep again when, again, the phone rang. This time it was another nurse with the results of a gas on Baby Torres. These results weren't so good, and we decided to turn up the oxygen concentration a little. I hung up and was nearly in dreamland when the phone rang a third time. Again and again through that night I tried to fall asleep and again and again, my sleep was interrupted by the phone ringing. Like Ray the night before, I had a benign, easy night, but failed to sleep for more than a half hour at a stretch.

The night seemed unending. Since there was no window in that on-call room, I had no way of knowing when dawn was breaking. But at 7 A.M., the nurse who called to report the results of a gas on Baby Argos mentioned that she thought it was time I got up. I dressed, stole some coffee from the urn in the nurses' lounge, and headed for the nurses' station to await the arrival of Ray, Terry, and Frohman.

Although I felt tired and a little cranky, I had the satisfaction of knowing that I had survived my first night on call as an intern. I still hadn't been tested in a real emergency, however, and knew that if the need arose for me to help a really sick baby, I had neither the skill nor the knowledge to do anything but freeze. Still, I had survived a big hurdle. But now came the hard part: to survive the day after a night on call. And it would be especially tough for me this day, because this day was Wednesday. And Wednesday was the day of my first follow-up clinic.

V

Wednesday, June 30
Attending Rounds

At ten o'clock, with work rounds finished, we all filed into Dr. Sullivan's office for attending rounds. After the new data on Baby Torres, still the sickest baby in the house, was presented and discussed, and plans were made for her management for the day, I presented my first admission, Baby Girl O'Hara, to Dr. Sullivan. I informed him of the basic history and pertinent physical findings.

"Duodenal atresia is fairly common in mongoloid babies," Sullivan said. "Duodenal atresia's a good lesion to have, because it can be fixed by even a third-rate surgeon. Problems rarely occur. Has a surgeon seen the child yet?"

"I called them yesterday afternoon but they haven't come yet," I answered. "But there's a little problem. I don't think Mrs. O'Hara, the baby's mother, will give her permission for the surgery."

"What do you mean won't give her permission for the surgery?" Sullivan asked. "Did you explain to her the baby will die without the operation?"

"I couldn't explain it to her because she wouldn't talk to me. But the nurse told me that that's what she wants. She wants the baby to die."

"What?" Sullivan shouted, his face turning a dull red. "What do you mean, she wants the baby to die? Who gave her the right to make a decision like that?"

"Although I don't agree with what she's saying," Dan said, awakening momentarily from his usual attending rounds stupor, "she is after all the child's mother. And as such, she is entitled to have some say concerning what should happen to the baby." Dan remained calm, but smiled, knowing that this simple statement of opinion would drive Sullivan absolutely crazy.

"She's the mother?" Sullivan shouted, not letting Dan down. "Great! Serving as an incubator for nine months suddenly bestows upon her the right to make decisions about life and death? Look, this is a perfectly viable child who has a congenital lesion that can be repaired by simple surgery. Withholding the operation is equal to murdering the child!"

"I know that," I answered meekly, "but Mrs. O'Hara says that this was an unwanted pregnancy. She feels it was God's will that she have a child with Down syndrome, and God's will that that child have a problem that would kill it, and therefore, God's will that the child die."

"Oh, even better!" Sullivan yelled again. "She doesn't want the baby, so she's standing behind God as an excuse. These are the facts: we have a child in my nursery who must have an operation; the mother must consent to the surgery; if the mother doesn't consent, we'll call Judge Isaacs and get a court order to do the surgery. And then after the surgery is done, we'll return the baby to the mother's custody. There are legal precedents for this. It may be God's will, but it sure as hell isn't Sullivan's will!"

The legal precedent Sullivan referred to resulted from a case strikingly similar to the Baby Girl O'Hara incident. A child with Down syndrome and duodenal atresia was transferred to the nursery at Johns Hopkins in Baltimore during the early 1960s. Like Mrs. O'Hara, the parents of this child refused to consent to the surgery, and the child was left to die. The parents, additionally, refused to take the child home. So the baby lived out its short life as a resident of the nursery.

The infant in that case took weeks to die. It was a hard and bitter agony for the baby and for the entire staff of the nursery. The director of that nursery, having no legal recourse but to allow the baby to starve to death, made home movies of the child's life. The resulting documentary was shocking. And since that time, judges throughout the country, in issuing court orders permitting the surgery to be performed, have vowed never to allow such suffering to occur again.

Rounds ended that day with Sullivan ordering me to find Mrs. O'Hara and inform her of the attending's decision. I was issued an ultimatum: either return to the nursery with a signed consent form or don't come back at all. Although I figured that Sullivan would not seriously consider firing me because this baby's mother continued to refuse to allow this operation to be performed, I thought very carefully about electively taking the second option without even attempting to fulfill the first. I hadn't before seriously considered just chucking the whole thing, just quitting my internship. But now I felt not only incompetent to carry out the technical part of my job, but I was dreading the social part, the dealing with the children's families, the thing I had always been best at, the part of this specialty that had caused me to choose pediatrics in the first place.

I was ambivalent about going to speak with Mrs. O'Hara. On the one hand, I understood at least a little of what she was going through and because of this I wanted to respect her wishes; but on the other hand, I could clearly see Sullivan's point, that not performing this simple operation would be tantamount to murder. I walked around the nursery for a while, trying to sort all this out in my own head, trying to figure out a mode of action. I finally decided that I couldn't make a decision, that I needed to speak to someone wiser than I. I needed to find Dan.

The well-baby nursery was down on the third floor. The doors of the elevator opened into a corridor that looked as if it were in a totally different hospital. I entered that corridor, making my first venture into the "old" St. A's.

The first thing that hit me was the heat. The new parts of the hospital, the Pit and the delivery suite were climate controlled, ensuring a year-round temperature of seventy-two degrees, regardless of weather conditions outside the hospital. But the old parts of the building weren't air-conditioned and so the air was already sweltering and stagnant in the corridor, even though it was still morning.

Other differences between the old and the new were also immediately obvious. The lighting, much less efficient, was far dimmer than that in the Pit. The walls were covered with plaster, cracked and chipped in many spots, and large chunks were coming loose. The entire place was in need of major repairs, repairs that I figured were kept in a low-priority position, as the hospital board struggled to pay for the upkeep of its prize perinatal center.

The third floor's central corridor led, at its end, to smaller corridors

that went off to the left and the right. At the junction of these corridors was the floor's nurses' station. I asked for directions to the nursery and the clerk pointed me to the right.

The nursery was off by itself, away from the patients' rooms, and roughly a third the size of the Pit. However, it clearly was home to more babies. The left wall as I faced in from the corridor had a large washbasin and an examining table attached to it. The right wall had a door that led into the nursery's small nurses' station. And between these walls, lying in hospital bassinets which had been haphazardly placed in every corner of the room, were over thirty healthy, screaming bundles of joy.

I stared through the glass for a while. These kids were really cute. They were pink and cuddly, and crying at the top of their lungs; I could have stood there watching them all day.

I found Dan, sitting in the nurses' station with his feet up on a desk, reading the Boston *Globe.* The only other occupant of the room was a clerk, who occasionally turned to glare at Dan. I'm sure she deplored this lazy behavior. "Bob," Dan said when he saw me at the door, "come in, make yourself at home." He offered me a chair next to his. "Thank you for not bugging me last night. I managed to get a pretty good night's sleep. Everything okay with you?"

"Actually not," I answered. "I need some help."

"Help?" he repeated. "I hope it's nothing too taxing. As you can see, I've got my hands full down here." He laughed.

"It's not too taxing," I said. "I've got . . . well, I guess it's an ethical dilemma."

"Oh, an ethical dilemma. I can see why you came to me then. I know for a fact that no one of any authority up in the Pit has any ethics! What is it?"

I explained the problem to him. "Sullivan ordered me to get consent for the surgery from Mrs. O'Hara. I'm not sure if I agree with him about how to do it."

"I know what he told you," Dan said. "I was at rounds this morning, remember?"

"Yeah, I know you were there," I answered. "But you looked like you were sleeping."

"I wasn't sleeping. I do that because it drives Sullivan crazy. But I hear everything, and I realize you don't think it's right to go into Mrs. O'Hara's room and demand that she sign a consent form or else."

"But I also know that if I don't get it, Sullivan will go crazy."

"Well, let's ignore Sullivan for a minute. How would you like it done if you were running the show?"

"I guess I agree that the surgery must be done. I agree that withholding it is like murdering the baby. I just don't think it's right to force it down the mother's throat right now, after she's just been through the section and all. I'd wait another day or two before bringing it up with her and try to feel her out about what she's thinking until then."

"So why don't you do that?" Dan asked.

"Because Sullivan'll go berserk if I. . . ."

"Screw Sullivan!" Dan interrupted. "Don't be a schmuck about this, Bob. Handle it your own way."

"Can I do that?" I asked.

"Sure you can. You can do anything you want; you're a doctor."

"That's it?" I asked.

"That's it," he answered. He went back to reading the paper.

"Thanks," I said. "Is this what you do around here all day?"

"All day," he said, looking up. "Those babies in there, they're so damned healthy it's disgusting. I have a lot of time to read and relax."

"Healthy babies," I said as I got up to leave. "It's hard to believe there's such a thing as healthy babies."

"Bob, that's the way most of them come out. You kind of lose perspective, working up in the Pit."

On my way out I again stopped to look at the babies. They were all quiet now; they seemed to all be asleep. I didn't want to leave them but Mrs. O'Hara had to be faced before follow-up clinic.

Mrs. O'Hara did not look well. She was not crying, but her face was pale, puffy, and drawn. I reintroduced myself.

"I know who you are," she said, not sounding angry or hostile. Her voice was soft and flat. She seemed somewhat resigned. "I'm sorry for my outburst last night. I'm . . . I'm not usually like that. I've been under a lot of stress since . . . since they told me that the baby . . . the baby. . . ." She couldn't continue. She began sobbing quietly.

I pulled a chair up to her bedside, sat down, and waited for the sobs to subside. She was calm again in another minute.

"How are you feeling?" I asked solemnly.

"Not so well. I have a slight temperature now and my stomach where they cut me hurts a lot. I've been getting the painkiller shots but the pain's getting worse. But I'll be okay, I guess."

We both were quiet now for what seemed like an eternity. I was afraid to start talking about the baby but I finally closed my eyes and began. "Mrs. O'Hara, I've really come to talk to you about the baby. First of all, she's doing well upstairs. We're giving her fluids through an IV in her arm, it's like yours," I said, pointing toward the IV in Mrs. O'Hara's left arm, "only smaller. We have done some X-ray tests that confirm that she does have the intestinal blockage. The Genetic doctors have come to see her and we all feel that the odds are that she does have Down syndrome, but we won't be positive until the blood test they did is completed. That'll take another few days yet."

She remained silent all through this. Her face was expressionless and seemed frozen in place. She did not look at me but stared up at the ceiling, as if she were daydreaming of something else.

I continued. "I understand you don't want the baby to have the operation and I respect your wishes. However, although I'm not going to tell you that you have to sign a consent form, I'd like you to reconsider your decision."

I stopped talking. I had already gone further than I intended to, further than Dan would have liked me to. I hadn't even meant to discuss the question of surgery at all, but it had just slipped out.

After a few seconds, she turned her head toward me. Tears were forming in her eyes. "Dr. Sharon," she began, "I've got two sons at home. One's sixteen and one's eighteen. They're all grown-up. My husband and I were looking forward to having the rest of our lives free from the responsibility of caring for children. And then I got pregnant. It was unexpected and unplanned. But we resigned ourselves to having the child. I swear, if I believed in abortion, I would've had one.

"Then I got the complication Dr. Krumholtz found and they told me what that meant and that the baby might be a mongoloid. These last four weeks since then have been the worst in my life. Not only were we going to have a baby, but that baby was going to stay a baby forever. Dr. Sharon, I'm thirty-seven. My husband is forty-five. We don't want to be taking care of a baby when we're sixty-five years old!" She began sobbing softly again.

I felt a lump in my throat and should have left her alone with her decision. But I continued talking, figuring that I had a responsibility to at least try to get her to see our argument about performing the surgery. "I understand what you're saying, Mrs. O'Hara, and I'm concerned about you and your husband both. But you have to look at it from our position. She's a human being. With a simple operation, she'll live. Without it, she'll die. But it won't be a quiet, comfortable death. It'll take weeks for her to die and all of us in the nursery will watch her get more and more wasted and hear her cry constantly for food. We're doctors. We can't stand around and let that happen! We have to fix what can be fixed."

Through this she was again staring at the ceiling. When I had finished, she looked at me with anger and cried out, "What will you do if I don't give my permission?"

I was stuck. I didn't want to threaten her and I didn't want her to think of me as the enemy. So I hedged. "We're hoping we won't be faced with that. We're hoping that after you've thought it through, you'll give us your consent."

"You'll get a court order, won't you?" she sobbed.

I sighed. I felt tears forming in my eyes and I felt the need to run out of this room filled with sadness and misery and cry my eyes out. Looking away from her, I said yes. "If you don't consent, Dr. Sullivan, the director of the nursery, will get a court order." I stood up from my chair. "We don't want to have to do that, Mrs. O'Hara. Please reconsider and give us your permission." I nearly ran from the room, not waiting for a response, ran down the hall, found the men's room, ran inside, and began crying. I cried for Baby Girl O'Hara; I cried for Mrs. O'Hara; and I cried for myself. At that immediate instant I could imagine no tragedy worse than the one befalling the O'Hara family.

VI
Follow-Up Clinic

By the time I composed myself in the men's room it was 1:10 P.M. I had been crying for over twenty minutes. I had missed lunch and was already late for follow-up clinic.

The old St. A's had always run a well-baby clinic. This was a clinic run by a nurse practitioner, a nurse who had trained to work as a physician and was watched over by a local pediatrician who donated a small amount of his time each week to the hospital. The babies enrolled in the clinic received routine pediatric care, including the required series of immunizations free of charge, and they were referred to the specialty clinics at the Medical Center if specific problems occurred.

With the founding of the new St. A's, the follow-up clinic was added. This was a clinic where graduates of the Pit could come for their care. Unlike the children who were enrolled in the well-baby clinic who were, for the most part, well and brought there because their parents could not afford the cost of private pediatric care, the patients in the follow-up clinic were never "well" and were brought not because of financial difficulties but because no private pediatrician wanted to take care of them. Follow-up clinic which met only on Wednesday afternoons was run by the senior resident and the interns who were working in the Pit. Only the intern who was to be on call that night was left inside the hospital in order to cover the nursery and the delivery room in case of emergency. The clinic was held in a small, wood frame house which had been purchased and refurbished by the hospital, and which stood on a plot of land adjacent to St. A's.

After entering the clinic building I found Frohman, Ray, and Dan in the clinic's nurses' station area. "Dr. Sullivan believes that this clinic can be a good learning experience for you interns," Frohman said as our orientation began. "You will see more pathology here in one day than you would in a month in any other clinic. There are about twenty patients scheduled for today. The nurse will weigh and measure all the children and then place them into the empty rooms. We just go from room to room and see the patients. Any questions?" Frohman hesitated, and the only sound was the noise produced by his fingers snapping rhythmically. "Okay, let's get started."

I got up and headed for a room. Dan remained sitting with his feet up on a chair. "You coming, Dan?" I asked, trying to rouse him.

"A good learning experience?" he asked. "Is that what he said?"

"Yeah," I answered, "that's what he said."

"Well, Bob, you tell me what you think. You come to me after you've been here for a while and you tell me if you think this is a good learning experience."

"Okay," I said. We headed for the examination rooms. I stopped at Room 2. There was a chart in the plastic holder attached to the door. I grabbed the chart and went inside.

The patient behind the door was Bernard Feldman, a four year old who had weighed slightly less than two pounds at birth and who had stayed in the Pit for nearly four months. He had been left with the most severe neurologic sequelae of prematurity: he was profoundly retarded, not toilet trained, not able to feed himself, not able to talk or communicate; cerebral palsy had turned his little body into a pretzel, causing severe contractures of the joints of his arms and legs, making them difficult and painful to move, and extreme curvature of the spine for which he had to wear a heavy brace around his midsection in order for him to sit upright in his wheelchair; and he had an intractable seizure disorder for which he was being treated with three different types of anticonvulsant medications, medications that made him drowsy, made hair grow everywhere, damaged his liver, made him anemic, and enlarged his gums to such an extent that unless the tissue was periodically hacked away by an oral surgeon, it made him appear as if he had no teeth. Bernie was due on that day to receive an immunization against diphtheria, whooping cough, and tetanus, and to have blood work done.

After my encounter with Mrs. O'Hara, poor Bernie almost tipped me over the edge. His parents had tried to care for him but Bernie's many medical problems made home care almost impossible. So he had been admitted to the Waltham Home when he was one year old.

The aide who accompanied Bernie and I tried to get the child out of his wheelchair and onto the examining table for a quick physical exam, but the child seemed to be in such pain at the sharp movements of his contracted, withered limbs that I finally decided to examine him quickly while he sat in the chair. Finding no abnormality for which I could offer any curative treatment, I retired to the nurses' station to prepare the injection and to gather the materials needed for blood drawing.

I ran into Ray, who was also preparing to give an immunization. "Ain't this great, Bob?" he said. "Aren't you real proud of the fact that you're working in this terrific nursery, saving the lives of premies so they can someday grow up and come to follow-up clinic?" With that, he walked away.

I finished my work and returned to Room 2. I stabbed Bernie with the immunization, drew off 5 cc of blood, filled out prescription blanks for refills of his medications, and gave him a return appointment for three months. These were the things the aide from the Waltham Home told me I had to do. I bid Bernie's aide goodbye and they went off back to the Waltham Home while I went on to the next examining room.

Ray and I saw four children each that first day of follow-up clinic. Frohman and Dan saw five each. All were variations on the same theme. Every one of them was retarded, some worse off, like Bernie, some better off. All were twisted and distorted by cerebral palsy. Most had seizure disorders. Some could feed themselves, some required assistance, some had to be fed through tubes, whereas others had feeding gastrostomies which are surgical openings through the abdominal wall into their stomachs into which blenderized foods could be shot through a syringe. Most wore diapers regardless of their ages and smelled almost constantly of urine and feces. Most came from families that had been broken up, usually as a direct result of their birth. Many had been placed at the Waltham Home or another similar facility.

By the end of that clinic, I felt suicidal. Ray had similar feelings. Frohman seemed happy, ready for his night on call, a chance to "save the babies," as he put it. I wanted to strangle him.

We started back to the Pit. Ray and I stayed behind Frohman, so we could have some time to talk with Dan. Dan appeared to have been totally unmoved by follow-up clinic.

"Well, Bob," he said, "how about that for a learning experience?"

"That was definitely the worst three hours of my life!" I said.

"It wasn't that bad, Bob," Ray said. "It could have been worse."

"How?" I asked.

Ray hesitated, and his face had a puzzled look. "I can't think of anything right now," he finally concluded.

"I don't know how I can possibly justify working in that nursery," I said very seriously, "knowing that this is what becomes of those kids."

"Well, Bob, you know this isn't what happens to all those kids," Dan said. "Only a very small percentage of the Pit's graduates go on to become regular customers of follow-up clinic. Most of the clients become solid citizens."

"Well I haven't seen any of them become solid citizens," Ray said. "All I've seen are GORKs!"

GORK, an eponym used mostly in adult neurology, is used to describe a patient who is neurologically impaired and answers the question, "Where is that guy's brain at?" The letters stand for "God Only Really Knows."

By this point we had reached the elevator. Ray and I took it up to five, and we said goodbye to Dan on the way, who got off at three to go back to his well babies.

Upon reaching the Pit, Ray and I signed out to Terry. She had just gotten back from the DR where she had attended one of Parris's C sections. She was white as a ghost and told a story strikingly similar to the one that I told the day before. We added our story of the horror of follow-up clinic to her story. Even though Ray and I embellished our story with lots of nauseating facts, I don't think Terry fully comprehended the misery that we experienced. But I figured she'd learn about it firsthand the next Wednesday when she would have to go to the clinic herself.

After signing out, Ray and I sat in the nurses' station staring silently

into the Pit through the glass windows, watching the buzz of activity that surrounded the first row of babies. Finally I said "I need a drink!"

"Let's blow this place," Ray said.

We ran for the elevator.

VII

After Hours

We walked from St. A's to Kelly's, the bar nearest the hospital. I bought the first round.

"What a day," I mumbled. "I'm wasted."

"You must be sort of hungry, too," Ray said. "Where were you during lunch?"

I told him of my visit with Mrs. O'Hara and how I had blown it.

"Oh, so you were all set for GORK clinic."

I smiled. So follow-up clinic had already become GORK clinic to us.

"You know, this is disgusting," Ray said as our second beers were poured. "Here we are, spending all these great summer days and losing sleep at night, and for what? I don't know anything about taking care of these babies, and I sure haven't learned anything while I've been at St. A's. Do you know what you're doing?"

"No," I answered. "I'm even less sure than I was when I came. Like I used to be pretty good at talking to parents. But I really screwed up with Mrs. O'Hara."

"Right," Ray said. "And even if we were learning, look at what we're doing! Sullivan doesn't care about anything except keeping these kids alive until they hit five pounds. He doesn't care if they have a brain, if they have working kidneys, if their parents want us to do any of this, or if they have a home to go to after they graduate. Do you know that every kid I saw today, every one of them came from a broken home? And you know why all those homes broke up? Because these kids had the disadvantage of being born too soon and then, before they could do the normal thing and go to heaven, they had the bad luck to run into Sullivan, who did everything he could to prevent them from dying only so they could end up as GORKs. I don't want to learn how to make GORKs. And I don't want to spend my time taking care of them."

"I know, Ray," I said, "but we're only here for a month. We'll soon be out of here and we won't have to deal with it."

"That doesn't make it right!" he answered. "Just because we're getting out of here soon doesn't mean we should just sit around and let this stuff go on. That obstetrician, Parris, he's gonna keep killing women who shouldn't be dead and Sullivan's gonna keep saving babies who shouldn't be alive! What they're doing is wrong, and just because we're only around for one month doesn't justify our sitting back and letting this go on!"

"Well what can we do?" I asked.

"We can stop doing what Sullivan tells us."

"No, that won't help," I answered. "We're not really doing anything now. We don't know how to do anything. The nurses are the ones who are important. And Kathy O'Connell sure as hell isn't going to tell them to stop listening to Sullivan's orders."

Ray reflected on this. "You're right," he replied, calmer. "But there's got to be something else we can do."

By the third round of beers, Ray and I started to move away from our worries. We looked around the room. It was a friendly-looking neighborhood pub with a long bar running the entire length of the room and a few tables scattered around, filling up the rest of the place. It was dark inside, and cool, and it wasn't very crowded yet. We turned to some gossip.

"I wish I could figure out what to do about that Lauren Feinman," Ray said. "She's really pretty, but that's not going to help me when I have a sick baby in the unit. I've got to figure out a way of making sure that she'll be around to help me when I need it."

"I wanted to talk to you about that," I said. "Last night when I was on, Dan and I had a little talk about her at dinner. I told him what had happened to you the night before, and he told me a few things about Lauren."

"Yeah?" Ray asked curiously. "Like what?"

"Well, apparently all the rest of the residents think she's a jerk. She's not very smart and they say she's incompetent. The story is that she screwed herself into medical school here by sleeping with just about every member of the admissions committee. Then when she was a fourth-year medical student, she got a job here as an intern by sleeping with the chief resident in Pediatrics!"

"That figures," Ray said. "She sold herself like merchandise. And that explains why she left me alone. She knows there's no way I could help her. So I guess I can forget about getting any help from her on the nights when we're on call together. How am I going to survive this?"

I thought for a minute and pulled on my beer. It was at this point that I went ahead and revealed the scheme Dan and I had cooked up the night before. "Ray, the best way we could fix this situation is to figure out a way in which you could help Lauren's career."

"Help her career?" he repeated. "How can I do that?"

"Well, Dan says she's interested in pediatric nephrology. She's applying for fellowships all over the place. Dan says the only chance she has of landing a good job is to make it in using something more than her record and letters of recommendation. So all we have to do is make you a famous renal physiologist."

"A famous renal physiologist?" Ray repeated. "How can I become a famous renal physiologist between now and tomorrow night?"

"Well, obviously you're not actually going to be a famous renal physiologist. We're going to make it all up. You got your PhD in renal physiology from, where did you go to medical school?"

"University of Michigan," he said.

"Right, the University of Michigan. And you've worked for five years doing research involving . . . . what? Name one portion of the kidney."

"The glomerulus," said Ray, starting to get into this.

"Right, the glomerulus. And you had to go to medical school in order to get an MD so you'd have a better chance of getting big grants from the government. So you're doing a pediatric internship to get licensed, but then you're going back to Michigan to continue your research. How does that sound?"

"Great!" Ray said. "I guess I'm a pretty fabulous guy. Only two problems: first, how do I get this information to Lauren?"

"Oh, that's easy," I said. "We start a rumor. We'll tell a few nurses, Dan'll call a couple of friends at the Medical Center, it'll get around."

"Okay. The other problem is that I don't know anything about the kidney. I haven't published any papers. How do I fake all that to someone who knows a lot about this stuff?"

"That's no problem," I answered. "From what Dan tells me, Lauren doesn't know anything about anything, including renal physiology. And he also says that she doesn't read anything, so she won't be surprised that she's never heard of you. As long as she knows that you could possibly get her a job in Michigan for next year, that should be enough to get her to do anything for you."

"Pretty devious, Bob. Not very nice but I think it's worth a try. I'm not really doing this for my own gain, I'm doing it so some baby won't be faced with only incompetent me when he arrests."

We had finished our third round and called for a fourth. Ray had started to hum a country song to himself. I realized that although I had just helped to invent a part of Ray's past, I actually knew nothing about his real life outside of work.

"You like country music?" I asked.

"Well," he answered slowly, "I used to hate it. But my wife sort of liked it and I used to be forced to listen to it. After a while I guess I got to like it too. Now I sometimes listen to it on my own."

"What's your wife do?"

"She lives back in Ann Arbor with our kid. I guess we're separated now."

"Oh. Sorry to hear it. When did it happen?"

"Last week. She didn't want to come to Boston. Since I matched here, I had no choice. But last week while I was packing, she said, 'You know, Ray, I've got a pretty good job at the library and I'm in line for a raise in another month. So I'm not going with you to Boston,' and I guess I said, 'Okay.' I'm not really upset. It's been coming for a long time. I'm just sorry that Katie's gonna be staying with her. I really miss that kid!"

"How old is she?"

"She's nearly five. A great age. She really got cute over the last few months. She's going to start kindergarten in September. I was looking forward to seeing her get on the bus that first day. Oh well, it's really not so bad. If she had come with me, I'd be working all the time and I wouldn't have much of a chance to be with her anyway. I guess it'll probably work out for the best this way."

"And I thought I had problems with my wife living back in New York because she has to finish the work for her PhD thesis."

"That's not so good," Ray said. "You ever gonna have a chance to see her?"

"She'll be coming up on weekends."

"Was coming to Boston your idea or her idea?"

"Well, all my advisers told me it would be very helpful to me if I were to do my residency out of New York City. Rachel wasn't very happy about me leaving since she had to stay, but I guess I argued her down enough. Hopefully, she'll be able to finish her lab work in the next few months and come up here full-time to write her thesis."

"That'll be good," Ray said.

"Boy am I tired," I said, and yawned. I looked at my watch. It was seven-thirty. I hadn't slept in thirty-six hours.

"Ray, how long do you think we can go without sleep?"

"I think we can probably go one more beer's worth." With that, the fifth round arrived.

VIII

Thursday, July 1
Morning Rounds

Terry brought two admissions up to the Pit during the night. Although the first admission was only a grower, a baby born slightly prematurely who weighed about four pounds at birth and who had no real medical problems, the second admission was a true sickie. This second child had been born thirteen weeks prematurely at about four in the morning and had taken the place of Baby Torres, who had been trying to go to heaven from midnight on and, when all efforts at resuscitation had failed, had finally been allowed to die at 3 A.M. Terry had become paranoid overnight.

"That Frohman is out to get me!" she whispered when Ray and I found her in the nurses' station at nearly eight o'clock. "He's been bugging me all night! First it was Torres. Ray, I'm sorry I let Torres die."

Ray nodded and made a gesture with his hands toward heaven. "These things happen," he said. "Thank goodness."

"Frohman told me he didn't think Torres looked right when we rounded at about midnight. I didn't notice any difference. She always looked as if she had recently died. But he told me to look her over. While I was checking her, her heart slowed down. I pulled on her big toe and the rate came back up. But then it dropped again and, while I was pulling the other big toe, Frohman came over and said, 'Hmm, bradycardia.' That was all. Then he ran to the nurses' station and called

Sullivan at home. He came back with about ten things Sullivan wanted done. Then the baby arrested.

"We started giving all sorts of medication and got her heart working again for a while. But then the heart stopped, so we gave her another round of meds and got her back. When the heart stopped the third time, we couldn't get it started again for all the medicine in the world. Frohman pumped her chest and shocked her a couple of times, but she didn't get any better. Finally he stuck a needle straight into her heart and gave a round of meds that way. When nothing happened, he pulled the needle out and told me I should do it because, 'If you don't learn on the dead babies, you won't know how to do it on the live ones.' After that didn't work, Frohman said we could stop. 'We gave it the old college try,' he said."

"I'm sure glad I didn't go to the same college as Frohman did," Ray interrupted.

"Then Frohman disappeared. He said he was going to call Sullivan to tell him about the death. I was actually happy he left for a while. With all that fidgeting and gesturing, he makes me so nervous I wind up chewing on my nails. Look." She held up her left hand to show how short her fingernails were.

"I was just beginning to recover from the Torres disaster when the next disaster occurred. This new baby was a mess! Lots of confusion in the DR, lots of screaming and yelling and crying, and that was just the staff! Frohman reappeared and he was standing right behind me, looking over my shoulder the whole time. Then when the baby was born, he pushed me away and did the whole resuscitation himself."

"Well, he did say you have to learn on the dead ones first," I said.

"I guess that's it. Anyway, we got the new baby stabilized at around seven. I haven't even creased the sheets on the cot. And every time I sit down, Frohman finds two or three things I should do!"

Ray and I calmed her down. We told her she should leave the hospital as soon as she could, but she didn't want to. She knew that if she were to leave, we would get stuck doing her work. We pushed her and ourselves through work rounds. I had no idea what to expect from Sullivan at his rounds. We hadn't had a death before.

As soon as we entered his office at around ten, Sullivan asked how Baby Torres was doing. Terry, Ray, and I looked puzzled. Frohman didn't, but didn't say anything. After some hesitation, Terry finally said, "The baby died this morning."

"He died?" Sullivan asked in a high-pitched voice. His eyes opened wide. "Dr. Frohman? Why wasn't I called at home?"

All eyes shifted to Frohman. He was rubbing the fingernails of his left hand against the fingernails of his right repeatedly, and this motion was creating a disturbing clicking sound that could be heard only now that everyone in the room was silent. His feet, meanwhile, were sliding alternatingly up and down the legs of his chair. After a slight hesitation, Frohman said, "Terry, you know that Dr. Sullivan says that he wants to be called at home if there's any major change in any of the babies. Why didn't you call Dr. Sullivan when Baby Torres died?"

Terry was really puzzled now. "You said you were going to call him," she said to Frohman.

"That's always been the intern's job," Frohman said.

Sullivan was really angry. "You screwed up, Dr. Costa!" he said. "I'm to be called at home when there's a major change in any patient's condition. And I would call dying a major change!"

"But Frohman said . . ." Terry started.

"I don't want to hear any excuses," Sullivan interrupted.

Terry stared angrily at Frohman who looked away. Sullivan leaned back in his chair and looked up at the ceiling for nearly a minute. Then he straightened up, looked at Terry, and began firing questions. "What change did you note before the arrest?"

Terry told him what Frohman had noticed around midnight.

"What did the blood gases show? Was there any change in them?"

Terry didn't remember; Frohman, usually the leader on attending rounds, was now not offering any information.

"You don't remember?" Sullivan asked vindictively. "That could've been the answer! That could've saved the baby's life! And you didn't notice whether the baby became acidotic before the arrest?"

"I didn't notice," Terry answered.

"Well, then tell me what you did notice?" Sullivan yelled. "You didn't call me so I sure wasn't around to notice anything. Don't you think noticing something like acidosis might be important?"

"Frohman was with me!" Terry said. She was remaining calm. "He was telling me what to do."

"Oh?" Sullivan asked. "Do you depend on Dr. Frohman for all your ideas, Dr. Costa? You are a doctor, aren't you?"

"Why shouldn't she depend on Frohman?" Ray asked Sullivan. "After all, Frohman depends on you for all his ideas."

Frohman glowered at Ray. Dan, who had been listening to all this with his eyes closed, finally seemed to wake up. "Please leave her alone, Dr. Sullivan," he said politely. "You know, at night here in the nursery, it is the resident who is the responsible party. So if you do want to yell at someone, the correct person would be Dr. Frohman. He was the one in charge."

Now Frohman shot daggers with his eyes at Dan. The rhythm of his nail clicking increased with his anger. Sullivan was ready to lower the proverbial boom. "Stay out of this, you asshole! I know damned well who's supposed to be in charge and what the intern's responsibility is!" he yelled at Dan.

I couldn't control myself and started to giggle, and Ray changed the subject. "Look, Dr. Sullivan," he said, "what difference does it make? Torres had a terrible prognosis. You said so yourself. If she had lived, she'd just be another one of the GORKs at follow-up clinic. It's for the best that she died."

"A what?" Sullivan asked angrily. Clearly he had never heard this term and was steaming. "First of all, Dr. Brewster, you, Dr. Costa, and Dr. Sharon have to learn what the procedure is when cases like this occur in the future. I must ensure that this kind of mistake does not occur again. Second, how do you know what Torres would have been like? How many twenty-six weekers have you taken care of, Dr. Brewster?"

"Well, none. But one day in follow-up clinic is worth a thousand twenty-six weekers! Even the twenty-seven and twenty-eight weekers end up retarded, have CP and seizures. This kid had no chance!"

Sullivan tried to calm himself. "I can see that pursuing this discussion further is pointless. And I can also see that you, Dr. Brewster, are not going to agree with my decisions. I've told you that if you listen to me, this can be a good learning experience. I hope you other interns don't follow Dr. Brewster's lead."

Terry and I looked away, not answering Sullivan's challenge. I knew I had already had enough of this man. I was sure Terry had also had enough of him. She didn't need all this abuse heaped atop a night spent without sleep.

And then, something weird happened. Politely, in a completely different tone of voice, Sullivan said, "Now, Dr. Costa, will you please tell us about Baby Singer, the new admission from last night?"

"Schizophrenic." I thought.

Terry, at first looking confused, launched into the story of her new sick premie. Sullivan listened, seemingly detached. He didn't interrupt Terry's story at all and there was no argument and very little discussion. He simply told Frohman what he wanted done, and that was all.

After Baby Singer was discussed, Sullivan turned to me and asked, "Have we gotten consent from the mother of that mongoloid baby yet, Dr. Sharon?"

I had been dreading this moment. "I had a long talk with Mrs. O'Hara yesterday. I told her that she had to sign for the operation. I figured it would be best to give her a day or two more to think about it."

Sullivan's eyes again opened widely. "Dr. Sharon, didn't I order you to come back with a signed consent, or not to come back at all?"

"Yes, you did," I answered. "But I thought it best . . ."

"Another one thinking?" he shouted, interrupting me. "Another one making decisions? Didn't I tell you three that I was the one who made all the decisions here? If I tell you to do something, I don't want you to think about doing it! I want it done, and done right away. Now get going, Sharon. Get down to that mother's room. I want that consent form signed immediately. And this is your last chance. If you don't do it, I'm going to have to do it myself."

And that was the end of rounds. When I went down to the third floor, I found that Mrs. O'Hara was in critical condition.

IX

Mrs. O'Hara

Sometime during the night, Mrs. O'Hara had cried out in pain and slipped into coma. Her deterioration seemed sudden but, in retrospect, it was clear that this had been developing since her cesarean section.

Some obstetricians use antibiotics routinely to prevent infection after they've performed a section. Parris, of course, hadn't been keeping up with the latest advances and so hadn't given Mrs. O'Hara any antibiotics. She had seemed fine right after the operation, except for her depression. However, even when I had spoken with her twenty-four hours after the delivery, she had complained of a slight fever and increasing tenderness at the incision site. As the day had worn on, her fever increased. Since she had been transferred back to the maternity floor in the old St. A's, the obstetric house staff no longer were involved with her case. Her care had become solely Parris's domain. Parris hadn't thought anything of Mrs. O'Hara's symptoms when he had made rounds in the afternoon. But during the early evening, her fever had risen to a hundred and three, she had complained of more and more pain and, at around ten o'clock, had become disoriented, not remembering the name of the hospital or, more troubling, the name of her husband. Mr. O'Hara, who had been allowed to stay since Mrs. O'Hara had been so depressed, demanded that Dr. Parris be called immediately. The nurse who had woken him up at eleven-thirty told him the problem. Parris, relieved that it was just a little post-op complication and not one of his patients annoying him by going into labor prematurely in the middle of the night, ordered some Tylenol for Mrs. O'Hara and that the nurse not wake him up again.

When it had become clearly evident that something was terribly wrong, the nurse paged the obstetric resident on call. Sheila Simpson, the resident, had come to see Mrs. O'Hara immediately and had suspected a wound infection which had led to sepsis, a bacterial infection of the blood. Sheila, hoping to catch the infection before it was too late, had immediately taken samples of blood, urine, the fluid coming from the wound, and cerebrospinal fluid for culture, and started Mrs. O'Hara on high-dose, broad-spectrum antibiotics. But it had already been too late. Mrs. O'Hara had lapsed into septic shock.

Dr. Simpson had known exactly what to do, and she had done it all well. Mrs. O'Hara had received a large quantity of Ringer's lactate, an IV solution designed to increase the circulating blood volume and the blood pressure, and a large dose of steroids. Oxygen had been administered by face mask and Mrs. O'Hara had been taken to the hospital's operating room on the second floor, where the incision had been reopened and a large quantity of foul-smelling pus had been drained. The wound had not been reclosed, but had been left open to allow more drainage of the infection. Finally, Mrs. O'Hara had been transferred back to the delivery suite's recovery room, the closest thing St. A's had to an intensive care unit for adults.

After listening in disbelief to this story as it was told by the nurses on the third floor, I came to see Mrs. O'Hara in the recovery room. I found her husband standing at her bedside. He was a tall, thin man. He had dark hair and was totally bald on top. He wore a three-piece, dark suit. He had been crying. I introduced myself.

"Hello," he mumbled. "Joan told me about you. How's the baby?"

"Okay," I answered. "About the same. How are you doing?"

He didn't answer but looked to his wife lying unconscious on the bed. She had as many tubes in her as some of the premies.

After some hesitation, I said, "Mr. O'Hara, if there's anything I can do to help you, please ask." He didn't answer. I turned to leave. I felt bad for him. At the nurses' station I stopped to read Mrs. O'Hara's chart. There was an intercom from Mrs. O'Hara's bedside and it was on. I heard Mr. O'Hara saying in a broken sobbing voice, "C'mon, Joan. Don't do this to me. You have so much to live for. Please don't die. . . ." His words broke off into loud sobs.

I went back to the nursery and sat in the nurses' station, peering in through the glass windows at the hubbub of activity. Sullivan, who was examining Baby Singer, Terry's new admission, saw me and came over. I was trying hard to fight off tears.

"Did you get the consent form signed?" he barked.

"Mrs. O'Hara is in septic shock. She's just come from the OR where they drained an abscess. She's unconscious."

"Was the father there?" he asked.

"Yeah. He was pretty broken up."

"Well, did you get him to sign the consent form?"

I looked at Sullivan in disbelief. "You're kidding, aren't you?" I asked.

"I don't joke about things like this," he answered.

"Haven't you been listening to what I've been saying?" I asked, even closer to tears. "Mrs. O'Hara may die. Her husband is at her bedside, crying. You think now is a good time to get him to sign the damned form?"

"Look, just because one member of the family is dying, that's no reason we have to let another one die!"

"Sullivan," I shouted loud enough to turn the head of every adult in the nursery, "you are a madman! You are absolutely certifiable! You're nothing but a machine. You are totally void of any human emotions!"

"Human emotions? Look, sonny, I've been saving babies for over ten years. I know what life and death is! I've had to tell a lot of mothers that their babies had died in that time! So don't you talk to me about emotions!"

"You are out in left field!" I yelled back. "I tell you one thing and you answer with a total non sequitur! Okay, I'll spell it out for you, nice and simple. If you want that consent form signed by the father, you go do it yourself! I refuse to even ask until Mrs. O'Hara is out of danger!"

Without another word to me, Sullivan stormed out of the nurses' station.

X

After Hours

I sat on a lawn chair on the patio in back of Terry's house in Brookline, drinking white wine while the coals were heating up in the hibachi. Terry was reclining on a chaise longue. She had invited me over for dinner to calm me down after my argument with Sullivan.

I was on my third glass of Chablis and was feeling better. I was beginning to realize that my internship might well turn me into an alcoholic. It certainly didn't look as if it was going to turn me into a competent physician! The only times I had felt at ease so far during this first week had been the times I had been drunk. Terry seemed to be drifting off to sleep.

"The coals look hot," I said, awakening her. "I'm going to put the hamburgers on." She nodded and fell back to sleep. But then Ray phoned with some interesting news.

"I'm sorry to interrupt your evening," he said after Terry had instructed me to pick up the extension phone in her bedroom, "but I have something to tell you. The O'Hara baby's father just punched out Sullivan."

"What?" we asked simultaneously. "You're kidding! What happened?"

"Well I'm not exactly sure about the whole thing but I guess after you and Sullivan had your little discussion in the nurses' station, Sullivan went to the recovery room with a consent form and he told Mr. O'Hara that he had to consent to the operation or that we'd do it anyway. I guess Mr. O'Hara didn't like being told what he had to do, especially with his wife lying there in a coma and everything, and so he leaned back and punched out Sullivan's lights. I guess our attending has a glass jaw."

I was trying to imagine the scene. I could visualize everything up to the point where Mr. O'Hara delivered the haymaker. He just didn't seem like that kind of man. "Well that's great," I said. "He probably deserved it. Anything happen when Sullivan came to?"

"Sure," Ray responded. "That was just the beginning. The nurses saw Sullivan go down for the count and they called the security guard stat! O'Hara, realizing what he'd done, went to Sullivan's side to sort of help him up. The guards arrived and I guess they thought O'Hara was trying to finish Sullivan off, so they jumped him, pried him off Sullivan, and hustled him out of the hospital.

"When Sullivan finally came to, he was madder than a hatter, as they say. He was yelling and screaming. It was pretty funny to watch. He says he's gonna press charges against O'Hara and he's already spoken to some judge to get permission to do the operation on the baby. The papers aren't all signed yet, but Sullivan told me to make sure the baby was ready to go to the OR tomorrow morning."

"What a jerk!" Terry said.

"I can't understand why Sullivan is still working at St. A's. In less than a week he's made enemies with three interns and got himself slugged by the father of a patient. You'd think someone would have enough sense to throw the guy out on his ear."

"Well I just wanted to let you know," Ray said. "I have to get back to work. There are about a million blood gas results waiting here for me and then I have to go to dinner with Lauren."

"Dinner with Lauren," I repeated. "It sounds like you're making some progress."

"Yeah, Bob," Ray said. "She already got wind of the story. The first thing she asked me tonight was whether it was true that I was some sort of brilliant renal physiologist from the University of Michigan. I sort of blushed and said that I don't like to discuss my life outside of the hospital, that I was just another intern."

"Just another intern, huh?" Terry giggled.

"Yeah. So after that, she told me she was interested in renal and maybe we should discuss it over dinner tonight."

"Wow," I laughed. "I never really thought it would work, and certainly not so fast! It sure tells you something about how rumors travel around this place!"

"Bob, it was a great idea," Ray said. "You are a genius."

"Yeah," Terry added. "Ray, you're a brilliant physiologist and, Bob, you're a genius. It's really terrific to be in such stimulating company."

"Yeah, it might be terrific," Ray said, "but the fact still remains that none of us knows what the hell we're doing when it comes to taking care of these damned babies. Well, I'm gonna go. Have a good night. See you bright and early in the morning."

"Bright and early," Terry said.

"Good luck with Lauren," I added as we all hung up.

I rejoined Terry out on the patio. The hamburgers had burned to a crisp while we were on the phone. "Damn," I said at the sight of the charred meat.

"Doesn't matter," Terry said, "I'm not hungry."

"Me neither." Since starting my internship I had lost my appetite.

"I tell my husband all about these things, but he doesn't believe me. Nothing like this ever happens at his hospital."

"Where's he work?" I asked.

"At Beth Israel. He's a medical intern. He's on call tonight. Do you realize, because we pulled different schedules this first month, that we see each other only one out of three nights? And we're so exhausted on that night that all we seem to do is argue and sleep. What a great life this is turning out to be."

I thought about this for a minute. "It's amazing. One week ago all three of us were leading seminormal married lives. And now, just because we started our internships, you see your husband every third night, I'll see my wife only on weekends, and Ray won't ever see his wife and daughter, except maybe during vacations."

"Ray said to me that it's good in a way he and his wife separated," Terry said. "He said living alone during an internship is less distracting."

"I have a feeling Ray would find something good in a pile of shit falling on his head," I said. "Well I guess this'll give me a chance to wash my hair." We both laughed.

We drank more wine and watched a rerun of "The Odd Couple" on TV. By seven o'clock Terry had fallen asleep with her head up against my right knee. Even though we had met only four days before, I already knew that I liked Terry very much. And I liked the feeling of being next to her, and of having her leaning on me, even if it was only her head against my knee.

At about seven-fifteen, I woke Terry and told her that I was feeling much better and that I was leaving. "Can't you stay a little longer?" she asked. "We haven't killed the bottle of wine yet."

"I'm already drunk," I answered, "and tired. I don't think I'd be able to get home if I drank any more."

"Okay," she said as she rose, and together we walked out to the driveway. We embraced tightly before I got into my car and, intoxicated and exhausted as I was, I felt my pulse quicken. But I fought off the urge that threatened to overtake me. We broke the embrace and I got into the car. She told me to drive carefully and then disappeared back into the house.

XI

Friday, July 2

Morning Rounds

Although the whole week was bad, Fridays were the worst simply because on the day before the weekend we spent a lot more time with Sullivan than usual. It was necessary for him to see every patient so he could tell us what was to be expected and what would have to be done over the next two days. As a result, more time was needed for rounds. They were extended to fill the time usually allotted for attending rounds. And then after we had dissected every patient in the nursery, one interesting case, which illustrated an important concept in neonatal medicine, was discussed in depth. This latter event, called "grand rounds," was billed as a teaching conference and occurred between eleven-thirty and one in the afternoon. Grand rounds were followed at one-thirty by the combined obstetric/neonatal rounds, a mammoth event where Sullivan got to argue with Dr. Adams, the chief of the perinatal obstetrics service, about which service actually was at fault in cases where the outcome was not as good as it should have been. The combined conference usually lasted an hour, so all in all, we would be spending about six and a half hours with Dr. Sullivan. None of us was looking forward to this overdose.

Ray again had had a pretty good night. He had gotten no admissions, and again, little sleep. Lauren had stayed with him until midnight and had spent the evening hounding him with questions about the nephrology program at the University of Michigan. Ray had continued to remain silent about his past, which had only served to reinforce Lauren's feelings that he was the key to her salvation.

The babies had all been stable through the night. Baby Singer, Terry's admission from the night before, was beginning to show signs of improvement; he looked like a real fighter and probably would do well.

Frohman showed up that morning wearing a small plastic pouch attached to his belt. Missing from around his neck was the stethoscope he usually wore. It was clear that that stethoscope was now kept in that belt pouch.

At a little after eight, Sullivan, accompanied by Kathy O'Connell, appeared in the Pit. The left side of Sullivan's face below his eye was black and blue and swollen. His eye was partly closed. It looked pretty painful. Terry and I tried not to laugh as Frohman began rounds.

Sullivan poked and prodded every baby in the Pit. Even the growers, who received only a quick glance on most mornings to make sure they were still with us, got their heads measured, their hearts examined, and their weight charts checked. Sullivan ignored us interns on rounds, speaking directly to Frohman and to Kathy, who was taking notes on a yellow pad of paper. Ray, Terry, and I did not in the least mind being slighted by Sullivan.

It was to be a particularly trying morning for Kathy. Word had come the day before that a bed had become available at the Waltham Home for Freddie Endicott. He was to leave that morning and so, while we were walking through the nursery, two nurses were packing all the belongings that Freddie had accumulated during his four-month stay at St. A's.

Rounds were stopped when Freddie was ready to go. The evening nurse who had cared for Freddie during his stay was ready to drive the baby to the Waltham Home. Kathy had brought a cake that she'd baked herself which had "Goodbye Freddie" written on it in frosting. Kathy had made sure not to use any milk products in making the cake, so that Freddie could have a little piece. The cake was cut and divided among the staff. Even Ray, Terry, and I got a slice. Dr. Sullivan took the opportunity to thank the nurses. "If it had not been for the outstanding nursing care Freddie has received, he never would have survived to reach this point. I thank you all."

"If it hadn't been for the horrible medical care Freddie has received," Terry whispered to me, "he would have gone home four months ago, a relatively normal child."

Freddie was dressed up in a little blue suit with a matching blue baseball cap and baby blue running shoes. Kathy lifted him out of his special crib (he was too big to fit on a warming table) and wrapped him in a light receiving blanket. Then still cradling the baby in her arms, she looked to Ray, Terry, and me and said, "I hope all you house officers remember Freddie! It was because Freddie was entrusted to doctors who couldn't recognize a child with galactosemia that he ended up this way. I hope none of you, if you're ever faced with a child with a similar problem, ever forget Freddie."

We stood frozen in our places. Kathy didn't sound angry or hostile, she simply wanted to make a point and, as I've already mentioned, that point was clearly made with me; I have never forgotten Freddie Endicott, and I have never missed the diagnosis of galactosemia.

Kathy, after her remarks, handed the baby over to the nurse who was going to drive him to the Waltham Home. We all waved goodbye to him as he and the nurse disappeared through the door.

I had trouble concentrating through the rest of rounds that morning. My mind was wandering; I was trying to imagine what Freddie's life was going to be like at the Waltham Home. Before starting at St. A's, I had never thought about the disasters our modern technology created. Now I was thinking about what this home must be like, a home that cared for maybe hundreds of GORKed-out babies, fulfilling their immediate needs of food, clothing, and a crib, but never able to fulfill their needs for love and attention, so necessary for young children.

I also was thinking about what had happened the night before when I was leaving Terry's house. I tried to deny it, I tried to minimize its importance, but I had felt something, a spark of electricity, pass between us when we held each other in that embrace. That feeling scared me because I hadn't felt anything like it since I had fallen in love with Rachel while I was a second-year medical student, and because of the threat that feeling posed to my relationship with Rachel, already threatened through the simple fact that we were separated by two hundred miles.

We didn't discuss Baby Girl O'Hara that morning because she was in the OR during our rounds, having her gut repaired, thanks to an order issued by a Judge Isaacs. I was happy that we didn't have to relive the events of the night before, not because I felt that I had done anything wrong, but because I was afraid I would break into uncontrollable laughter if Sullivan mentioned his encounter with Mr. O'Hara.

Near the end of rounds that morning, we were interrupted by the appearance of two visitors. "Good morning, Dr. Sullivan," one of the visitors, a man of about sixty-five who was wearing a black suit and a clerical collar, said. "You remember Mr. Stone?" His eyes seemed to twinkle as he said this.

The other visitor, a man in a conservative gray pin-striped suit who was in his late fifties, put his hand out and said, "It's very nice to see you again, Dr. Sullivan."

Sullivan did not offer this man his hand; instead, he looked to the man in the clerical collar and said, "Monsignor Vitale, I believe I have asked you at least three times in the past not to disturb me while I'm busy on rounds. I'm afraid I can find no other way to make that any clearer to you."

Monsignor Vitale moved back a step and his eyes widened and lost a little of their twinkle. "Dr. Sullivan," he seemed to spit as he spoke, "please mind your tongue! I am afraid there was no other time Mr. Stone could come by to see you. I'm truly sorry that we are disturbing your rounds, but some things must take precedence."

"Kissing up to Stone takes precedence over the babies?" Sullivan shouted at Monsignor Vitale. "Look, Monsignor, I have a nursery full of sick infants here. I won't get anything accomplished if I have to stop everything and kiss the ass of every bastard who comes through here promising to donate some money to keep this place running! So if you don't mind, the door is that way!"

Monsignor Vitale glared at Sullivan. He turned to Mr. Stone and said, "I apologize to you, sir, for Dr. Sullivan. His behavior is . . ."

"And don't apologize for me!" Sullivan shouted. "I said what I meant! If I want to apologize, I'll do it for myself."

Mr. Stone, whose facial expression didn't change during the monsignor's conversation with our attending, simply put his hands up in the air and said, "Don't worry about it, Monsignor. I've had some past dealings with your Dr. Sullivan, and I know he's full of hot air." Sullivan glared at him. "Dr. Sullivan, it is a good thing you are a good neonatologist because, if you were not, and you persisted with this attitude of yours, you can be sure you would have been out of a job long ago." Now he turned again to the monsignor. "Monsignor, my daughter-in-law is due to deliver my first grandchild in less than a month. I hope you will make sure that Dr. Sullivan here treats my grandchild in the manner I would expect."

The monsignor smiled at Mr. Stone. "You can be sure your grandchild will get the royal treatment," he said. Before Sullivan could answer, they walked out of the Pit.

"Those bastards!" Sullivan said as they vanished behind the door. "Those rich bastards who, because they're in a position to give away a lot of money, think they can come in here and run the whole show! I hate every one of them! Pushy sons of bitches! And that monsignor, kissing his ass like he was the Pope or something! You can bet, that grandchild of his is going to get treated like it was any other baby! Royal treatment, my ass!"

We remained silent and frozen all through this interruption. And then, just as it had started, it ended. Sullivan, with the same expression he had worn before the meeting with the monsignor, continued rounds and we finished a few minutes later.

Grand rounds were held in Dr. Sullivan's office. Dan, who had not appeared during morning work rounds, still hadn't shown up.

For this day's grand rounds, Sullivan had prepared a slide presentation. "Since none of you has chosen to listen to my orders over the last week," he said, looking toward us interns, "I got to thinking about how I could convince you that my way is best. I realize that since this is your first rotation, you've seen none of the products of our nursery except for our failures, the children who attend follow-up clinic. So for today's grand rounds I've assembled a series of before-and-after pictures and I'm sure that after you see these slides, you'll all see my point and the arguing and bickering will cease."

I was stunned to hear normal and reasonable words coming out of his mouth. He flashed the first slide up on the wall near the door. It showed a small baby in an incubator. The baby was breathing on its own, without the help of a ventilator. Sullivan was also in the picture, looking younger and thinner, and his hair was fuller and less gray. He was listening to the baby's chest with his premie stethoscope.

"This is Roy Darren," he said after turning the office lights off. "He weighed eleven hundred grams when he was born in January nineteen seventy-three. He spent a month and a half as a patient here." Sullivan clicked the projector and the next slide appeared. It showed the same child standing with his arm around Sullivan's leg. "And here's Roy, age two, at this year's Premie Picnic which was held a few weeks ago. The picnic is a yearly reunion for all the patients and the staff. It gives us a chance to view the fruits of our labor. As you can clearly see, Roy is a happy, healthy, normal child now."

Another click of the carousel projector and a picture of a premie lying on a warming table, looking very much like Baby Summlitz, flashed on the wall. "This is Andy Sterling. He weighed nine hundred grams at birth, required ventilator support, and had a fairly rocky course during his four months here in nineteen seventy-two. His parents kept asking me why I was doing all the things I was doing. They wanted me to let him die." The projector moved again and another picture taken at the recently held Premie Picnic appeared. "And here's Andy at the picnic. Although he has some residual lung disease, still occasionally requires ventilatory assistance, and has a tracheostomy to allow his parents to hook him up to his home ventilator, you can see that he will be a normal member of society. His parents wanted to kiss my feet at the picnic because I hadn't given in to them and allowed Andy to die."

Sullivan continued on like this. He presented pictures of a dozen premies, all of whom had come into the Pit as small, frail chicken wings and had gone out as nearly normal children. Most of these children had some residual defect, a tracheostomy, mild heart disease, an eye problem, a colostomy, to remind them of their stay at St. A's. All, however, seemed totally normal in their development.

After the slides were completed, Sullivan sat back in his swivel chair and said, "So, you can all see why it is mandatory that everything be done for every baby at all times. Even after all these years, and all the babies I've taken care of, I still can't tell who's going to survive and who is not. And I truly believe that none of you, or any other doctor, can either."

I was truly impressed by this presentation. These children certainly weren't the GORKs we had seen in follow-up clinic. We were silent for a few seconds. I was suddenly feeling a little better about spending this July at St. A's.

But Ray brought us all back down to earth. "That was sort of nice," he said, "but I have one question. Did any of those babies have any neurologic complications while they were patients here? Did any of them have intracranial hemorrhages or seizures?"

"No," Sullivan responded, with a questioning look on his face. "As far as I can recall, all were normal neurologically. What are you getting at?"

"Well that's a problem," Ray said. "I can understand doing everything at all times for every baby who is neurologically normal. I can understand doing everything even when there's a question but no proof of neurologic problem. But where we're sure a kid has burned out his brain, you must admit that that kid isn't going to contribute much to society. And I think that doing everything at all times for that kid is wrong."

Sullivan remained calm, but he lost the contented expression he had worn during most of the grand rounds presentation. "Well, Dr. Brewster," he said, "I'll agree with you that doing everything for a child who we're sure is going to grow up to be severely handicapped is, in theory, wrong. But, as I said before, I can't be sure which of these babies will be and which won't be severely handicapped, even when there is some evidence of abnormal neurologic functioning. And it is my feeling that it is better to err on the side of being too conservative and save a percentage of infants who eventually grow into damaged children, than it is to err on the side of being too liberal, and withhold treatment from even one baby who may survive intact."

"Again," Ray said, "I disagree. In a baby like Torres, where we knew the prognosis was terrible from a day or two before the baby died, I feel we shouldn't go all out on a baby like that. I think we have to think about the quality of life that's going on, and I think we should direct some of our energies on sort of preparing the family in a situation like that."

"Again the family!" Sullivan shouted. "All you interns ever think about is how this is going to affect the poor family. Haven't I already convinced you that the families don't have enough smarts to know what should and shouldn't be done? If I had listened to the Sterling family, Andy would have been left to die. He may grow up to be president of the United States for all we know. I swear, if you three spent as much time learning about how to take care of these premies as you do being concerned with how we're torturing the families, we'd all be better off!"

Ray, Terry, and I looked at each other. I think it was at this point that we first realized that Sullivan was not a person with whom we could civilly discuss our point of view. The man was beyond reason. And so for the rest of grand rounds, which soon ended, we kept our mouths shut.

Combined obstetric/neonatal rounds, which began about a half hour after grand rounds concluded that day, were held in the auditorium on the first floor of the hospital. The auditorium seated about three hundred people, and thus the twenty or so of us who showed up were just about lost in the room. As I entered, I saw Sullivan with Kathy by his side in the first row on the left side of the aisle, the section that had over the years become the pediatric area. Sullivan's counterpart, Dr. Adams, the chief of the perinatal service, sat opposite Sullivan in the obstetric section on the right side of the room. Seated next to Adams was a woman who looked just exactly like Kathy.

The room looked as if it had been decorated by a color-blind interior designer. The curtains which hid the stage were of orange, green, and blue check. The walls were dull orange cinder block with green trim. The seats were upholstered with a faded, dull blue cloth. While I was trying to imagine the person who consciously tried to get this effect, I saw Dan seated in the fourth row on the pediatric side of the room, with his feet sprawled over the seat in front of him. I sat next to him, and Ray and Terry sat next to me. Frohman sat by himself, between Sullivan and us, in the second row.

"I didn't think you were going to show up today," I said.

"Oh I've been here since eight," Dan said. "I'm boycotting Sullivan. I decided I couldn't stand being around him."

"Well, if you're boycotting him, what are you doing here?"

"Are you kidding?" he asked. "I wouldn't miss this conference for the world! This is usually the best theatrical event in the whole Boston area on Fridays. Wait'll you see what happens."

"Who are those people?" I asked, gesturing toward the obstetric side of the room.

"The obstetric house staff," he answered. "A lot of their nurses come to this thing too, if they can get off work. It really is very entertaining. You see that guy sitting opposite Sullivan?" He pointed to Adams. "That's Dr. Adams. He's a world famous perinatologist. He's great!

And he's the reason these rounds are so good. Watch what he does to Sullivan in the next hour."

"Who's that woman sitting next to him?" I asked.

"Oh, that's a good story too," he answered. "Who does she look like?"

"Like Kathy," I answered. "Only better looking."

"Right. She's Donna O'Connell, Kathy's sister. She's a nurse midwife. She and Adams have been having an affair for at least as long as I've been here. It drives Sullivan crazy. . . ."

"How come?" I asked.

"Well, I don't know if you've had time to notice it yet, but Sullivan's dying to get into Kathy's pants. She won't let him though. She told one of the women who was a senior resident when I was an intern that, although she thinks he's a great doctor, and although she'd follow any order he gave her when it came to taking care of the babies, she'd never go to bed with him because he's married. But it drives Sullivan crazy that her sister is screwing around with Adams, who's also married."

"This is like Peyton Place. How do you know all this stuff?"

"You gotta keep your eyes and ears open, Bob," he said, as Sullivan rose and walked slowly to a podium that had been set up at the front of the room.

"Let's get started," Sullivan said, and everyone in the room quieted down and turned to face the front. "Because the interns have just arrived on service, I will present today's case." As he reached into his pocket and removed a piece of note paper, I thought that something struck me as being different about Sullivan. I couldn't put my finger on it, and he began to read his prepared notes. "The patient, Baby Boy MacArthur, was born by spontaneous vaginal delivery to a twenty-eight-year-old woman. The baby was the product of a twenty-six-week gestation, by dates, size, and developmental assessment. Because of severe asphyxia suffered while in utero, the baby was born with evidence of severe neurologic damage. All efforts to resuscitate the child in the delivery room were unsuccessful. The baby was pronounced dead thirty-two minutes after delivery.

"The reason we're presenting this case today," Sullivan continued, now looking at Dr. Adams, "is to question why the mother was managed in the way she was. From the notes in her chart, it is apparent that signs of fetal distress were present on the fetal monitor recordings as soon as the mother appeared in the delivery suite. In spite of these signs, the labor was not managed aggressively, but rather the mother was permitted to continue to labor until conclusion. I believe that this baby would have survived had this woman had a cesarean section as soon as the problem was first detected."

Sullivan, having concluded his presentation, replaced the paper from which he had read back into his pocket and, while he was returning to his seat, Andy Schwartz, the chief obstetric resident, took Sullivan's place at the front of the room. This was the first time I had seen Schwartz wearing something other than dirty, bloody scrubs, as he had worn during the delivery of Baby Girl O'Hara; he still looked like a bear. Schwartz was prepared to discuss the Obstetric Department's side of the case.

"Mrs. MacArthur was a high-risk patient, followed here in the St. Anne's clinic," he began. Unlike Sullivan, he did not refer to notes, but stood slouching, with his hands in his pockets, and stared straight ahead. "The reason she was originally referred here was because of her diabetes. She has been an insulin-dependent diabetic since the age of nine, she has evidence of ocular disease and pretty significant renal disease. During the pregnancy just reviewed by Dr. Sullivan, her diabetes had been in fairly good control, but she required a couple of hospitalizations for better glucose control during the second trimester. Her renal function has been drastically deteriorating in the three weeks prior to delivery, and it looked as if we were going to have to dialize her if the pregnancy continued.

"When she appeared in the delivery suite in labor, exam revealed that the fetus was smaller than it should have been for her point in gestation. An ultrasound exam confirmed our impression of intrauterine growth retardation. When we hooked her up to the monitor and found late decelerations, I consulted with Dr. Adams who agreed with my impression that Mrs. MacArthur was not a candidate for a section, since the procedure might jeopardize the survival of the mother and since the baby was extremely premature and showed evidence of growth retardation. So we allowed her to labor and to deliver the child vaginally."

Diabetes during pregnancy presents many problems to the mother, to the fetus, and to the perinatologist caring for them. In the present case, there was evidence even before she got pregnant that Mrs. Mac-

Arthur would have a lot of problems. She already had some of the complications that are seen usually only in people with long-standing, poorly controlled diabetes. These problems, all resulting from damage to blood vessels, include eye problems that lead ultimately to blindness, and renal disease that leads ultimately to chronic renal failure and death. These vascular problems also contributed to the damage that Mrs. MacArthur's fetus had apparently suffered while still in the womb.

The fetus relies on the placenta for its supply of oxygen and nutrients. The placenta, a highly vascular organ, is made up of collections of blood vessels, some fetal and some maternal in origin. Although these two circulations don't actually touch, they are close enough to assure that substances can pass between the two compartments. Like all the other blood vessels in diabetic women, the ones in the placenta are abnormal and, as a result of this, the fetus can be deprived of the oxygen and nutrients it requires during the critical period before birth. This leads to the growth retardation seen in the MacArthur baby, brain damage caused by lack of oxygen, and congenital malformations. Since evidence of at least one of these abnormalities was documented in the fetus, the obstetric staff had decided to do nothing heroic to save the fetus, but rather to preserve the life of the mother.

At the conclusion of his discussion, Schwartz asked, "Any questions?" To be sure, Sullivan had a few.

"Dr. Schwartz," Sullivan began, standing at his place and rocking gently back and forth, "I don't fully under . . . understand how you reached this decision." He seemed to be slurring his words a little. "Babies given to us at this gestational . . . gestational age have a fifty percent chance of survival. Our statistics show that those babies who were delivered by section did better than those who were delivered vaginally, so your decision to let this woman deliver vaginally essentially sentenced this child to death."

"I can't believe he's arguing about this," I whispered to Dan. "The mother would have died if they had done that section. He sounds like he's drunk or something."

"Shhh," Dan whispered back. "This is where it starts getting good."

"Again, Dr. Sullivan," Schwartz said patiently, "we felt that first, the operation would endanger the life of the mother and, second, the child had already been significantly damaged by the metabolic milieu."

"Metabolic milieu, my ass!" Sullivan shouted. Dan was grinning. "You guys simply chose to save the mother at the expense of the baby. And I want to know who gave you the right to make that decision!"

"Again, Dr. Sullivan," Schwartz repeated, still calm and patient, "the decision was a judgment call on our part. We felt the mother's chance of survival without the operation was better than the fetus's chance if the operation had been performed. Based on this judgment, we elected not to proceed with a section."

"This is bullshit!" Sullivan shouted, his face turning red. "I keep asking the same . . . the same question, and you keep giving me the same bullshit answer. You obstetricians don't care what happens to the babies. You're only concerned with the mother's welfare. This case makes that obvious. Who is the advocate for the fetus when these decisions are being made by you? I'll tell you who! No one! What chance do the babies have in these cases? I'll tell you again! None!" Sullivan's rocking was becoming more and more exaggerated.

Now Dr. Adams rose to his full height. He stood straight and tall. "Oh boy," Dan whispered to me, "here it comes!"

"Dr. Sullivan," Adams began, "there are civilized human beings present in this room. Please attempt to refrain from swearing."

"Don't give me that," Sullivan yelled over to his counterpart. "You just tell me why you continue to make these decisions without consulting me."

"Dr. Sullivan," Dr. Adams said calmly, "are you an obstetrician?"

"You know I'm not. That doesn't have anything to do with it!" Sullivan's face was getting more flushed by the minute.

"Dr. Sullivan," Adams continued, "do you have any special training in medical ethics?"

"You're not answering my question, Adams!"

"Dr. Sullivan, if you have no training in obstetrics or in ethics, what qualifications do you have to make decisions in the delivery suite?"

"I care about the babies!" Sullivan screamed back. "I have a vested interest in how these fetuses turn out, 'cause I'm going to be caring for them upstairs. And I just want to make sure I get the best baby I can. That's my qualifications."

"I see," Adams said, still calm. Dan was eating this up. "Well, Dr. Sullivan, I too have a vested interest in what happens to the babies. After all, I take care of the mothers and if their babies are sick, my mothers are going to have a much more difficult time in their postpartum recovery. So using your logic, I should be involved in making decisions in your nursery. Is that right?"

Sullivan became wary. He realized he had backed himself into a corner. "That's not what we're discussing here! That's not the point!"

"Dr. Sullivan," Dr. Adams said calmly, "I understand that you have the baby of one of my mothers in your nursery who has been significantly damaged because you and your residents did not pick up the fact that the child had an inborn error of metabolism until it was too late." Adams was referring to Freddie Endicott who, in fact, was no longer in the Pit. "I want to ask you why you didn't consult me about that child's early problems. I know the symptoms and signs of galactosemia." Dan and the obstetric staff laughed.

Even though he knew he had lost, Sullivan would not give up. "You are not trained in neonatology," he said, now cautiously. "You don't have the experience. . . ."

"Aha," Adams shouted, interrupting Sullivan's meanderings. "And as I said before, Dr. Sullivan, you are not trained in obstetrics, nor do you have the experience that I do. And that is why you should not be involved with the care of the mothers. That's the way it's always been and frankly, Dr. Sullivan, knowing about some of the things that have happened in your nursery, I wouldn't be so willing to criticize other services if I were you. Any other questions or comments?"

Sullivan seemed stunned and staggering and I had never seen him at a loss for words before. "Okay," Dr. Adams said when nobody spoke up, "I guess that concludes this week's conference." The crowd began to leave.

"Amazing," Dan said to me, "it's absolutely amazing!"

"Yeah," Terry said, "how can Sullivan argue about something like saving a premature baby when the mother's life is in danger?"

"No, that's not what's amazing," Dan said as he rose from his seat. "That's expected. What's really amazing is how this same thing happens every week. Every week at this conference, Sullivan criticizes the obstetric service for something they did to a patient, and every week Adams proves that Sullivan's a moron in front of all members of both services. It's astounding how Sullivan can keep it up week after week. Anyone want to go eat lunch?" We all did, and so we headed over to the cafeteria. Before we got there, Dan's beeper went off, notifying him of an outside call and he went off to answer it while Ray, Terry, and I continued to the cafeteria, where we couldn't wait to verbally tear Sullivan apart.

"It's clear to me that he's downright crazy," Ray announced. "A sane man wouldn't do the things he does. He's egotistical, power-hungry, and he won't listen to reasonable people, which I guess we are, who suggest reasonable things. Normally, none of this would matter much; being crazy and not listening to reason isn't a crime. But in Sullivan's case, being crazy and doing unreasonable things means that some poor kid who shouldn't be kept alive will be, even when the mother's health is at stake, and some families, who have normal kids in addition to their sick kid, are gonna be screwed up, both from an emotional and a financial standpoint."

"Well what can we do about it?" I asked. "We can't go to Sullivan and tell him he's got to change. He'd just answer us with something off-the-wall, like 'What do parents have to do with anything?'"

"Well I guess the only way around Sullivan is to go to a higher authority," Terry said.

"But Sullivan said he doesn't think that God has any place in the nursery," I answered.

"Well then we'd better go to someone between God and Sullivan," Terry said. "How about the hospital board?"

"Hmmm," I said.

"Hmmm," Ray said. And after lunch we went to the administrative office on the first floor and were told that the next regular meeting of the hospital board was scheduled to occur the next Wednesday afternoon. We made an appointment for four-thirty.

"What is this in reference to?" the secretary asked while she penciled Terry's name into the appointment book.

"Intensive care nursery policy problems," I answered, sounding official.

"Then we'll expect Dr. Sullivan to be attending?" she asked.

We looked at each other and smiled. "No," Ray answered, "just us interns."

"All right," she said, "be here next Wednesday at four-thirty sharp."

It was that easy. "Great," Ray remarked as we walked out of the office, "right after GORK follow-up clinic. We'll be coming in with a full head of steam."

Terry and I looked at each other and laughed. Ray asked what was so funny. Terry didn't answer but asked him, "Ray, what would you say if a pile of shit fell on your head?" Ray didn't respond but laughed along with us.

XII
On Call

Everything remaining fairly stable, Ray and Terry signed out early and left me alone in the nursery. It still spooked me to be the only doctor in this room where disaster could hit at any minute, even though I knew that if anything were to happen, the nurses would know what to do and would do it well, in spite of me. However, I felt better when I was away from all the noise and the beeping, and so I decided to go visit Mrs. O'Hara. I figured that someone else's misery was a little more comfortable than my own terror and feeling of inadequacy.

Mrs. O'Hara was still in the recovery room. She had not yet regained consciousness. Mr. O'Hara was again at her bedside, still pretty depressed but physically none the worse for wear, considering the main event that had occurred the night before. I said, "Hello."

"Hello, Dr. Sharon," he answered somberly. He didn't seem angry or resentful, but he was very sad. "How is the baby doing?"

I told him that she had done well in the OR and was now back in the Pit in fairly good condition.

"How long will it be before she's ready to come home?" he asked.

"It depends on how long it takes her to heal after the operation. We'll have to be very careful when we start to feed her. I'd say it'll probably take a week or two. But I'm surprised you are asking about her. I thought you and your wife had decided you wouldn't be taking the baby home."

"Well, Dr. Sharon," Mr. O'Hara replied, "we're religious people.

We believe that God has a reason for everything He does, be it good or bad. I've been talking with our priest and he's helped me come to this decision. I've decided that if the baby is going to survive the operation, then it's God's will that we raise her up. She's been placed on this earth as our burden to bear, as a way of testing me and my wife." Tears began to fill his eyes. "We must accept that burden. . . ." He was too choked with tears to continue. I put my hand on his shoulder.

Mr. O'Hara composed himself and continued. "Dr. Sharon, I'm not a violent man. Before yesterday, I had never struck another man in all my adult life. But when that Dr. Sullivan came in here, into this room where my poor Joan is lying, and when he insulted me and told me that I wasn't man enough to accept the responsibility of a damaged child, and that I was hiding behind God, well, I just couldn't restrain myself. I hit him, and I'm glad I hit him. I would do it again if we had that situation back. How can a human being, and a doctor at that, someone who's supposed to be compassionate and sensitive to the feelings of others, how could he have said those things? What kind of a man is he?"

I took a deep breath and I did something at that point that I didn't think I could do. I defended Dr. Sullivan, in a manner of speaking.

"Mr. O'Hara, this is extremely difficult for me to do," I began. "I'm only an intern and brand-new at taking care of these babies, and Dr. Sullivan is my attending and my superior in both position and experience. But I want to apologize to you for him and try to explain some of his motivation to you. He feels like a father to all the babies in the nursery. He loves his babies and he wants them to survive regardless of anything else. And because of this desire, he has become a cruel, insensitive, inhuman beast when dealing with the real mothers and fathers of the babies. See, with his wish for survival of all the babies, he's lost the perspective to tell when saving a baby is good and when saving a baby is not so good. So you have to accept that what he was doing yesterday was trying to do what he thought was best for your daughter." I finished talking and took a deep breath.

Mr. O'Hara was very quiet when I had finished. He looked somewhat surprised at what I said. "You mean he was trying to help our daughter, not make a fool out of Joan and me?" he asked.

"Just trying to help the baby," I answered.

"Well, that's something I hadn't even thought about. But I can see what you're saying. I guess it makes sense. Thank you very much for explaining this to me, Dr. Sharon. You may be new at caring for these babies, but you sure seem like you know how to talk to people a lot better than your boss does!"

I tried not to change my expression at this compliment. "Have they told you anything about Mrs. O'Hara?" I asked.

"Well, Dr. Fredericks, he's here tonight. He's been the one who's been the straightest with me. He talks like you. He was here a little while ago and told me that Joan was stable, not much better than yesterday, not much worse. He said it's too early to tell what's going to happen. If she doesn't wake up," his eyes started to cloud over again, "I don't know what I'll do." He broke into tears.

I went over to Mr. O'Hara and again put my arm around his shoulder. We sat like that for what seemed like an eternity.

Fredericks was sitting in his on-call room easy chair, watching a rerun of "The Odd Couple" on TV. He didn't seem too interested in the show, he'd probably seen this episode a hundred times before, and so was glad to see me. "Sit down, Bob, sit right down. What's going on in Dr. Sullivan's fifth floor sideshow tonight?"

I told him the only news of the Pit that I had. "That baby with Down's syndrome who was born after you refused to assist Dr. Parris the other day had her duodenal atresia fixed today. Pretty soon she'll be eating like a normal person."

"Well that's food for thought, Bob, food for thought." I groaned. "That's what I get for watching this damned TV all the time," he said. "Do you know that Mr. O'Hara flattened Sullivan in the recovery room yesterday afternoon?"

"Yeah," I answered. "I was going to tell you about it."

"Well I was at ringside when it happened, and let me tell you, Sullivan really deserved it. He was bugging the hell out of that poor man."

"I don't know if you saw it at the conference but Sullivan looks like he was the loser in the heavyweight title fight. How is Mrs. O'Hara doing?"

"Well, she's not great, Bob, not great at all. She's still growing bugs in her blood, even though we're giving her mammoth doses of all kinds of antibiotics, but she is out of septic shock, so I guess that's a good sign."

"Think she'll make it?" I asked.

"Still touch and go, Bob. People have been known to survive septic shock. If she does die, I think we should have that damned Parris assassinated. You realize that none of this was necessary, don't you?"

"Is anything going to happen to you for walking out on Parris like that?"

"Well, he's bringing me up in front of the hospital board next Wednesday. Accusing me of disobeying orders and insulting him. Sounds like a court-martial. I guess we'll see what happens."

I told Fredericks that we also would be at the hospital board meeting on Wednesday. "Ahh," he responded, "it'll be like a family reunion."

I got up to leave and said, "By the way, Tom, is there anything doing around here?"

"Pretty quiet. We've got a woman coming in by ambulance from New Hampshire. She's about three weeks overdue. They did a nonstress test up there and got a real bad new tracing. So her private doc is sending her down for management. She should get here in about an hour, I guess."

The nonstress test is one method of ascertaining fetal well-being. In the test the fetal heart rate is monitored through a sensor in a belt that fits around the mother's abdomen. It tells the obstetrician whether the fetus is healthy enough to remain in the womb or if it is unstable and requires immediate delivery. The fetus from New Hampshire was telling the doctors up there that it needed to be delivered, and soon.

I bid Tom farewell and headed back to the Pit. I found Frohman signing out to Dan in the nurses' station.

"Afternoon, Bob," Dan said after his sign-out was completed.

"Hi, Dan. We missed you at lunch."

"Yeah," Dan responded, "sorry about that. It was a call from Dr. Jennings. Sullivan, that schmuck, called Jennings to complain about my so-called disruptive behavior. I wish he would just vanish out of here!"

"Well, Dan, I agree with you but I do think you're bringing a lot of this on yourself."

"What do you mean?" he asked with a smile.

"Well you're always getting into arguments with him on rounds. You provoke him."

"Bob, I'm surprised at you. You're not paying attention. I never provoke him. I never start fights with him; he's always starting them with me. I'm sitting there calmly, minding my own business and, zap, I'm being attacked. What I'm doing is just defending myself."

"How about yesterday morning?" I asked. "You hadn't been attacked yesterday morning."

"Yeah," he said, thinking back, "but Terry was getting killed in there and she hadn't done anything wrong except for having the misfortune of being on call with Frohman, another schmuck. So I guess you're right; I guess I will start a fight to help someone else out."

"Sullivan really hates you, doesn't he?" I asked.

"This is true," Dan responded. "And I know why. But I still can't tell you why yet."

"Come on!" I responded. "If you and Jennings are worried about us being destroyed, it's already too late. We all hate our lives, our jobs, the babies, everything. And we hate Sullivan so much we even made an appointment to complain about him to the hospital board."

"The hospital board?" Dan asked with surprise. "Really? Nobody's ever tried complaining to the hospital board about the schmuck. Nobody's ever done anything about him."

"Why is that?" I asked. "Dan, it's clear to us, even after one week, that this man is downright dangerous. How is it he's gotten away with this for so long?"

"Well, basically, the majority of the house staff is like Frohman, afraid of their own shadows and, even if some of them have felt like us, they've resigned themselves to not doing anything—we're each only here a month at a time."

"Why hasn't anyone from the Medical Center tried to stop him? Dr. Jennings must hear the stories you guys have brought back. Why doesn't he get rid of him?"

"It's not that simple. Sullivan's an employee of St. A's and Jennings has nothing to do with his hiring or firing. St. A's likes the way Sullivan conducts business. He saves babies and that's a pretty marketable trait in a Catholic hospital. So it comes down to the fact that it's Sullivan's ball and, if you don't play by his rules, he'll still keep it alive with a ventilator. I don't think the board will do any good, but it'll be interesting to see what happens."

"Why don't you think it'll do any good?" I asked.

"Well like I said, the fact that Sullivan saves babies is very appealing to the board members. So if you go to them complaining that he's saving too many babies, they'll probably wind up firing you guys and giving Sullivan a raise."

My spirits sank a little. "I guess you're right," I said. "I guess we'll have to come up with another idea."

"As long as we're on the subject of schmucks this evening, maybe it's a good time for your second installment of pediatrics, the Berkowitz way. As you remember, the last time we met, we spoke about certain pieces of equipment that are the intern's friends. Not only is it important to know the ins and outs of the equipment, it is also important to know the ins and outs of the staff, who, like the equipment, can either be the intern's friend or the intern's enemy. Unfortunately, here at St. A's, you'll find that the latter outnumber the former by about fifty to one. For instance, let's take Simon Frohman. No one is sure how Simon got to be the way he is, but the rumor is that while pregnant with him, his mother was frightened by a giant asshole." Dan stopped to laugh. "Frohman is an unpleasant person on every level, who is always out for himself, and who will do anything to get what he wants. Keep this in mind and clear a path when he's coming for something. It'll save you from having to wipe the footsteps off your back later."

"We've already seen him in action," I responded. "You know yesterday morning when he accused Terry of forgetting to call Sullivan after Baby Torres died? Frohman had told Terry that he would take care of calling him."

"Right," Dan said, "that's the kind of thing he's famous for. He figured if he had called Sullivan at home, Sullivan would get angry with him for letting one of the babies die on his time. By not calling, he got Sullivan to yell at someone else."

"How has he gotten through two years of residency?" I asked.

"Simple. He kisses ass. Look how he's acted since you got here; everything out of his mouth is 'Sullivan says this' and 'Sullivan says that.' Sullivan thinks he's molding Frohman into being just like him. And then to top it off, Frohman comes in wearing a stupid belt pouch, just like Sullivan's. When I saw that, I couldn't believe it. I wonder if

Simon keeps the same stuff in his pouch that Sullivan keeps in his. . . . Come to think of it, that might explain a lot."

"I just have one question about him," I said. "Why is he so nervous?"

"All the fidgeting and stuff?" he asked. "You'd be nervous, too, if you were a senior resident and you hadn't yet made any decision other than what to eat for lunch. He's scared shit about next year, when there isn't going to be an attending around to tell him what to do. Simon's at the edge, let me tell you, Bob. It's not going to take much to send him over."

Dan and I kept an eye on the Pit together that evening while he told me more unbelievable stories about people with whom I was working. At six we ate dinner, and then passed the time until our beepers went off simultaneously at about nine. "Dr. Sharon, go to the DR stat!" mine screeched. We ran down the stairs and burst through the doors of the delivery suite, almost colliding with the gurney being pushed toward DR 3 by Fredericks and Schwartz. Upon seeing us, Fredericks shouted, "Crash section! Fetal distress! Move it!"

Dan and I reached the locker room, put on scrubs over our clothes, and reached DR 3 as they cut skin. The residents hadn't scrubbed.

We prepared for the baby. I turned on the warmer over the table. Dan took out the intern's friends, an endotracheal tube and an umbilical artery catheter, and made sure that the medications for resuscitation were drawn up in syringes. I walked over and stood by Fredericks while he cut and told us all the history he had. "Three weeks postdates, from Nashua, New Hampshire. Came down by ambulance. Damned thing broke down on the way in. Trip took three hours. She ruptured membranes somewhere north of Boston. Lots of meconium. She got here twenty minutes ago. We attached an internal monitor and got her ready. With the last contraction, severe fetal bradycardia. Heart rate never came back up. So we called you guys and brought her back here."

This was the woman Tom had mentioned to me earlier in the evening. What he meant by the story was that the bag of amniotic fluid had ruptured while on the trip from New Hampshire. Rather than being clear, as amniotic fluid should be, the fluid that had gushed out contained meconium, the greenish substance that represented the fetus's first bowel movement. The presence of meconium in amniotic fluid implies that the fetus is, or has recently been, in distress. Often low concentrations of oxygen in fetal blood will cause the passage of meconium while the fetus is still within the womb.

In addition to being an indicator of fetal distress, the presence of meconium in the amniotic fluid poses another problem. Since the fetus breathes soon after birth, if meconium is present in the mouth, it may get aspirated into the lungs. This causes a horrendous pneumonia and respiratory distress, which sets in motion a whole series of physiologic pathways that lead to more problems for the fetus.

Because of the presence of meconium in the amniotic fluid, Fredericks and Schwartz had hooked the mother up to a monitor as soon as she got to St. A's. With the next contraction of the uterus, that monitor had revealed that the stress caused the fetal heart rate to drop. Often the heart rate returns to normal after the contraction ends. In this case, however, it stayed down at an abnormally low level.

My legs shook as I watched Fredericks and Schwartz work. Their instruments moved rapidly, the reflection of the bright lights off the dancing surgical steel was dazzling. The baby's head appeared through the incision in the mother's abdomen less than six minutes after the skin had been cut. I was handed the baby and ran with it over to the warming table. It was limp and it was not breathing.

Dan told me to wipe the baby off with a towel. I dried the thick, greenish fluid off the baby's lifeless body while Dan placed a laryngoscope, an instrument designed to push away the tongue and allow direct visualization of the back of the throat, into the mouth and passed the endotracheal tube through the baby's vocal cords and into the baby's windpipe. Dan instructed me to listen to the heart with my stethoscope and to bang out the rate with my index finger on the side of the warming table.

The heart rate at that point was about thirty. Using a special catheter threaded through the endotracheal tube and a vacuum hose, Dan suctioned a large amount of the thick meconium that had passed into the baby's windpipe and lungs. He then shot a small amount of sterile water through the endotracheal tube, using the pressure generated from the ambu bag. He again suctioned, this time getting only a small amount of meconium back. He did it again, and the water that returned was unstained by meconium. "Okay," he said to me, "the airway's clear."

He then attached the ambu bag, through which 100-percent oxygen was flowing, to the endotracheal tube and shot oxygen into the baby's lungs about forty times a minute. I continued tapping out the baby's heart rate, which had come up to about sixty beats per minute but seemed stuck there and would not go any higher. Dan pumped on the ambu bag for another minute, but when the heart rate remained at sixty, he realized he had to try something else. The baby was three minutes old.

Shaking all over, I took Dan's place at the head of the warming table, as he ordered. Dan, not shaking at all, grabbed a bottle of antiseptic solution and poured the stuff over the baby's abdomen. He tied what looked like a ribbon around the lower end of the stump of the umbilical cord, about an inch above its junction with the abdominal wall, and, after pulling the ribbon tight, cut the umbilical cord about two inches above the ribbon with a sterile razor blade. In the stump of the umbilical cord, he found the wide-bored, thin-walled umbilical vein and tried to pass the umbilical artery catheter into it. His first attempt met with resistance. He pulled the tube out, pushed some normal saline solution through the plastic catheter, and tried again. This time the tube passed easily. He attached a syringe to the end of the catheter and pulled back on its plunger. Dark brown blood filled the catheter. "I'm in," Dan said.

As I continued pumping up the lungs, Dan began to push medications through the line. First he gave some sodium bicarbonate, then some epinephrine, then some calcium, and finally a solution containing glucose. He then stopped, pulled my stethoscope from my ears, and put the earpieces in his own. He listened for the heart rate. Then he tapped it out with his finger on the side of the warming table. It was a little over a hundred beats per minute. He stayed like that, looking straightforward, listening intently, and tapping for about another minute. The heart rate slowly but steadily slipped back down to seventy. "Damn," he groaned as this occurred, "Round two, coming up!" He again pushed the medications, bicarb, epi, and calcium, through the catheter. He listened and tapped out the heart rate again. This time it was a hundred and twenty. He waited another minute and, when he was convinced that the rate was remaining steady, he said to me, "Let's get him upstairs!"

While I continued pushing oxygen into the baby's lungs forty times a minute, Dan wheeled the transport incubator into DR 3. He picked up the baby and set it down on the transporter's mattress. My arms and legs continued to shake, and the continuous, repetitive motion of bagging made my arms feel like hundred-pound weights were suspended from each one. The circulating nurse removed from its nipple on the wall the hose that was feeding oxygen into the ambu bag and reattached it to the portable oxygen tank which was located in the transporter unit. With me pumping the bag and with Dan pushing the incubator, we ran from DR 3 through the empty lobby area of the delivery suite and into the elevator, which was being guarded by the delivery suite's clerk, who has passed the time waiting for us by reading a copy of *McCall's.* The elevator doors closed and in seconds opened again on the fifth floor. We pushed out, ran down the hall and into the Pit. The nurses and Dan picked the baby up, placed it on a scale to weigh it, and then plopped it down on the warming table that had been prepared for it in the first row. I continued to work the ambu bag.

Within seconds Angela Meroni and the other nurses were swarming over the baby, attaching up the ventilator which relieved me of my job, gluing cardiac monitor leads to the chest, sticking a temperature sensor through the skin at the left shoulder, washing off residual meconium, and taking the baby's vital signs: heart rate, respiratory rate, blood pressure, and temperature.

Dan and I, relieved for a few seconds, moved a few steps away from the baby and took a breath. I had at last stopped shaking.

"You did good, Bob," Dan said with little emotion.

"I didn't do shit! You brought that baby back from the dead!" I answered. "You were great! I'll never be able to do all the stuff you just did, even if I were to stay here all year."

"No. You'll learn," Dan said, his tone unchanged. "We all learn, sooner or later."

"No, Dan," I responded. "While watching you work in there, knowing exactly what to do and staying calm, I really realized how little I know and how little I can do."

"Well, don't pat me on the back yet. We're not exactly out of the woods. Bob, it's going to be a long night."

Dan took me over to scrub at a sink in the corner of the Pit. We washed our hands for ten minutes up to the elbow, as if we were preparing for surgery. Then we put on sterile disposable paper gowns and plastic gloves and, with Angela's help, removed the catheter that Dan had placed in the baby's umbilical vein that was intended only for emergency use and tediously replaced it with a more permanent umbilical artery catheter. When it was in place, Dan drew off a sample of arterial blood to check if the baby was getting enough oxygen. The blood was more brown than red, which made it clear that not enough oxygen was getting into the baby's blood. And the baby was, at that point, breathing air composed of 100-percent oxygen.

Dan outlined the problems we were up against and gave Angela and me an idea of what the rest of the night was going to be like. "This baby has clearly aspirated meconium and has gotten the damned stuff down pretty deep in his lungs. I think most of this happened before the kid was born. Bob, did you see how much gunk I got up from the ET tube? And that was before the kid even had a chance to breathe. The main problem now is that the lungs won't work right. The meconium makes them real stiff, so in order to get the oxygen down into them, we'll have to push it down there with a lot of pressure. Now that's fine except for one thing. Think of it as a balloon. You can blow air into a balloon with a lot of pressure, but sooner or later you get to a point where the pressure is too much and the balloon pops. Lungs can do that, too. So our job is just to keep the pressure below the point where the lungs pop. Got it?"

"It seems logical," I said. "I guess so."

"Yeah, it's logical," Dan continued. "Only problem is sometimes you need more pressure to get the oxygen into the blood than it takes to blow out the lungs. In that case, you just have to explode the lungs. Is that clear?"

This also seemed perfectly logical, of course, but not totally consistent with life as we know it. "I think I lose you there, Dan," I said. "It seems to me, if you explode the lungs, the baby dies. At least that's what I learned in medical school!"

"Right," Dan said. "But like most things you learn in medical school, it's not completely right. The baby won't die if one lung blows up, as long as the second lung still works. And you can reexpand the collapsed lung by putting in a chest tube. Of course, if the second lung collapses before the chest tube gets in, the baby immediately goes to heaven. But you have to remember that the kid'll also die if he doesn't get enough oxygen. So we don't have much choice."

"Dan, why aren't you giving this baby tolazoline?" Angela asked. I didn't even know what tolazoline was.

"Well, Angela, I've been burned by tolazoline before. When I was an intern, I had a kid who went into shock and died from the stuff. So I'd like to push the ventilator to the limit before using it, even if it means blowing out a pneumothorax or two. How has your experience been?"

Angela wrinkled her eyes. "It's been mixed. Some people give it right away, they swear by it. And I've seen a lot of shock in the babies. And some people are like you. I don't think there's any difference in how the babies do."

"Well, either way we do it, guys," Dan said, "we got problems. We're sort of stuck."

Stuck was exactly what we were. The baby's initial blood gas had an oxygen value of thirty-two. Eighty would have been normal, sixty acceptable, but thirty-two just wouldn't do. So we increased the pressure on the ventilator a little. On the next blood gas measurement, the oxygen level rose to thirty-eight. We increased the pressure a pinch further and the oxygen in the blood went to forty-five. One more increase and the blood gas oxygen was fifty-five.

"I think we're gonna make it!" Angela said as she wrote the results of this last gas on the flow sheet attached to the baby's bedside clipboard.

"I think you're right," Dan answered. "Let's keep him on these ventilator settings for a while and we'll send another gas in about an hour. If that one's okay, we'll turn the pressure down a little. Keep your fingers crossed!"

With that, Dan went off to his on-call room to get some sleep. With my fingers crossed, I walked into the deserted nurses' station. I began to write an admission note on this new baby. I looked at my watch. It was 2:25 A.M. The completion of my work and the chance for sleep was only about a half hour away. I had almost made it.

At about two forty-five Angela called me from across the Pit. "Get over here stat, Bob. He's blue and in a lot of distress!"

I ran over to the baby, whose mouth, nose, hands, and feet were becoming dark blue. His breathing, at a rate of about a hundred per minute, was very labored. I was so sleepy I could barely keep my eyes open. My first reaction was to panic and run from the room, but I fought that off and remembered Dan's lecture to me on the care and feeding of the ET tube: "If the baby suddenly crumps, think of the tube." I asked Angela to send off a blood gas; when she pulled back on the plunger of the syringe attached to the UA line, the blood that returned was dark brown. The baby was in a lot of trouble.

"Somebody call Dan," I shouted. Another nurse went to do that.

"He's blown out a lung, Bob," Angela said.

"Right," I responded. "Let's light up the chest." I got the Shun gun, the bright light source that Dan had demonstrated to me the last time we were on call together. This instrument was really just a fancy flashlight that was bright enough to light up the entire state of Rhode Island. I pushed the flashlight up against the baby's chest while someone turned off all the lights in the Pit. In that eerie darkness, lit only by the red emergency lights on the ventilator control panels, the left side of that baby's chest lit up like a three-hundred-watt light bulb. Because of the pressure we were delivering through the ventilator, we had blown out the baby's left lung.

Dan entered the nursery at this point, on the dead run. He saw the chest lighting his way from across the room. "And you said you'd never be able to do any of this stuff," he said, huffing and puffing. He grabbed a wide-bored needle from off the code cart, attached a 60-cc syringe to it, and plunged the needle through the ribs on the left side. Immediately the plunger on the syringe shot back to the 50-cc mark. All at once, the baby's color improved.

"Tension pneumothorax!" Dan said. "Good pickup, Bob!"

"It really was Angela's pickup," I said.

"Don't be silly, Bob," Angela said with a smile. "You did all the right things!"

"Well, so this is the critical point," Dan said. "We have to take out that needle and put in a chest tube right away. If the other lung blows out before we get a chest tube in, the baby dies!"

We scrubbed again while Angela set up for the chest tube. Again we gowned and gloved. Dan did the procedure. He made a small slit into the skin right next to the needle site with the blade of a scalpel and immediately pushed the tube through the slit and through the space between the ribs, into the chest cavity. The force that was necessary to push the damned thing through the chest wall was amazing! I was sure Dan would wind up with the tube in the baby's heart. But he didn't.

The baby's color remained good. The right lung continued functioning normally. We had made it over the hurdle. But the night was still far from over.

The blood gas that Angela sent at the start of the crump came back with an oxygen of twenty-eight. It also revealed, not surprisingly, that the baby had severe acidosis, acid in the blood, brought on by chronically low oxygen. Dan gave the baby a dose of a drug called Tham, a buffer designed to improve the acidosis. The repeat blood gas, drawn after the Tham revealed that the acidosis had resolved and that the oxygen was fifty-seven.

"Let's turn the pressure down a little," Dan said. "I'd rather deliver a little less oxygen than risk blowing out the other lung."

"Do you want to start tolazoline yet?" Angela asked. She didn't seem at all sleepy. Of the three of us, her thinking was by far the clearest.

"Not yet," Dan answered, a little less sure of himself. "We've gone this far without it. Let's give him another chance."

It was now 3:45 A.M. Dan said he was going to try to get some sleep. I said that I'd try to lie down on the cot in my on-call room for a while. We had almost made it to the door when Angela's yell again broke the air.

"Get over here stat!" she yelled. "He's blown the other lung!"

We ran back to the first row. Of course Angela was right. We again shone the Shun gun onto the chest and, of course, this time the right side lit up. I groaned. I really needed to get some sleep. But instead, again, Dan and I scrubbed, gowned, and gloved.

It was an awfully strange feeling, working on this baby in the middle of the night. I could barely see straight. I felt sick to my stomach because of fatigue and wanted to go vomit in the bathroom. But my adrenal glands kept pumping out adrenaline, and the adrenaline was driving me on. I just kept on working.

While we were scrubbing, Dan said, "Well, Bob, you've seen one chest tube inserted. This one's yours!"

"What?" I asked, a little startled. The opportunity Dan was dumping on me didn't do much for the feeling in my stomach. "You think I'm ready for that?"

"What, ready?" he asked. "You saw me do it. It's the simplest thing in the world. And I'll be here to tell you what to do. It'll be a breeze. It'll make you happy you stayed awake!"

"I doubt that," I said. I finished scrubbing, and gowned and gloved and with Dan at my side telling me exactly what to do, I made a slit in the skin between two ribs on the right side of the chest. I put the chest tube into the slit and pushed. But the damned thing wouldn't go in.

"C'mon, Bob," Angela said. "You gotta put some muscle behind it."

I pushed a little harder. It still wouldn't go through.

"More force, Bob," Dan said. "Don't be afraid. You won't hurt anything!"

I was putting so much force behind the tube that I was sure I was going to kill the baby. Finally, I felt the chest give way and the tube popped in. The sudden release of resistance almost made me topple over. Again, almost instantly, the baby's color improved, but this time the improvement wasn't as marked as it had been the first time we relieved the tension pneumothorax. He still was tinged blue around the mouth, hands, and feet. We sent off a blood gas and this time, the oxygen level was only forty-five.

It was nearly 5 A.M. The first light of day was beginning to brighten the sky over Boston. The sun was just beginning to come up. It was going to be a hot, humid summer day. And all I could think about was how much I wanted to get to sleep. To hell with this damned baby! But those adrenal glands kept pumping away, and I finally knew that I wasn't going to get any sleep on this night on call.

"We've got to do something quick," Dan said. He was looking a little sleepy, too, and seemed a little panicked. "It's time to start tolazoline. We'd better do it before the baby's brain gets any more damaged from lack of oxygen."

"I'll make up the drip," Angela said.

"Okay," Dan smiled. "I'll give Bob the lecture. Bob, you know how tolazoline works?"

"No," I answered. "I don't even know what the hell it is."

Dan then went through what seemed like an endless, detailed description of how, physiologically, the drug worked. I was far too sleepy to understand what he was saying, or to even care. I just knew that if it was going to make the baby well enough to allow me to get some sleep, I was all for giving it.

In order to give this drug we had to start an IV separate from the UA line. Tolazoline was one of the few drugs for which umbilical artery administration was prohibited. Realizing that at least to start the IV would probably take me all the time remaining between then and 8 A.M. when our relief showed up, Dan did it himself. He got the needle into a vein in the right hand on the first stick.

Angela attached the solution to the tubing end of the needle. Dan, Angela, and I stood and watched in wonder. In the time it took for the tolazoline to make one circulation through the blood vessels of the lungs, an incredible change came over the baby. The skin, which had been mottled and tinged with blue, suddenly became bright pink! It was as if we had sent this baby to Miami, and he had been out on the beach for a few hours too long!

"I think it's working!" Angela said.

"I think you're right," I added.

"There's just one problem we have to look for now," Dan said. "This drug can cause severe hypotension. It can be enough to throw the baby into shock. We have to follow the blood pressure pretty closely."

As Dan was saying this, Angela was taking the baby's blood pressure. "Guess what," she said, as she finished her reading. "Blood pressure is thirty over ten."

The baby was in shock. If this continued for any appreciable period of time, the baby's brain would be destroyed.

"What do you want to do?" Angela asked.

"Dopamine. Stat." Dan answered.

"I've already got some made up," Angela said as she produced an IV bag.

"Great," Dan said. "I'll start another line." Working quickly, Dan cleared off the back of the baby's left hand, put a tourniquet around the wrist and, when a vein popped up, plunged a needle into it. While he taped the new IV down, Angela hooked the dopamine-containing IV solution up to the needle.

We waited another minute until the dopamine had had time to make a pass through the baby's circulatory system. "Check the BP, Angie," Dan ordered.

She did and responded, "BP's sixty over thirty. He's okay."

We all breathed a sigh of relief. "He'll be okay for now," Angela said reassuringly.

"I just hope we started the tolazoline in time," Dan said.

Angela sent off another blood gas. The oxygen this time was seventy-two, the best since the baby had been born, so we turned down the ventilator's pressure a little, enough to give us and the baby a little breathing room against a third pneumothorax. For the first time since birth, the baby was finally stable. At seven-fifteen, I looked out the picture windows; the day was now almost fully developed.

Dan went to his on-call room to get a half hour of sleep. "I just hope we didn't start that tolazoline too late," he said again on his way out.

After he was gone, I looked the baby over gloomily. He had been born a few hours before, like all babies, devoid of tubes or other extraneous apparatus. He now had an endotracheal tube, a nasogastric tube, three cardiac monitor leads, a heat sensor, two chest tubes, a UA line, and two IVs. He had now, in a very short time, become clothed in the costume of the neonatal ICU, the style that was always popular regardless of the season with the premies and unfortunate others who inhabited this place. "I just hope we didn't start that tolazoline too late." Dan's words rang in my head.

After signing out to Gloria Higgins, the day nurse who would be caring for this baby, Angela came to my side and put her arm around my shoulder. "You did a good job last night, Bob," she said. "You stayed with that kid all night, you didn't let him down when he needed you. I've seen interns and residents and attendings faced with the problems you faced last night. None of them cared about a baby anymore than you did." She gave me a hug.

I was too tired to respond. I smiled at Angela and gazed into her big brown eyes, but I just couldn't protest, or thank her. I was just too tired.

I went about my morning scut in a haze. By 8 A.M., with my head spinning, my belly aching, feeling rotten, I was sitting in the nurses' station, ready for Terry's arrival.

"You made it to the weekend," Terry said, smiling as she breezed into the nurses' station.

"Oh yeah. It's Saturday. Terrific!" I answered with all the strength I could muster. And with that, I burst into tears.

XIII

Saturday and Sunday July 3 and 4

It's amazing what a night without sleep can do to a human being. Sleep deprivation can take a well-balanced, relatively intact person and change him into a raving lunatic. And so on the morning after my first on-call night spent without sleep, I was an uncontrollable emotional cripple.

Not unexpectedly, Terry was surprised by my sudden outburst of tears. I was too, but I just couldn't control myself. I needed to get out of the nursery; if I didn't, I would suffocate. So I signed out as quickly as possible, just giving Terry the bare facts about what had happened during the night and introducing her to the new baby and, when done, I fled from the hospital and drove to the airport to pick up Rachel. Although I felt I could now breathe, my crying did not cease during the short car ride.

By concentrating all my strength, I managed to stop crying by the time I saw Rachel standing outside the Eastern Airlines terminal at Logan Airport. I don't think I was ever so happy to see anyone before. I stopped at the curb by the sidewalk where she was standing, got out, and fell into her arms. When the embrace ended, we got into the car, me behind the wheel, Rachel in the passenger seat.

"How are you?" she asked with a smile. "I've missed you so much!"

Like a dam breaking, I burst into tears again. My wall of concentration cracked and I sat behind the wheel and cried unashamedly; I cried for Mrs. O'Hara, I cried for all the babies in the Pit, I cried for all the babies in follow-up clinic and at the Waltham Home; but the longest and loudest wail, the most sustained and most gut-wrenching yell, the hardest and the heaviest cry I cried for myself.

So began Rachel's first weekend in Boston. In the years we've spent together since then, through the good and the bad times, we've never discussed that weekend. She had to think that they had taken her husband and had changed him; that the rest of her married life, or at least the time until I was finished with my training, she would have to live with a man who had become an emotional lunatic. But she didn't show any of her shock or upset during that weekend; instead she stood by me and helped me through. She probably saved my professional life.

In the car Rachel put her arm around me, hugged me, and comforted me. We sat like that, outside the terminal building for nearly an hour. The hustle and bustle of a day coming to life at the airport went on all around us but we stayed there, embracing, not making a sound except for the sounds of my crying.

When I had calmed a little, she moved me out of the driver's seat, took her place behind the wheel, and drove the car out of the airport. The silence in the car continued during our trip to the apartment we had rented in Watertown. In the parking lot outside the house, Rachel helped me out of the car, brought me upstairs, and put me to bed. I fell asleep almost immediately. I slept fitfully and the nightmare of having a normal baby die in my arms recurred.

Rachel woke me at 6 P.M. I had slept for eight hours. Still unsure of what had happened, or what she could do about it, she crawled into bed next to me and asked what was wrong. I was feeling a little better after my sleep and could finally tell her what had happened to me. The words flowed like the tears had earlier in the day. I told her about the babies and how sick they were. I told her about Freddie Endicott and how his life had been destroyed because the doctors had failed to make a correct diagnosis. I told her about Sullivan, and Kathy, and Frohman, and Parris, and how everyone in a position of authority at St. A's seemed to be crazy. I told her of the O'Hara family and of the struggle through which they were living. I told her of the GORKs at follow-up clinic, and of what their lives must be like. And finally I told her about me. "I'm twenty-nine years old. I've been in school, preparing to be a doctor my whole life. I'm just beginning a full year of internship, I'm only one week into it, and my internship year will be followed by two years of residency. I'm already exhausted. I've already seen I don't have the technical skill or the know-how to take care of these babies. I've screwed up in relating to parents. I don't know if I can make it! I don't even know if I want to make it, if what I'm going to wind up doing is taking care of kids like these all my life! I just don't know."

Rachel could have said a lot of things then. She could have told me how it would have never been like this had I stayed in New York during my internship, that if I had listened to her, rather than to my advisers, and taken a job at Jonas Bronck Hospital that, even when times got bad, she would be there to help me through them, to calm me and console me every day, not just on weekends. But she didn't say anything; she took me in her arms and the late afternoon sun came in through the windows as we made love. It seemed to last a long time and it felt good, better than it ever had before. Just for a fleeting instant, I had an image of Terry lying next to me on her couch, and that image made me shudder with guilt, but it passed away and soon Rachel and I fell asleep, and we slept through the rest of the night, oblivious to the loud crashing of the fireworks going off all around us as the Boston metropolitan area celebrated Independence Day.

By Sunday morning I had recovered. With the restoration of my mind and body by sleep, I became more like the man Rachel had married. The crying was behind me, at least for now. We celebrated the Bicentennial by going out for brunch and Rachel, seeing that I was in a better mood, gave me a pep talk. "Look, Bob, you're only a week into this thing. Whenever things are new, you always feel like you'll never get the hang of them. It's the loss of control, I think, that makes you feel that way. But you did very well in every rotation in medical school, you even got honors in a lot of them. You just have to give it a chance, work through this adjustment period. You'll do fine."

I didn't respond. I wasn't as sure about my future as Rachel seemed to be, but I sure hoped she'd be right.

We went to a movie in Chestnut Hill. How long it seemed since I last was surrounded by so many normal, nonmedical people. Although it had only been a week, it seemed like months.

The weekend flew by and before I knew it, it was Sunday evening and, as firecrackers were going off all over Boston, the butterflies in my stomach and the dull headache gradually and steadily returned.

BOOK II

The ulcer pain started to hit me just south of Bridgeport, Connecticut. I think it was a combination of things that caused it; certainly the rush hour traffic wasn't helping. But the main factor was this exercise in memory, my attempt to recall everything that had happened during that first week at St. A's. Thinking back to those days made me realize how idealistic I had been, how naïve, how ignorant to the way things happen in academic medicine, and to the consequences of those events. I came into the Pit knowing so little, and was hit with so much disease and pathology, and not just from my patients.

If the first week I spent in the Pit was highlighted by my feelings of incompetence and of helplessness, the middle part of my stay was punctuated by my attempt to fight back, to try to make things better both for me and for my patients. I met with a lot of discouragement during this period, and my feelings of helplessness continued. The middle part of the month was a little better than that first week. But it couldn't have been much worse; nothing could have been worse!

I found some Di-Gel in a truck stop off the highway. I chewed it and within minutes the pain was gone. Contemplating the miracle of medicine, I headed back to the highway, and memories of that second week kept flooding back.

XIV

Monday, July 5
Morning Rounds

I dropped Rachel off at Logan to catch the shuttle back to New York and, feeling much stronger after the rest and relaxation of the weekend, managed to say goodbye without tears. We held each other tightly, then I watched her pass through the electric doors and vanish into the Eastern building.

I drove into the parking lot at St. A's as Terry was getting out of her Toyota. She waited as I parked my car and caught up with her. Putting her arm around my back, she gave me a hug.

"How you doing?" she asked. "I was worried about you."

"I'm better," I said, managing a smile. "Guess I scared you on Saturday morning."

"You bet," she answered. "I thought you'd never come back to work."

"I was thinking of chucking it. I was on the ropes on Saturday morning, and I thought I was going down for the count. Thank goodness for Rachel. And for sleep."

"Yeah," Terry said, "I thought you'd be okay as soon as she got here. It looked like you really needed to be taken care of."

We had by this point entered the building and were waiting for the elevator to arrive. "How was your weekend?" I asked.

"Saturday shat. That new kid you brought up was sick as a dog. But yesterday, Cliff had the day off too, and it was great. We stayed in bed all day, read the papers, and watched old movies on TV. The only thing that could've made it better was if we had a maid in the house to bring us our meals. Then we wouldn't have had to get out of bed at all!"

In the elevator on the way up, we both thought of Ray. "I'm dying to find out what happened with Lauren last night," I said. "She really took our bait."

The doors opened, we left the elevator, and entered the nurses' station where Ray was sitting with an odd smile on his face.

"Hi, Ray," I said, "you look like you had a pretty good night."

"Not sure about good," Ray responded, "but it sure was interesting. On paper, it doesn't sound so good. That kid from Friday night was a pain in the ass all day, but that wasn't so bad because Laurie really broke her neck to help me out."

"Laurie?" I asked.

"Yeah, she told me to call her Laurie. Says all her friends do. Anyway, she couldn't do enough for me! She even wanted to spend the night in the intern's on-call room, so I wouldn't get woken up for every blood gas."

"Spend the night in your on-call room?" Terry asked. "Uh oh. Ray, you sure you want to get into this any further?"

"Well it never got to the point where we were talking about whether I would be in the room with her. I sort of told her not to be ridiculous, that I was just a regular intern like Bob or Terry and that she shouldn't have to do my work. It really didn't take too much to talk her out of it; I guess she sort of felt like she should volunteer."

"I guess we've really convinced her that you're Ray Brewster, the famous renal physiologist," I said.

"We sure did. I'm starting to feel a little guilty about this. After all, I'm sort of deceiving her."

"No sort of about it, Ray," Terry said. "You are deceiving her."

"Well, I'm not sure what to do about it," Ray responded.

"Look, nothing's happened," I said. "You're using her the same way she uses other people. Forget it. Did you get any admissions yesterday?"

"Yeah," Ray said with that weird smile. "Two. Sort of."

"You're going to drive me crazy with all these 'sort ofs,' " Terry said. "Admissions are all or nothing things; there's no 'sort of' about them."

"Well, come and look," Ray answered coyly. He led us to the chronics row and there on a warming table were his admissions. They were conjoined, or Siamese twins. I did a double take when I saw them, and I thought Terry's eyes were going to pop out of her head.

"Ah, I see what you mean," Terry said after catching her breath. "I guess this does qualify as 'two admissions, sort of.' "

"I got a call from Sheila Simpson, who was covering obstetrics yesterday, telling me that they needed me and Laurie for a section. When we got there, they told us they had a woman with twins who was in labor, but that the kids weren't coming down right. So they did the section and when they pulled one of the kids out, the other one sort of came with her. It was then that we all noticed the kids were attached. So I brought them up here to figure out what to do with them. I guess they'll have to be separated or something."

"How many admission notes did you write?" I asked.

"Interesting question, Bob. Things are complicated with these two, scut-work-wise. They were put on only one warming table, so they were assigned only one admission number, and the clerk made up only one chart for them. So I wrote only one admission note. But when the X-ray technician came up to take some pictures, he counted the number of abdomens and came up with two, and he told me if I wanted X rays of both, I'd have to make up two requisitions. Since there's only one chest, he was satisfied with one form for that. So it's sort of confusing."

"Hmm," Terry mused, "blood work must be pretty hard to interpret. I mean," she asked, "if you draw a blood gas from that arm," pointing to the right arm of the baby on stage left, "would it also reflect the values of that one's blood?" pointing to the baby on stage right.

"Luckily that hasn't been a problem," Ray said. "Other than having their chests stuck together, they're in good shape. We haven't had to do anything for them except feed them and change their diapers. But these guys are going to be interesting. I'm glad I got them for admissions, instead of that dead kid you brought up Friday night."

Our discussion of these joined creatures was interrupted by Frohman who wanted to begin work rounds. Dan was around and so he came with us and, for some reason, Lauren decided to make rounds with us, too. She seemed to be spending most of her time hanging around Ray.

Rounds that morning were pretty depressing and it was mostly because of the very sick baby I had brought up on Friday night. Our discussion of his problems took over a half hour. Even though I had hoped it would not be so, it was clear that we had started the tolazoline too late; in fact, looking at the baby that Monday morning, it appeared that it might have been too late even if we had started the drug as soon as the baby had come into the Pit.

Although he had had a few hours to improve, the child began to require larger and larger doses of the drug to keep the blood oxygen content in the normal range. And with the higher doses of tolazoline, the baby's blood pressure dropped lower and lower, and so it became necessary to increase the rate of the dopamine drip until the maximum dose was reached. But none of this really mattered anyway, because, although we were oxygenating his blood, the baby's brain, kidneys, and intestines were giving us signals that they had been severely and probably irrevocably damaged.

On Saturday afternoon Terry had been called by Gloria Higgins because the baby had had a convulsion. Terry and Frohman, who was always looking over her shoulder, found the child shaking his arms and his legs. They began giving medications to stop the seizures; through the UA line they gave Valium, but the seizure wouldn't stop. They gave a large dose of phenobarbitol, but the seizure wouldn't stop. They gave a large dose of Dilantin, but the seizure still wouldn't stop. Finally, because it was bothering Frohman so much to have a baby in the nursery seizing while he was in charge, they gave the baby Pavulon, a drug that paralyzes all muscles. The baby stopped shaking, but it was clear that the baby's brain was still convulsing.

Convulsions in a baby following an episode of low blood oxygen are a bad sign. They imply that the brain has been damaged. The fact that the seizures in this baby were so hard to control despite all the drugs the baby had been given was a terrible sign, implying that the baby had suffered severe anoxic brain damage, either before or after birth. In cases like this, the prognosis for the baby is very bad.

Because of this evidence of anoxic brain damage, on Saturday morning Terry and Frohman began to look for evidence of damage to other organ systems. That evidence was not hard to find. They examined the bedside clipboard, found that the infant had passed no urine since the time of birth, and reasoned that the kidneys had shut down, had stopped working because they had not received the oxygen they had needed. And on Sunday, while making rounds, Ray and Lauren, noticing that the baby's abdomen had become very distended, had ordered an X ray and had found the presence of free air in the walls of the intestine, a sign called pneumotosis intestinale, indicative of a serious disorder called necrotizing enterocolitis which causes destruction of the intestine. Like the brain damage and the kidney failure, necrotizing enterocolitis is caused by lack of oxygen.

Because of the involvement of these three critical organ systems we came to the conclusion on work rounds that morning that this baby was significantly damaged. "I guess we started the tolazoline too late," I whispered to Dan.

"We couldn't win, Bob," he responded. I wasn't exactly sure what he meant by this at the time, but I would soon find out.

"Since this baby is so bad," Terry reasoned, "shouldn't we stop the dopamine which is keeping up the blood pressure and let the kid die?"

"That's not our decision to make," Frohman snapped back. "It's Sullivan's. And when I spoke to him about the baby on Saturday afternoon, he said he wanted everything done. He was also pretty pissed off at you two guys because you never called him on Friday night to tell him about this baby. He said you were both pieces of shit."

"Damn," I whispered to Dan, "we forgot to call him."

"I didn't forget," Dan whispered back.

"You called him?" I asked.

"No," he answered, "but I never intended to call him. I don't like speaking to Sullivan."

"Well, we'll just have to wait and see what Sullivan has to say about this baby during attending rounds." Frohman continued. "We can't make any decisions until then."

I was convinced that even Sullivan, when confronted with a baby with evidence of so much damage to so many organs, would not hesitate to discontinue vigorous life support. At least that's what I thought.

After we finished with this new baby, rounds went pretty smoothly. All the other babies in the first row were getting better. Over the past week we had been able to wean Baby Summlitz off the ventilator and probably would be able to take the endotracheal tube out of her windpipe and let her breathe like a regular baby sometime that day. We didn't pull out the tube during work rounds, as we probably should have, because Frohman again said that this was Sullivan's decision to make and therefore would have to wait for attending rounds. Baby

Singer, Terry's premie who had been born the previous Thursday morning, was also making giant strides toward normal respiration. Through the weekend Ray and Terry had been able to lower her ventilator settings to the point where she, too, was essentially breathing on her own. We guessed that her tube would be ready to come out the next day.

And finally we hit Ray's new admissions from the day before, the Siamese twins. Upon seeing these creatures, Frohman lost his breath. We hadn't mentioned them earlier and he was momentarily speechless. Even Dan was floored. "These are . . . Siamese twins," he announced.

"I know," Ray answered. "They're sort of stuck together."

Dan approached the babies and started touching them. "Pretty damned interesting!" he said. We all agreed.

Frohman had finally recovered enough to say, "Uh, we'd better hold the discussion of these babies for attending rounds. I bet Dr. Sullivan will have something to say about them." Actually, Sullivan did have a lot to say about them, but little of it was medical, and none of it was directed at us.

After work rounds ended, we went directly to Dr. Sullivan's office. Kathy was already there. After we got ourselves comfortably seated, Sullivan began discussing the baby I had admitted on Friday night, and he quickly made me feel uncomfortable again. "I understand a baby who aspirated meconium was admitted to the unit on Friday night," he began slowly and calmly, looking directly at me. "I only found this out, however on Saturday, when Dr. Frohman took it upon himself to call me to discuss the case on Saturday afternoon. Did you forget to call me, Dr. Sharon, or did you do it intentionally?"

"I forgot," I answered meekly.

"Well, don't forget again!" he snapped. "What did you do for the baby on Friday night?"

I began to tell him the story. "The baby was born by emergency section on Friday night, after the mother had been transferred in from New Hampshire because of a bad nonstress test. She ruptured membranes in the ambulance and the fluid was reported to be as thick as pea soup. They attached an internal monitor when she got here and there was bad bradycardia that didn't improve after a contraction, so they did a stat section. We resuscitated the baby in the DR and brought him up here. Through the night, the blood oxygen stayed between thirty-five and fifty-five, despite maximal ventilator support. The baby had two pneumothoraces and we put in two chest tubes. . . ."

"Did you start tolazoline?" Sullivan asked calmly.

"Not until five on Saturday morning," I answered.

"I see," Sullivan responded. He wrote this down on a pad in front of him. "And what happened after you started the tolazoline?"

"Well, the baby became bright pink. His blood oxygen stabilized in the normal range, but his blood pressure dropped very low. So we started him on a dopamine drip. The baby was stable by the time I left on Saturday morning." At least, I thought, he was more stable than I was!

Terry took up the story from there, without hesitation, and without giving Sullivan a chance to respond. "After Bob and Dan left on Saturday, we repeated the blood gas and found that the oxygen had dropped back down to forty-eight. So, as you ordered when Simon called you, we increased the tolazoline and the dopamine. We kept having to do that all day. The oxygen kept going up with the higher dose, but then would drop down in the forties again a little later.

"I was called to see the baby at about two in the afternoon because of a seizure. As you told Simon, we tried Valium, phenobarb, and Dilantin, but we couldn't stop it. We finally resorted to paralyzing the baby; that was the only way to stop the convulsions.

"Then later I noticed that the baby hadn't put out any urine since birth, and we diagnosed renal shutdown. He hasn't passed a drop, even to this morning."

Ray then finished off the story of the weekend. "On Sunday Laurie and I continued pumping in the tolazoline and dopamine and we had to keep the kid paralyzed or else he'd start seizing again. Also, we noticed that his belly was blowing up like a balloon so we got an X ray. It showed air in the wall of the bowel, so I guess he's got necrotizing enterocolitis, too."

When Ray had finished, Sullivan was quiet for a minute. We were all quiet and still, except for Frohman, who was hitting his thumbs against the side of his chair nervously. Then Sullivan looked directly at me and asked, "How long was it you waited before starting the tolazoline, Dr. Sharon?"

"The baby was about four hours old at that point," I answered. I knew he was about to start laying into me. I just hoped I could weather the storm.

"I see. And why is it you waited that long?" he asked coldly.

"We were pushing the ventilator to its limit in trying to oxygenate him up to that point," I responded.

"I see." Sullivan was now sneering. "Who made that decision?"

"Well, we talked it over. I guess mainly Dan."

"I see. Do you think you did a good job oxygenating this baby?"

"No," I answered. I was holding up pretty well so far.

"Well, why the fuck did you wait that long?" Sullivan's voice was rising. "Why did you wait until the infant was five hours old before you started the damned tolazoline? While you were thinking and making decisions on your own, this baby's brain and all his other organs were being deprived of oxygen. While you waited, he was running the risk of becoming even more brain-damaged!" Dr. Sullivan's eyes were now wide open, his face bright red, his voice reaching a crescendo. "Dr. Sharon! Do you realize your procrastination caused this child to be brain-damaged?"

I couldn't cry. I wanted to, but I was too shocked. Ray and Terry were also stunned. Frohman, though, was not shocked. He seemed happy.

Thank God for Dan, who came to my defense. "You sure about that, Dr. Sullivan?" Dan asked, much calmer than Sullivan. "You sure the baby's problem resulted from our not giving the tolazoline in time?"

"You keep out of this, Berkowitz!" Sullivan shouted. "I'm not talking to you!"

"No, I won't keep out of this. I was on with Bob, and he's my responsibility. I'm the one who said no tolazoline at first. So if you want to accuse someone of starting it too late, accuse me! And if you're accusing me, I'm asking you a question, Are you sure that the baby's problem resulted directly from starting the tolazoline too late?"

"I'm telling you," Sullivan yelled, "stay out of this!"

"You're not sure, are you, Sullivan? You're definitely not sure. You just wanted a reason to yell at an intern, someone who wouldn't talk back to you like I would. Well, you picked the wrong topic. Sullivan, I bet this baby would have wound up the way he did even if we had started that tolazoline as soon as the baby was born. That baby was damaged before we got a hold of him, he was damaged right in the womb. That's why there was so much meconium to begin with. But I know one thing: if we had started that tolazoline right at birth, you would have yelled at Bob for that too. The baby would have gone into shock and you would have said, 'Why did you start a drug with so many side effects when you hadn't even tried him on the ventilator?' And you would have said, 'Dr. Sharon, your starting that drug so soon caused that baby to develop brain damage.' You just wanted a chance to yell at somebody."

"Get out of this office!" Sullivan shouted at Dan. "Get out now! And don't come back!"

Dan rose to leave with an angry glare at Sullivan. "Look, you guys," he said as he strolled toward the door, "don't let this bastard get you down. He needs to make you feel like shit in order for him to feel like a man."

"Get out!" Sullivan shouted again.

Sullivan sat back in his chair and looked at the ceiling. "Dr. Sharon," he finally began, more calmly now, "why didn't you call me at home? We could have averted that whole scene."

"Like I said, Dr. Sullivan, I forgot in the excitement. And like Dan said, we felt we were justified in what we were doing."

Now Kathy joined in. She had been silent through Sullivan's initial outburst. "Justified," she shouted. "A house officer justified in making a decision that could mean life or death to a patient? Listen, before you are justified to do something like that, you'd better be sure you have enough experience. And you and your friend, Berkowitz, you sure don't have that kind of experience. Even I don't have that kind of experience. In this nursery, Dr. Sullivan's the only one who's justified in making those decisions."

"Thank you, Kathy," Sullivan responded, still calmer. "I'm going to tell you three one more time, and I'm not going to tell you again. I am to be called at home for all admissions, and for any change in the status of any patient already here. Do you understand? If this happens again, I will report the incident to Dr. Jennings, and he will take whatever punitive action he deems appropriate."

Ray, whose anger was building through this, could contain it no longer. "I don't understand this," he said. "This baby was on death's door all weekend. Terry and Bob and I and the residents we were on with did a damned good job just keeping this baby alive so we could even have this argument today. Where I come from, you get commended for doing a good job. But all you can do is yell!"

"Oh, terrific," Sullivan screamed back at him, "you want a pat on the back for producing a baby with brain damage, as well as with kidney and intestinal damage!"

Terry got into it at this point. "We didn't produce this kid!" she yelled back at Sullivan. "He was handed to Bob and Dan this way!"

Sullivan sighed, shook his head, laughed to himself, and looked to the ceiling. He was silent for about another minute, but he kept shaking his head. Finally, calmly he turned back to us and said, "Well, I can see there's no use discussing this any further with you three. Some people just can't be taught anything. Well, Dr. Frohman, since you still seem to be with me, let me tell you what must be done for this baby: we continue the tolazoline and keep the oxygen over fifty; we continue to maintain the blood pressure with dopamine; we follow the blood electrolytes for a rise in potassium. If the potassium gets too high, we'll have to dialyze him. Hopefully, with antibiotics the intestine will heal on its own and we won't have to do surgery. But keep an eye on that gut and get an X ray every day to see what's happening."

Frohman wrote this down, word for word, on a piece of paper attached to his clipboard. Ray, Terry, and I, although outraged by these orders to continue aggressive care of this baby, remained silent.

"Now," Sullivan said after Frohman had completed writing, "anything else happen over the weekend?" He was calm and sounded friendly again. This man could go from furious to best friend in ten seconds.

"Well, Ray admitted a very interesting baby . . . or rather babies yesterday," Frohman said.

"You didn't call me for another admission?" Sullivan asked. "Kathy, were you told. . . ."

"No, I wasn't told," she answered.

"What can you do?" Sullivan sighed, looking toward heaven. "Oh well. Dr. Brewster, tell me about this admission."

"Why bother?" Ray mumbled.

"What was that?" Sullivan was angry again.

"I said, 'Why bother?' Why should I bother telling you anything?

You'll just find something to yell at me about and then make any irrational decision that pops into your head."

"All right, Ray," Frohman said, "let's not have any more fighting. Just tell the story."

Ray glared at Frohman and then started the story. "Mrs. Srnivasan was referred here by her private obstetrician in Worcester for management of her twin gestation. She had an ultrasound at thirty weeks and the twins were diagnosed at that time. The pregnancy went to full term and was otherwise uncomplicated.

"The staff here decided to let her try to deliver vaginally. She went into labor but the babies just wouldn't come down into the pelvis so, after sixteen hours or so, they decided to deliver her by section. At the time of delivery it was noted that the twins were sort of joined at the chest, so we brought them. . . ."

Sullivan, who had been listening to the first part of the story with a detached, "I wish I were somewhere else" look on his face, suddenly perked up. His eyes opened wide and a smile appeared on his face as he shouted, "What? You mean we have a set of Siamese twins? Why didn't you tell me before? Let's go see them!"

Without waiting for Ray to finish the rest of the story, Sullivan, like a little child with the promise of a new toy, sprinted out of his office and into the Pit. We all followed at a slower pace. He found the two little girls himself, took his stethoscope out of his pouch, along with his wallet and a Mobil road map, and started examining them. He turned them on their backs and on each side, he looked at the bridging part from every possible angle, he looked at what was separate and what was shared. All through the exam the babies cried and cried while Sullivan muttered, "Oh this is great, this is just terrific," over and over again to himself. And then to Kathy, who stood across the warming table from him, he said, "Have you ever? Have you ever seen anything like this, Kathy?" The two of them were transfixed.

After a few more moments in ecstasy, Sullivan addressed us, never taking his eyes off the babies, who had suddenly become his prized possessions. "This is tremendous! Viable conjoined twins are incredibly rare. This is the first pair I've ever seen. It looks like they might share a common heart, since they're joined at the chest. Dr. Brewster, what did the X ray show?"

"It does look like there's a shared heart," Ray answered quietly.

"Ah yes," Sullivan said, proud of his clinical acumen. "We should let the cardiologists from the Medical Center see this . . . er, these babies, for their own education. There's no way I'm going to let them do anything but look, though. Once those guys see these two, they're going to want to cath them and do an echocardiogram, and the first thing you know, they'll be talking about wanting to separate them. But there's no way we're going to allow them to be separated. And now, I'm going to my office to call the newspapers and TV stations. This kind of thing is great publicity for us." And with that, Sullivan left the Pit.

"That sure was an educational discussion," Terry immediately said to me. She, Ray, and I, with attending rounds now over, adjourned to the cafeteria for lunch.

"We're stuck with a resident who's a worm and with an attending who is irrational and who looks at the birth of Siamese twins as a publicity stunt," I said as we sat down with our trays.

"Oh well, it's not so bad," Ray responded. "At least he didn't go to his office to call the papers to tell them we were killing babies by not giving them tolazoline in time."

"Yeah, I can see it now," I laughed. "INTERNS KILLING BABIES AT THE ST. ANNE'S HATCHERY!, a banner headline across the front page of the *Herald American.* Actually, maybe we should call the papers ourselves and tell them that Sullivan is keeping dead babies alive. NEONATOLOGIST FILLS BEDS AT WALTHAM HOME BY PRODUCING GORKS AT ST. ANNE'S. Now that would sell papers."

"You know," Terry added quickly, "that's not a half bad idea. If we do it right, that kind of yellow journalism could be just the thing needed to get the hospital board to throw Sullivan out on his ear."

"I've been thinking about our date with the hospital board," I said. "I think we're going to need some kind of publicity stunt like that, because I don't think we're going to get anywhere with the board."

"Why not?" Ray demanded.

"I talked it over with Dan and he said the members of the board like the fact that Sullivan saves babies, and that they probably looked all over for a guy like Sullivan who would be crazy enough to keep a dead kid alive. So, if we go to them and complain that he's saving too many babies, they'll probably wind up giving Sullivan a promotion."

"Good point," Terry said, a little disappointed. "I hadn't thought it all the way through."

"So I don't think we can rely on the hospital board. I think we can do something, but we have to do it ourselves and not rely on anybody else. I can't really think of anything. Any ideas, Ray?"

Ray had fallen asleep in his chair. Terry and I laughed, but neither of us had the heart to wake him up.

On my way back to the nursery, I stopped in the recovery area. Mrs. O'Hara, although weak and worn, was wide awake and responsive; she had regained consciousness sometime during the preceding night.

"Dr. Sharon," she said slowly, "it is good to see you."

"It's even better to see you," I responded.

"My husband told me you've been a comfort to him during my illness. I'd like to thank you for that."

"Oh, you don't have to thank me. It's enough just to hear your voice again. How are you feeling?"

"So-so. Dr. Fredericks tells me that I'm getting better. I guess I gave everyone a bit of a fright last week."

"I'll say," I responded.

"How is my little daughter doing?"

"Just fine. She seems to be a fast healer. I think we'll be able to start feeding her formula later this week."

"That's good. If it is at all possible, Dr. Sharon, I would like to give her her first bottle."

"I think that can be arranged," I smiled. "When are they going to let you go back to your room?"

"Dr. Fredericks says later on today. But I think they'll want me to keep out of the nursery for another two days yet. They don't want me spreading my germs to the little ones."

"If I may say so, I'm happy to see the change in your attitude about the baby."

"Well my husband told you of his decision. He's the boss in our house and what he says goes. I'm not looking forward to raising her, but if I have to do it, I will. And this decision my husband made, it has nothing to do with that terrible man, Dr. Sullivan."

"Mrs. O'Hara, I have to go now," I said. "I want you to know how happy I am you're better. I'll look forward to seeing you in a day or two up in the nursery."

"Thank you again, Dr. Sharon, and God bless you! Outside of you and Dr. Fredericks, not a soul here has been decent to either me or my husband."

I left the recovery area with a weird, ambivalent feeling: I felt good that I had somehow come through for this family in their time of need but, at the same time, I felt horrible that I could have good feelings about an incident that had been so poorly managed. I returned to the Pit and found Ray and Terry sitting in the nurses' station, observing the circus that seemed to have pitched its tents right inside our unit.

The nurses had cleared room around the Srnivasan twins to prepare for the onslaught of media people. While we watched, reporters from the two daily newspapers, the *Globe* and the *Herald American,* were interviewing the nurses who were caring for the babies and Dr. Sullivan, who had changed out of his usual crumpled white shirt and tie into a more official-looking surgical scrub suit for the benefit of the photographers.

There were two photographers in the Pit, indiscriminately snapping away. They took pictures, not only of the twins, Dr. Sullivan, and the nurses, but also of some of the other babies, of the equipment, of the view out the windows, in fact, of just about everything except the interns.

The newspaper people remained in the unit for about a half hour. They were soon replaced by a mobile team from "Channel 6 Eyewitness News," who arrived with bright klieg lights, which they set in strategic positions around the Pit, makeup, which they applied to Sullivan's face, and a reporter I had seen on the news named Mary Jane Doherty. Mary Jane, who looked attractive and vital on the tube, looked molded out of plastic in real life. Most of the time she looked human, but if you happened to catch her from just the right angles, you'd swear she looked like she was painted on cardboard.

When everything was set up and ready, they began taping. We interns moved our vantage point from the nurses' station to inside the Pit so we could hear as well as see what was happening. We did stay a safe distance away from the action, however, and also stayed away from Kathy, who was looking on anxiously, somehow hoping that Mary Jane would interview her.

"I'm Mary Jane Doherty," Mary Jane said with the camera pointed at her, "here in the newborn intensive care unit at St. Anne's Hospital in Cambridge, where a very unusual set of twins were born yesterday. The babies are Siamese twins, joined together at the chest. These small creatures, born to an Indian couple from Worcester, are totally normal in every way except for an area of skin that joins their breastbones."

Dr. Sullivan, being cued by the director, now stepped to the right of Mary Jane. "Joining me now is Dr. John Sullivan, professor of Pediatrics at the New England School of Medicine and director of the nursery here at St. Anne's. Dr. Sullivan, is this the first pair of Siamese twins who have been born here at St. Anne's?"

Perspiration stains were starting to darken the olive green of the enormous surgical scrub suit Sullivan had put on. "Well, Mary Jane, not only are these the first Siamese twins born here at St. Anne's, but they are the first I've ever seen in my career. In fact, the last pair born in Massachusetts occurred in Springfield in nineteen sixty-three."

"That long ago!" Mary Jane exclaimed with theatrical surprise. "I guess they are quite unusual."

"Yes they are, Mary Jane," Sullivan answered, "but they do occur more commonly in India. And these twins are ethnically Indian."

"Can you tell us something about the twins' medical status?"

"Of course, Mary Jane. These twins are in excellent health. They've needed no extra help, but we have performed some tests. I have personally been supervising their medical care."

"Bullshit!" Ray whispered loud enough for Terry and me and a few nearby observers to hear.

"I see," Mary Jane said. "Dr. Sullivan, can you tell us when you plan to perform the surgery that will separate these two?"

"We have no plans at this time to separate the twins, Mary Jane. You see, this type of conjoined twinning, called 'thoracopagus' or 'joined chest' has, as one of its frequent complications, a single shared heart. Because of this fact, we have performed X-ray tests that have shown that there is only one heart beating in the single chest. Because of this, only one twin could survive a procedure that separated them."

"Can they live a life together? Aren't there problems associated with not separating them, Dr. Sullivan?" Mary Jane asked, concerned.

The enormous green scrub suit was now soaked through with sweat as Sullivan responded. "Well, Mary Jane, the term Siamese twins comes from the most famous pair of conjoined twins that ever existed, Chang and Eng, the renowned circus performers of the nineteenth century. Like these twins, Chang and Eng were thoracopagus, and they were never separated. Yet they lived full, normal lives, both in and out of the Big Top, and each even fathered children of his own. So Mary Jane, I would expect these two to be able to live long, fulfilling lives in the joined state."

"Finally, Dr. Sullivan, when do you anticipate that these babies will be ready to go home to their parents?"

"Pretty soon, actually, Mary Jane. Since there are no medical problems, we'll probably release them from the nursery in three or four days."

"Well thank you, Dr. Sullivan." Mary Jane looked back at the camera, which closed in on her plastic face. "The birth of Siamese twins, a wonder of nature. For 'Eyewitness News,' this is Mary Jane Doherty, reporting from St. Anne's Hospital in Cambridge."

The bright lights went off and the cameraman changed his position in order to get some close-ups of the babies. "Thank you again, Dr. Sullivan," Mary Jane said, this time without her usual painted-on smile. "You did a fine job."

"Thank you!" Sullivan smiled, wiping the doughy mixture of sweat and pancake makeup from his forehead and leaving the nursery.

"A fine job," Terry said. "Ray, would you call Dr. Sullivan's performance a fine job?"

"I don't think Sullivan's gonna win any Academy Awards for it," Ray responded.

"I'm going to get you on TV, Ray," Terry said, and she approached Mary Jane, saying, "Excuse me, Ms. Doherty, but I'm one of the interns working here in the nursery. Dr. Brewster," she motioned to Ray, "was the pediatrician in the delivery room when the twins were born. He worked through the night stabilizing them. Why, without him, these twins wouldn't be alive today," she lied.

"Yeah?" Mary Jane asked matter-of-factly. "So what?"

"Don't you think you should interview him?" Terry asked.

Ray stepped forward. He looked terrible. Mary Jane took a close look at him and said, "Are you kidding? He's disheveled, covered with blood and sweat and Lord knows what else, his eyes are bloodshot, and it looks like he hasn't slept in a week."

"But he was there!" Terry responded excitedly. "He saved their lives. Can't you fix him up with some makeup or something?"

"Makeup?" Mary Jane asked. "No way. Makeup can cover a lot of problems but . . . well, there's just no way we could get anyone to believe that someone who looks like this is actually a doctor!"

We hurried out of the Pit and convulsed with laughter in the hallway. "We're the ones who stay up all night, we're the ones who do all the dirty work while Sullivan sleeps comfortably in his warm bed every night," I observed, "and when the time comes to get interviewed for the TV news by Mary Jane Doherty, who do they pick? Clean, well-rested Sullivan! They won't interview us, 'cause we're covered with so much shit no one will believe we're really doctors."

"Oh well," Ray said philosophically. "It's not so bad; at least I won't have to stay awake until six-thirty to see myself on the damned news."

XV

On Call

As Ray and Terry were signing out to me that evening, a second television news crew appeared at the door of the nurses' station. By the time Ray and Terry left, Sullivan, after having exchanged his sweat-soaked scrub suit for a new clean and dry one, had begun to go through his act again. I couldn't bear to watch this a second time, and so I went down to the fourth floor to visit Tom Fredericks; as usual, I found him in his on-call room in front of his color TV.

"Hello, Bob, how are you? Ready for another night at fabulous St. A's?"

"As ready as I'll ever be, Tom, as ready as I'll ever be." Tom's pattern of speech had become infectious. "How are you?"

"I'm great," he answered. "And I'm great because things here are great, as great as they ever get. It looks like we saved Mrs. O'Hara from almost certain death. Damn, was she sick! It's at times like this that you feel good you became a doctor. I feel like I really helped save that lady's life."

"Yeah," I said dreamily. I of course had not yet experienced the exhilarating feeling Tom was describing, and I was beginning to doubt that I ever would. After all, I hadn't even successfully started an IV yet.

"And not only that, Bob, not only am I feeling great because of how well Mrs. O'Hara's doing but, to top it off, it's been pretty quiet down here all day and I know it's going to stay that way because today's the first day of the quarter moon."

"What does that have to do with anything?" I asked.

"Plenty, Bob, plenty. I've found, through my extensive one-year experience here that more babies are born during the first phase of the new moon than during any other time. Take last week for instance; we had a couple of premies, the new mongoloid, that dead kid you brought up to the Pit, a set of Siamese twins. . . . That's busy for us, Bob, real busy. But with a quarter moon, that'll all settle down. There probably won't be any deliveries tonight and tomorrow, none at all, except for maybe that pig Parris's patients, but his deliveries don't depend on anything except on when Parris wants to operate. I'll be right, Bob, you just wait and see."

"Why is that?" I asked, certain that Tom was pulling my leg.

"Don't know, Bob, I just don't know. Just the way it is, I guess. Might be sunspots, might be gravitational pull on the uterus, or pressure pockets, or maybe hormone changes caused by the phase of the moon; hell, it might have something to do with werewolves. Don't know why it is, just know it happens every month that way. If you can figure it out, you'd probably win yourself a Nobel Prize."

"I don't know about this, Tom," I said, "but I hope you're right. I could sure use an easy night."

"Me too," Tom answered, "and I will be right. You just wait and see."

I wandered upstairs where I found Dan nearly asleep in the nurses' station. "Evening, Bob," he said when he opened his eyes.

"Evening, Dan," I answered.

"It looks like this place has turned into a soundstage," he said. "When I got here, there was a crew from Channel 10."

"Yeah, that was the second one, and that's not counting the newspaper reporters."

"They all came to see those twins?" Dan asked.

"Yeah," I responded, "after you left rounds this morning, we told Sullivan about the Siamese twins and he's turned into a media freak."

"Thought having the twins here would be great publicity for him and the hospital, huh?" Dan asked.

"Yep, that's exactly what he said."

"That figures. Bob, do you have any idea about whether he went down to talk with the babies' parents to tell them exactly what was happening with the twins? Did he get their permission to call the newspapers and TV stations?"

"I don't think so," I answered. "I think he just went ahead and called them."

"That figures too. Do you know if Ray spoke with the mother yesterday or today?"

"I don't think so. He had his hands pretty full last night with the Dead Kid we brought up on. . . ."

"The Dead Kid?" Dan interrupted.

"Yeah. Everyone seems to be calling him the 'Dead Kid.' "

"It's got a nice ring to it." Dan repeated it over and over to himself. "Yeah. It's not exactly nice, but it sure is true."

"Yeah. Anyway, Ray had his hands full with that kid and he was so tired today that he fell asleep during lunch in the cafeteria."

"Fell asleep in St. A's cafeteria?" Dan asked. "That could be dangerous. He could wind up as dinner." He laughed.

"Anyway, I don't think he spoke to the parents. Why?"

"Well, Sullivan didn't talk to them, that's for sure. And the same is true for Kathy and Frohman. So if Ray didn't go and tell them what's happening . . ."

"Then the parents may not know the babies are joined," I said, completing the sentence Dan had started.

"Right. But if they have the TV in the mother's room turned on, they'll find out pretty soon."

"Oh shit!" I said, banging my head with the palm of my left hand. "It's six-thirty and time for Mary Jane Doherty and the news."

" 'Oh shit' is right," Dan repeated.

"Along with everybody else in the greater Boston area, this is how they're going to find out that their twins are joined."

"We'd better run downstairs and see if we can get to them before they see it." Dan rose to his full height and, as he started moving for the elevator, I followed.

While we were waiting for the elevator to arrive, I said, "Dan, I want to thank you for defending me in front of Sullivan during rounds today. You just about saved my life."

"Oh come on, Sharon," Dan said as the elevator doors opened and we got in, "there's no way I saved your life. Sullivan hasn't murdered even a single house officer yet."

"You know what I mean," I said.

"Well, I wasn't really defending you, anyway." The elevator opened on three and we stepped out in the ugly corridor with the peeling paint, poor lighting, and sweltering temperature as Dan continued, "I was defending myself. After all, it was me, not you, who made the decision to start the tolazoline. So he wasn't really attacking you, he was attacking me through you. He knew if he attacked me directly, I'd really give him a hard time; also, it's easier to get you upset."

By this point we were at the nurses' station. I got Mrs. Srnivasan's room number from the ward clerk, and Dan and I walked down the hall toward the room. We didn't exactly enter her room at the best moment. The television was on. Mrs. Srnivasan, whose face was puffy and tear-streaked, obviously the result of long hours of crying, was lying in bed, staring in disbelief, her mouth and eyes wide as saucers, at the screen. Her husband, sitting in a chair next to the bed, had a similar look on his face while on the tube was a picture of Mary Jane Doherty, looking great, interviewing Sullivan, who looked fatter and sweatier than he did in person. They were informally chatting about thoracopagus twins.

"I think we're a little too late," Dan whispered as we stood at the open doorway, surveying this scene. We turned to leave but were again too late. Mr. Srnivasan was staring at us.

"Mr. and Mrs. Srnivasan?" Dan asked, once he realized we couldn't turn back. Now they both looked toward us, but the expressions on their faces did not change. "I'm Dr. Berkowitz and this is Dr. Sharon. We're two of the doctors who are taking care of the babies upstairs."

"They are alive!" Mrs. Srnivasan said in a monotone. She had very long, stringy black hair and very dark skin. "You tell me they are dead. But they are alive."

Dan and I were quiet. At first I thought she was addressing us, but I was wrong.

"I tell you they are dead because that is what doctor told me," Mr. Srnivasan said.

"Which doctor?" Dan asked. "That one on TV?"

"No, not him. That doctor with blond hair, he tell me they are dead."

"Dr. Brewster spoke with you?" I asked.

"Yes, that his name. He came the night they are born. He tell me something is very wrong with them, that they have a condition, that everything not be okay. So I tell my wife they are dead. But now Mary Jane Doherty show them on TV. They are not dead?"

"No," Dan answered, "they're both fine. But as you see on TV, they are joined together at the chest."

"These people lie to us," Mrs. Srnivasan said to her husband. "They tell us baby are dead, then they show them on TV. They say one thing, then do another. And now everyone in Boston know about my baby before I do!"

"Please to get out of here!" her husband said. "You both please to get out now!"

Without uttering another word, Dan and I turned on our heels and left the room. Outside the door, Dan said, "Damn, we really blew it this time!"

"I feel terrible!" I said.

"So do I," Dan added. "But what can we do? There's no way we could have prevented this. It's all that damned Sullivan's fault. It was more important for him to be on the Mary Jane Doherty show than it was to talk with the parents!"

We walked back to the Pit, defeated, and sat around in the nurses' station talking about this screwup and about what we could do in the future to prevent this kind of thing from happening again. At about seven-thirty, the door to the nurses' station opened and a tall, thin, bald-headed man walked in. Dan rose when he saw him and his face brightened as he said, "Hi, Dr. Channin. What brings you out to this wasteland?"

"Hi, Dan. I'm here to do a consult. Is this new meat?" Channin asked as he looked toward me.

"Yes, sir. This is Bob Sharon. Bob, this is Harold Channin, pediatric cardiologist par excellence. Dr. Channin is one of the few physicians at the Medical Center whose head is screwed on right."

"Actually, Bob, Dan only likes me because I'm one of the few attendings who still is talking to him." He offered me his hand. "Pleased to meet you, Bob."

I shook his hand but didn't say anything.

"You're making a great first impression, Bob. Tell me, do you always look this happy?"

"Actually," Dan answered before I had a chance, "Bob and I just had a little problem with one of the patient's families. Sullivan screwed things up pretty well."

"What?" Channin asked with feigned shock. "Sullivan screw up? Is such a thing possible?"

I didn't laugh.

"All the interns are having a little bit of trouble with Sullivan," Dan said. "It looks like they're already onto him."

"Not surprising, Dan. You guys have been here for a week already, right?"

I nodded in the affirmative.

"Well I would think it shouldn't take longer than twenty minutes to figure out that Sullivan's from outer space! But enough of this character assassination of my colleagues. Men, I'm here for business. Dr. Sharon, I understand you have a baby for me to see."

"Well, actually there are two babies," I said, brightening a little.

"Two? My secretary told me only about one. A Baby Girl Srnivasan?"

"Well, there are actually two babies named Srnivasan. However, they possess only one heart." I was smiling now.

"Oh I see. Dan, I have always said that it is a mistake to start new interns at St. Anne's. It does something to their brains that seems irreversible. It must have something to do with the Cambridge drinking water."

"I agree with you, Dr. Channin," Dan said, also smiling. "But in this case, Bob is correct. There are two babies named Srnivasan here, but only one Srnivasan heart."

"Senior's aren't immune from it, I guess," Dr. Channin said. Without another word, I led them both to the Srnivasan twins. Dr. Channin hid his surprise well. After the initial shock, he adopted a look that suggested he was thinking, "Oh yeah, another set of Siamese twins."

After a short hesitation, he asked, "Dr. Sharon, do you realize that these two babies are joined together?"

"Yes, sir. That's what I was trying to tell you."

"Ahh, I see, I see. Have you, by any chance taken any X rays of these babies?"

"As a matter of fact, I have a set of X rays right here." I handed him the packet that I had carried from the nurses' station.

He held the films up to the light. He studied them for a good long time. He measured, using his free hand, the size of the single heart; he traced the vessels that led to and came from the organ; he looked at the lungs and compared their size with the size of the heart. Finally, he handed the X rays back to me, produced a stethoscope from his jacket pocket, placed the stethoscope's bell on the chest over the heart, and listened.

"Let's do an EKG," he said after listening to the chest for a while. I got the electrocardiograph machine from its corner of the Pit and Dr. Channin applied the leads and ran the test. Usually, the technician who performs an EKG puts one lead on each extremity and one more at different positions around the chest; with the Srnivasan twins it was more complicated, since there were twice the normal number of limbs for the number of chests, but Dr. Channin appeared to know what he was doing. After finishing, having produced a long strip of paper with a lot of squiggly lines on it, he took off the leads and played with the babies for a few seconds.

"By any chance," he asked Dan earnestly when he was all finished, "do these babies have the same mother?"

"Yes they do," Dan answered. "They are twins."

"I see. Tell me, Dan, has anyone spoken with her yet?"

"Interesting you should ask. Up until about an hour ago, nobody had said a word to her. But then Bob and I tried to speak with her."

"She was too angry to talk with us," I said. "She threw us out of her room."

"Angry at you?" Channin asked. "Why?"

"Because Sullivan decided it was more important to speak with Mary Jane Doherty from 'Channel 6 Eyewitness News' than it was to speak with Mrs. Srnivasan," Dan answered.

"The mother saw the twins for the first time on TV," I added.

"Oy vay!" Channin groaned.

"And that's not the worst of it," Dan said. "Through some sort of misunderstanding the mother had been told that the twins had died. Then when she saw Sullivan explaining to old Mary Jane how the babies were in excellent health, she was, to say the least, a little surprised. As a result, she's decided there's no one working at this hospital who's trustworthy. That's why she threw us out of her room."

"A wonderful situation," Channin said. "Just wonderful! I hate to tell you guys this, but I think the mother is going to have less reason to trust anyone working here after she finds out what I'm going to recommend. I'm not exactly sure about this yet, I've got to get an echocardiogram and a cardiac cath done, so I wouldn't say anything to her right now. But I'm pretty sure we're going to have to have these babies separated."

"Separated?" I asked. "Won't separating them kill one of them?"

Channin looked at Dan. "Dan," he said, "it looks like they got a smart one when they got this guy!" Then, looking at me, he continued, "Yes, Dr. Sharon. Unfortunately, if you have two babies and only one heart between them, when you separate the babies, one of them will get that heart, whereas the other one will get nothing. Now regardless of what you hear from the neurologists about the brain being the most important organ, if you don't have a heart, you can't live. So, unfortunately, one of the babies will have to be . . . sacrificed."

"But can't we keep them together?" I almost pleaded, not liking the sound of that "sacrifice." "That way, they'll both survive."

"Well I don't know about that. We could keep them together. But if we did that, they'd both die within a month or two. See, I'm not exactly sure of this yet, and that's why I have to get some more tests, but it looks like the way the whole system is set up, there's going to be too much strain on the single heart. I just don't think it will be able to support both circulatory systems for any length of time. So I think the only way the parents are going to get a viable child out of this deal is if one of the twins is sacrificed so that the other one can survive."

I understood what he was saying, but I was having some trouble accepting it. "Dr. Channin, how will you decide which twin will be allowed to live and which will die?"

"When you put it that way, Bob, it makes me sound like I'm playing God. Actually, I'll only be an observer in all this. The twins will probably let us know themselves. The echocardiogram and the cardiac cath will tell us which twin has the larger portion of heart in her chest and, therefore, which will have the better chance of survival. I think the surgery's going to be pretty tough."

"I think we're going to have a pretty rough time even before we get to the surgery stage," Dan responded. "The parents don't trust us now because they think we told them that the babies had died; now, how can they believe us when we tell them the twins both will die unless they have an operation that is guaranteed to kill at least one of them?"

"Well, I wouldn't tell them anything yet, Dan," Channin answered. "I may be totally wrong about this, hard as I know that is to believe. We have to get those tests done first."

"I don't know if any of this is going to matter, anyway," I said. "It's all academic; Dr. Sullivan said he would never allow these babies to be separated. He wants them both to live."

"Well, Bob, even Dr. Sullivan can't always get what he wants," Channin responded glumly.

While Channin was writing his findings in the twins' chart back in the nurses' station, I considered his recommendation. This was really going to be rough on two fronts: Sullivan would be hard to control after he read Channin's official consult note; and dealing with the Srnivasans would be a whole other thing.

After he had finished writing, Dr. Channin turned to me. "These parents are going to need a lot of attention, Bob. They're confused, angry, and feel like they've been lied to, all during a time when they're finding out, in a miserable way, that their babies are freaks. I'm sure that poor woman is scared to death that she's produced some awful monster and it's because of this that the whole staff is avoiding her and lying to her. The best thing to do in cases like this is to bring the mother up here and let her see the babies for herself. That way she'll know what the truth is. I think if that's done, she'll feel better about things, and that will make it easier for us to talk with her about the rest of the workup and about the possibility of surgery. It is essential that she find at least one staff member of this godforsaken institution who she can trust, but after she saw the Mary Jane Doherty show herself, I don't know if that'll be possible. I'm available at all times to serve you in any way I can." And with that, Channin rose, said goodbye to Dan and me, and left the Pit.

"A prince," Dan said after Channin had gone. "A true prince." And although I thought Channin's sense of humor seemed a little inappropriate at times, anyone good enough for Dan was good enough for me.

When we returned to the nurses' station after dinner, I noticed that a man was standing at the Dead Kid's bedside. Angela, who had come on duty while we were at dinner, entered the nurses' station and asked, "How are you doing tonight, Bob?"

"I'm better than I was the last time I saw you," I answered.

"I thought you'd be, after a nice weekend off. You looked like you could have used a little rest."

"Yeah," I answered, "a little rest! Well, I guess you can see, it looks like we started the tolazoline a little too late."

"Bob, you can never tell," she responded. "You know, I've seen this same kind of thing happen even when the tolazoline was started right away. You guys did what you thought was right; I wouldn't have let you get away with it if I thought you were wrong."

"Thanks for saying that," I said. "And thanks for saying what you did on Saturday morning. I know I didn't say anything at the time, but it did make me feel better."

"I wouldn't have said it, Bob, if I didn't believe it. You are good. Don't get down on yourself!"

"I don't have to get down on myself," I said, blushing. "Sullivan and Kathy are around to do that for me."

"Ah, don't pay any attention to those two! I got a lot of flak myself from Kathy this afternoon. She called me at home, wanting to know why I didn't force you to call Sullivan when that baby was admitted, and how I could allow an intern to get away with doing things that could hurt one of her babies. That Kathy's quite a piece of business! You know, outside of Sullivan, she doesn't trust anyone!"

"Well, it's good to know we interns aren't the only ones being abused by our superiors," I said. "You nurses have your problems too, huh?"

"Oh, it's awful! The way Kathy carries on, with her constant second-guessing and her threats of disciplinary action, she's caused a lot of good nurses to quit their jobs here."

"That is pretty bad," I responded. "It sounds like she's got a lot of rules and regulations."

"Oh yeah. One of her rules is the reason that I came in here to talk to you. You see that guy out there?" She pointed to the man standing beside the Dead Kid's warming table.

"Yeah?" I answered.

"He's that poor baby's father. He's asking some questions about the baby's condition. Kathy has ordered us never to talk to parents but instead to send them to the intern. And the intern's supposed to send them to Dr. Sullivan. It seems kind of silly to me."

"Okay," I said, "I'll go talk to him."

"There's something about him," Angela said. "I don't know. . . . There's something strange about him. The poor man! This is the first time he's seeing his child. But he doesn't seem to be acting right. I'm not sure what it is, but he's acting . . . different from how most parents I've seen react."

"Well, I'll go talk to him," I repeated.

When I joined the man at the baby's bedside and introduced myself, I could immediately understand what Angela was talking about. He was not just unusually calm, an already uncharacteristic appearance for someone who was surrounded, for the first time, by so many small, seriously ill newborns, but he didn't seem frightened or put off by the appearance of his own child, who had all kinds of tubes coming out of and going into him and already looked as if he'd been dead for a few days. The man must have realized that the child was extremely ill and that he probably would die, but he didn't seem morose.

A partial explanation for this behavior came when the man returned my introduction. "I'm pleased to meet you, Doctor," he said. "I'm Steve Smith. I'm an orthopedic surgeon and the father of this child. Would you be kind enough to answer some questions for me?"

My gut felt queasy as I said, "Sure, Dr. Smith. What would you like to know?"

"Well, first off, I can see that this child is pretty sick. Can you give me a rundown of his problems?"

I told him, and I didn't pull any punches. I used all the medical jargon I could remember. I told him that the brain didn't work, except when it came to having convulsions, that the kidneys hadn't produced a drop of urine since birth, that the intestines were damaged with necrotizing enterocolitis, that the lungs were all clogged with meconium, and that we were still using very high ventilator pressures to force oxygen into the blood, that we were using tolazoline and dopamine and antibiotics and anticonvulsants.

"I see," he said when I finished my little dissertation. "Doctor, what you are really telling me is that this child is essentially dead." No change in emotion was registered in the deep blue eyes behind Dr. Smith's wire-rimmed glasses. "But I come here and see that you are keeping the child alive with dopamine and a ventilator, and none of this was discussed with me or my wife. Can you explain to me the rationale for doing these things?"

I told him about Sullivan, about his view of neonatal intensive care, about his belief that everything must be done for every baby at every moment.

"But certainly he would not do everything possible on a baby who has no chance of survival if that child's parents strongly object to the use of extraordinary heroic measures," Dr. Smith responded.

I sighed. "Dr. Sullivan has told us," I answered, "that as far as he is concerned, parents have no right to make any decision concerning the care of critically ill babies in this intensive care unit."

"Why not?" Dr. Smith asked, outraged.

"Because he feels parents having no previous exposure to sick newborns are so frightened that they cannot make rational decisions."

"How about if the parent is a physician?"

"I don't think it would make any difference to Dr. Sullivan."

"He's crazy!" Dr. Smith said, getting red in the face. He was a tall, powerfully built man, looking more like a defensive lineman for a pro football team than a physician. Excited, he looked even bigger. "I am not only the parent of this critically ill child, but I'm also a physician. I know full well what to expect from a baby like this. I operate on the legs of children with cerebral palsy who are miserable, and those are the children who are only minimally affected. I think what you're telling me is, if this child were, by some twist of fate, able to survive, he would be able to lead at best a totally vegetative existence. Is that right?"

"I'm not sure," I said, "I've only been working here a short time. But I guess that's probably true."

"Then I want full life support stopped," he ordered, "and I want it stopped right now!"

"Dr. Smith," I sighed, "I agree with you fully, and if it were up to me, we would not even be having this conversation now, but I can't do anything about it. I have been ordered to continue full life support."

"Dr. Sharon," Dr. Smith said, regaining his composure and cool detachment, "you're an intern, correct?"

"Correct," I answered meekly.

"I fully understand your position. I only finished my training three years ago and I haven't forgotten what would happen if an intern disobeyed a direct order from an attending." He smiled. "How can I get in touch with Dr. Sullivan?"

"Well, he's gone home for the night. He'll be in tomorrow morning at around nine."

"I'd really like to settle this immediately. Is there any way of reaching him at home?" Dr. Smith knew the answer to this question was yes.

"I guess I could try his home number. . . ." I said.

"I'd appreciate that, Dr. Sharon. Normally, I would wait until tomorrow, but I feel the longer this affair drags on, the worse it'll be for everyone involved."

"All right." I walked to the nurses' station, where Angela was sitting.

"How'd it go, Bob?" she asked.

"Terrific!" I answered. "He's a doctor and he wants to talk to Sullivan at home. Tonight."

"Sullivan's not going to be too happy about that! He doesn't like to be disturbed about these kinds of things."

"Well, what can I do?" I asked. "The guy wants to talk to him. You know where they keep his number?"

She showed me the listing on a three-by-five file card taped to the wall over the clerk's desk. I dialed the number. After three rings a woman's voice said, "Hello?"

"Hello," I said back. "May I speak with Dr. Sullivan please?"

"Who's calling?" the voice asked.

"Dr. Sharon from the St. Anne's nursery. It's about a patient."

The voice sighed, "Okay, hold on." After about a minute the receiver was picked up by Dr. Sullivan. "Yes, Dr. Sharon," he said, somewhat irritated, "what is it?"

"Sorry to bother you at home, Dr. Sullivan," I said, not in the least bit sorry. "I was asked to call you by Dr. Smith, the father of the very sick baby. He would like to speak with you."

"You called me at home because a parent wants to speak with me?" he asked, annoyed. "Can't it wait until tomorrow?"

"He insisted on speaking with you right now."

Sullivan hesitated a moment. "I'll speak with him this once, but in the future, Dr. Sharon, the use of my home number is to be reserved for emergency situations involving the health of the babies. You better not abuse it again for some damned social problem."

I signaled for Dr. Smith to come to the phone. As he was taking the receiver from my hand, one of the nurses called me to check the UA line in Baby Singer which didn't seem to be working properly. I went over and fiddled with it. I don't know what I did, but for some reason, the damned thing started working again.

The shouting began about five minutes after Dr. Smith had started his conversation with Sullivan. I heard Dr. Smith's shouts and hurried back into the nurses' station. I could hear only Dr. Smith's half of the conversation, but it was enough to understand the whole picture.

"Who the hell are you to say something like that?" Dr. Smith said. And, "You have no right to make decisions like that without consulting me or my wife first!" And finally, "I want this baby out of this nursery immediately and into a place run by a competent neonatologist!"

Dr. Smith had, at least momentarily, again lost that detached physician approach he had been using with me. In our discussion he had been acting as if the baby lying on the warming table were not his child at all, but rather an anonymous patient upon whom he had been called to consult. But after speaking with Sullivan, the whole experience had become very personal. After finally hanging up the phone, Dr. Smith, in a very agitated state, shouted at me, "That Sullivan is an utter madman!" Everybody in the nursery at the time heard him.

Trying to calm him down, for the second time since starting my internship, I launched into my Sullivan apology speech, the one that had been so successful with Mr. O'Hara the week before. Although I still hadn't successfully started an IV or intubated a baby, I was gaining vast experience at making excuses for the bizarre behavior of my attending. "Dr. Smith," I began, "this is very difficult for me to do. Dr. Sullivan is my superior in both position and experience. But I want to apologize to you for him and try to explain his actions. See, he loves these babies, the babies like your son for whom he's responsible. He wants them all to survive and to ultimately lead normal lives, regardless of what the cold, hard facts might be, and because of this, he has become a cruel, insensitive, inhuman beast when dealing with the real parents. See, he's lost the perspective to tell when saving a baby is good and when saving a baby is not so good. He feels that what we're doing for your son, Dr. Smith, is what's best for the child."

Well, this speech, which had stopped Mr. O'Hara in his tracks as if he were an elephant and it was a tranquilizing dart, had an interesting but different effect on Dr. Smith. At first, he had a questioning look on his face and, then, as if he had remembered the title of a song that had been playing on the radio, he smiled. When I completed the whole speech, he asked, "Is Dr. Sullivan an alcoholic?"

"No," I said, puzzled. "At least I don't think so."

"It's funny. I knew that speech sounded familiar. When I was a resident, we had an old orthopedist on staff who was a drinker. He used to destroy bones rather than fix them. And, after just about every operation he did, the resident who had scrubbed in with him would have to go out to the family and tell them that he had done what he thought was right and that, as sometimes happens, it didn't work out for the best. I bet Sullivan's an alcoholic."

"Well . . . I just don't know. . . ."

"Look, I understand what you're trying to do; you're trying to tell me he means well, that he's just lost his perspective. I can see it's not just a matter of perspective. The man's crazy. The guy's playing God and I don't want him playing anything when it comes to doing what's best for me and for my family. I know what's best! What's best is to let that child in there die. And if Sullivan doesn't agree to do that, well, then I'll find a neonatologist who does. I'm going right now to call around Boston and find another place. I'll be back tomorrow to make all the arrangements." And with that, he stormed out of the nursery.

As Dr. Smith was leaving, Dan sauntered back into the Pit, eating an apple. He watched Dr. Smith cruise out and said, "Ah, looks like another satisfied customer," as Dr. Smith disappeared down the hall.

The rest of the night passed without much excitement and without any calls to the delivery room. However, during that night I did pass a notable milestone in my career as an intern. At about ten o'clock, the IV in the back of the Dead Kid's left hand, through which he was receiving his tolazoline, blew up like a balloon and had to be removed. Angela asked me about it and asked if I wanted her to call Dan.

"No," I said, "I'll do it."

And I did.

I got to bed in the on-call room at eleven-thirty. Tom's prediction of a quiet night was correct. At around two, for some reason, the nurses stopped waking me for blood gases. I was allowed to fall into a deep sleep that lasted for two hours. I was awakened at four-thirty for a volley of results, but then fell back to sleep and slept intermittently until seven, when I awoke to greet the new day. "Ahh," I thought, "free from night call until Thursday." I arose from the on-call room cot that morning in a good mood. That good mood remained with me all the way through work rounds with Frohman and up until attending rounds. But attending rounds brought Sullivan.

XVI

Tuesday, July 6
Attending Rounds

"Dr. Sharon, I want to start off this morning by reiterating to you the fact that I am available to be reached at home only for medical emergencies. I am not some damned social worker or psychiatrist who can afford to spend time talking to any parent who wants me to do this or doesn't want me to do that. Being the director of this nursery is a very demanding job, and it is imperative that when I am away from here, my time be spent relaxing, not going one-on-one with some parent who wants to discuss some social issue. If ever these problems do arise at night, you tell the parent that it can keep until the morning, and you refer them back to me during regular working hours. Is that clear?"

I didn't argue. We interns had decided collectively that morning before work rounds that arguing with Sullivan about matters such as this was, as Sullivan would say, in nobody's best interest. We decided we'd bring up the issues of Sullivan's apparent lack of concern with the family's role in the management of the newborn, and his lack of concern for the quality of life with which the children that he had "saved" would lead their lives, when we went to the hospital board. So, in response to Sullivan's tongue-lashing, I replied, "Yes, Dr. Sullivan. I am truly sorry for disrupting your evening, but I must tell you that after getting off the phone with you, Dr. Smith has vowed to have his baby transferred to another hospital as soon as possible."

"What nerve!" said Kathy indignantly. "Imagine an orthopedic surgeon thinking he knows more about the care of sick newborns than Dr. Sullivan."

"That doesn't matter," Sullivan responded. "Let the guy try to get that kid out of here! No one in New England would accept a baby like that. And besides, he's far too sick to be transported. No ambulance company in its right mind would even attempt to move that child, even if Smith found another nursery that would accept him. And if Smith tries something stupid, like signing the baby out of the hospital and taking him home, I'll just pick up my hotline to Judge Isaacs." Sullivan had a sinister smile on his face as he said this. "That baby's not going anywhere. Not until I say he's ready."

I decided again not to pursue the matter any further with this maniac. "Well, I apologize again for calling, Dr. Sullivan. It won't happen again." Ray and Terry had to cover their faces with their hands.

"Well, John," Kathy said to Sullivan with a smile on her face, "it looks as if maybe at least one of these interns may be salvageable."

"Yes, Kathy," Sullivan said, "maybe you're right." I held my breath. "Now then, did anything else happen last night, Dr. Sharon?"

"Yes, sir. Dr. Channin, the cardiologist, came to examine the Srnivasan twins."

"Was he appropriately impressed?" Sullivan asked, now sitting back in his seat, with a broad smile on his face. "I know the rest of the Boston metropolitan area was. I received a number of calls from interested people who would pay good money just to have a look at those twins. We might just have to set up an exhibition for the general public here at the hospital."

"Dr. Channin was impressed, Dr. Sullivan," I continued, "but he feels they must be separated or else both of them will die."

"Separate them?" Sullivan shouted. "Never! Why, we'd have to kill one of them if we were to do that! And there's absolutely no need to separate them. As I told Mary Jane Doherty when she was interviewing me, they can live normal lives together, just like Chang and Eng."

"Yeah," Ray muttered, "normal circus freaks."

"Dr. Sullivan," I said quickly, "Dr. Channin feels that the single heart the babies share is not strong enough to support the two circulatory systems. He says he's almost certain that if the surgery is not performed, the heart will give out within a month or two and both twins will die."

"That's bullshit!" Sullivan shouted. "How can he say such a thing? How many sets of Siamese twins has he taken care of in his career?"

"He didn't say," I answered calmly.

"None, I bet," Sullivan shouted again. "That asshole. And tell me, if we were to allow him to do the operation, which we're not, how would he decide which twin would live and which would die?"

"He said the decision will essentially make itself as a result of what shows up on the echocardiogram and the cardiac cath he wants to do. Those studies will show which twin will have the best chance of survival."

Sullivan leaned back on his swivel chair and looked up at the ceiling. He was silent for a moment, but then he leaned forward again and looked into my eyes. "Well, like I said, Channin doesn't know everything, and he's a cynical bastard, too, just like that damned Berkowitz. Berkowitz probably put Channin up to this. They probably just want to separate the twins because they know I want to keep them together. Well, I'm not going to do something just because that's what Channin decided has to be done. I want another opinion. I want a competent cardiologist and a cardiac surgeon to see these babies."

Frohman studiously wrote "get another cardiology and cardiac surgery consult" on the sheet of paper attached to his clipboard that had the words "Srnivasan twins" at the top of it.

"And if those guys tell you they should be separated, are you going to get more people to see them until you find someone who tells you what you want to hear?" Terry asked angrily.

Sullivan didn't pick up on her tone. "Well I sure as hell am not going to make a decision based on what that asshole Channin says."

And with that Sullivan swiveled around in the chair, turning his back to us, and looked out the windows at downtown Boston. We all understood that attending rounds were over.

XVII
Afternoon and Evening

After doing some scut work in the Pit, we went to lunch. "Did you guys see the newspapers this morning?" Terry asked when we got settled at our table. "The twins made the front page of both the *Globe* and the *Herald American.*"

"What do you expect?" Ray responded. "I only admit celebrities to the Pit. Not like Bob here who'll admit any dead kid who comes along."

"Hey, Bob," Terry asked, "what's the story with that cardiologist?"

"Channin?" I asked. "He's a really great guy."

"I figured that," Ray interrupted, "since Sullivan sounded like he hates Channin's guts." Ray and Terry laughed.

"Anyway, he said somebody responsible has to talk with the twins' parents. I guess it's common knowledge among pediatricians in Boston that Sullivan doesn't talk to his patient's families. Channin felt that someone else has to establish a strong, close relationship with the Srnivasans since a lot of important decisions are going to have to be made over the next few days."

"Damn!" Ray said, slapping his forehead with the palm of his left hand. "I knew I forgot to do something yesterday. I had meant to talk with the Srnivasans. I spoke with the father the night they were born, but I had the feeling that he didn't understand what I was saying. I think he sort of figured that he had produced some sort of comic book monster or something, so I wanted to go back and see how they were doing. Damn! I was just too damned tired yesterday afternoon."

"I'll say you were too tired," Terry responded. "You fell asleep over lunch."

"Well that wasn't so bad," Ray returned. "I was dreaming I was eating lunch at Maxim's in Paris."

"Ray, I guess there's no way out of telling you this," I began. "Last night, Dan and I figured that you had been too tired to talk to Mrs. Srnivasan, so we went to see her. Unfortunately, we got to her room just after she and Mr. Srnivasan had watched Mary Jane interview Sullivan. And you're right about the father misunderstanding, because he told the mother that both babies were dead. So they were surprised to see their babies on the news. Now the parents won't speak to any of us. They don't trust us and they threw Dan and me out of their room."

"Great!" Ray hit himself on the head again. He thought for a few seconds. "I guess I really screwed this one up."

"It's not your fault, Ray," I said. "You were too sleepy yesterday to do anything. And it was Sullivan's job to talk to those parents, but he thought it was more important to call Mary Jane and the rest of the media first. So it was really Sullivan's fault."

"Well," Ray sighed without responding to what I had just said, "I guess the only thing I can do now is go to the Srnivasans, try to explain what happened, and hope they'll forgive me. And then, if it's all right with you, Terry, I'd like to sign out early. I sort of hate this place."

"Me too," I said.

"Okay, okay," Terry answered, throwing her hands up in the air, "you guys finish your work and get out. That's okay! That's fine! There's nothing I like better than to be left alone here for sixteen hours at a time with Simon Frohman looking over my shoulder."

"He sure is a weirdo!" I said. "Why is it he never eats lunch with us?"

"When we're on together, he doesn't eat dinner with me either," Terry added.

"I'm not sure," Ray said, "but I think the explanation lies in Frohman's physiology. See, I don't think he eats at all. That's because I don't think he's really human. I sort of think he was sent from another planet or something to torture us for things we three did a long time ago, maybe in another life."

"Ah yes," I said, "the famous renal physiologist's paranoid schizophrenic theory of the extraterrestrial origin of Simon Frohman."

"Exactly," Ray responded. "It also explains why he's so nervous. Simon's afraid he won't ever get home to his mother planet."

"I sometimes really worry about that guy," Terry said. "I mean, he's a pain in the ass and all, but he doesn't have any friends here, he's always fidgeting so much, he doesn't know how to make decisions or how to be a doctor. He can't be too happy with his life."

"He's a worm," Ray said. "Look what he did to you the night Baby Torres died, telling you he was going to call Sullivan. He went out of his way to screw you."

"That makes him all the more pathetic," Terry answered. "At first I was pissed off about that, but then I realized that's his only way of making people like him, by making other people look more incompetent than he is."

"Dan told me no one back at the Medical Center likes him either," I added, "and that Dr. Jennings doesn't exactly consider him one of the best house officers he's ever seen."

"I'm just afraid that, sooner or later, something terrible's going to happen to him," Terry said.

"I agree," I said. "It's only a matter of time."

"I just hope it doesn't happen on one of these nights that we're on together. Do you think there's anything we can do for him?"

"Do for Frohman?" Ray asked, surprised. "Aren't we sort of having enough trouble here ourselves? I don't feel very good about my own ability to take care of the things that we're assigned to take care of in the Pit. I don't think I want to add Frohman and his problems to my load right now."

"Ray's right," I said. "Right now, we have to worry about ourselves. Our appointment with the hospital board is coming up tomorrow, and we'd better discuss what we want to tell them."

"Good idea," Ray said. "I think we should just tell them about cases. Like the O'Hara story, with emphasis on the part where Mr. O'Hara decks Sullivan. I bet the hospital board won't look kindly on an attending who gets a parent so mad that the parent actually physically punches him out."

"And the Dead Kid," Terry added. "They should know that even when the kid's father is a qualified physician who knows something about premies, Sullivan not only won't let the man participate in the decision-making process, but he so insults the man that he's looking to find another hospital to transfer the baby to."

"I think cases are fine," I said, "but I think the only way we're going to score any points with the hospital board is to mention the cases where it looks like the parents might sue. Intern and patient satisfaction might not mean shit, but a million-dollar lawsuit, now that's something a hospital board member will listen to."

"That sounds sort of reasonable," Ray said.

"It sounds like you have some experience with this kind of thing," Terry added. "Have you ever done this before?"

"No, but my brother's a doctor in Washington and he's on the board of a hospital down there. He's always told me that money talks louder than anything else."

"Okay," Terry said, "then that sounds like the way we should go. I have a morbid question for you two."

"Morbid?" I asked. "I think we're just the right crowd for morbid."

"Well, I've been thinking about the Dead Kid and his father. I think that, God forbid, it could be any one of us in that same position, and if it were me, I'd come to the intern and ask him to help the baby go to heaven. Do you think we should do that?"

"You mean, disconnect the ventilator by accident or something like that?" Ray asked.

"Yeah," Terry responded, "but disconnecting the ventilator is too easy to figure out and too easy to fix. I was thinking more along the lines of a pinch too much KCl added to the IV solution."

KCl, the chemical shorthand for potassium chloride, is an essential compound necessary for the control of a number of body mechanisms. However, an overdose of the compound, when given rapidly by vein, causes the heart to cease beating almost immediately. The cause of death is not easily diagnosed, unless the level of KCl is measured directly in the postmortem blood.

I sighed at the suggestion. "I've given it some thought, too, and I don't think I could do it. Although I know in my heart that the kid's death would be the best thing for everyone involved, giving an overdose is like murder. It's not the same as withholding something like dopamine."

"I guess I agree," Ray said. "Besides, it's probably not a good idea to kill a kid before any of us have saved one. And so far, not only have I not saved a kid, I haven't even done any good for one."

I smiled. "I started an IV last night."

"Yeah?" Terry responded. "On who?"

"On the Dead Kid."

"That's great," Terry said.

"I called my wife in New York to tell her, but she wasn't very excited about it. She just didn't understand."

"But it is a milestone in your life," Terry said. "Your first IV in the Pit. We should have had a cake to celebrate."

I sat back on my chair, smiling and reflecting on this ridiculous accomplishment.

I was sitting in the nurses' station writing the daily progress notes we were required to write every day on every active patient. It was about 3 P.M. when I looked up from Baby Summlitz's chart and saw, coming into the nursery through the side door, Mrs. O'Hara. She was sitting in a wheelchair which was being pushed by Mr. O'Hara. The discomfort that she felt was obvious in her face. A nurse was pushing an IV pole from which hung the bottle of IV solution in which Mrs. O'Hara's antibiotics were dissolved. I went into the Pit and joined this group.

"Hi," I said with a smile. "Welcome to the nursery."

"Hello, Dr. Sharon," Mrs. O'Hara responded, looking up at me and taking my left hand in hers. She looked paler than she had the last time I had seen her, but she managed a small smile. "We've come to see our daughter."

"Well, come on," I said, "she's over here." I led the three of them over to Baby Girl O'Hara's warming table in the chronic row.

Although she approached the warming table with a frightened look on her face, a small smile appeared as soon as she saw her baby. "Oh," Mrs. O'Hara said with a sound of surprise, "she's cute."

"Of course she's cute," I said with a grin. "What were you expecting, Mrs. O'Hara?"

"Well, I don't know," she responded softly. "When I heard she was a mongoloid, I thought . . . well, I thought she was a monster or something. But she's not. She's really cute. Hi, baby," she said, looking at her baby.

The baby, who looked fine except for the IV in her left arm and the gauze wrapped around her abdomen at the site of her surgery, took that moment to open her eyes and look directly at her mother. Both baby and mother stared into each other's eyes.

Mr. O'Hara also smiled slightly. He seemed very ill at ease, both because of this nursery and because of his daughter. "Why is she on that thing?" he asked, pointing to the warming table.

"Oh, just because it's easier to get at her this way," I answered. "We have to be able to check the IV and take blood from her for tests. All the babies in this nursery are on these tables."

"You know," Mr. O'Hara said, "she really is pretty cute. We had prepared ourselves for her to be very ugly."

The baby looked toward the direction this new voice was coming from and, for the first time, saw her father. Mr. O'Hara looked away, toward Mrs. O'Hara, when the baby's eyes fell upon his.

"Would you like to hold her?" I asked Mrs. O'Hara.

"Do you think I should?" she returned. "With the infection?"

"Sure," I said, as I gently lifted the baby off the mattress and placed her into Mrs. O'Hara's lap.

"Oh, she's so small," Mrs. O'Hara said. I could see the tears coming. "Oh baby, baby, baby!" she cried in a burst of tears, cradling the baby's small head in her hands. The baby began gazing into her mother's eyes when Mrs. O'Hara started talking and now couldn't take her eyes off her mother's face.

By this point we were all misty-eyed. I was new and still very inexperienced at Pediatrics that late afternoon when Baby Girl O'Hara with Down syndrome finally met her mother but even now, years later, I still feel a tear come to my eyes when this strange, beautiful event occurs at the very beginning of the life of a newborn.

"I'll leave you all to get acquainted," I said as I started back to the nurses' station.

"Thank you again, Dr. Sharon," Mrs. O'Hara whispered.

I went back to my charts. Every few minutes I'd look up from the note I was writing and gaze through the windows into the Pit at the O'Hara family. Mr. and Mrs. O'Hara had been with the baby for about a half hour when the nurse came over to get me. I followed her back to the O'Haras and took the baby from her mother and placed her back onto the mattress of the warming table.

Mr. O'Hara seemed more uncomfortable so I asked him if he had found anything wrong with the baby. "No," he answered, "the baby's fine, better than we could have expected. Dr. Sharon," he continued, now with a stern tone, "you and Dr. Fredericks have been the only two people who have treated us like human beings through this ordeal. The nurses, Dr. Parris, they all treated us like we got some disease or something since we had a baby with mongolism. And Dr. Sullivan . . . well, you know what I think about him. If it hadn't been for the caring of you two, why, I think I would've gone crazy."

"I didn't do anything special," I said quietly as I felt my face turn red. "I was just doing my job."

"No, you did more than just doing your job. And we wanted to find some way of repaying you. Joan," he gestured toward his wife, "and I want to name the baby after you and Dr. Fredericks. If it's okay with you, we'd like to call her Sharon Frederica."

I was stunned; I hadn't expected him to say anything like this. "You don't have to do that," was all I could manage to say.

"We want to do it," Mrs. O'Hara said, smiling, "so that we'll always remember you and Dr. Fredericks."

"Okay," I said very quietly, still shocked, "that's very nice of you."

We were then silent and uncomfortable for a few seconds until Mrs. O'Hara finally said, "I've got to get back to bed now, Ron, I'm feeling very weak."

I felt the same way as I walked them to the door. "We'll see you tomorrow," Mr. O'Hara said, shaking my hand. "Take good care of our Sharon."

I watched them disappear into the elevator and then returned to the nurses' station and my waiting charts. I felt a sudden, intense headache coming on. "I've got to get out of here," I announced to Terry, who was sitting next to me, working on her charts.

"What happened?" she asked. "You're as pale as a ghost."

"The O'Haras just told me they are going to name the baby after me and Tom Fredericks. Sharon Frederica they're going to call her."

"Wow," Terry said, her eyes opening widely, "that's pretty heavy!"

"It's unbearably heavy. I need a drink."

Just then Ray walked in, looking terrible. "Drink?" he asked. "Did someone say drink?"

I nodded yes.

"Let's go," he answered, "I gotta get out of here!"

We both signed out quickly, got into my car, and drove the two blocks to Kelly's. As we had got out of the doors of St. A's, Ray had asked, "What happened to you?" I told him about the O'Haras naming their baby after me.

Ray laughed. "That's great. What's wrong with that?"

"Ray, they named the kid after Tom Fredericks and me because the rest of the staff of this damned hospital has treated them like shit. I didn't do anything special for them, I just treated them like humans. Last week they were going to let the baby die, and now they're naming her after me. Like Terry said, that's pretty heavy. I'll always know in the back of my mind that there's a child with Down syndrome out there somewhere named after me. What's wrong with you?"

"A few things. I won't be able to talk about it until I get at least two drinks into me."

"I noticed," I responded. We passed the rest of the short trip to Kelly's in silence.

Inside Kelly's, which was empty because of the fact that it was still before 4 P.M., we seated ourselves at the bar and ordered scotch. Straight. As soon as the bartender put the glass in front of him, Ray picked it up and downed the contents. "Another," he said before the bartender even had a chance to step away. I could see there'd be no keeping up with Ray that day.

"What's up?" I asked.

He started on the second glass and began talking. "First, it's the Srnivasan family. I'll bet you they're not going to name either of their kids after me! I walked into Mrs. Srnivasan's room this afternoon and just introduced myself, and right away she started yelling at me in some foreign language. I didn't understand what she was saying, but I could sort of tell she wasn't telling me to have a nice day."

"Oy," I said.

"I tried to sort out what had happened with her; I told her I had spoken with her husband on the night the babies had been born, and that I had told him the babies were pretty much all right, but that he must have misunderstood me or something. But she said I was like everybody else at that damned hospital, a liar and a phony, that I was only interested in making money off her kids by exhibiting them on TV, like they were in the circus. I tried to explain that I had nothing to do with the circus exhibit part of the deal, that that was Sullivan's work, but she wouldn't hear of it. I tried to explain again that everything was all a big misunderstanding, but I couldn't get a word in edgewise. Boy, I really screwed this one up, Bob!" he said as he downed his third glass of scotch, and I, my second. We called for another round.

"You screwed up?" I asked. "How do you figure it was you who screwed up? You did your job; you talked to the father and told him what had happened. It isn't your fault he didn't understand a word you were saying."

"No, Bob, it is my fault. If I had gone back and talked with the parents the next day, I would have found out about the misunderstanding and would have set things right before they saw Mary Jane's show. That way, at least maybe they would have trusted me."

"Ray, how could you have talked to that mother and made her understand yesterday? You were a wreck. You were so tired you fell asleep eating lunch. I didn't even understand what you were saying yesterday, so how would you expect a woman whose native tongue isn't even English to figure out what you were saying? And besides, it's not your place to talk to the parents about issues like this; it's Sullivan's place. He should have gone to those people and spoken with them before he called Mary Jane and those newspaper guys."

"Sullivan's place? That's a joke. You know we can't rely on Sullivan to do anything that's rational." He was shouting directly into my face. "We have to take these matters into our own hands."

"Ray, we're only interns, and we're only in our second week. We're not competent enough to be left alone to baby-sit for a healthy two year old. How can we take matters like these into our own hands?"

"Bob, we may not have the technical skill Sullivan has, but we know the difference between right and wrong. You don't even have to be an intern to know what to do if you see someone abusing another human being. But Sullivan's lost his ability to distinguish between right and wrong and so we have to do what we think is right, and what was right yesterday would have been for me to have gone to see Mrs. Srnivasan before the damned news show had come on. So I have to take responsibility for the whole fuck-up."

"Ray, we're only interns," I said again, a little more forcefully this time. "We can't take responsibility for something like this. We're still amateurs at this stuff."

"No, Bob, that's no excuse. I'll just have to live with this screwup and try like hell not to make the same mistake again."

We finished the drinks that were in front of us. I had lost count by this point and was feeling very tipsy, but Ray called for another round. "Anything else bothering you, Ray?" I asked.

He sighed. "Look at this," he said as he pulled an envelope from his back pocket, which was addressed in crayon in very primitive writing. "I got it last night when I got home from work." He handed the envelope to me, and I opened the flap and pulled out the contents. The letter consisted of one piece of heavy construction paper, the kind kids in kindergarten use. It said:

Dear Daddy,
I LOVE YOU
I MISS YOU
COME HOME SOON
KATIE

That was all.

"Oh God" was all I could say, and I felt as if I had been whacked in the belly with a baseball bat.

"Her mother or someone must have helped her with the writing, I guess," Ray said slowly. "Katie can't write that well yet." He had lost the anger that had filled his voice when we had spoken about the Srnivasans, and his eyes got misty. "Oh boy, I sure miss that kid!"

"How did you get out of bed this morning?" I asked. "I would've been too depressed to get up."

"Well, Bob, I guess I am pretty depressed, but I've got to go on. It's not so bad, really. At least I'll see her during vacations."

"Ray, this, for one thing, really is so bad! You love that kid. Being away from her is going to kill you. Isn't there any way you can get her and your wife to come out here, at least to talk about getting back together?"

"Not much chance of that, Bob. Karen and I, we weren't really right for each other from the beginning. We only got married in the first place because Karen was four-months pregnant with Katie, but we never really loved each other and we sort of didn't even like each other much. I guess we both knew this wasn't a permanent thing, but we were just going along for the ride because of Katie."

"Still, it's a shame you'll be separated from her for so much time. Have you thought of taking this year off and trying to get an internship for next year in Ann Arbor?"

Ray sighed again. "How old are you, Bob?"

"Twenty-nine," I answered, not understanding this change of direction. "Why?"

"Well I'm thirty-one. I've wanted to be a doctor ever since I can remember wanting to be anything. I was premed in college and sort of screwed around. I got into drugs for a while, met Karen, got her pregnant, married her, and basically got lousy grades, so when I applied to medical schools, I got rejected by all of them. I tried again the next year and got rejected again, so I decided to go to grad school and to try a little harder. I did well. I applied to med schools again and this time I finally got in. I did okay in medical school, good enough to get an internship at this hot-shit Boston teaching hospital. It sounds sort of hokey, I guess, but I always wanted to be a doctor so I could help people. I don't want to be forty before I get to take care of real patients. And I'm starting to get old. So doing this internship this year is important to me. I don't want to screw up again, I don't think I can afford to lose another year. I've got to stick this thing out."

"I know what you're saying," I said as I began to feel the room spin. "We shouldn't have to worry about whether we're going to be able to stick the internship out. It should be a good experience for us, we should be learning how to take care of these sick kids. But we're not. I feel like this month has been arranged just so Sullivan can have somebody new to abuse."

"They should have put something about that in the catalog they sent out to us when we applied for internships here: 'The neonatal experience at St. Anne's Hospital offers the intern a unique opportunity to be abused both psychologically and physically by a nationally known neonatologist.' "

"That's right," I laughed. "They should at least be honest about this place. Damn, if I had known it was going to be like this, I never would have even considered coming here."

"Well, Bob, I'll tell you, I'm not going to let this happen to the guys who are going to apply this year. I'm going to tell the intern applicants the truth. I don't want any of them coming here under some false pretense. They ought to know about the senior residents, too, that they can't make any decisions and they're not helpful, except, of course, if you find one who wants to do a renal fellowship and you happen to be a famous renal physiologist." He laughed.

"How's that working out?" I asked.

"That Lauren's pretty funny," he answered, beginning to slur his words. "On the one hand, she's this beautiful woman who got to where she is by selling herself to get what she wanted; but then, on the other hand, she's pretty pathetic, like Frohman in a way. She doesn't have any friends and she's got a terrible reputation, and she's sad about that. She seems to me like she's a really needy person."

"Uh oh," I said, "it sounds like you like her."

"I think I do, and I feel sort of bad that I'm deceiving her."

"But, Ray, she's deceiving you also," I responded. "Don't you remember? At first she wouldn't even talk to you, but when she found out you were a famous renal hit man from Michigan, suddenly she can't do enough for you. She's trying to use you like you're using her."

"I guess you're right, Bob. Still, I think I've got to tell her about what I'm up to."

"Okay," I said, "if it'll make you feel better, tell her. But don't be surprised if, after you do, she develops a headache and you never see her again."

We had finished the drinks in front of us and the bartender asked if we wanted another round. With the room spinning, we both said, "No thanks."

"I feel better," Ray said.

"I feel nauseated."

"Do you like pinball?" Ray asked.

"Pinball? I love pinball."

"You ever play Pop-a-Card?"

"Yeah," I answered, "I love Pop-a-Card."

"You ever play Pop-a-Card when you were so drunk it seemed like the balls were sort of moving up and down through the glass as well as back and forth?"

"No," I answered, "never that drunk."

"Let's go," he said. And off we went.

XVIII

Wednesday, July 7

Morning

The day of the hospital board meeting dawned hot and humid, and Ray and I arrived earlier than usual to find Terry relaxing in the on-call room. It had been the second night of the quarter moon, and Tom Fredericks's prediction was still holding up; Terry had had an excellent night. While waiting for eight o'clock to come, we went over our strategy for the meeting and, at eight on the dot, we walked into the nurses' station for rounds.

There really wasn't much going on; all the patients were either stable or improving, except for the Dead Kid who was continuing to demonstrate what could be done with a ventilator and some medications. We were monitoring him closely and providing heroic care, despite the apparent futility of it. The day before, Gloria Higgins, the Dead Kid's primary nurse, told me she had not given the baby any of the paralyzing medication in over a day and he had not again begun convulsing. We concluded that the child's brain had ceased sending out the signal to convulse, usually a good sign but, in the Dead Kid's case, a bad one, since now in addition to the child not convulsing, he wasn't moving at all; he had become brain-dead.

The Dead Kid, who was now five days old, still had not produced a drop of urine; his kidneys, like his brain, just didn't work and the potassium was beginning to rise to unsafe levels in his blood. It was beginning to look as if it would not be necessary to give the infant an overdose of potassium chloride, as Terry had suggested the day before;

his lack of kidney function would cause the toxic waste product to slowly rise until it reached a level at which point his heart would completely cease beating. The only possible remedy to lower the level of potassium in the Dead Kid's blood would be to perform a dialysis treatment, a process used in patients with kidney shutdown to artificially remove the poisonous waste products of metabolism. We were all sure that Sullivan, upon hearing of the elevated potassium level from Frohman on rounds, would order that dialysis.

So far there had been no signs of the return of Dr. Smith but, according to Gloria Higgins, Angela had received a call from him the night before. He wanted to know whether the baby was still alive or not; he did not mention whether he'd been able to locate another facility that would accept the Dead Kid, nor did he mention when he would be back.

Baby Singer, Terry's premie from the week before, was now extubated and only requiring a little extra oxygen, blown in the direction of his face through a device called a head box. He'd probably be able to breathe straight room air within a week, and he would then be transferred to the growers row.

Sharon Frederica O'Hara was also doing pretty well. On rounds that morning, I could have sworn that she smiled at me. It probably was only caused by a little gas, though, but that wasn't a bad sign in a baby who had had intestinal surgery; it was an indication that Sharon Frederica's intestine was beginning to function again following the trauma of the surgery. Sullivan's plan was to start her on some sterile water by mouth the next day, as a test, and if she tolerated the water for twenty-four hours, we would switch her to formula and take out her IV.

"Anything new on the Smith baby?" Sullivan asked as soon as we had settled in for attending rounds.

"No," I answered quickly.

"Well," Frohman cut in, looking at me with displeasure and rubbing his palms together, "I wouldn't call a potassium of 6.6 nothing new."

"The potassium's rising?" Sullivan asked.

"Yes, sir," Frohman answered, as if he were proud of the fact.

"Well, we'll have to have the kidney boys come over and dialyze the baby, but fast," Sullivan responded with an evil smile. "None of my babies are going to die because we overlooked the potassium." Frohman carefully wrote "get renal consult stat!" on the page of his clipboard marked "Baby Boy Smith."

"And when they're here," Kathy added, "make sure you tell them Dr. Sullivan wants the attending to do the dialysis. They always let the fellows do them, and they inevitably screw it up. When they're working on these little ones, the person putting in the catheter should be the most experienced person there is."

"Good point," Sullivan said as Frohman added "get the attending to do it" to the note he had just written. "And that dictum holds for any of the specialty services who do consults on our babies. Only the most competent person should work on the patients. We don't want to introduce any unnecessary risks."

None of us objected. Ordering a dialysis treatment for a baby who was brain-dead was irrational enough in and of itself, but to order that the seniormost person do the procedure, to deprive a more junior person who could use the experience of a chance to do it, was almost criminal in a teaching hospital. But this was just another one of those irrational moments, in a place filled with irrational moments, that Terry, Ray, and I had decided not to raise a fuss about; it just wasn't worth the trouble. In this particular situation, I did see a glimmer of hope, though; I didn't think any nephrologist, in his or her right mind, would allow a dialysis treatment to be done on a brain-dead child. As it turned out, I was right; the nephrologist who did eventually dialyze the Dead Kid was not in his right mind.

After that decision was made, Sullivan moved on to discuss the Srnivasan twins. "Did the cardiac surgeon come to see the twins?" he asked.

"A surgeon and another cardiologist both," Terry responded with a gleam in her eye. "Dr. Dover from cardiac surgery and Dr. Chin from cardiology both came late yesterday afternoon. And they both concluded that the twins had to be separated. Dr. Dover also said he'd love to do the operation."

Dr. Sullivan took a deep breath, hesitated for a second, and then with annoyance, said, "Well Dover isn't going to get that chance. Those babies are not going to be separated."

"Channin probably spoke to those two before they came," Kathy said indignantly. "He probably put them up to this."

"You're right, Kathy," Sullivan responded, "we can't trust anyone."

Ray had had enough. He couldn't contain himself through another one of these paranoia-filled moments. "You're both right!" he shouted. "Everyone's out to get those twins! They want to take them away from you so they can exhibit them themselves and get all the glory! But I have an idea! Why don't we just kill them ourselves? That would stop everyone from plotting against you and them. Neither of you two wants them to survive anyway, so why don't we just give them a bolus of KCl and get it over with?"

"Dr. Brewster," Sullivan shouted, "you are mistaken! I want those twins to live. And they will live, too, just like Chang and Eng!"

"Just like Chang and Eng, huh?" Ray responded. "I did a little reading about your Chang and Eng last night and, you're right, they did survive and live full lives. But Chang and Eng were a little different from these twins; they didn't share a common heart or any other organ. They were just joined by skin and connective tissue. So you can't use Chang and Eng to make any predictions about what's going to happen with these twins!"

"That doesn't matter, Dr. Brewster. I want them to live and that's the way it will be."

"Oh, that's a very realistic attitude, Dr. Sullivan," I said, trying to come to Ray's aid. "You will something to happen and it happens, huh? Regardless of what all the experts in the field have to say. You are right and that's that, and anyone who disagrees with you is either crazy or plotting against you. Well, you know what? I've had enough of these ridiculous attending rounds. I'm not learning anything and I'm just wasting time listening to you make these stupid, paranoid, irrational decisions! I'm going to do my work!" I rose and walked out of Sullivan's office.

I walked into the nurses' lounge and found Dan sitting on a couch, flirting with Maureen, the red-haired nurse. "Hey, what are you doing here?" Dan asked when he saw me. "You're supposed to be at attending rounds."

"I quit attending rounds," I said angrily.

"You can't quit attending rounds," he answered. "You have to be thrown out like I was." He and Maureen giggled.

"Well, I quit," I repeated. "I just walked out."

At that point we were joined by Ray and Terry.

"You all left?" Dan asked, smiling.

"Yeah," Ray and Terry answered.

"It looks like a mutiny," Maureen said.

"Even worse," Dan said, "Sullivan'll think it's a conspiracy."

"Look, we're here to do our work and to learn," I said, almost preaching. "Although there're only a few things we know how to do, we still try to do our best. But we don't have to participate in the workings of that maniac just because he's in charge here."

"Right," Terry said. "We'll get him at the hospital board meeting."

"This is the best thing we've done so far," Ray added. "It'll give us an extra hour to get our work done so we can get out of this hellhole earlier. And Dan can teach us everything we need to know."

"Great," Dan said, "now I'm part of the conspiracy, too."

"You kidding?" I asked. "You're the leader of this conspiracy."

"Are you the same guys who were scared to touch these babies last week?" Dan asked.

"Yeah," I answered.

"And now you're revolting against a full professor? Boy, it looks like Sullivan created himself a monster."

"That's right," Ray responded, "we sort of are monsters."

We went back into the nurses' station and went about our work. For some reason, I even called the nephrology office at the Medical Center and told the secretary that we needed a consult. After the secretary assured me that someone would be over to see the baby that afternoon, I began writing my progress notes, trying to get everything done before follow-up clinic, so I wouldn't have to return to the Pit after the hospital board meeting.

Frohman came back into the nursery at a little after eleven. "Sullivan's sure pissed off at you guys," he told us.

"Drop dead!" Ray said to Frohman, not very politely.

"No need to get angry at me! I have nothing to do with your beef with Sullivan."

"You're a fart, Frohman, you know that?" Terry said.

"What's wrong with you guys? Come on, I'm on your side."

"Bullshit!" I said angrily, looking directly into Frohman's eyes. "You're on your own side! You do whatever's best for you. If it weren't for you, and your inability to make a decision, we wouldn't be so bad off. You do things only to gain points with the attending, so you'll get a good recommendation from him. You're disgusting!"

He was astonished by my hostility. "Disgusting?" he repeated, his facial muscles in constant, nervous, involuntary movement by this point. "What's wrong with trying to gain points with the attending? Isn't that what it's all about?"

"No!" I yelled. "You do what's best for your patients!"

"Well, don't you think the attending has a better idea of what's best for the patients than you or I do?"

"Are you kidding?" Terry asked. "The three of us have been here only a week and a half and we already know that Sullivan's a paranoid schizophrenic. He and Kathy are living in a little dreamworld where everyone's out to get them."

He looked even more surprised. "Well, if they're both paranoid schizophrenics, how is it they got to be in charge of this nursery?"

"We don't know!" I answered. "It's amazing to me. But we're going to try and find out at the hospital board meeting this afternoon."

"The hospital board?" he repeated, grimacing. "It does sound like you three are out to get him. Listen, I'm going to let you in on a little secret I learned through my years of residency: if you listen to what the attending says and do what he tells you, everything'll work out right. It's when you don't follow orders that you get into trouble."

"You think Sullivan's plan for the Dead Kid is a good one?" Terry asked. "You think that baby should be dialyzed?"

"I don't know. Sure, why not?"

"Because the baby's brain-dead!" she responded.

"I don't know that. I'm not a neonatologist or a neurologist, and neither are you. But I'll tell you what; I'll bet everything comes out all right with that kid, or else Sullivan wouldn't be doing it."

"You know, you're really crazy!" Ray yelled. "You are a zombie! You don't have a mind of your own. What's going to happen to you next year when you don't have an attending to tell you what to do and what to think? You haven't made a single decision in your whole medical career, and in less than a year you're going to be the one people are going to turn to to tell them what to do. What's going to happen then?"

Frohman's eyes opened wide and a look of stark, naked terror came into them. "I don't have to listen to this," he stammered, and stormed out of the Pit.

"Ah, Ray," I said after Frohman had gone, "I think you struck a raw nerve."

"Did you see the look on his face?" Ray asked. "That guy is scared out of his wits!"

"I'm really worried about him," Terry said. "He's really in bad shape. He's getting more fidgety by the minute. He needs help and fast!"

We slowly turned back to our work. I kept thinking about that look in Simon Frohman's eyes and how close to the breaking point he seemed.

XIX
Follow-Up Clinic

It had started raining. The rain was pouring down heavily, cooling off the hot, humid July afternoon. We ran next door to the little house in which follow-up clinic was held, but we got soaked anyway. I hoped the rain would hold down the number of patients who would show up for clinic, which was to be Terry's first.

It didn't. There were already twelve patients strewn around the waiting room when we arrived. Terry gave a quick look toward the masses of twisted, distorted human flesh seated in wheelchairs who had arrived for clinic, then stepped up her pace, following me into the nurses' station area. Frohman, who apparently was not speaking to us, was already there sitting at the desk, with a cup of coffee in one hand and an old copy of the *New England Journal of Medicine* in the other. His eyes were glazed but no longer showed that frightened expression.

I showed Terry around and told her how things worked. The nurse was wheeling the first patient into an examining room. I took the chart and followed them into Room 1.

This patient was Jessica Rosado, now a four-year-old girl, who had been full-term at birth but had been born, much like the Dead Kid, through a sea of thick meconium. She had had some of the same problems as the Dead Kid but hadn't been as sick, and had subsequently done fairly well. Her convulsion which occurred on the second day of life had been easy to control. She had left the Pit after about a month and a half. She had been left with moderately severe cerebral palsy, was twisted up in her wheelchair, and had a seizure disorder which caused her to jerk her arms and legs and lose consciousness at least once a day. She was, however, better off than most kids who came to follow-up clinic. She could speak.

"Hi, Jessie," I said after the nurse who accompanied Jessie, a woman named Betsy Campbell, told me about her speaking ability. I hadn't spoken to any of the patients I had seen the first week.

"Hi, Doctor," she said in a slow, slurred, barely understandable voice.

"How are you feeling today?" I asked slowly and clearly.

"Fine!"

Betsy Campbell explained to me that Jessie's parents had institutionalized her upon her discharge from the Pit. They felt they could not fulfill Jessie's needs, medically, educationally, or emotionally, and still care for their other four children. So Jessie now lived at the Home as a member of Ms. Campbell's unit. Ms. Campbell was the director of the highest functioning patient group at the Home. "Some of my patients," she told me proudly, "are even toilet-trained!"

"Who's your best friend, Jessie?" I asked as I went about examining her.

Jessie thought for a minute. "I don't have a best friend," she said finally. "No one likes me."

"Oh come on, Jessie," I said. "You seem like a nice girl. Everyone must like you!"

"No. They don't like me 'cause I can't walk and I talk funny and I have dark spells every day." Jessie started to cry.

"Don't cry," I said to Jessie, "I'll be your friend."

She stopped crying and her face brightened. "You will? You really will? Will you come and visit me, too? I get lonely a lot."

"I'll try to," I said sincerely, but in my mind doubting that I ever would. "I'll try to come visit."

As I went about my work, filling out her form for school and reviewing her anticonvulsant medications, I tried to imagine what life must be like for Jessica, being one of the lowest-functioning members of the highest-functioning unit at the Waltham Home. And then I remembered Freddie Endicott again, and his galactosemia, and figured there'd be no way he'd ever be able to make it to the highest-functioning unit as Jessica had done.

When I finished Jessie's paperwork, I gave Ms. Campbell some prescriptions for the child's medications and sent them off on their way with an appointment to return to clinic in three months.

"Promise you'll be my friend and that you'll come visit?" Jessie asked as she was being pushed out of the room.

"I promise," I responded, and I bent down and gave Jessie a little kiss on her cheek. Her eyes glowed and a big smile came to her lips which just about tore my heart out.

I returned to the nurses' station and waited for the placement of the next patient in a room. Dan was sitting in there, also waiting. "Great teaching opportunity, huh, Bob? That Frohman! What a barrel of laughs!"

"Yeah," I answered, "like he said, I'm seeing more pathology here in one week than I'd see in a month at another clinic. And more than I want to see in my whole lifetime."

Just then Terry entered from her room, obviously shaken. "This is terrible," she said, her voice breaking and her eyes welling up with tears. "These poor kids! They're disasters. Why are we doing . . . this?"

"Welcome to follow-up clinic, Terry," Dan said.

Terry started crying. I put my arms around her and held her, trying to console her. "It's not so bad, Terry," I said softly. "It's only a once-a-week thing."

"It's not just this clinic," she cried, "it's this whole place. Why are we working in the Pit? That kid I just saw, he wasn't even so . . . so bad. He was a thirty-weeker with just a little respiratory problem. Now he's . . . he's a GORK. And if he's a GORK, what becomes of the twenty-six weekers and the twenty-seven weekers? What kind of life are they going to lead? This is just . . . just terrible." She held on tightly to me and dissolved into tears.

Dan seemed truly touched by Terry. "This happens to everyone who comes through here," he said gently. "The only way to make it through this is to think abstractly; don't think of them as children. Think of them as poorly made pieces of furniture that are here to get polished. Think abstractly and hold on to your friends."

She clutched me tighter and said, "Okay, Dan. I'll try."

When Terry was able to again gain control, I went off to see my second patient. This one, thank goodness, could not speak. I went through five patients that afternoon; Terry saw four, crying after leaving the room after each one; Dan saw five, putting a good shine on the coffee tables and bookcases; while Frohman, ignoring the rest of us completely, saw six.

When it was over, Terry and I sat in the nurses' station, alone. She had finally stopped crying but was obviously still very upset.

"It's like a Grade B monster movie," she said, "only the monsters are real live children."

"And here we are, Terry, spending our days and nights making more of them."

I looked at my watch and saw it was four-fifteen. "It's getting late," I said. "We'd better get over to the meeting."

We got up to go. "Would you do something for me, Bob?" she asked. "Would you just hold me for a little while?"

We embraced. And we stood there, me hugging Terry tightly in the empty clinic area, crying together in the dark.

XX

The Hospital Board Meeting

The front entrance lobby of St. Anne's Hospital had not been renovated in a long time. Like the rest of the old St. A's, the lobby was rundown and seedy, with a few hard-backed benches, a few tattered upholstered chairs, and an old oak table, its finish cracked and peeling, on which long out-of-date issues of *Time* magazine and *Sports Illustrated* sat, untouched and gathering dust. There was a bank of telephone booths in one corner and two newspaper machines dispensing the *Globe* and the *Herald American.* The information desk, which looked like the registration desk in a red-light district fleabag, except that it was manned by an elderly nun, occupied the area farthest away from the main entrance. Whenever I entered the front door of St. A's, I always had the feeling I was walking into an Alfred Hitchcock film.

We found Ray sitting on one of the hard-backed benches. "I was afraid you guys had chickened out," he said when he saw us.

"Clinic ran late," I answered.

"I thought Dan was going to come with us," Ray said.

"He thought it would be better if we three went alone," I responded.

"Why?" Ray asked.

"He said something about the members of the hospital board knowing him from when he was an intern, and that he thought if he went in with us, they'd think that he had put us up to it."

"Did he say why the members of the board know him?"

"He didn't specify," I answered. "Something to do with what happened between him and Sullivan, I guess. And the secret."

"I wish I knew what that secret was," Ray answered. "Maybe Sullivan's selling GORKed-out babies to the Waltham Home so they can be used in research?"

I laughed. "No, I kind of doubt that that's it."

Terry didn't laugh, nor did she respond. She was silent all through this conversation, staring straight ahead like a zombie. "You okay, Terry?" Ray asked.

"Okay" was all she was able to manage in return.

"She had a bad time at follow-up clinic," I explained. I was afraid that all of Terry's fight had been drained from her by the GORKs and that she wasn't going to be much help in the meeting room.

"Well, it's getting late," I said. "We'd better go in."

We walked down the hall and entered the administrative office, where the secretary, who was seated behind her desk, noted that we had arrived, wrote something in the memo book in front of her, and told us to have a seat. We sat on a couch opposite the door that led into the inner office. We were silent. I was tense and I could feel that Ray was tense also. Terry, who was sitting between us, was limp, and she sighed occasionally.

In a minute or so, the door to the inner office opened and Parris came out. He was wearing a tan, three-piece suit made of lightweight material, and white shoes. The vest of the suit seemed to accentuate his potbelly. I had never seen him dressed in anything other than a surgical scrub suit, and in this getup he reminded me of a rich plantation owner in the antebellum South. All that was missing was a mint julep in one hand, a long cigar in the other, and a straw hat on his head. Parris was smiling from ear to ear, as if he had recently caught one of his slaves involved in a heinous crime and had had him castrated.

Soon after Parris cleared out of the office, Tom Fredericks came through the door. Tom was not smiling. I got off the couch, walked up to Tom, and said, "How'd it go?"

"Not bad, Bob, not bad at all. Thanks to Dr. Adams, they decided not to have me hanged, although they were seriously considering that for a while, Bob, they really thought about it. They finally decided to put me on probation. All because of that asshole Parris."

"Probation?" I asked. "What does that mean?"

"A lot of things, Bob. First, they put it down on my record, so if I apply for a job in academics that record'll be seen by the folks who want to hire me. Plus, if I do anything wrong, Bob, if there's another complaint lodged against me, I'm fired. At least I got away without being restricted to quarters or anything like that."

"I'm sorry this turned out this way for you," I said.

"Well, Bob, I'd have done it again if I had to. They can do whatever they want to me, Bob, whatever they want, but I'm never going to resort to practicing medicine like Parris does. Well, I've got to go home now. I'll see you tomorrow. I'm going to take a bath and try to forget about all this. Good luck in there." And Tom walked out of the office.

I sat back down on the couch. Now I was really worried. If they could do something like that to Tom, what chance would we have?

In another minute the secretary's phone rang and, after picking it up and listening to it for a few seconds, she said, "You can go in now." With Ray leading, we walked through the door and entered the hospital board room. In contrast to the outer office and the main lobby, this room had been recently and exquisitely redecorated. The floor was covered with a blue carpet which had white polka dots patterned through it; the walls, mahogany-paneled with light blue trim, were covered with framed, enlarged photographs of the hospital during its stages of construction, during its early years of operation, and during the reconstruction of the perinatal center.

The center of the room was occupied by a massive oak conference table. Seated around this table were seven men and a woman. We were told to take seats at the foot of the table and did as we were told. All I could think about was the scene in *The Wizard of Oz* in which Dorothy and her friends approach Oz, the Great and Powerful, in order to get their wishes granted.

Only two people at that table were instantly recognizable: Monsignor Vitale, the man who had interrupted Friday morning rounds earlier in the month, was seated at the head of the table. Next to him sat the man who had accompanied the monsignor during that visit, the man named Mr. Stone who had done a good job in putting down Sullivan. "Good afternoon," the monsignor said to us, "it's nice to see you three young people here. I'm Monsignor Vitale, I'm the chairman of the hospital board." The monsignor, wearing his black suit and clerical collar, and with a few wisps of white hair around the sides of his head, did resemble the Wizard of Oz. "What brings you young doctors down to see us today?"

I started. "Monsignor, we are working on the fifth floor in the intensive care nursery. We are here today to lodge some complaints against our attending, Dr. Sullivan." I was speaking in a very high-pitched voice, the way I always do when I'm nervous.

"Complaints?" the monsignor asked with a very serious expression. "Shouldn't Dr. Sullivan be present to address these complaints?"

"We felt it would be best to do it without his being present," I said.

"It doesn't seem fair to make accusations against someone without allowing that person to defend himself," he said in a very gentle, but firm voice. "What are these complaints?"

"Dr. Sullivan, in our opinion, is making life-and-death decisions every day on babies in the nursery without ever consulting the parents of those babies as to what they would like done. These decisions often strongly influence what the life of the child, and of the whole family of that child, will be like in the future. Both we and the parents are very upset about this policy. Some of the parents are so upset, in fact, that they've mentioned the possibility of suing Dr. Sullivan and the hospital." I took a deep breath after getting all this out.

"Suing the hospital," the monsignor repeated, and the board members who had been fidgeting came suddenly to attention and instantly appeared concerned. "Certainly we need to investigate this if there may be lawsuits. Can you give us some examples of what's been happening, Doctors?"

Ray now picked up the flow. "Last week a baby was born with Down syndrome and an intestinal blockage. . . ."

"Yes," the monsignor interrupted, "the O'Hara case. Dr. Parris was just in here about that. That baby seems to have swirled up a lot of dust on the fourth and fifth floors!"

"Yes," Ray continued, "it is the O'Hara baby. When Mr. and Mrs. O'Hara refused to consent to the operation that would relieve the obstruction, Dr. Sullivan insulted Mr. O'Hara and provoked him into hitting Dr. Sullivan in the jaw." Everyone around the table laughed.

"Yes," the monsignor said, "I think we have all observed that Dr. Sullivan can bring out the worst in people."

"I've heard Dr. Sullivan's side of this case, Monsignor, and I agree with him," a man sitting to Mr. Stone's right said. This was Dr. Alphonse diGregario, a pediatrician in private practice who was affiliated with the old St. A's.

"Right or not, Dr. diGregario," the monsignor countered, "provoking a fistfight with the father of a patient does not seem to be in the best interest of that patient or of the hospital."

"That's exactly how we feel," Ray said. "Dr. Sullivan must be instructed that he deal with these problems on a more adult level rather than resorting to name-calling and insults. Although Dr. Sullivan may have made the right clinical decision, he was totally wrong in the way he managed this family."

"And that seems to be the case with most patients," I continued. "Although he is extremely competent technically in managing problems in these newborns, he pays little attention to the families and to the social problems they might be facing."

"I see," the monsignor responded. "It sounds like this O'Hara case was botched from start to finish. I better pay a visit to the family personally and try to soothe their feelings."

"Monsignor, that would be like putting a Band-Aid on a festering abscess. There are so many examples of Dr. Sullivan's bumbling of cases that you would have to spend your whole day soothing feelings. Here's another example. A baby born late last week with problems that have left him essentially brain-dead, in renal failure, and with problems in every organ, is the son of a physician who has expressed the wish that no heroic measures be taken to prolong his child's misery. However, Dr. Sullivan, after hearing the father say this, insulted the man's intelligence and has vowed, just to spite him, to do everything within his power to maintain the baby. The father's been trying since that time to find another hospital to which he can transfer the baby and has told me that, if necessary, he will bring a lawsuit against the hospital and Dr. Sullivan for wrongful life and will seek a court order to have all life support discontinued." As this was going on, my voice was returning to its normal pitch; telling these stories, I wasn't so nervous anymore, nor was I as concerned about the outcome. How could they ignore all this?

"You must admit," the man sitting at the monsignor's left began, "these cases contain extremely emotionally charged issues." This man was Father James McMurphy, a rugged, healthy, and muscular man who looked to be a few years older than Ray, Terry, and I. "The question of whether severely damaged children should be kept alive through modern technology has been hotly debated, but you also must realize that the Catholic faith looks upon life as sacred. We as Catholic clergymen must stand behind Dr. Sullivan and support him in the position he has taken in these cases and, historically, in all cases he has managed since our neonatal unit opened."

"As Dr. Brewster pointed out earlier," I said, "whether Dr. Sullivan is right or wrong, clinically or ethically, is not the question. What we are concerned about, what is at the heart of this is should Dr. Sullivan be allowed to treat patients the way he does?"

"Well to me, that seems to be an important, but secondary issue, Doctor," Father McMurphy responded. "Monsignor, I feel very strongly that if we were to take any action against Dr. Sullivan at this time, if we were to question any policy that he has adopted, we would be undermining him, and that would be in direct opposition to the teachings of Jesus Christ."

I was seeing all hopes of returning to Kansas gone forever, when another voice spoke up. "We must consider money matters," said a sixty-year-old man wearing a dark suit and sitting to Dr. diGregario's right. This was Dr. James Patrick, an obstetric attending who had been on the staff of St. A's for over twenty years. Dr. Patrick looked nervous and frazzled, as if he hadn't slept in a long time, and he had looked at the watch on his left wrist at least five times during the early part of the meeting. "These boys," he continued, obviously ignoring Terry's presence, "have come to tell us there may be trouble ahead because Sullivan's been upsetting the parents. Lord knows, we've heard these complaints before. As you all know, we've been sued because of this kind of thing more than once in the past, and each time we get hit with a suit, Sullivan's insurance premiums go up a few thousand bucks. If this goes on for much longer, he's going to lose his insurance coverage, we're going to be out an awful lot of money, and Mr. Stone here and some of his friends might not be so willing to bail us out. And I don't need to tell you, gentlemen, that if we don't have money, we don't have a hospital. So although I agree with you, Father James, that taking a stand against Sullivan may not be the best thing religiously, I think it makes a damned lot of sense financially."

"Yes, that's true," the monsignor said thoughtfully. "Doctors, how many other incidents like these are there that you are aware of?"

"We've only been working in the nursery for ten days," I responded, "and in that time there've been two cases in addition to the two we've already told you about. In one of those," I said, remembering poor Baby Torres, "the baby died. That father did not express any interest in suing but he was, in our opinion, badly treated by Dr. Sullivan. The other case is still evolving, but it may turn out to be the ugliest of them all. It involves a pair of Siamese twins born last Sunday."

"Oh yes," the monsignor interrupted with a smile, "the Siamese twins. I watched Dr. Sullivan being interviewed by Ms. Doherty on the news Monday night. Great publicity for the hospital."

"Unfortunately, the parents were also watching the news on Monday night," I responded. "I say 'unfortunately' because that was the first they heard about the babies. Through a misunderstanding they thought the babies had died. Dr. Sullivan never bothered to speak to them, to explain the medical situation, or to even ask permission to have them shown on TV."

"Oh dear!" Dr. Patrick said. "He never talked with the parents? That's unbelievable."

"No, it's not unbelievable," Ray answered. "From what we've been seeing, it's sort of routine. Sullivan never talks to parents."

"And the parents of these twins, Mr. and Mrs. Srnivasan, are so angry at the way they've been treated, they've refused to talk with anyone connected with the neonatal unit. Mrs. Srnivasan will probably only be satisfied when she can transfer the babies to another hospital."

"I see," the monsignor said, rubbing his chin. "A very volatile situation!"

"Why is it, Monsignor," began the only woman board member in the room, "that we have not heard complaints like these from previous interns?" This was Sister Mary Theresa, head of nursing at St. A's and, as such, Kathy's boss. Sister Mary Theresa, dressed in her habit, was sitting next to Father McMurphy. Although she wore a smile on her face, her voice had an accusatory tone.

I answered her directly. "Although our predecessors have had similar complaints, they've all felt that since we're here for only a month it just didn't pay to make waves. We're speaking up at this time because we feel we have a moral obligation to do so."

"That's very admirable," said the monsignor. "Any other comments?"

"Yes, Monsignor," Mr. Stone said, "when I joined this board at the beginning of this month, I was told that important issues are discussed at these meetings. So far, however, all we've discussed has been the social habits of these residents. Either the attending doctors are angry at the residents, or the residents, like these three in front of us, have something they don't like about the attendings. I am a busy man; I do not have time to sit here and listen to these long harangues if nothing is going to come of them."

"I understand your concerns, Mr. Stone," the monsignor responded, "and I just beg your indulgence for a little longer. Believe me, we do get down to topics that will interest you and will make it worth your while. Thank you, Doctors, for coming and bringing this matter to our attention. Other factions have raised questions regarding Dr. Sullivan and perhaps it's time we as a board discussed these problems. We will inform you three when we come to a decision. Thank you again."

"Thank you for your time," I said as we rose from our chairs and backed out of the room, much like Dorothy, the Cowardly Lion, the Tin Man, and the Scarecrow had when their audience with the Wizard was at its end.

"I think we lost," I said when we reached the hall outside the office.

"You can't tell, Bob," Ray answered, "they might come through. That stuff that guy said about without money they don't have a hospital sounded sort of good."

"That Stone made me feel like two cents," I said.

"Are you okay, Terry?" Ray asked. She looked glazed over.

"No," she said as she fell into my arms and started crying.

I let her cry for a few minutes. Ray got beeped to the DR, apparently Parris was going to celebrate his victory by performing a late afternoon section. I said goodbye to Ray while Terry continued to cry.

When she had calmed a little, I asked if Cliff was scheduled to be on call that night. "Yes," she said through the tears, and I told her I would take her home.

XXI
After Hours

The rain had stopped by the time we left the hospital but Terry was in no condition to drive. We left her car in the lot and together drove in my car to a Mexican restaurant I had found on Commonwealth Avenue not far from Terry's house in Brookline. She continued to cry off and on in the car.

I was silent during the initial part of the trip; I didn't know exactly what I could say or do to make Terry feel better. Having spent my entire life up to that month as a student, I not only was not prepared for caring for the babies in the Pit, I also was unfamiliar with dealing with real-life experiences. I just didn't know how to comfort a friend who was obviously in need.

But Terry spoke first. "So terrible," she said in a wavering voice, "all those little twisted bodies with so many problems!" I remained silent.

"Why are we doing this, Bob? Why are we working so damned hard to keep these damned babies alive? All that's going to happen is we're going to create more GORKs." Her tears bubbled out again.

After her crying subsided a little again, I said, "Terry, you're very tired. When you're tired, you lose all the normal defense mechanisms you use to protect yourself from the horrible stuff. Normally, you'd make a little joke about this and just go on with your life. But today you're too tired to joke, and the bad images stay with you. Try to relax. Forget about work."

"That doesn't help, Bob," she responded. "Just because I'm tired and can't use my normal defenses doesn't change the fact that we're working to perpetuate the need for that follow-up clinic!"

"Terry, it really isn't all that bad. Sure, a certain percentage of these kids end up as GORKs. But as Sullivan says, a lot of them end up totally normal, and some of those normal kids would have died just a few years ago. Just think about how exciting that could be, to be able to produce a normal life out of a child who should be dead."

We were silent through the rest of the trip to the restaurant. I felt so sorry for Terry, and I so wished I could just reach out and say something, or do something to make everything all right. I parked on the street just outside the restaurant, which was really a dump, a run-down bar with a few tables strewn around in back. But the food was delicious and I remembered that Terry had said that the one thing she truly missed about living out west was good Mexican food. The place, dark in the bright late afternoon light, was empty. We sat at one of the tables and I ordered a pitcher of margaritas.

"Thanks for bringing me here," she said. "I'll feel better after I eat."

"You know," I said, "Rachel coming to see me last weekend really saved my hide. I thought I had bought it last Saturday morning. I guess we all have to go through it once. I'm worried about you with Cliff being on call tonight."

"I'm learning to adjust to being alone," she sighed. "So many things have changed since we got here. In Seattle, we worked our schedules out so that we were never apart for more than one night a week. I thought medicine was wonderful. But now . . ."

"It's different," I said.

"You can say that again." Terry was sounding a little better and had stopped crying. "Do you know, this whole month there's not one night when we'll both be home together and be well rested? We haven't even finished unpacking our stuff yet. And we may never get a chance to do it either! I don't know. . . . Everything's so . . . so complicated now. . . ." She started crying again.

"Is something else wrong?" I asked.

"It's hard to talk about," she said after some hesitation.

"Terry," I began, holding her hand, "we're friends. We've been through a lot already, and we've only known each other two weeks. What's wrong?"

"Well, that O'Hara baby. It's really upset me. . . ."

"It upset you that we threatened to get a court order?" I interrupted.

"Not that. It's just . . . . the mother; she was over thirty-five. Cliff and I, we want to have children, but, I don't know. Last year, we had this little fight. He wanted me to take this year off to have a baby. He said he was afraid if I waited too long, we'd have a kid with a birth defect or something. I told him there'd be plenty of time to have children after I finished my residency. But after that baby with Down syndrome was born, I got to thinking. I'm thirty-one now. I'll be nearly thirty-five when I'm done with the residency. Bob, that's just two years younger than Mrs. O'Hara. Maybe I should have listened to Cliff. Maybe I should have taken the year off." She dissolved into tears.

"I'm really worried about you, Terry," I said. "When Rachel came, I didn't have enough strength to talk to her, but just knowing she was around made me feel better. Is there anyone you can stay with tonight?"

Terry thought for a minute. "There's my friend, Joannie. She's a surgical intern at the Medical Center. We went to med school together. I guess I could stay with her. I'll give her a call after we finish eating."

"Good," I responded as the margaritas arrived. I poured, and we ordered dinner and drank. By the time she was into her second drink, she seemed much less depressed.

"You know," I said, "the only times I've felt halfway decent since starting this damned internship have been when I've been blasted. I've never really been a big drinker, but I've been drunk four times in the last ten days."

"Me too," Terry responded. "Alcohol seems to numb my pain. And I've been feeling a fair amount of pain over the past two weeks."

"Yeah," I said. "The Pit is a terrible place to work. Is there anything you can think of to make the rest of the month survivable?"

"I don't know," Terry answered as our order of nachos arrived and we set about devouring them. "What do you hate most about St. A's?"

I thought and chewed for a few seconds. "Two things," I finally answered. "First, I hate Sullivan and Kathy, and their attitudes. . . ."

"Me too! They're part of what's bugging me. I mean, how can they make these decisions without giving any thought to the quality of life they're saving?"

"You know, I never really thought about this much before I came here. To use technology to save someone of any age who is going to end up a vegetable, I just never thought about it one way or the other. But having been here two weeks, I now think about nothing else. And the more I think about it, the more I'm sure we have to do something about it."

"What else do you hate?" Terry asked.

I hesitated. "It's not really St. A's," I finally said. "I think it would be anywhere. I have the feeling that I can't do anything helpful. I keep having this dream. . . ."

Terry's eyes widened. "A dream?"

"Yeah. I've had it a few times already. I'm handed a perfectly normal child in the DR and, right in front of me, the kid dies. I can't do anything to help it. I have the feeling I'm paralyzed and impotent."

"That's weird," Terry said, her eyes still wide open. "I've been having a dream just like that. It's been scaring me to death!"

Our dinners had arrived. We stared down at our plates for a long time, not moving to reach for our forks, suddenly not wanting to eat. "Have they gotten us?" I asked.

"It's weird, Bob. Really weird."

"What does it mean?"

"I don't know. Stress? Fear?"

"We better eat," I said. I picked up my fork and began slowly transferring food from my plate to my mouth. I ate the entire plateful without looking up, without saying a word to Terry. She did the same. I was worried about both of us. Bad dreams are bad things to have. And then the margaritas hit, and suddenly we were both happy again. I forgot all about the dreams and we talked about other things, happier things.

"Bob," Terry asked after the plates had been cleared away, "why did you come to Boston if your wife's in New York?"

"It was a screwup," I sighed. "At the time I had to send in my match list last winter, Rachel thought she'd be finished with her PhD work by the spring. Although she wanted us to stay in New York, she caved in, after everyone else told me it would be best for my career to do my residency in Boston. She even got a postdoc at MIT."

"What happened?" Terry asked.

"What happened? Her lab blew up."

"Blew up?"

"Poof! Blew right the hell up. Nobody knows exactly why it happened. One night last January she comes home from work, everything's fine, next morning she goes back, everything's blown up. The explosion destroyed the stuff she was working on and a couple of the notebooks with her data in them, so she's got to repeat a lot of the stuff she already did. Now, she won't be finished in the lab until next summer."

"That's awful! And they wouldn't let you change your match list?"

"Nope. I called the Medical Center and told them what happened, I called the computer service and explained it to them, but they said sorry, the choices had already been made, there'd be no way to change the matches without upsetting the balance of nature in the Western hemisphere. I didn't want to do that, so here I am."

I poured the last round of margaritas from the pitcher and, now feeling plastered, asked, "Dessert?"

"No, I'm Terry."

"No, I wanted to know if you wanted dessert."

"Oh."

"Do you?" I asked after she hesitated.

"Do I what? . . . Oh, want dessert? No, I don't think so. Do you?"

"Not really," I answered.

"Well, drive me back to my house and I'll make some coffee."

"Okay," I said. "Let's blow this place." I paid the bill and we slunk out, trying not to act drunk, the way people do when they're drunk. But we were trying so hard not to act drunk that it was immediately obvious to anyone who passed that we were very, very drunk indeed.

I managed to drive my car the few blocks to Terry's house, but I don't remember the trip at all. I shouldn't have been driving, that's for sure, but we made it in one piece. While Terry put a pot of water on to boil, I sat in the living room. She soon joined me and we watched a dumb "made for TV" movie as we sipped our coffee.

After a time I had sobered up a bit and felt that I could probably drive. "I've got to go, Terry," I said. "How are you feeling?"

She was sobering up too, and with her sobriety came the return of her depression. "Why don't you call that friend?" I suggested. "I'll drop you off on my way home."

She looked up the number in her little brown address book and tried calling, but there was no answer. "Maybe she's on call," Terry said.

"Is there anyone else you can stay with?" I asked.

"No. I don't know anyone else in Boston. Except you and Ray."

As luck would have it, just then on the TV a public service announcement for the United Cerebral Palsy Foundation came on. Terry saw the children on that commercial and started crying again. Her crying was loud and strong, as it had been during the afternoon outside the hospital board office.

I embraced her again and she fell into my arms. Her embrace was strong, she hugged me tightly, her tears dampened the right shoulder of my shirt. We fell to the living room floor, still in an embrace, and began kissing. Her lips felt good against mine. "Don't leave me, Bob. Please stay with me," she pleaded again and again. Her crying had stopped.

Neither of us planned it, but it happened. I unsnapped the button of Terry's jeans and undid her zipper. I pulled down her pants and caressed her. She began to unbutton my shirt. Within a very short time, we were both naked and we made love for a long, long time.

. . . I am in the delivery room. Parris hands me a baby. Heart rate normal. Respiratory rate normal. Baby's face begins to turn blue. Hands and feet turn blue. Heart rate drops below a hundred. All respiratory effort ceases. I put ambu bag over baby's face and breathe for it. Face and hands become a robin's egg blue. Heart rate below fifty. I start to pump the chest. Heart rate still dropping. I bag baby more. Face, hands, and feet become darker, darker. I put a needle in the umbilical vein and inject some drug. I don't know what it is. The baby is dead. . . .

It was nearly midnight when I awoke. Terry was still asleep lying next to me on the living room floor. I had a bad headache and felt hung over. The dream had been intensifying; now there was a clear character in it—Parris. It was becoming more real, more lifelike, and more scary.

I turned off the TV, woke Terry up, and together we went up to the bedroom. "Bob," she said slowly as we got into the queen-sized bed, "you had the dream!"

I didn't answer. I didn't need to.

"I did too," she said as she started crying. I held her again. She embraced me tightly.

XXII

Thursday, July 8
Morning

I awoke early, at 6 A.M. I found the shower and took a long, cool one. The day was going to be a scorcher. I found a bottle of aspirin and Cliff's razor in the medicine chest. When I was finished in the bathroom, I went back into the bedroom and found Terry still asleep. It was getting late now so I nudged her awake and her eyes opened. She didn't smile as she said, "Morning."

"Good morning. It's getting late. We'd better get moving."

"I don't want to go to work today. I'm sick. I've got a headache."

"You're hung over," I responded. "So am I."

"So let's both stay here. Let's never go outside."

"Not fair," I said. "That's not fair to Ray."

"Oh," she responded slowly, sighing, "you're right."

She got out of bed and went about her usual morning routine. I dressed, went down to the kitchen, and warmed up the coffee that had been left over from the night before. In a few minutes Terry came down and I poured the warmed-over coffee.

"You're on tonight," she said. "What are you going to do for clean clothes?"

"Terry, I didn't learn a lot in medical school, but I did learn that an intern always needs to carry a toothbrush, a can of Right Guard, and clean underwear. With this stuff, you're ready for just about anything."

Terry tasted the coffee. "Yecch," she groaned. "What is this stuff?"

"Coffee," I answered. "I warmed up last night's. It may not taste good, but it's got caffeine, the intern's friend."

"Great," Terry said as she poured her cup down the sink. Even I had to admit that it tasted pretty awful, but I drank a whole cupful.

We were silent for a little while, until Terry said, "Look, Bob, I know this is awkward, but I really want to thank you for last night."

"Don't mention it," I answered, my face turning red.

"No, I don't mean it that way. I really needed someone to be with me last night. I needed a body who I knew cared about me, and you were there when I needed you. It really meant a lot to me."

"I know," I said. "I really needed someone too. I guess we both happened to be in the right place at the right time."

"Exactly. I hope what happened last night doesn't change our friendship. Although I only met you and Ray a short time ago, you two really mean a lot to me."

"I don't think anything will change. What happened last night was just two friends helping each other in an emergency, only the way we did it was a little . . . unorthodox."

"You know, Bob, it's just like two interns to totally intellectualize away sleeping together." We both giggled and Terry took my hand and squeezed it for a second.

"I guess that's part of the process," I said. "We have to learn to intellectualize away all our emotions. That's the only way to get through all the depressing stuff."

We drove to the hospital in silence. I parked in the lot and we headed up to the Pit. Ray, again looking very well-rested, was sitting in the nurses' station. "How was the night?" I asked.

"Great," he answered. "Great and interesting both. I got six continuous hours of uninterrupted sleep, and only one DR call in the late afternoon, for a Parris section. I could do it all over again tonight."

"I'm willing to give up my night on call for you, Ray," I offered seriously.

"I wasn't being serious," Ray responded.

"What was the interesting part?" Terry asked.

"I think I'm in love," Ray answered.

"Oh no" was all I could say.

"Yup. I had a talk with Laurie at dinner. I didn't exactly tell her I wasn't a famous nephrologist, but I did say I didn't think I could be of much help to her. You know what she said?"

"What?" I asked.

"She said it didn't matter. She said I was different from everybody else." Ray had a weird expression on his face as he said this.

"You're different all right!" I responded.

"Did anything happen?" Terry asked. I guess she had noticed the weird expression on Ray's face, too.

"Well, we sort of spent the night together," Ray answered.

"Oh no," I said, hitting my forehead with the palm of my hand. "Ray, what are you getting yourself into?"

"Nothing bad, I think. She likes me, Bob. And is she great in bed!"

Just then Frohman arrived and we started rounds. Ray continued to walk around with that lovesick cow expression all day long.

Again that morning most of work rounds were taken up discussing the Dead Kid and the Srnivasan twins. Frohman tried his best that morning to ignore us, and we tried to ignore him, but we were all unsuccessful.

I noticed there was tape around the Dead Kid's abdomen. "Oh no," I said in Ray's direction, "don't tell me somebody actually dialyzed the Dead Kid."

"Yep," said Ray. "Yesterday afternoon Laurie and I were sitting in the nurses' station when about twenty people showed up. Laurie rushed over to them and started gushing and cooing; it was the guys from renal. I don't know how they all got here, they must have taken a bus or something, but anyway, they all came into the nursery. There were attendings and fellows and medical students and social workers and stuff like that. Laurie went right for the head guy, Rickover, or Rickunder, or something like that. . . ."

"Dr. Rickhofer," Frohman interrupted.

"Anyway," Ray continued, "this guy with Laurie at his side sort of saunters over to the Dead Kid and asks real loud, 'Who's in charge of this baby?' I went over and told him I was covering. He asked me what was wrong with the kid, so I told him he was sort of dead except his heart didn't know it yet, and the guy looked at me like I was crazy and ordered me to explain. I gave him a blow-by-blow description of all the kid's problems, including the fact that he was in renal failure. When I said those two words, 'renal failure,' it was like a bell rang in this

Rickunder's head because his eyes perked up and he suddenly wanted me to show him the kid's numbers, his electrolytes, and stuff like that. After looking all this over, he said, 'It's a good thing you called us, this baby is very sick and will die if we don't dialyze him right away.' I explained again that the baby was sort of already dead, but Rickunder gave me a dirty look and said, 'Nonsense, if Dr. Sullivan wants him dialyzed, then the child must be all right. Dr. Sullivan is a good man.' This Rickunder must be related to Sullivan or something."

"He is," Frohman interrupted again, snapping his fingers repetitively.

"What?" Terry asked, acknowledging Frohman for the first time.

"He is related to Sullivan. Dr. Rickhofer is Dr. Sullivan's brother-in-law."

"Well, that explains it," Ray said. "After Rickunder decided they would dialyze the kid, all the fellows and medical students and social workers huddled around Rickunder and he told them what he wanted to do. One of the other guys, I guess he was a fellow, argued a little with Rickunder about doing the procedure on a kid who was such a bad risk, but Rickunder told him, 'Nonsense, this baby will die if his potassium gets too high,' and that was all the flak he got. He must have had those other guys hypnotized or something.

"Anyway, Rickunder gets the whole thing set up and Laurie says, 'Can I do it, Dr. Rickunder, please, can I please put the catheter in?' And Rickunder thinks about it for a minute and then says, 'Sure, Lauren, since you're going to be a fellow somewhere next year, you should take this opportunity to learn the procedure.' So Laurie . . ."

"Wait a minute," Frohman said, his twitching increasing in intensity, "didn't you tell Dr. Rickhofer that Dr. Sullivan wanted him to do the procedure?"

Ray just glared at Frohman and continued, "So Laurie gets ready to do it with her hands shaking, she was so nervous. Rickunder tells her to stick the thing in here and push it in this far. . . ." Ray measured a distance of about one inch between his forefinger and his thumb. "Laurie's really shaking, but Rickunder's standing next to her, yelling, 'Stick it in, stick it in, farther, farther.' "

"Sounds pretty sexually provocative," Terry said.

"Yeah, I was getting pretty hot watching it," Ray responded. "Anyway, Laurie finally stabs the catheter trochar in and, of course, the damned thing went in too shallow. So Rickunder grabs her arm and pushes it down really hard. They take out the trochar and what do you think flowed out of the catheter? Meconium, of course. They had pushed the damned thing through the peritoneum, where it was supposed to be, and hit the intestine. Laurie ran out of the room screaming, like she had seen a ghost or something, and Rickunder says, 'Uh oh.' Then he pulled the whole thing back out and pushed it in through another spot. This time, he didn't get meconium out, and he said, 'Well, sometimes, these things happen.' "

"So what you're telling me, Ray," I said, "is that we now have a patient with necrotizing enterocolitis who we were managing conservatively, trying to avoid surgery, who now has a clearly perforated and probably ruptured bowel?"

"Yeah, I guess that's right," Ray answered. "But they did successfully dialyze him. They got his potassium down to 3.2."

"Great," I responded. "At least he'll die with normal electrolytes."

"What happened to Lauren?" Terry asked, more interested in the soap opera part of the story than the medical part.

"That has nothing to do with rounds," Frohman said. "Sullivan's going to be pretty angry about all this. We'd better get moving."

"She was pretty broken up for the rest of the evening," Ray said, completely ignoring Frohman. "She said, 'Now I'll never get a fellowship here' and 'Maybe I ought to look for something else to do next year.' I told her that was all bullshit, the fact that she hit gut the first time she tried to put in a catheter didn't mean a thing about what kind of nephrologist she was going to be. And then I told her I thought she'd make a damned good nephrologist anyway. She was really surprised."

"It must have meant a lot to her, you being a famous renal physiologist and all," Terry said, smiling.

"I think you're in love," I said to Ray. He didn't answer.

Peritoneal dialysis was to the nephrologist what ventilators were to the neonatologist. For patients with renal failure, when used properly, peritoneal dialysis saved lives. The idea was simple: put fluid with a low concentration of something, say, potassium, under the abdominal wall but above the membrane covering the intestinal organs called the peritoneum. Potassium and other waste products of metabolism that are usually excreted from the body by the kidney will flow from the blood, where they are in relatively high concentration, through the peritoneal membrane and into the fluid that has a lower concentration. Eventually, equilibrium is reached; the level of the poison in the blood equals the level in the peritoneal fluid. At that point, the fluid is withdrawn through the catheter through which it was initially introduced. Obviously, this is not curative. A few days after the dialysis is completed, the waste products will build up to unsafe levels in the blood again, and the whole procedure will need to be repeated.

The major complications of this technique include damaging an underlying organ during the introduction of the catheter, and infection of the peritoneum, called peritonitis. The former complication had already been accomplished when the metal part of the catheter, called the trochar, had been introduced through the peritoneum and into the intestine. And it was probable that the latter complication, infection, would soon follow.

Frohman had moved on, had removed his stethoscope from the Sullivan-like pouch he was wearing attached to his belt, and was examining the next patient while we were discussing Ray's love life; and finally, we moved on too. The rest of rounds proceeded smoothly until we reached the Srnivasan twins. Ray then became very solemn. "I tried talking to Mrs. Srnivasan again yesterday afternoon," he said. "She won't listen to anything I have to say. The whole thing is bad, really bad!"

"Ray, you can't blame yourself," I said, patting Ray on the shoulder. Just then Frohman's beeper went off. He walked to the phone in the nurses' station and dialed the operator.

"Listen, I have a great idea," Terry said. "It might get us out of this whole mess so Ray won't have to face the twins every morning. Mrs. Srnivasan won't speak to anyone because she doesn't trust people who work here, right? How about if we get someone who doesn't work here to come and talk to her? Do you think that would do any good?"

"It might," Ray answered. "But who do you have in mind?"

"Channin," Terry answered proudly.

"Channin," I echoed, "a great idea. Mrs. Srnivasan will talk to him because he doesn't work here, he works at a real hospital. And while he's in with her, he can get her to consent to transfer the babies out of here and over to the Medical Center, where they can get the workup and surgery that everyone except Sullivan says they need."

"Great!" Ray said. His face, which had been wearing that weird expression during most of rounds, now broke into a real smile. "This way Sullivan won't have anything to do with making the decisions. Let's call Channin right now."

But before we could make a move toward the phone, we saw Frohman coming back toward us, so we decided to put off making the call until after work rounds were over. With Frohman back, we moved on to the next patient, continuing rounds. After rounds were completed, we did indeed call Channin's office and put into motion the gears that we hoped would eventually lead to the separation of the Srnivasan twins.

XXIII
Attending Rounds

Ten o'clock came, and Terry, Ray, and I sat in the nurses' station, working on our daily progress notes. Keeping our vow of the day before, none of us was going to attending rounds. We worked in silence, charting the inputs and the outputs, the results of the latest blood electrolytes, and blood counts on all the "active" babies. In the Dead Kid's chart, I added a new problem category: 7. Infection (following 1. Fluids; 2. Electrolytes; 3. Respiratory; 4. Renal; 5. Gastrointestinal; and 6. Social). Under this heading I documented that the peritoneal dialysis catheter had invaded the sanctity of the already compromised bowel and, as "plan" for problem seven, wrote "obtain blood, dialysis fluid, and stool of culture and observe."

By ten after ten Sullivan had realized we weren't going to show up, so he sent Frohman out to fetch us. "It's ten after ten," Frohman said as he reached the nurses' station, "time for attending rounds."

"Eat shit!" I said.

"Suck on it!" Ray added.

"Blow it out your ass!" Terry concluded.

"All right," Frohman said, throwing his arms up into the air, "I tried and that's all I'm going to do. I don't have to take this shit from interns!" He stormed out of the nurses' station.

A minute passed and Sullivan himself appeared. "Would you three please come into my office?" he asked in a calm, polite voice. "I have something important to discuss with you all. I understand that you're very upset and I want to get the whole thing out in the open."

He sounded coolly reasonable. I looked at Terry who looked at Ray. We nodded, agreeing that it seemed worth another try. We followed Sullivan into his office.

When we were all seated, Sullivan said, "I am very hurt. I understand that you three went to lodge a complaint against me at the hospital board meeting yesterday. Nothing like this has ever happened before, and I want to find out why exactly it has happened this time." He sounded sincere.

"Are you kidding?" Ray asked.

"No, Dr. Brewster. I simply don't understand what you have to complain about."

"Well, you must have seen that we've been pretty upset with the way things have been going around here," I said.

"Sure, I've seen you've been upset, but being upset during one's first rotation is something that's almost expected in interns. Interns are people who used to be smart medical students, and one thing about smart medical students is that for their entire lives they've been in control of everything. But then they come in here and find they have control over nothing; the first thing I tell you is that I'm the boss and I make all the decisions. So you interns become rapidly frustrated and, naturally, you take your frustrations out against the authority figure who, in this case, happens to be me. I understand all that. But what I don't understand is why you took your frustration and anger to the hospital board? Why not just come to me and discuss it?"

"We've tried to discuss these things with you, Dr. Sullivan," Terry said sincerely. "But you've refused to listen to the things we've had to say. You've just decided to continue carrying on with your plans regardless of how strongly we protested against them. We went to the hospital board because we needed to discuss our objections with somebody else in authority here. We weren't being satisfied by you."

"I see," Sullivan said with a thoughtful look. "Well, do you have any suggestion about how we can remedy this situation?"

"Although none of us is very technically adept," I said, "we all have very strong feelings about the ethics of the decisions that get made. You could include our opinions in your thinking when you make plans about our patients."

"How?" Sullivan asked. "Can you give me an example?"

"Like with the Dead Kid. You could . . ."

"The Dead Kid?" Kathy interrupted.

"That very sick baby. Baby Smith."

"You call him 'the Dead Kid?' " Kathy asked.

"Yeah," I said, trying to continue. "We feel . . ."

"That's disgusting!" Kathy said. "You have no respect for these patients!" Sullivan didn't change his expression.

I didn't respond but continued. "We feel the baby is brain-dead and that all the aggressive treatment he's receiving is in direct opposition to all the principles we were taught in medical school. We feel like we're needlessly torturing the baby!"

"You treat the patients as if their death would be a personal disgrace to you," Terry said. "In some situations death is the best thing that can happen!"

Sullivan was now getting upset, but he was still keeping his anger under control. "I strongly disagree. Death is never the best thing for a baby. I keep telling you three, no one can predict which babies will survive to live a normal life and which will not. I still get surprises, almost every day, and I'm sure none of you are better at predicting than I am."

"Dr. Sullivan," Ray began, "we've had this discussion over and over again. Certainly there are kids you can't be sure about. But the Dead Kid . . . look, he's brain-dead. He's not gonna grow up to be a normal citizen unless you do a brain transplant on him. And until you're able to offer that kind of treatment, you shouldn't be using your supertechnology on these kids just to keep their damned hearts pumping."

"Well, I continue to disagree with you!" Sullivan said. His anger was beginning to bubble through his calm exterior. "And as long as I'm the boss here, things'll get done my way. But I do think I understand your position a little better now. And I'm not angry with you for going to the hospital board. I know in your need to rebel against authority you'd probably want me to get angry with you. But I'm not. I won't give you three that satisfaction."

"Not angry with us!" I yelled. "Who the hell cares whether or not you're angry with us? We're concerned with the quality of life our patients will be left with after you get through with them, not with

"Oh God, maybe Sullivan is right about you guys. That's new meat, son."

"Oh right. Anyway, Ray's blaming himself because he feels that if he had gone to talk to the mother the next day, none of this would have happened. But he was really tired. He even fell asleep over lunch!"

"Ah, just like an intern to blame himself. If something goes wrong and there's an intern around, it must have been the 'terns fault!"

"Well, anyway, Mrs. Srnivasan won't talk to us and that suits Sullivan just fine because, although he got your opinion as well as Dr. Dover's and Dr. Chin's, he still doesn't want them separated."

"What a medical giant that man is!" Channin boomed. "A medical giant and a saint as well. Oh well, so how do I fit into this soap opera?"

"We interns figured that Mrs. Srnivasan would speak to you because you don't work here, you just come here to visit. And while you're talking to her, you know, medically explaining the situation, maybe you could get her to consent to transfer the babies over to the Medical Center. That way they could get the workup and surgery that everybody except Sullivan thinks they need."

"I see," Channin said with a smile, "you called me here to steal the patients away from Sullivan for their own good, right?" I nodded. "You sure you haven't been talking to Dan about this?"

"No," I said. "It was all our idea."

"This sure smells of his work. I remember once he drove a patient over to my office in his car when he was working here as an intern. Told the nurses he was taking the kid downstairs for some X rays. I could never figure out how he got the portable ventilator into his Volkswagen. Well, Bob, I don't know if stealing a patient is really very ethical, but since it is for the patients' own good, I'm willing to give it a try." And with that, he turned and went to find Mrs. Srnivasan.

I sat in the quiet of the nurses' station, supporting my head with my left hand and, staring at the Dead Kid's bed space, began to think through all that had happened. Two weeks before, I was a reasonably happy, reasonably confident medical school graduate, leaving a wife, whom I loved and who had not wanted me to leave in the first place, to move over two hundred miles north to start an internship in a program I actually knew little about. And now my confidence crumbled, my state of mind was bleak; unsure of my ability and of my future, I sat staring at a child, with painfully obvious brain damage, who was being kept alive by technology I didn't fully understand, and by ethics I didn't accept. And additionally, a formal complaint charging me with incompetence had been lodged against me, a complaint that would follow me through every job application I ever made out. How had all this happened?

I was trying to work through all the steps that had led up to my fall from grace when Dan came into the nurses' station, huffing and puffing. His face was red. "Bob," he gasped, "come on quick! I have to show you something really interesting!"

"What's up?" I asked, following Dan, who had already started out of the nurses' station.

"There's a kid down in the well-baby nursery I want you to see. You have to guess his diagnosis."

I followed Dan, who was running a few steps ahead of me, down the steps to the third floor and then through the corridor leading to the well-baby nursery. We entered a nursery packed with bassinets. Census was above 100 percent.

Dan led me to the bassinet of Baby Girl Donovan. He picked up the baby and carried her to an examining table that was adjacent to the nurses' station. "Tell me what you see, Bob," he said, placing the infant on the table.

I unwrapped the receiving blanket in which she was wrapped and set about examining her. "She looks pretty good," I said after a minute or two. "She's cute."

"Keep looking," Dan ordered, "it's kind of subtle. But you should get it."

"Well, she's not funny-looking." I stuck my finger in her mouth. "She has a good suck and there's no cleft of the palate." I felt the soft spot on top of her head. "Her fontanel is open and it's soft." I listened to her heart with my stethoscope. "She doesn't have a murmur." I felt her belly and said, "Her abdomen is soft and she has normal female genitalia." I moved both arms through their normal range of motion. "Her joints work okay and she's got the right number of fingers and toes. So far I don't see anything wrong." All through this examination the baby was screaming, I was sweating, and Dan was smiling.

"Maybe you need a little more light," Dan said as he picked the baby up and carried her closer to the window. "Like I said, it is kind of subtle. See anything now?"

"Well, I'm not sure, but her feet look a little blue. I'm not sure if that's normal at this age or not."

"Do her hands look blue?" Dan asked, his smile broadening.

"Nope," I answered, "just her feet. And the more I look, the bluer they look."

"Anything unusual about her breathing?" Dan asked.

"Let me see," I responded as I carried the baby back to the examining table and laid her down. After listening to her chest with my stethoscope for a while, I said, "Well the lungs are clear, but she's breathing kind of fast."

"Yeah," Dan said. "This baby was born three days ago, and I was just doing the predischarge physical. Do you know what's wrong?"

"Let me think. No murmur but rapid breathing. Blue feet but pink hands. That rings a bell, but I can't remember. . . ."

"What system?" Dan interrupted. "What organ system is abnormal?"

"Well . . . the heart?" I answered. "The cardiac system?"

"Right. You got the system right. Now, when you do a cardiac examination, what do you have to do?"

"Listen to the heart?" I asked.

"Sure. You did that and you said it was normal. What else?"

"Feel the pulses?" I asked.

"An excellent idea," Dan answered. So I started to feel the baby's pulses. I started at the elbows. Although I hadn't felt too many newborns' pulses before, these felt a little stronger than I thought they should have. "They're full," I said, thinking out loud. Then remembering my cardiovascular physiology from medical school, I asked, "Is it aortic regurgitation?" a problem with the valve that separates the main pumping chamber of the heart, the left ventricle, from the aorta, the blood vessel that carries blood to the rest of the body.

"Good thought," Dan answered, "but wrong. Keep feeling."

I then tried to palpate the left femoral pulse, the pulse in the left groin. I felt and I felt for it, but I could not find it, so I tried for the pulses in the knee and on the foot, but I couldn't feel any of them either. "I must have my anatomy all screwed up," I said. "I can't feel anything."

"You have to learn to trust yourself more, Bob," Dan said, patting me on the shoulder. "Maybe you're right; maybe they're not palpable."

"Of course!" I yelled. "That's why the feet are blue! This baby's got a coarct!"

"I think that's it," Dan said, "I think she's got a coarctation of the aorta. What would you like to do right now to confirm that diagnosis, Bob?"

"The next part of the exam," I said, now almost as excited as Dan. "Take the baby's blood pressure." He nodded, and we went to get the blood pressure machine from the nurses' station. We checked the pressure first in the right arm; it was 110/60, somewhat elevated for a newborn. Then we checked the left arm; here it was 160/110, enormously elevated. Finally we measured the pressure in the legs and found a reading of 50/30 in both, which confirmed the diagnosis.

Just then Dr. Channin entered the nursery, saying, "What are you guys doing down here? I've been looking all over this hospital for you."

"Dr. Channin," Dan said, his smile broadening even more upon seeing the cardiologist, "what are you doing here?"

"This young impressionable intern called me and asked me to come over to hijack one of Sullivan's prized possessions. What in God's name are you two doing to torture these well babies?"

"They're not all that well," Dan responded, "and, let me tell you, am I glad you're here. You're just the man we need. Come and look at this baby."

As ordered, Channin approached Baby Girl Donovan. It took him only a few seconds of observation to make the diagnosis. "Jesus Christ," he said, "does she have a coarct?"

I was blown away. "That didn't take you long," Dan said. "I thought it was pretty subtle."

"Well it is subtle," Channin responded. "I probably wouldn't have picked it up if I were the first one to see her. But since you especially asked me to look at this baby, and since you're smiling so broadly I can just about see the fillings in your molars, I figured it had to be something unusual and something pretty subtle. What's her blood pressure?"

"In the left arm, 160/110, 110 over 60 in the right, and 50/30 in both legs," Dan responded.

"Must be preductal," Channin said thoughtfully. "You guys probably just saved this baby's life."

The aorta, the large blood vessel that carries oxygenated blood from the left ventricle of the heart to the rest of the body, is usually of fairly uniform width throughout its course from midchest upward toward the neck, then downward again through the chest and abdomen. Rarely, one small section of the aorta will be narrowed and this narrowing, called a coarctation, if severe enough, can cause inability of blood to get from the heart side of the narrowing to the leg side of the narrowing. If the narrowing happens to occur in the lower chest or abdomen, the presenting symptom is usually high blood pressure above with normal or low blood pressure below. Usually, in this form of the disorder, there will be no other cardiovascular complication; blood can reach the legs through the major blood vessels that take off from the aorta above the narrowing. But in rare cases, the narrowing will occur in the segment of the aorta that is adjacent to the heart, the region before the takeoff of any of these major blood vessels and, when this happens, blood will flow to the rest of the body only as long as a fetal structure, called the ductus arteriosus, remains open. The ductus, a structure that serves in fetal life to shunt blood away from the lungs, where it is not needed since the fetus receives all the oxygen it needs from the mother's blood through the placenta, usually closes within the first three or four days of life.

Babies born with preductal coarctation of the aorta do well until the ductus closes, but then they run into a lot of problems. Baby Girl Donovan, now three days old, had a preductal coarctation and a closing ductus and she was heading for big trouble.

"What do we do now?" I asked Dan and Dr. Channin.

"We've got to get this young lady back to the Medical Center," Channin said, "and fast. It's a good thing I already ordered an ambulance."

"Why'd you call an ambulance?" Dan asked.

"Well, I wasn't going to take the Srnivasan twins back with me in my car," he answered. "And when the patients are this big, there's always room in the ambulance for one more."

"You're taking the Srnivasan twins back tonight?" I asked excitedly.

"Sure," Channin answered. "It worked out very well. I don't know how ethical it is, but the mother sure is happy. I had a nice talk with her, told her what the problems were and what we needed to do. We became such good friends that she even invited me to her house for dinner after she gets discharged. And by the way, Bob, you were right; she sure hates all your guts."

"You mean you're transferring the twins without telling Sullivan?" Dan asked, piecing together the story.

"Yeah," Channin responded, "and when I heard Bob's plan, I was almost positive that you had to be involved, Dan. You know these guys have already had formal complaints lodged against them by Sullivan, don't you, Dan?"

"Sullivan complained to Jennings about you guys?" Dan asked me, the smile vanishing from his face. I nodded yes.

"And I don't think Sullivan'll be exactly ecstatic when he finds out you've moved the twins," Channin added.

"Can they get fired for having two formal complaints within a month?" Dan asked.

"I don't really know," Channin responded after some hesitation. "As far as I know, it's never happened before. But, we'd better come up with some plan. Let me think about it. I've got to go talk to the mother of this baby. The child will need a cath tonight and may need emergency surgery. I'll be back in a few minutes."

After Channin was gone, I sat in the nurses' station and watched Dan write a short note in Baby Girl Donovan's chart explaining his findings and their significance. On our way back to the Pit, I said, "You are amazing!"

"Why do you say that?" Dan asked.

"You picked up that coarctation. You saved that baby's life. That's terrific."

"Oh, come on, Bob, you got the diagnosis, too."

"Yeah, but I knew there was something wrong with that baby, and I still had to have you tell me what to look for. Even Dr. Channin said he wouldn't have picked it up. I'll never be able to do what you just did."

We entered the Pit to find that the ambulance driver, who was being assisted by Dr. Channin, was transferring the twins onto a gurney. Mrs. Srnivasan was standing by, watching the scene, as were a number of the nurses. The driver and Channin moved the gurney to the door and then stopped, and Channin approached Dan and me. "We're on our way," Channin said. "I've spoken with Mrs. Donovan. She was shocked about what I told her, but I got her to believe that the transfer was necessary, and she signed the consent form. Bob, I even figured out a way to ensure that you and the other two accessories to this crime will avoid having a pink slip signed by Jennings attached to your first paycheck. You just tell Sullivan, when he goes apeshit tomorrow after he realizes that his favorite pair of Siamese twins have been stolen, that this was all my idea and that I arranged the whole thing. The worst that can happen to me is that he'll call Jennings to complain about my unprofessional behavior and then vow never to speak to me again. I can easily handle the first of those and would gladly welcome the second. Well," he said as he began pushing the gurney out, "wish me luck."

"Good luck," I said as we walked to the elevator, "and thanks."

"Just remember one thing, Dr. Channin," Dan added. "Always face forward in the ambulance. If you face back, you'll puke on the patient."

"I'll keep that in mind," Channin responded. "And, guys, don't hesitate to call again if you need another set of Siamese twins kidnapped. The AAA Ambulance Company and I are experts in the field of Siamese twin removal." And with that, the elevator doors closed.

Dan spent the rest of the evening in his on-call room as there wasn't much going on. By eleven-fifteen I finished all the scut work Ray and Terry had signed out to me and decided to check the DR to see if anything was brewing down there.

I found Tom Fredericks right where he should have been—sitting in the easy chair in his on-call room, watching TV. The Red Sox were playing the Oakland A's in California. When I walked in, the game was in the top of the third inning, and the Sox had the bases loaded with two outs and Carlton Fisk at the plate. The game was scoreless. Tom saw me and signaled for me to sit down.

The count on Fisk was two and one. All of Tom's energy was concentrated on the TV screen, and he said softly, "C'mon, Pudge, little bingo, little bingo, let's go, clean up those bases, let's go, babe."

The next pitch was a called strike, and the count went to two balls and two strikes. "C'mon, Pudge, it only takes one, let's go, babe, a single brings in two, c'mon, babe," he droned on.

The next pitch was a called strike on the outside part of the plate, and Fisk didn't even argue the call with the umpire. He threw his bat away and was replaced on the screen by Jim Rice eating a hot dog in a commercial. "You bastard!" Tom shouted, standing up. "You damned bastard! You strike out and leave three men on base? And they're paying you over a hundred thousand bucks a year? Ah well . . ." Tom remembered I was in the room and turned his attention to me. "Hi, Bob, how're you doing?" I nodded. "That Fisk, that damned Fisk," he continued, "what a bastard. Well, how are things with you, Bob, how are things with you?"

"Fine," I said, "pretty busy, but fine."

"I know what you mean, Bob, know what you mean. The first quarter of the moon's past and it's the time of the month to get on with babies being born."

"How are things with you?" I asked. "With probation and all?"

"So far, there's no difference. Only thing I can't do is talk back to Parris, which is fine since he's leaving on vacation a week from tomorrow and won't be back until the middle of August. How'd things go during your meeting with Murderer's Row?"

I told him everything that had happened to us involving Sullivan, both during and after the hospital board meeting. "Sounds nice," Tom said after I'd finished, "sounds real nice. Maybe we'll all get thrown out of here together and we can start our own hospital somewhere, with you guys taking care of the babies I deliver. And we won't let Parris in."

"Or Sullivan," I added.

"Or Sullivan, right." The game was back on with Oakland now at bat. The first batter hit a fly ball to center field that was misplayed by Fred Lynn into a two-base error. "Shit," Tom exclaimed. Then to me, "Bob, you like the Sox?"

"Well, you know I was born in the Bronx and I spent a lot of time there, so actually, I'm a Yankee fan," I said quietly. I had learned that admitting out loud to being a Yankee fan while in Boston could be hazardous to my health.

"Shit," Tom exclaimed again, "a Yankee fan? Well . . . I guess I can't hold that against you much since my wife likes the Yankees, too. She's from New Jersey."

The next Oakland hitter hit a ground ball through the legs of the pitcher and out into center field for a single. The runner scored from second and Tom exclaimed "shit" for the third time, as he jumped out of his chair and switched off the TV. "Gotta go make rounds," he said.

"Anything going on?" I asked.

"Well, we got a twenty-four weeker out there," he answered. "Kid's not viable, I don't think, not viable at all, so I don't think she's going to be a problem for you guys. It's sad, though, this lady's lost a lot of pregnancies in the past. She hasn't had a kid who's been viable yet. Besides her, there are a couple of patients of private docs out there lying around in labor. Including one of Parris's. Bob, is he going to be pissed when he gets my call about her, the night before he's supposed to go on vacation. But I'll love calling him, Bob, I'll just love waking him up."

"I guess I'll see you later then," I said. And I left the delivery area.

I went back to the Pit and walked around the sickie row, making sure all the disasters were stable. As I was finishing my rounds, on my way to the on-call room and dreamland, I got beeped to the DR. It wasn't a stat page, so I called 3434 and waited.

After speaking to the clerk, Tom came on. "Hi, Bob, how are things?"

"Okay," I answered. "What's up? What are the Sox doing?"

"Getting creamed, Bob, getting creamed. I'm sorry to bother you but you know that twenty-four weeker I told you about?"

"Yeah," I answered, "the one that's not viable?"

"Right. Well, she's about to deliver. You want to come, just in case the baby's bigger than I think it is?"

"Sure," I answered, "I'll be right down." I hung up and called Dan in his on-call room. He said he'd meet me in the DR in five minutes.

I got down there before Dan. The patient had already been brought to DR 2. I changed into a green scrub suit that had been washed probably close to a million times and had shrunk down to the point where it was only laughingly too large, and proceeded to the DR. Tom was sitting on a stool, facing the woman's perineum, patiently waiting for the next contraction. The woman began sobbing when the next contraction came.

Dan entered, his eyes drooping, looking even sleepier than he usually did. I had everything set up by that point, so we just waited together. The contractions were coming about every two minutes. We saw the top of the little head peak through the vagina with every contraction, and watched it disappear again when the contraction ended. Finally, Tom said, "I think this next one is going to be it."

And with the next contraction, the baby was forcefully expelled from the birth canal and landed in Tom's waiting hands. Tom suctioned some amniotic fluid from the baby's nose with a bulb syringe, clamped the still-pulsating umbilical cord in two places, and cut the cord between the clamps. He carried the baby to our warming table.

He was so tiny! Dan was reluctant to do anything. We talked in whispers so the mother, who was sobbing quietly, would not hear.

"This baby can't weigh more than a pound," Dan said. The baby, who didn't move at all, except to make some gasping motions, looked literally like a fish out of water.

"Well, he's trying to breathe," I said, pointing to the chest which was pulling in and pushing out regularly. "Should we give him some oxygen?"

"Sure," Dan said and he got the hose through which 100-percent oxygen flowed from the nipple in the wall and placed it up near the baby's nose. Dan began to examine the child. "See this?" he asked, demonstrating that the eyelids wouldn't open. "The eyelids are fused. That's a sure sign that the baby's less than twenty-six weeks. Babies less than twenty-six weeks aren't viable. You want to try intubate him? For practice?"

"I'll try," I said. While I was messing around with the laryngoscope and the smallest endotracheal tube I could find, attempting to place that tube down into the baby's windpipe, Dan walked over to the mother's side and put his hand on hers. "The baby's very small," he said firmly. "There's not much we can do for him."

The mother was Puerto Rican and barely understood enough English. "Oh please, Señor Médico," she said back to Dan between sobs, "please no throw my baby in the garbage." She then went back to sobbing.

"No, no, don't worry, Señora," Dan responded. "We'd never throw the baby in the garbage."

He left the mother and came back to me and the baby. "Having trouble," he asked, noticing I had not yet passed the tube. I could tell by his voice and the look in his eyes that he was fighting off tears. I didn't have to answer his question; all I had to do was leave the bewildered look on my face that had appeared as soon as I began trying to pass the tube. "It's pretty easy," he said, now getting a better grip on himself. "Push the tongue away with the laryngoscope. Now look in the back of the throat. There should be two openings. You see two openings?" I did. "The one in the back is the esophagus. Don't put the tube in there. The other one looks like it's got strings around it?" I nodded. "Those strings are the vocal cords. The hole between them is the trachea. Put the tube in there." Dan was now back together. He was amazing; he was able to bury all his emotions when technical work had to be done.

I put the tube between the strings. And the tube passed in.

"Okay, put the ambu bag on the end of the tube and start pushing on it." I did as ordered and the chest expanded. "Mazel tov, Dr. Sharon," Dan said, "you've now successfully intubated a baby!"

I had. I really intubated this tiny baby. I began pushing 100-percent oxygen into the lungs via the ambu bag and the ET tube. Dan, listening to the chest, found the heart beating around fifty times per minute. "Bob, you can see all that oxygen's not doing anything. The baby's still pretty blue, but he's got a heart rate and so we have to take him up to the Pit and keep him there until the heart stops." Dan went back to tell the mother we were taking the baby upstairs.

"Oh thank you, Señor Médico," she said with some hope in her voice. "Baby will live?"

"The baby is very small and very sick," Dan said again. "I don't think he'll make it, but we'll do our best."

The mother sighed. "Thank you for not throwing baby in garbage, Señor Médico. The way they do in Arecibo."

Dan sighed, did not answer, then turned back to me. Together we put the baby in the transport incubator and took him slowly up to the Pit. Dan told me not to bother bagging the baby, because it was obvious that this was not helping, so I just placed the 100-percent oxygen hose near the endotracheal tube opening. Angela met us when we reached the Pit and Dan instructed her to keep the baby in the transport incubator, with the oxygen running in, and to monitor the heart rate every hour. It was still, at this point, about fifty beats per minute.

"This is terrible," Dan said to me and Angela, "these are the cases I hate the most. This baby isn't really alive, but he's not truly dead either. Even with all the technology Sullivan has, there's nothing he could do to keep this baby alive for long. Sure, with massive, expensive, and painful care, he could probably manage to keep the heart beating for a day or two, but physiologically, it's impossible for this kid to survive. So what can we, as rational people, do? We have to sit here and let him die with as much dignity as possible. My policy is no blood work, no IVs, no respirators, just keep the baby warm and comfortable and call the priest."

The priest was called and the baby was baptized. The oxygen was continued and the temperature was maintained at ninety-eight degrees. I sat on a stool at one end of the transport incubator, and Dan sat on a stool at the other end. Intermittently, Angela came and stood vigil with us. And we waited for the baby to die.

Even with all the technological advances that had been made to keep premature babies alive, any baby born more than fourteen weeks prematurely cannot survive. This is because of a physiologic phenomenon. The lungs are made of millions of tiny air sacs called alveoli which are in close proximity with tiny blood vessels called capillaries. In the mature lung, the alveoli and capillaries are so close that gases such as carbon dioxide and oxygen can flow unrestricted between them. Before twenty-six weeks of gestation, the distance between the capillaries and alveoli is too great to allow transfer of these gases. Therefore in babies like this one, gas exchange is impossible, and the babies die with too much carbon dioxide and not enough oxygen in their blood.

Through this long night, while we waited for this poor baby's heart to cease its beating, Dan napped while I read from Berenson's textbook on neonatology, chatted with Angela, and napped myself. The baby survived for five more hours. The morning sun was pouring through the Pit's picture windows and I was asleep on my stool when Angela nudged me to tell me the heart had finally halted. I listened with my stethoscope. Nothing. I woke Dan and he listened with his. Nothing.

"I hereby pronounce this baby dead," Dan said solemnly.

"Amen," I added.

"You know, it's kind of funny," Dan said. "We usually lose sleep trying like hell to keep these babies alive. Tonight, we lost sleep to make sure one died."

Dan went back to his on-call room to get an hour more of sleep. Angela came over to me and together, for a few undisturbed minutes, we studied this infant in silence. Then Angela said, "I've been working in ICUs for four years. I've been working in this Pit for fourteen months. I don't think I'll ever get used to them dying."

"It's for the best," I said. "He's so small."

"It's usually for the best. But still, it's not like any other feeling I've ever had. They're so small, so helpless. Are you guys going to get into trouble for letting him die?"

"I don't think so," I answered naïvely. "I don't think even Sullivan would be angry. The baby just wasn't viable."

"You'd be surprised," Angela answered. "That man's crazy. And so is Kathy, who'll do just about anything he asks. They're the reason I asked to be put on nights."

"Yeah?" I asked.

"Yeah. I never worked nights before coming here, but two weeks working with those two during the day and I'd had enough. I had to reorganize my whole life to work nights, but I think it's worth it."

"Why do you stay?" I asked. "Why not go to another unit?"

"Well, in spite of Sullivan and Kathy, this place is still the best center in New England. And the pay here is excellent. So it's worth it, even with those maniacs."

Angela went back to care for the living and the near-dead while I continued to examine the dead infant in front of me. I looked closely at his fingers and toes, so small and yet so perfectly formed. His face was the face of a fetus, but with all the features programmed to mature into those of a full-term infant, then a child, then an adult, and finally those of an old man. And because this child was born a few weeks too soon, because he had been removed from the protecting, nurturing environment of his mother's womb, this preprogrammed growth, the maturation of the fetus, the miraculous reproduction of the adult human, which brings about and guarantees survival of our species, would never occur in this tiny, lifeless being.

I inspected this baby closely, these thoughts percolating through my tired mind on that very early Friday morning for nearly forty-five minutes. And then, as eight o'clock neared, I went off to brush my teeth.

XXV

Friday, July 9
Morning Rounds

Terry came in first. She found me sitting in the nurses' station, hunching over a cup of black coffee. "Hi," she said, "how was it?"

I thought for a second and then responded, "Don't ask.".

"That bad? Get any sleep?"

"Not really."

At that point Ray came strolling in and repeated the question, "How was it?"

"Well, on paper, it doesn't sound bad. We have two heads fewer than we had yesterday at this time. However, I did get one admission who died this morning, Dan made a terrific diagnosis that saved a baby's life, and that child as well as a pair of Siamese twins were transferred to the Medical Center."

Ray's and Terry's eyes lit up. "Would the twins you're referring to happen to be the Srnivasans?" Terry asked.

"That is correct," I answered. "Dr. Channin came yesterday afternoon, listened to the plan, and didn't object. He talked to the parents and they loved him. They even invited him to their house for dinner. Not only that, Mrs. Srnivasan was more than happy to consent to transfer the babies out of here, so Channin called the AAA Ambulance Company and they all disappeared into the sunset."

"Hot damn," Ray said. "Bob, you just made my day."

"Well, it's still pretty early," I responded, "I still have a lot of time to ruin it." We all laughed. "By the way, Channin was very upset that

Sullivan had lodged a formal complaint against us, and he was afraid that if another one got called in, we might all get automatically fired. So he told me to blame the whole transfer on him. He is terrific!"

"He sounds terrific," Terry said. "I hope I get a chance to meet him before we get thrown out of here. Sullivan's going to be crazy when he hears about this. You transferred out another kid?"

"Yeah," I answered, "great case. Dan was doing a discharge physical on a baby in the regular nursery and he noticed the kid's feet were blue. So he checked the pulses and they were strong in the arms and absent in the legs. Then he checked the blood pressure and found hypertension in the arms, and . . ."

"You mean he diagnosed a coarctation of the aorta on routine physical exam?" Ray asked.

"Yeah," I answered, "and he saved the baby's life."

"That's great," Terry said. "Lord, that's terrific. That's like being . . . like being a real doctor!"

"Yeah, instead of being a real scut carrier like we are," Ray added.

"I was really proud of Dan. Even Channin was impressed."

Our conversation was interrupted at this point by the appearance of Frohman, Kathy, and, of course, Sullivan. They were all ready to begin gargantuan Friday morning rounds.

We interns didn't exactly know how best to play this; after the blowup in Sullivan's office the morning before, none of us wanted to have anything to do with our attending. However, we did need to discuss our patients in order to decide on a plan of management.

It turned out that Sullivan wanted to have as little to do with us as we wanted to have to do with him, but he needed to get the story on most of the patients concerning what had occurred since Thursday afternoon. That information, of course, was only available from me. Without any discussion of the matter, we hit upon a compromise: we ignored each other and spoke through the most neutral entity. That entity was Frohman. The situation was very maturely handled.

On rounds that morning, Frohman and Sullivan led the way. Unfortunately for me, the first stop we made was at the transport incubator in which the very premature baby had died. Because I had been standing over the baby, musing for nearly an hour after the baby's death, Angela hadn't been able to prepare the body for its trip to the morgue. When the nurses had changed shifts, the day nurses, trying to first dispense the care necessary for the more alive patients, had not yet gotten around to disposing of the child. So there he lay, dead as a proverbial doornail, in the transporter.

When Sullivan saw the body, he did a slow burn. In a hushed, very serious voice, he said, "Dr. Frohman, what is this baby doing here?"

"I don't know, Dr. Sullivan," Frohman said. "Berkowitz didn't sign this baby out to me."

"Where's Berkowitz? Why isn't he at rounds?"

"I don't know, Dr. Sullivan," Frohman said. "He said he had something more important to do."

"I'll bet," said Sullivan. "Well, which one of these shining examples of humanity was on call last night?"

I was surprised that Sullivan had to ask this question. Ray and Terry had slept at home in their beds the night before and they looked relaxed and well rested. I, on the other hand, was wearing a sweaty, blood- and meconium-stained green scrub suit, was unwashed, uncombed, and unshaven, and had bloodshot eyes with dark circles under them. But still, Frohman had to say, "Sharon."

"Well, Dr. Frohman, perhaps Dr. Sharon will tell us what this baby's doing here."

Frohman really did ask. "Dr. Sharon, what is this baby doing here?"

I couldn't resist. "Nothing," I said directly to Frohman. "He's dead."

"Dr. Frohman," Sullivan returned, obviously waving simultaneous translation, "I can see that this baby has . . . passed. Why is it, Dr. Frohman, that I was not called at home concerning this baby? I have said this so many times that I wonder why I keep repeating it. I have left explicit instructions that I should be called whenever a sick baby is born. And yet, I come in this morning and find this."

"I don't know why you weren't called, Dr. Sullivan," Frohman responded. "I didn't get any sign-out."

"Well, perhaps Dr. Sharon will tell you."

And again Frohman asked, "Dr. Sharon, why wasn't Dr. Sullivan called?"

"Well, Simon," I answered, "we didn't call Dr. Sullivan at home because this baby was not viable. He was only twenty-four weeks by dates, he weighed only fifteen ounces, and his eyelids were fused."

"I see," Dr. Sullivan said solemnly. He looked to the ceiling for a few seconds and then said, "Dr. Frohman, did the baby have a heart rate at birth?"

"I don't know, Dr. Sullivan. I didn't get . . ."

"Yes," I interrupted. I couldn't go through this nonsense anymore. "The heart rate was sixty in the DR. The baby was intubated, by me and bagged with 100-percent oxygen. But the heart rate and color did not improve, so we brought him up here to await . . ."

"Dr. Frohman," Dr. Sullivan interrupted me, "have you ever seen a baby with fused eyelids survive for any length of time?"

"No, sir," Frohman answered. "They all died."

"I have," Sullivan returned quickly. "I've kept babies alive for weeks who were born with fused eyelids, and I'm sure it is conceivable that some of these children may survive much longer. So you see, Dr. Frohman, I can't understand how an intern can independently make a decision to do nothing because he feels, with his vast experience, that the child is inviable."

I wanted to go for his jugular, but even in my debilitated, sleep-deprived state, I managed to hold myself back. Instead, I went for the textbook, the copy of Berenson's I had left on the stool on which I had been sitting. Without directly responding to Sullivan's challenge, I read the following passage from the chapter entitled "Evaluation of Gestational Age":

> Generally speaking, the best parameter to utilize in the delivery room when presented with a very premature infant is the presence of eyelid fusion. This fusion, which normally persists until the gestational age at which the alveolar-capillary distance has become small enough to support mature gas exchange, is an easily-observable marker of physiologic viability.

I also read another passage, "No baby with a birth weight of 500 grams or less has ever been reported to survive the neonatal period." "Dr. Frohman," I said at the conclusion of my reading, "I will admit that I do not have nearly the depth of experience that Dr. Sullivan has, but I'd bet that Berenson does. Is Dr. Sullivan telling us that he knows more than the author of this textbook and the man considered the father of neonatology?"

Neither Frohman nor Sullivan answered. I knew I had him, just like Dr. Adams had him every Friday afternoon. Sullivan, rather than responding, simply walked on to the first bed in the first row of babies. I had succeeded in shutting him up, at least temporarily, and in getting rounds moving again.

Rounds continued for a good long time after that without incident. We spoke about the Dead Kid, whose condition hadn't changed any and who was to be getting another dialysis treatment that afternoon from the crack nephrology group. Dr. Sullivan had had the baby started on heavy-duty antibiotics as a prophylactic measure because he was afraid the baby would die of an overwhelming infection, resulting from the spearing his intestine had received during the first dialysis. We made a stop at the bedside of Terry's premie, Baby Singer, who was now able to breathe room air and who would be transferred to the growers row in a day or two. Sullivan examined Sharon Frederica O'Hara's belly and pronounced it good as new, while Kathy noted how fulfilling a case like Sharon Frederica's was because it really gave us a chance to do something to save a baby and to make her normal. The baby was now taking fluids through a bottle and the intestine was holding up so well that she'd be ready for discharge sometime during the following week.

After what seemed like forever, we finally reached the empty warming table on which the Srnivasan twins had recently resided. At first Sullivan didn't seem to notice that they were gone; he went right on to the next patient. But then after a short time, the conspicuousness of their absence hit him. "Dr. Frohman," he said, just slightly panicked, "where are my twins?"

Frohman thought for a few seconds, then said, "Why, I don't know, Dr. Sullivan. They weren't signed out to me."

This time I wasn't about to volunteer any information.

"Perhaps Dr. Sharon knows where they are," Sullivan said, losing patience.

"Yes," I returned thoughtfully, "I do know that."

"Well?" Sullivan asked.

"Well?" Frohman asked.

"Well what?" I answered, trying to be cute.

"Where are they, Dr. Sharon?" Sullivan asked testily, not appreciating my cuteness. "What have you done with my twins?"

"I haven't done anything with your twins. They've gone to the Medical Center."

Sullivan, his face turning bright red, looked to the ceiling. He seemed to be holding his breath, but then he looked directly into my eyes for the first time that morning and, shouting, asked, "Dr. Sharon, who authorized the transfer of those twins to the Medical Center?"

"The mother signed a consent-for-transfer form," I answered.

"No, Dr. Sharon. I mean, which attending physician asked her to sign the consent? It certainly wasn't me and, last time I checked, I'm the attending-of-record in this nursery."

"Dr. Channin got the consent form signed," I said, trying to look and sound as innocent as possible.

"So it was Channin!" Sullivan roared. "That shit! Who gave him the right to steal my patient?"

"He didn't steal your patient," I replied calmly. "He told Mrs. Srnivasan that he thought the babies needed a more complete workup. It was the first time she had had the opportunity to talk with any attending. He recommended that the babies be transferred to the Medical Center and, since she had heard no opinion to the contrary from you or anyone else, and since she was so overjoyed to have the opportunity to speak with an attending, she signed the consent form right away and Dr. Channin took the twins over last night. They left at about ten o'clock. So, if you want to blame somebody, blame yourself for not going to talk to the mother personally."

Sullivan was livid! He looked at me, at Kathy, at Frohman, back at me, and, finally, at the empty warming table. After staring into this void for a few seconds, he turned and stormed out of the Pit.

"You idiots!" Kathy yelled at us after Sullivan had departed. "How could you do such a thing to those babies? Dr. Sullivan wanted to make sure they both survived, and you've fixed it so that at least one of them will surely die! And knowing the way that Dover operates, neither of them will probably make it out of there alive! You interns are all alike! Nobody other than Dr. Sullivan should be trusted to take care of these babies!"

"Shut the fuck up, Kathy," Terry yelled back at her, with fire in her eyes. "I've had about enough of you, too. We're doing what we think is best for our patients! And we tend to trust Channin more than we trust you or Sullivan, that's for sure. It's you and that maniac who shouldn't be allowed to take care of these kids! You're both crazy!"

Kathy sneered. "You interns will never learn!" And with that, she, too, stormed out of the Pit. We assumed, at this point, that morning rounds had come to an end.

XXVI

Afternoon

We didn't have grand rounds that Friday morning; when we tried to get into Sullivan's office, we found the door locked. So we went to the cafeteria and ate lunch instead, and it was a far better way to use the hour. After lunch we went to the auditorium on the first floor for the combined obstetric/neonatal conference.

Dan was already in the room when we arrived, and we sat down next to him. "How'd rounds go this morning?" Dan asked. "I was tempted to show up in person, just to watch Sullivan go crazy when he saw the twins were gone. It must have been great."

"He went crazy all right," Terry said. "He's a pretty scary guy."

"That asshole," Ray said. "I've had it with him. Dan would you like to replace Sullivan as our attending for the rest of the month?"

"Sure," Dan answered, "but do you really think you need to replace him?"

We didn't get a chance to respond, as Sullivan entered the room at that point, yelling to Kathy, "Those fucking interns better keep their mouths shut! 'Cause if any of 'em makes a sound, I'm gonna break his face!"

"Oh, Christ!" Dan sighed. It was obvious, from his tone of voice, from his staggering gait, and from his appearance, that Sullivan was drunk. No doubt while we had been in the cafeteria eating our lunch, he had been in his office drinking his. As they made their way to the front of the room, Kathy supported her boss as if he were a sack of potatoes.

The rest of the staff soon arrived and the conference was begun by Dr. Adams. "We'd like to discuss the case of Mrs. Smith," he said. "Dr. Fredericks will present the case."

"Great," Dan whispered. "I wish I had some popcorn."

Fredericks walked to the front of the room and reviewed the Dead Kid's journey from Nashua, New Hampshire, where he had been a fetus in some distress, through the ambulance ride, and finally to the point where the infant was handed to Dan and me in the DR. "Thank you, Tom," Dr. Adams said upon the completion of Tom's discussion. "Would the pediatric house officer involved in the case like to give us an idea of how the baby is presently doing?"

"Sure," I said as I rose from my seat and walked slowly to the front of the room, keeping my eyes on Sullivan during the trip to see if he was going to try to stop me. He didn't, and I completed the report of the Dead Kid's journey. "The baby had severe meconium aspiration syndrome and suffered a long period of hypoxia. As a result, he now has renal failure, for which he's being dialyzed, he's brain-dead, he's got necrotizing enterocolitis, and he might be septic."

"I see," Dr. Adams said. "What is currently being done for him?"

"Well, he's getting the dialysis treatment, as I've already said, he's ventilator-dependent, with no spontaneous respirations of his own, he's on a dopamine drip to maintain his blood pressure, and on tolazoline."

"So what you're saying, Doctor," Adams said with a pained look on his face, "is this baby is dead but is not being allowed to die."

"That's essentially correct," I answered.

"That's bullshit!" Sullivan shouted from his seat. "The only thing wrong with that baby is he had an incompetent intern and resident takin' care of him the first night after he was born. The only problem is they didn't call me so I could tell 'em what to do! None of my babies are safe up there. I can't trust any of these house officers." Sullivan was slurring his speech.

"John, control yourself!" Adams ordered, shocked by Sullivan's speech and his behavior. "I think it is clear, from Dr. Fredericks's description of the prenatal course, that this baby was significantly damaged intrauterinely. What I don't understand is why you are now torturing him by not allowing him to die. Would you address that, John?"

"Why are we doin' what we're doin'?" Sullivan slurred. "It's none of your damned business!"

"John, one of the reasons I decided to discuss this case today is because I received a call earlier this week from Dr. Smith, the baby's father. He asked me to intercede in this case. So, as the father's advocate, it certainly is my business!"

"The father called you?" Sullivan screamed. "Okay, if you wanna know why we're doin' what we're doin', I'll tell you, and you can tell that damned father so he'll get off my back. We're doin' what we're doin' 'cause we're gonna make this baby normal again. We're gonna make him into a normal baby!"

"A normal baby?" Adams asked. "John, the baby's brain-dead! All you're doing is flexing your technological muscle. He'll never be normal." Then gently, kindly, Adams said, "John, if you don't mind my saying so, I think you need a rest. Your behavior here, your judgment, I think you're under a lot of stress."

"I don't have to take this shit!" Sullivan shouted, rising clumsily from his seat. "You can't talk to me like that! You stand there so damned self-righteous, like you can judge me, like you're better than me, and you tell me what I need and what I should do. I'm getting the fuck out of here!" And he lumbered out of the auditorium, stumbling occasionally, weaving down the aisle.

After he had gone, Adams said, "I tried. That's all I could do," to Tom Fredericks. I returned to where Dan, Terry, and Ray were still sitting. "Well, we've just seen history," Dan said.

"History?" Terry asked.

"That's the first time Adams has actually succeeded in getting Sullivan to walk out. I really think Sullivan's flipped. He used to be able to contain the drinking so that just about no one could figure out that he was doing it, but now it seems like he can't control it anymore."

"You mean he drinks that much?" I asked, surprised.

"Well, I might as well tell you now," Dan said, "since the cat seems to be out of the bag; that was my secret about Sullivan. One night when I was an intern, they were painting the intern's on-call room and I had to sleep in his office. I wasn't trying to find anything; it was early in the month and I hadn't even learned to hate him yet, but I found an empty pint bottle of gin in the garbage can. It might or might not have been Sullivan's, I didn't know, but I decided to watch him very carefully and I noticed, as you guys have, that Sullivan's very unpredictable; one minute he'll seem crazed with anger, the next he's like your best friend. And then near the end of the month, I walked into his office, which is usually locked in the afternoon but wasn't that day, and found him sitting at his desk, alone, drinking out of a hip flask. I'll never forget the look on his face. First he looked guilty and ashamed of himself, but then his face twisted up with anger and he got up and yelled, 'Get the fuck out of here,' at me. I knew then that he must have been drinking all month long, and that was why he was so inconsistent."

"That's the secret?" Ray asked. "That's all it was? That Sullivan's an alcoholic?"

"That's all," Dan said.

"And he's not a homosexual or an ex-convict, and it had nothing to do with whether or not he went to medical school?" Ray asked.

"No, just that he's an alcoholic," Dan answered. "It is kind of sad. . . ."

"Yeah, it is kind of sad," Terry said, "but it's also frightening that an alcoholic can be given so much power, and be able to make life-and-death decisions."

"I sort of agree with Adams," Ray said, now over his disappointment. "I think Sullivan needs a long vacation."

We interns returned to the Pit to finish our work. The worst part of a night on call without sleep occurs the next afternoon. The brain doesn't want to do any more work until it gets to sleep for a while. I was sitting in the nurses' station, trying to write some progress notes, but I kept getting distracted; I'd write a line and then have to stop to admire the pen I was using; I'd write another line and then look up and stare off into the Pit at a baby drinking from a bottle. As a result, getting my work done wasn't going to be easy.

"Dial ninety-nine for an outside call," my beeper squawked. I thought about the tremendous tone the beeper had for a while and almost forgot to answer its call, but I finally dialed the number and said, "Hello?"

"Bob?" the voice said. "This is Harold Channin. How are things over there?"

"Here?" I repeated. "Fine. I'm a little tired, but things are fine."

"A little tired?" he repeated. "You're supposed to be a little tired, aren't you? That's the natural state of the intern. I'm calling to find out if Sullivan's taken a contract out on you guys yet."

"Nope," I answered. "He was pretty mad, but he had no reason to be angry with us. I blamed everything on you."

"Oh good. That makes me feel very comfortable. He'll probably take out a contract on me. Anyway, I have a few things to tell you. First, I've already been subpoenaed to appear in Jennings's office this afternoon about this whole mess, but that won't be much of a problem. Jennings can't really do anything to me, but he's got to make it look like I've been disciplined so that Sullivan won't bug him forever. The big news is that that damned Berkowitz was right! I cathed that baby last night, and damned if she didn't have a preductal coarctation. The narrowing was so severe that there was just about no blood getting through, so Dr. Dover took her to the OR last night and he fixed her right up! The baby's fine today. Dan definitely saved her life," Channin said excitedly.

I even got excited, though one could barely tell in my debilitated condition. "That's great," I muttered.

"Well, don't run out and celebrate," Channin said back sarcastically. "You sound like death warmed over."

"I'm just really tired," I answered, "but I really am excited. By the way, how are the twins doing over there?"

"They're stable, and with all the excitement about the other baby, we haven't had a chance to do anything with them. They seem to like it here just fine, but they miss Sullivan and Mary Jane Doherty. I'll probably get around to cathing them next Monday."

"Okay," I said, "thanks for calling, Dr. Channin. And good luck with Jennings this afternoon." We both hung up. "Well, Dan was right," I turned and said to Ray and Terry, who were sitting next to me.

"The baby had a coarct?" Terry asked.

"A preductal coarct," I answered. "Channin said Dan definitely saved that little girl's life."

"Wow!" Ray said. "That was a good pickup."

"Good?" Terry repeated. "That was outstanding. God, that must be a great feeling. To be able to know enough to save a kid's life, just by doing a physical exam."

Ray and I agreed, and we all went back to writing our progress notes.

After finishing my work, I went to visit Mrs. O'Hara, who was sitting in a chair, alone in her room. "Hello, Dr. Sharon," she said with a smile on her face. "Everything all right with our little girl?"

"She's just fine," I answered. "How are you feeling?"

"Good. Pretty good. They stopped the antibiotic medicine this morning. See?" She raised both arms to show that they were no longer restrained. "No IV. And they tell me if everything goes okay, I'll be leaving tomorrow. I can't wait to get out of here. It's been such a long time since I've seen those boys of mine. I miss those kids a lot."

"Well, it's good to hear you're finally getting out of here. The baby will probably be able to go home early next week."

"That's good," she responded with a small amount of enthusiasm. "I've got a lot to do yet to get her room ready for her. She seems like a nice, friendly baby."

"She is," I answered. "She even sleeps through the night most of the time, and she hardly ever cries, except when she's hungry."

"I've been meaning to talk to you about a problem, Dr. Sharon. I don't know exactly what to do about a pediatrician for the baby. The doctor I used for the boys, well, he's a good doctor when the kids are pretty healthy, but he gets uneasy with kids who have complicated medical problems. I got the feeling from talking to him about Sharon that he didn't want to have anything to do with her."

"That's too bad," I said.

"I was thinking," she continued, "do you see private patients, Dr. Sharon?"

I blushed. "Well, Mrs. O'Hara, you know I'm just an intern. I can't really see private patients, but starting next month when I get back to the Medical Center, I will have clinic sessions once a week where I can see patients. Would you like to bring the baby to that?"

"I sure would," she said with some emotion. "It seems only right that Sharon be taken care of by the doctor she's named after."

I blushed again. "Okay," I said, "we'll make arrangements for her first visit when she goes home."

We talked for a few minutes more about infant care problems (Mrs. O'Hara was asking me questions, but it was clear she knew more about feeding and diapers and rashes than I did at that point), and when her telephone rang, I took the opportunity to say goodbye and leave the room.

There still was another patient's family I had to see that afternoon. I wasn't looking forward to this visit. It was with Mrs. Gonzalez, the woman who had delivered the very premature baby who had died that morning. Mrs. Gonzalez, in another private room on the third floor, was lying in bed sobbing when I entered the room. Her husband was sitting in a chair beside the bed. With a blank look on his face, he was staring up at the room's TV, which was tuned to "General Hospital."

"Mrs. Gonzalez," I said, standing close by the door, "I am Dr. Sharon. I took care of the baby while he was upstairs." My introduction brought a rise in Mrs. Gonzalez's sobbing, and Mr. Gonzalez turned off the TV by its remote-control switch and looked toward me; neither of them said a word.

"I'm sorry," I said after a long and awkward period of silence, "there was nothing we could do. The baby was too small and premature."

The sobbing crescendoed, and Mr. Gonzalez continued to stare at me with glassy eyes. Save for Mrs. Gonzalez's crying, we remained frozen in these positions, in silence, for nearly two minutes. Finally, Mr. Gonzalez spoke, "We are sorry, Señor Médico, to be too upset. We have no children. My wife, she be pregnant six time, and she lose every time the baby. This baby, she lose him later than the other ones. We both think, 'Good, this one be okay.' But then she begin having the pain, and she lose this one also."

"I'm sorry," I said again. "There was nothing we could do."

Mr. Gonzalez stared at me. We both listened to his wife cry. In a minute more, I said I had to go and left the room. I stood outside in the hall for a while without moving, listening to Mrs. Gonzalez's crying, mourning the loss of a baby, a very wanted baby, who was born too soon. I felt the familiar lump rise in my throat, but no tears came to my eyes, and I realized I was not able to cry. In these first two weeks of my internship, working with all the misery and the death, and the successes and normal babies produced by our modern technology, I had made the first step in the transition—the transition from the sensitive, feeling, and vulnerable medical student who had first walked into this strange place two weeks before, to the hardened, calloused, impenetrable house officer who would eventually walk out of the Pit for the last time in two more weeks. I did not welcome this transition. It was unfortunate, but it was a necessary change in order to function successfully in the world of medicine.

I headed back to the Pit, where in the nurses' station Ray and Terry were talking with a man who was wearing a clerical collar. I recognized the fat, friendly, and handsome face but could not place him. I overheard him say, "I understand what you three were trying to do at the meeting, and so I felt I should come and talk with you three about it. Is there a place we could be alone?" Ray suggested the on-call room and led the way.

When we were all seated, this man said to me, "I'm Father Walsh," and I then recognized him as the one member of the hospital board who had remained silent during the time we were in the meeting room. "I apologize for not speaking up for you during the meeting," he continued, "but I am really out of place on that board. The members don't want to be bothered by the recommendations of a patient's advocate. I used to speak up all the time when I was first appointed, but they all ignored what I had to say anyway. They just think of me as one more troublemaker, but I wanted you interns to know that I agree with you. I support you. It took a lot of guts to get up in front of that group in the first place. No other group of interns or residents has had those guts before. I think you three are special.

"I feel you three should know what was decided at the meeting. I'm telling you this as a friend, not in any official capacity. The decision was to table action on your complaint until a meeting sometime next month, when you three are gone and will, therefore, no longer represent a problem to the board. So, essentially, they've voted to do nothing about your complaint."

I took this news badly. I felt as if I had been kicked in the stomach. I also was feeling a little dizzy and I wasn't sure whether this was because I was upset, or just because I was so sleepy.

"Why exactly are you telling us this, Father?" Terry asked.

"Because, as I said, I agree with what you are trying to do. I've been involved in too many cases in which parents have been dissatisfied with Dr. Sullivan to believe that these are accidental or the result of isolated foul-ups. In dealing with patients and their families, Dr. Sullivan's record is disastrous. Something must be done about him, and I wish I could be the one to do it, but my resources and my powers are extremely limited. I was hoping that if I told you not to expect too much from the board, perhaps you would investigate using alternative avenues for your protest. Do you have any other plans?"

"It might be a good idea to try the newspapers," Terry said sadly.

"I must urge you to be very cautious with the press," the priest said. "A newspaper reporter, getting hold of the wrong piece of information, can have a devastating effect on the wrong people. You may wind up wounding Dr. Sullivan, but in the process risk destroying an innocent family."

"Well, maybe we'll just chain ourselves to the door of the delivery room and prevent any woman from getting in," I said, and we all laughed, but the on-call room was filled with depression. "We have to do something," I continued. "It's apparent to us that Sullivan is downright crazy, and he's getting worse all the time."

"Well, let me know if there's anything I can do to help," Father Walsh said, rising and walking toward the door.

"Thank you, Father," I said. "And thank you for coming." He nodded and left the room.

We sat in silence. Finally, Ray said, "You know, that's not a bad idea." I looked at Terry and she looked at me; we had absolutely no idea what Ray was talking about.

"What's not a bad idea?" Terry asked.

"Bob's idea about chaining ourselves in."

"You're joking," Terry said.

"Forget it," I responded. "It was just a little joke."

"No, really," Ray continued undaunted. "It'd get a lot of attention, I guess. You know, newspapers and TV coverage, stuff like that."

"You're crazy, Ray," Terry said. "It's unprofessional and they'd have to fire us."

"Well, I think we should consider it," Ray concluded.

We sat silently for a few more minutes. It was three-thirty when I next looked at my watch. "Holy shit!" I said, "I've got to get out of here. I've got to pick Rachel up at the airport at four." I ran into the nurses' station, got my sign-out sheets together, and gave them to Terry.

"Have a good weekend," she said with a gleam in her eyes. I smiled back, gave her a kiss on the cheek, and headed out of the hospital.

XXVII

Evening and Saturday, July 10

I made my way in the slowly building Friday afternoon traffic, through the Callahan tunnel and to Logan Airport. Rachel, looking weary, was waiting outside the Eastern terminal building.

"Hi," she said, a little annoyed as she got in. We hugged and kissed. "Where have you been?"

"Sorry," I responded. "I got a late jump from the hospital. It's been a long day. It's great to see you." Being as tired as I was, I said this pretty unconvincingly.

"You look awful," she said.

"Thanks," I answered, but she was right. I was covered with the dried gore and blood of a night on call. I was disheveled and I probably smelled pretty bad.

"At least you're not crying this week," she said with a smile.

"I didn't sleep at all last night," I said. "I need to go home and just crawl into bed."

"Before you crawl into bed, you need to jump into the shower."

I turned the car onto the expressway and headed toward the Mass Pike. The five-mile trip to the Watertown exit was spent in bumper-to-bumper traffic. Sitting in the midst of this chaos, we spoke mostly about Rachel's work. Although she was working in a biomedical science and I was in medicine, we spoke of our work in different languages; I couldn't understand her when she spoke in the language of molecular biology and she couldn't understand my long clinical harangues. Still, we tried to communicate.

"How'd your work go this week?" I asked. "Any closer to finishing?"

"Well, I had one big success this week and two big setbacks. I isolated a great batch of DNA on Tuesday and now have enough to last for the next two or three experiments. That'll save me some time."

"That's the success?" I guessed.

"Of course," she answered, "but something got screwed up when I nick-translated my probe on Wednesday and Thursday. I don't know what went wrong, so I'll have to set everything up again and start that over."

"I think what you're saying is, you're no closer to finishing than you were last week?" I really couldn't tell what this meant.

"I guess you could say that," she said. "It's so damned frustrating. I did all this stuff before. If it hadn't been for that damned explosion, I'd be out of there by now."

By this point we had reached the apartment complex and I parked the car. We walked inside, arm in arm, me carrying my doctor bag which was filled with dirty laundry, and Rachel carrying her overnight bag. When we reached the apartment, there was an embarrassing three-day collection of mail, consisting of nothing but a circular from a local supermarket.

"Would you like something to eat?" Rachel asked, but when she opened the refrigerator, she found the food we had bought the week before, still in its wrapping, untouched by human hands and beginning to look like a junior high school science project. "Yecch," she said, "this milk is just about ready to speak by itself. I think we've proven the theory of spontaneous generation."

I didn't respond. I shed my clothes and took a long, hot shower, washing down with soap four or five times, trying to remove the grime, sweat, pain, and tears that had accumulated since Thursday. After what seemed like an hour, I turned off the water, dried myself with a towel, put on clean underwear, and got into bed. I was nearly off in dreamland when Rachel pounced.

"Oh no you don't, Sharon!" she yelled. "You don't get to go to sleep yet. I only see you once a week, so you have to at least eat with me."

"Tomorrow," I said, and rolled over onto my belly, but Rachel started to tickle me about the ribs. Through years of experience, she knew where I was most vulnerable, and I convulsed with laughter. Finally, she stopped, I rolled over, and we made love.

I felt some pangs of guilt, and I found myself comparing my experience with Rachel with that with Terry on Wednesday night. But the guilt feeling didn't last long, and I fell soundly and deeply to sleep. I don't remember dreaming that night, but I do remember waking up the next morning at 11 A.M., having been asleep for over fifteen hours.

Rachel, fully dressed, was lying next to me in bed, reading a book on gene expression, light Saturday morning reading for her. "Welcome back to the kingdom of the living," she said when she realized my eyes had finally opened.

"Ugghh," I responded, always very personable when I awoke.

"I thought you were in coma. If you weren't awake by noon, I was going to call an ambulance."

"What year is it?" I asked, checking my chin to make sure I had not grown a long, white beard. "Am I still an intern?"

"Yep. But there're only fifty weeks left, counting vacations."

I embraced Rachel tightly and she hugged me back. "I miss you," I whispered. "I don't know if I can take a whole year like this."

"I know I can't," she whispered back. "This isn't how life is supposed to be lived."

I sighed. "I'm sorry I ranked the Medical Center. If I had listened to you, we'd be back in New York, happy and well rested."

"Don't be a schmuck, Bob. The only reason we're not together is because of what happened in the lab. I would have been done, and we would have been together up here. If that explosion hadn't happened!"

"Well, is there anything we can do now?" I asked.

"I don't know," she said. "I've been thinking about taking a leave of absence."

"But you're nearly finished. If you stop, you may never get done."

"Things haven't been going well lately. Before the accident, I was pretty enthusiastic about my work. Now . . . I don't know, my heart isn't in it anymore. Maybe if I take the rest of the year off, I'll get excited about science again."

"Well, don't do anything for another week or two. I may get fired by then." I smiled sheepishly.

"Fired?" she repeated with surprise. "You can't get fired."

"Sure I can. If Ray and Terry and I cause enough trouble, they can fire us."

"Holy cow!" Rachel said, sounding just like Phil Rizzuto, "what have you done?"

"Well, we're always getting into fights with our attending, and disobeying his orders and complaining about him to the hospital board, and then he got really upset when we transferred out the Siamese twins. . . ."

"Transferred out the Siamese twins? What are you talking about? Is that medical slang for something?"

"Didn't I tell you about the twins? They were born last Sunday and they're joined at the chest. The cardiologists all say they have to be separated or else they'll both die, but Sullivan wants to keep them together, so we transferred them out to the Medical Center for their surgery without telling Sullivan about it."

"Can you do that?"

"We did it."

"Are you sure you guys are doing the right thing? I mean, Bob, this doesn't sound like you. You never had trouble like this with an attending before."

"I've never met an attending like Sullivan before."

"But he's an attending, and you're just barely an intern. Doesn't he know better than you about these kinds of things?"

I thought for a minute, then said, "You know, Rachel, before starting this damned internship, I would have agreed with you; sure, he's been an attending for years, he's got to know what's right, but since starting, I've realized something. There are two parts of medicine: there's the part that's involved with the technical stuff, like putting in lines and figuring out what to do with a ventilator, and Sullivan's got that stuff all over me; but there's a second part that may be more important. It deals with morality, and no matter how long you've been a doctor, you don't get better or worse with experience. If your heart's not in the right place, if you're immoral, then no matter how much experience you have, you can't make a better decision than someone who's just starting out. And Sullivan's immoral; he doesn't consider the family, he doesn't consider what the quality of the baby's life is or is going to be, he always decides to do the same thing, to keep the baby alive, regardless of anything else and, Rachel, that's wrong. Ray, Terry, and I feel we're better at this than he is, and so we've taken matters into our own hands."

"What are you planning to do?" she asked worriedly.

"Well, we already complained to the hospital board, but they're not going to do anything about Sullivan. So we've been thinking of calling a reporter to see if he would like to do a story about him."

"And if he doesn't? Then will you stop all this?"

"I don't know. Ray thinks it's a good idea to chain ourselves across the delivery room entrance and close down the hospital."

"Chain yourself to the delivery room? Bob, what are you saying? You're not being rational. What's happening to you?"

"I've spent two weeks in the Pit. I've been insulted, sleep-deprived, made to feel like a piece of shit, told I don't know anything and can do even less, just to name a few things that have happened. Rachel, after the Siamese twins were born, a TV news team came to cover it, and they wouldn't even interview Ray, who had been on call the night the twins were born, because he was so dirty and disheveled; they said no one would believe he was a real doctor."

"Bob, you don't have to tell me things are bad with you; I've spent two weekends with you. Last week, you cried nonstop. This week, you're raving like a lunatic and you seem to be heading for self-destruction. Do me a favor; before you do anything crazy that you may regret, call Dr. Cozza and talk things over with him."

Now this was a great idea and I was surprised I hadn't thought of it myself. Dr. Cozza, the chief of Pediatrics at Jonas Bronck Hospital, the main teaching hospital for Einstein, had been my internship adviser during my senior year in medical school and had become a good friend. I promised Rachel I would call him on Monday.

"Well, what do you want to do today?" Rachel asked, changing the subject.

"I want to lie in bed," I answered pathetically. "I want to be taken care of."

"Oh no you don't. I didn't spend all that time, not to mention money, flying up here so I could take care of you while you lie in bed. We at least have to go food shopping." She pushed me out of bed and into the bathroom and supervised while I got dressed, making sure I didn't sneak back into bed.

We went to the Star Market near Watertown Square and bought

another huge quantity of groceries to take the place of the stuff that had sat untouched in the refrigerator until it was nearly ready to have the penicillin harvested from it. I told Rachel it was silly to buy more groceries, since, in the few hours I had for free time, I would not be inclined to either eat or cook, but she would have none of it; she had been brought up believing that a house must be well stocked with food, and well-stocked it would remain all year long.

After dumping the stuff at home, we went to Cambridge and caught the matinee of the film, *"Nosferatu the Vampire,"* at the Orson Welles Cinema. In the theater I found myself able to forget about my internship for short periods, but then the reality would return, and I would twitch in my seat when I remembered that I would be on call the next day. All through that month, St. A's was no more than a few moments away.

After the movie we went to Legal Sea Food for dinner, and while we waited in line for a table, Terry and Cliff came in. It was a little embarrassing at first and I'm sure I blushed, but everything seemed to go well, and we had dinner together.

Right from the beginning, Rachel and Terry seemed to hit it off well, and they spent the best part of dinner involved in conversation. I tried to eavesdrop on what they were talking about, being a little concerned about whether their conversation might get around to how Terry and I had spent the preceding Wednesday night, but Cliff, trying to be friendly, sustained a dialogue about the Boston sports and cultural scene with me. So, although I was able to catch little bits of conversation here and there, mostly inconsequential stuff like the type of research Terry did before she started medical school, I had real anxiety that I had missed the important topic. But I was sure that if anything disastrous had been discussed, I'd hear about it from Rachel before we reached home.

Our conversation in the car on our way home was disturbing to me, but not for the reason I thought it might be. "Terry and her husband seem nice," Rachel began as soon as we left the restaurant's parking lot.

"Of course they're nice," I responded. "Did you think they were going to be monsters?"

"Bob, I didn't know what to think. You're so . . . different. It's like I don't know you sometimes and it worries me. When I was back in

New York last week, all I could think about was how you had become so strange. I couldn't concentrate on my work. You seem to be a little better this week, but you're still talking crazy. I've been with you all through medical school, and you've never acted like this during all that time. So I had to assume it wasn't the work that had changed, but the people you were working with and I guess I figured Ray and Terry and Dan were some kind of evil witches who had cast a spell on you. But meeting Terry and hearing her tell the same kind of stories as you, I guess maybe there really is something wrong with this Sullivan."

A little angry that Rachel would think I could be naïve enough to be swayed by contact with "evil interns," I was relieved that Rachel's feelings were at last out in the open. "I know it's been hard for you," I said. "I'll try to act more normal."

"And now I realize how hard that might be for you. Bob, I can understand, by having talked to Terry, what pressure you must be under. And I also realize that sometimes when people are under a lot of pressure unusual things can happen to them."

Very confused, I parked the car in the lot outside our apartment house and we went up to our apartment. We spent the rest of the evening watching TV, with me trying to figure out what Rachel's comment had meant and, alternatively, thinking about how soon I'd have to say goodbye to Rachel and reenter the Pit. By 10 P.M., we were already in bed. "Our time goes by so fast," I said before falling asleep.

"I love you," she said.

"I love you too," I responded, and I kissed her good-night.

Sometime during that night, the nightmare recurred. This time, in addition to Parris being in it, a figure appeared floating above the warming table. This image, just a face really, smiled at me as I panicked, and as the heart rate dropped, that smile widened. As the baby turned a deeper blue, the mouth of the image began to grin. And finally when the baby was dead, the image uttered a hearty laugh.

I awoke in a cold sweat. I recognized the face. It was John Sullivan's.

XXVIII

Sunday, July 11 On Call

When I arrived on Sunday morning, Ray and Lauren were sitting in the nurses' station. Ray looked great; no matter how it happened, being on with Lauren really seemed to agree with him. Ray was writing an admission note on a new premie when I came through the door. "Hi," I said.

"Hi," Ray answered. "How are things out there?"

"Hot," I responded. "It's going to be in the high nineties today. How was your night?"

"Pretty good," Ray said. "We got a thirty-two weeker who came up around 5 A.M., but before that everything was pretty quiet. It was sort of a good night."

"Yeah," Lauren agreed, "it was sort of good," and they both laughed.

"Oh God," I thought to myself, "this is all I need." Then out loud, "I don't know if it's safe having you two on at the same time."

"Oh it's safe," Ray said. "We're a great team."

Lauren left at that point to go find Dan so she could sign out to him. "What the hell's going on?" I asked after she had gone.

"What do you mean?" Ray responded.

"Between you and Lauren. What's going on?"

"We're getting along pretty well, Bob. We're spending the rest of the weekend together."

"Did you mention to her that you're not the hot-shit nephrologist she thinks you are?"

"Well . . . not exactly. Not in so many words."

"Ray, you're deceiving her and you're both going to get hurt."

"I'm not sure about that. She likes me and I don't think it has anything to do with whether I'm a nephrologist or not."

"I think you're being naïve, Ray," I said. He seemed wounded by this. "Look, there's one way to find out for sure: tell her the truth."

"I plan to tell her today," Ray responded, "but like I said, I don't think it's going to make any difference."

Ray finished his admission note and we made rounds on the babies in the first row. Included in the sickies that day were the still critically ill Dead Kid; Ray's new thirty-two weeker, a boy named Manfred; Baby Singer, who was extubated but still required supplemental oxygen; and a thirty weeker named Dogras, whom Terry had brought up on Friday night and who was intubated and required some ventilatory assistance. For St. A's, this was a fairly quiet time in the Pit.

In a short time Lauren returned, collected Ray, and together they left. Soon after Dan appeared, asking, "Ready for your first Sunday on call?"

"I guess," I answered.

"I hate being on on Sundays," Dan said. "When you're on on Saturday, at least you get to go home Sunday morning and get some sleep. Being on call Sunday, you work all day and night alone, and then you have to hang around to start the week on Monday. Your whole week is screwed up because you're always tired. It sucks."

"Great," I said. "I had enough trouble leaving my wife this morning. And on top of that, it's going to be a shitty day."

"Sorry to bring you down," Dan responded, "but that's just the way it is. Do you know what's going on between Ray and Lauren? She told me they're going to Rockport together. What's happening to that boy?"

"He thinks he's in love with her."

"In love with her? Doesn't he realize she's only playing with him because she wants him to get her a job? Know what she told me? She said she thinks she's going to like living in Michigan next year."

"I told him. He's having a hard time telling her he's not really a nephrologist."

"He'd better tell her. He took advantage of her, and that wasn't very nice, but if he doesn't watch out that bitch is going to really destroy him."

"I think he'll tell her today. At least, that's what he told me."

"Good. Any problems in the Pit?" I shook my head no. "Okay. I'm going to my on-call room to read the paper. Call me if you need me and remember, keep smiling; if you get depressed, Sunday'll seem to last forever."

He was right. Right after he left I got depressed. I began doing my morning scut work, drawing blood from babies who didn't have UA lines, going to the labs to check results of tests already done, and basically waited for things to start happening. I felt lonely, and time seemed to stand still.

I was in the lab at around ten when my beeper went off, directing me to call the DR. When I called the number, I got Fredericks. "Hi, Bob," he said. "We have something pretty interesting going on here, very interesting. Can you come down?"

"I'll be right there," I responded. I hung up the phone, took the elevator up to the fourth floor and, upon entering the delivery suite, found Tom sitting next to the ward clerk at her desk, reading one of her copies of *People* magazine. He looked up when I entered.

"Hi, Bob," he said, "nice to see you. You ever read this magazine?"

"No," I responded, "I never did."

"It's great, just great. It gives you the lowdown on all your favorite Hollywood stars. Oh well, I guess I'd better get on with work." He handed the magazine back to the clerk and said, "Thanks, Marie."

"What's up?" I asked.

"We seem to have a problem, Bob, and I'd like to get you involved. Come with me, Bob, just come with me." He led me into one of the labor rooms where on the bed a very pregnant woman about thirty years old was rolling around and screaming.

"You ain't cuttin' me open. I ain't gonna have no fuckin' operation for no fuckin' kid. If he wants to come out so bad, he can fuckin' come out the right way. I ain't havin' no operation," she screamed.

Tom led me back out into the hall and said, "Well, Dr. Sharon, that's our Mrs. Grant. What do you think of Mrs. Grant?"

"It seems to me that that lady is drunk."

"Very astute pickup, Bob, very astute. She's as drunk as a proverbial skunk. We've been following her through this pregnancy in high-risk clinic because she's a chronic alcoholic who already has two kids with the Fetal Alcohol Syndrome. You know what that is, Bob?"

"I do," I answered. I knew a lot about FAS because I had done a project on this subject as my senior thesis for medical school. It is known that women who consume a lot of alcohol during their pregnancies frequently deliver children with an unusual but easily recognizable pattern of malformations, which include an odd facial appearance, low birth weight and, most significantly, variable degrees of mental retardation. The reasons that these malformations occur—whether they are due to the toxicity of the alcohol itself or whether the alcohol causes some problems with the mother's system and therefore indirectly causes problems with the fetus—is not fully understood.

"Well," Tom continued, "every time she's come for her regular clinic visits, every time, she's been smashed. She fights with us regularly, and I mean fist fights, Bob; she won't do what we tell her to do and she won't stop drinking, even though we've told her over and over that drinking would cause this baby to be born like her other kids. She just won't stop drinking."

"So you're calling me to tell me to get ready for a baby with FAS?" I asked.

"Not exactly, Bob, it's not that easy. See, we brought her in here today for some tests, you know, a Fetal Activity Tracing, the test where we see if the baby's heart is doing okay. Well, we finally got her to cooperate, and the FAT was horrendous, so we did an oxytocin challenge test to see if the baby's heart could stand the strain of labor and delivery. And that was pretty lousy also, so our attending made the decision that we'd better get the baby out of there now!"

"So you're calling me to tell me to get ready for a baby with FAS who's going to be delivered by section?"

"Not exactly, Bob, not exactly. You're anticipating. See, although we've decided the baby's gotta be delivered, and soon, the mother won't consent to a section. You heard her screaming in there. 'If that kid wants to come out, he'll have to do it the right way,' she's been saying."

"I see. Well, what are you going to do?"

"It gets trickier and trickier, Bob, trickier and trickier. Under normal circumstances, we'd probably call the hospital administrator and the judge and get a court order to do the surgery, but in this case, nothing's normal. I mean, she's already had two kids with FAS, and she's been drunk all the way through this pregnancy also. That kid must be pretty well pickled in there by now."

"Ah, I see. So you have to decide whether it's worth getting a court order to deliver by section a child, against the will of the mother, who may have Fetal Alcohol Syndrome and, therefore, who may well be a damaged child. On the other hand, the kid may be normal and, if he is, delaying the section may cause him to be born damaged."

"Well, that's about it, Bob. You got it in a nutshell."

"Tough decision. What are you going to do?"

"Not much we can do. Dr. Adams is thinking about the case, but I think he'll want to deliver the baby by section. Then it'll probably take a couple of hours to get the court order. And you know, Bob, in obstetrics, you can't always wait around a long time making decisions. Things usually happen so fast that if you hesitate, the decisions get made by nature."

Just then Tom was called for a phone call from Dr. Adams. I left the DR at this point and returned to the Pit.

Dr. Smith was standing by the bed of his son, the Dead Kid. He looked anxious and was tapping his fingers against the metal corner of the warming table, the way we do in the delivery room to tap out the beat of the heart. The clerk in the nursery's nurses' station told me that Dr. Smith had been asking to see me.

"Hello, Dr. Sharon," he said solemnly as I approached.

"Hello, Dr. Smith. How are things?"

"Not well. My life and those of my wife and our other child have been lousy since this baby was born. And it's all the fault of that jerk who runs this place. What luck to have a critically ill baby born in a hospital whose nursery is run by a madman!"

"I apologize again," I said. "If there's anything I can do. . . ."

"As a matter of fact, there is something you can do. I'll tell you, I've called all over New England trying to find a nursery that would accept this baby as a transfer. They all turned me down. They told me that it sounded like the baby was too sick to be moved. I feel like I'm trapped in a catch-22. And so we're stuck with keeping the child here with that maniac.

"Since he won't do anything, I'll have to ask you. You realize, I know, that the continuation of this child's life is a totally pointless and empty exhibition of what Sullivan can do with a ventilator and some drugs. But it is only harmful to the child and my family. Therefore, as a brother in medicine, I plead with you to terminate this child's life!" Dr. Smith was calm and seemed pathologically detached during this speech. He had managed to totally ignore the fact that the Dead Kid, the child whose life he was asking me to end, was his own son.

I thought about his request for a while. On the one hand, I agreed with his reading of the situation, that no good could come from the continuation of the Dead Kid's life. On the other hand, I had been charged by Dr. Sullivan with the responsibility of caring for these children and carrying out his orders, no matter how illogical they seemed. Now it's true that Ray, Terry, and I had transferred out the Siamese twins in direct opposition to Dr. Sullivan's orders. However, I felt that situation was different; with the twins, there was a possibility of saving one if we transferred them. With the Dead Kid, if I were to turn off his ventilator and end his life, I could be tried for murder. I decided finally that I could not carry out Dr. Smith's request.

He looked at me for a few seconds after I told him my decision. "I understand," he said finally. "I think I would probably have said the same thing if our positions were reversed." He arose from the stool on which he was sitting and offered me his hand. "There are some things you just can't ask anyone else to do. Thank you for your time."

I took his hand and shook it. "I'm sorry."

He walked out of the Pit. As I returned to my work, I kept thinking about Dr. Smith and the poor Dead Kid. His phrase, "there are some things you just can't ask anyone else to do," kept reverberating through my head. I went back to the nurses' station and, with some of the data I had collected during my trip to the lab, began to write progress notes on the active patients.

Soon Dan, bored after spending the morning in his on-call room reading the New York *Times* and hungry for lunch, came to find me.

"Lunch?" he said.

I nodded yes. Together, we went to the cafeteria. But as we got settled at a table, my beeper went off again. "Dr. Sharon, call 3434," it said.

I called the DR from the phone in the cafeteria and Tom answered. "Hello, Bob?" he asked. "We've got some great action going on over here, great action. We're going to have a regular courtroom trial, like out of 'Perry Mason.' We'd like you guys to be here, because if the judge finds in our favor we're going to take Mrs. Grant to the DR for a crash section."

I said we'd be right there. Dan was as excited as I when I told him. "Great," he said, "a real-life drama, just like on TV."

We wolfed down lunch and in less than ten minutes were walking into the delivery area. The ward clerk directed us to Mrs. Grant's labor room.

The room had been redecorated for the occasion. The furnishings now consisted of the labor bed bearing Mrs. Grant, the comfortable chair on which Tom usually watched TV, a table in front of that chair, and four folding chairs. Sitting on Tom's TV chair was a man in his sixties with long gray hair, who was thin and wearing a fashionable three-piece suit. His briefcase was opened on the table before him and seemed to contain a lot of official-looking papers. Tom and Schwartz, still looking like a bear, were sitting on two of the folding chairs across the table from this man. Dan and I took our places in the other two folding chairs. Everything seemed very dignified and solemn, except for the ranting and raving of Mrs. Grant and the beep-beep-beep beeping of the fetal heart monitor that was attached by a belt around Mrs. Grant's protuberant abdomen. Mrs. Grant was squirming around the bed, trying to free herself from the fetal heart monitor. Tom had already ordered that her arms and legs be restrained.

"You fuckin' bastards," screamed Mrs. Grant. "You can't come into this fuckin' room with me in here. You get outa here before I call a fuckin' cop." This would continue until she had a labor pain. Sometime between the moment that I had first laid eyes on Mrs. Grant that morning and now, she had slipped into labor spontaneously. She was having labor pains about every six to seven minutes. When the pains came, she would let out a bloodcurdling scream which would last about thirty seconds. The screams would nearly drown out the "beep-beep-beep" of the baby's heart. The sounds of the heart seemed to respond to the screams by slowing down to almost none, as if the baby was stopping its heart in hopes that its mother would stop screaming. And when the contraction ended, Mrs. Grant would return to her "you fuckin' bastards" tirade and the baby's heart, relieved by the four-letter words, would pick up its rate somewhat.

"Let's get started," said the man behind the table. "I know that this is a bit unusual, but I am holding this hearing so that I can learn the facts in this case before deciding whether to sign an order allowing the obstetric staff of St. Anne's Hospital to perform an emergency cesarean section on Mrs. Grant in order to prevent damage to Fetus Grant, the baby Mrs. Grant is carrying. Please proceed, Dr. Schwartz."

"Thank you for coming here today, Judge Isaacs." So this man was Judge Isaacs, the man who had allowed Sullivan to get Sharon Frederica O'Hara's belly fixed. "Mrs. Grant, as you can see, is inebriated. She came to the hospital today, alone, for some tests to monitor whether the fetus she was carrying was healthy. Those tests showed that the fetus seemed to be getting into some trouble, and further, that the fetus probably would suffer significant trauma if delivered by natural means. Therefore, a cesarean section is essential for the welfare of this unborn child."

Mrs. Grant, upon hearing this, began screaming, "You ain't cuttin' me open, you fuckin' bastards. I ain't lettin' you near me with a fuckin' knife."

Judge Isaacs waited for this outburst to end and said, "Dr. Schwartz, have you fully apprised Mrs. Grant of these findings?"

"Yes, your honor, I have, and I explained to her clearly and simply, in layman's terms, the significance of them. However, she still refuses to allow the cesarean section and, as time goes by, the baby is in more and more danger."

I counted the beeps coming from the fetal monitor. They were now down to eighty per minute.

"Has any effort been made to contact other members of Mrs. Grant's family? Particularly, has Mr. Grant been called?"

"Yes, your honor, yes indeed," Tom answered. "I called and spoke with Mrs. Grant's mother. She was of no help."

"Did you explain the gravity of the situation to her, Doctor?"

"Yes, sir, yes, I surely did."

"And what did she say?"

"I don't think I should repeat it here, your honor. Let's just say that she won't allow the section to be done either."

"And Mr. Grant? Has he been contacted?"

"No, sir," Schwartz said. "He has been out of the picture since early in the pregnancy. He has left Boston, according to Mrs. Grant, for parts unknown."

"And good riddance to the fuckin' bastard," Mrs. Grant added.

"I see, Doctors." At this moment Mrs. Grant let out one of her better screams and I was sure my blood had curdled. The baby's heart rate dropped to fifteen per minute during the second half of the scream but then slowly came back up to around sixty-five.

Judge Isaacs continued his interrupted speech. "Doctors, what are the chances that this baby will be born normally, by natural means?"

"Very poor," Schwartz quickly answered. "There is a good chance that, if left to natural forces, the baby will be born dead."

"And if the cesarean section is done now? What are the chances for a good outcome?"

"That's a difficult question," Schwartz responded more slowly. "The baby may have already been damaged by the delay in delivery and the slowed heart rate."

"Also," I added, "from what I've been told, Mrs. Grant is a chronic alcoholic. There is a very good chance that this fetus may be affected with the Fetal Alcohol Syndrome, a disorder which, among other things, is associated with significant mental retardation."

"I see," Judge Isaacs said. He stopped for a few seconds and looked down at the papers which he had removed from his briefcase. Finally he began again. "This is very difficult for me. I always hope that these problems can resolve themselves without the intervention of the court. Usually we can get some relative or a priest to bring the patient around. But in this case, I am satisfied that you have run out of other options.

"The law in the state of Massachusetts is clear—that fetus inside Mrs. Grant's womb is entitled to all the rights granted in the Constitution. Therefore, being born alive is its inalienable right." At this point Mrs. Grant let out another gut-wrenching scream, which again caused the fetal heart monitor to dip down, this time to about ten beats per minute. The contraction seemed to last for a longer time. When it was over, the heart rate recovered to only about thirty per minute.

Judge Isaacs picked up the discussion where he had left it. "And so I must grant a court order allowing Fetus Grant to be delivered by cesarean section against the wishes of Mrs. Grant." Isaacs immediately signed the document which he had been clutching in his hands.

When pen hit paper, Schwartz, grabbing the head of the labor bed and Tom, grabbing the foot, quickly whisked Mrs. Grant out of the room and toward DR 3. Mrs. Grant screamed, "You assholes, go away, you fuckin' bastards," all the way down the hall. Dan and I ran into the locker room, changed our clothes, soon joined the obstetricians in the DR, and got prepared for the birth of Fetus Grant.

Mrs. Grant had already been anesthetized by the time we arrived. Tom and Schwartz began operating. After the warmer was turned on, the endotracheal tube and the UA catheter unbagged, and the meds prepared, I took my place next to Tom. Their instruments, again almost a ballet of stainless steel, moved like lightning and, within minutes, I was handed the lifeless body of Baby Grant.

Dan and I jumped on the baby. Dan put the laryngoscope in the baby's mouth, passed the endotracheal tube, and began pumping oxygen down into the baby's lungs. I listened for the heart but heard nothing. "No heart rate," I told Dan, and I immediately set to work passing an umbilical vein catheter. I poured the antiseptic solution liberally over the lower abdomen, tied off the umbilical cord near its base with the ribbon tape, cut the long stump of the umbilical cord just above the tape, found the thin-walled, wide-bored opening of the umbilical vein, and passed the catheter. At this point the baby was about one minute old.

Dan was still pumping oxygen through the endotracheal tube. I again listened for the heart. Still nothing.

"How is it?" Dan asked with a frown on his face.

"Nothing," I replied.

"Push meds," Dan ordered.

I did. Bicarb, 1 cc. Dan said to give 2, so I pushed the plunger of the syringe down until it reached the "2-cc" mark. Then epinephrine, again to the 2-cc mark. Then calcium, then glucose.

"Listen again!" Dan ordered after all the meds had gone in.

I put my stethoscope on the chest. Again nothing.

"Damn it," Dan hissed as he handed over the ambu bag to the anesthesiologist, who had left the mother to come and help us with the resuscitation of the baby. Dan began to perform cardiac massage. He pushed down on the baby's breastbone at a rate of about a hundred and twenty per minute. He counted out, "One, two, three, four, five," repeatedly. The anesthesiologist inflated the baby's lungs with the pressure generated from the ambu bag every time Dan said "five." The baby was now about two minutes old.

"Push round two, Bob," Dan said while continuing to pump.

I followed Dan's orders—bicarb, epi, calcium, glucose. I pushed them all in through the catheter in about forty-five seconds. When they were all in, Dan stopped pumping the chest and told me to listen again. Again I put the end of the stethoscope onto the baby's chest but heard nothing. I shook my head, no.

"Damn," Dan responded again. He continued pounding the chest in time with the bagging by the anesthesiologist while I just stood there waiting to push another round of medications. I looked up and discovered that Tom and Schwartz had come over to watch us, leaving Mrs. Grant, her abdominal wall still gaping open, attended only by the surgical scrub nurse.

The baby was about three and a half minutes old when Dan again stopped pumping. He put the bell of my stethoscope back on the baby's chest. Again I heard nothing. I shook my head again. As if not believing me, Dan tore the stethoscope's earpieces from my ears and put them into his own. He also heard nothing. "Damn!" he said again. Then he ordered me to give the third round of meds and went back to his pumping.

For the third time, I repeated the order—bicarb, epi, calcium, glucose. We waited a few more seconds and when the baby was five minutes old, Dan listened again. Again nothing.

"The baby's dead," Dan said. "Only one thing left to try: intracardiac meds. I've seen it work once in a dead kid."

Dan ordered me to take his place, pumping the chest while he prepared. He pulled the long, thin cardiac needle from its sterile test tube. He poured antiseptic over the baby's chest. He attached the epinephrine syringe to the hub of the cardiac needle. He was ready.

He ordered me to stop. He stuck the needle under the skin below the baby's rib cage on the left. Pointing the needle upward toward the left shoulder, he plunged the needle deeply into the baby's chest. He pulled back on the syringe's plunger and advanced the needle deeper and deeper until blood appeared mixed with the epinephrine. He then emptied the remaining 4 cc of epinephrine into the baby's heart.

Dan withdrew the needle and listened again for the heart beat. He listened intently, all of his energy focused on the sound of the heart, but he heard nothing, only silence. He listened for nearly two minutes. Finally he shook his head, took the stethoscope off the chest, and took a step back, away from the warming table.

"He's dead," he said.

The anesthesiologist, releasing the ambu bag he had been clutching, slowly turned and went back to the mother. Schwartz and Tom walked back to the operative field and, with much less speed, set about repairing the damage they had done to muscle, fat, and skin.

Dan sat on a stool about five feet away from the warming table, visibly shaken. I examined the dead baby, a handsome, well-formed, good-sized boy. He had none of the stigmata of the Fetal Alcohol Syndrome; somehow, he had been able to protect himself from the harmful effects of the massive quantities of Johnnie Walker Red that his mother had consumed. After a few moments Dan rose, put his arm around my shoulder, and led me out of DR 3. We walked to his on-call room which was located on the third floor in a virtually abandoned part of the old St. A's.

Looking like a seedy hotel room from the 1940s, the room was much different from the intern's on-call room. There was a real double bed with an oak headboard, a night table also made of oak on which an old desk lamp sat, and a few run-down, moth-eaten chairs were spread around. The floor was covered with a faded, dirty green wall-to-wall carpet and, for effect, there were sections of the Sunday New York *Times* strewn on the floor.

I sat on one of the chairs while Dan, sitting on the bed, reached into his overnight bag and pulled out a pint of bourbon. He opened the top, took a pull, then handed the bottle to me. I took a pull and handed it back to him.

"You did good in there, Bob. You're a damned good intern."

"Shit," I said back, "the kid died. And it was normal too, you know?"

"Of course I know. You think I would have spent so much time and energy trying to resuscitate a kid who would end up retarded? I didn't even think it was right to force a section on that bag of shit if all we were going to get out of it was a kid with Fetal Alcohol Syndrome. Oh well, it just shows you, even I can be wrong." He took another pull from the bottle and handed it to me. I took a second drink and handed it back.

"Do you always drink when you're on?" I asked.

"Me? No. I always have a pint with me, but I only use it for emergencies."

"I don't understand," I said innocently. "What's the difference between when you drink and when Sullivan drinks?"

"You're comparing me with Sullivan?" Dan asked, and for the first time during that month seemed angry with me. "There's no similarity. Like I said, I keep this bottle in my bag, and I only bring it out in the rare situation where I feel I need some help coping. Sullivan keeps his flask in that damned pouch he keeps on his belt, and he literally always has the stuff at his side. Sullivan needs the stuff just to get through the day; he can't work without a drink."

I sighed and apologized. "I hate this," I added.

"This place stinks," Dan responded, straightening up. "Look at me, Bob, here I am, thirty years old, taking call every third night, for sixteen thousand bucks a year, getting abused by just about every damned pediatric attending in Boston. I've really had it; I'm down, and I think this time I'm out for the count."

"Dan, you mean it doesn't get better after internship?"

"No way! Not here. It just keeps getting worse. You don't do as much scut work and shit like that, but there are more people for you to fight with, and you get more and more tired as time goes on. I should have gotten out of here. I should have done my senior year someplace else."

"Aren't all places like this?"

He gave me a questioning look and said, "Bob, you came from Einstein. Did you know any interns or residents at Jonas Bronck Hospital who were as miserable as you or I am right now?"

I thought for a second. "No," I finally said.

"It's Boston medicine. The medical community here feels it has a right to make the house staff feel like shit. They say Boston has a magic name in medicine, all the hotshots are here, so they take advantage of us, figuring we're going to take advantage of them when we go to look for a job."

"Is it worth it?"

"Hardly. That magic bullshit is only a myth, perpetuated by the Boston medical community. If you apply for a job in California, it doesn't matter whether you did a good job in Boston or New York or Washington or Philadelphia."

"Well, why did you stay here this year?"

Dan, looking ashamed, said, "I didn't get my applications for other programs out in time. I didn't have any choice."

"If it's really so bad, you could have taken the year off."

"Maybe I should have done that. Maybe I still will," Dan responded dreamily. "And if I were you, I'd look elsewhere for next year starting right now. You, Ray, and Terry are not exactly considered 'most valuable players' back at the Medical Center. It's a small program, word travels fast, and you've gotten a lot of bad press; people think you are troublemakers. I don't think there's anything wrong with that, but a lot of other people sure do."

"Great news. Thanks for telling me, Dan."

"Don't mention it."

"Oh well," I said, "I'd better get back to the Pit."

"Drop in anytime. And don't hesitate to call if you need me. I'm always at the end of my beeper." With that, I left Dan with the half bottle of bourbon.

The rest of the afternoon and night were mercifully peaceful and quiet. I returned to a nursery where every patient was stable, and I set about completing the scut work that had accumulated over the afternoon and finished the required progress notes. At 6 P.M. Dan, the effects of the pint of bourbon having worn off, reappeared and we went for dinner. After eating, Dan returned to his on-call room and I went to the delivery suite to check in with Tom. I found him sitting in his usual position, seated in the Judge Isaacs Memorial Chair watching "60 Minutes" on TV. I took my usual position and, comfortably seated on the bed, waited for the commercial.

"Well, Bob, you guys looked real professional working on that kid this afternoon," Tom said at the commercial break. "Too bad, though, too bad we were too late."

"Tom, you know that baby was normal. It didn't have FAS."

"I had a feeling, Bob, I had a feeling. I don't know why, but I thought the kid was going to be normal. That makes it worse."

"How is she now?" I asked.

"The mother? That dirt bag. She's hung over. Has a terrible headache and we're not giving her anything for it."

"Is she upset the baby died?"

"Nope, Bob, at least not yet."

"Anything else going on down here?"

"No. Looks like it's going to be a nice quiet Sunday night."

The commercial over, Tom went back to watching "60 Minutes" and I returned to the Pit. I got to sleep at ten-thirty and got a full night's sleep with only a few minor interruptions. By eight the next morning, I was awake and refreshed and ready to start my third week of internship.

XXIX

Monday, July 12

Attending Rounds

We three interns were all pretty well prepared to begin the new week, ready to face whatever the apparently psychotic Sullivan had to dish out. At least that's what we thought.

Terry had been greatly refreshed by her weekend off. Through brilliant manipulation of the Beth Israel interns' schedule, Cliff had accomplished the monumental feat of arranging to have both Saturday and Sunday off, and they had spent the weekend getting acquainted with Boston. Terry returned to the Pit on Monday looking tanned and happy.

Ray also had had a nice time on Sunday. As planned, he and Lauren had spent the day at Rockport, on the north shore. Ray had also stayed Sunday night at Lauren's apartment. He hemmed and hawed when I asked whether he had told Lauren he wasn't really a nephrologist; he still hadn't told her, but he, too, was more relaxed on that Monday morning.

Although I wanted to talk with Terry in private before rounds began that morning, the chance never presented itself. I was very anxious to find out what Terry had discussed with Rachel during dinner at Legal Sea Food. I hoped the opportunity to talk would come up sometime that day.

Work rounds went off that morning without much incident. Because we had asked him to be our substitute attending for the rest of the month, Dan accompanied us for the first time in over a week. Frohman, who had also had the weekend off, didn't seem as nervous as usual and he even tried to make some little jokes that morning. It was as if he had returned, at least briefly, to the human race. All the patients were either stable or getting better that morning; at least no one was in danger of dying. The only planned event for the day was the discharge of Sharon Frederica O'Hara.

When ten o'clock rolled around, Ray, Terry, Dan, and I went to the intern on-call room and Dan began to give us a little lecture he called "the Berkowitz approach to the very premature baby." We ate it all up, even the bad jokes; we were happy to at least be getting a little education. We all hoped that Sullivan wouldn't find us, but even if he did, with the door locked, he wouldn't be able to get at us.

At ten after ten, just as Dan was getting into it, a knock came on the door. "Who is it?" Terry asked.

"Simon," Frohman answered.

"Go away," Ray replied, "we're having a private conference in here, and we're not coming to attending rounds."

The door opened (I, having been the last person to enter, had forgotten to lock it) and Frohman and Sullivan entered. Sullivan looked terrible; he was pale and wan, his eyes were bloodshot, and he looked thinner.

"Dr. Sullivan wants to talk to all of us," Frohman said.

"In all my years of medicine," Sullivan started slowly and with a calm voice, "I have never heard of or experienced a situation like this before. You people dislike me; that's okay, I've had interns not like me before and that doesn't bother me. You interns are usually more trouble than you're worth, but that's to be expected. What's unique here is that this is the first time I've ever felt uncomfortable leaving my babies in the care of an intern. In the past I've known that even if the intern was technically inept and maybe not the brightest person in the world that the nursery would not be deliberately sabotaged. But that's exactly what happened last Thursday night when I left the nursery with Dr. Sharon in charge." Sullivan, though still calm, was building up a pretty good head of steam by this point and was starting to sweat. "On Thursday night I left my Siamese twins, thinking they would still be here when I returned on Friday. But what did Dr. Sharon do? He called Channin and coerced that jerk into coming out here to take the twins back to the Medical Center."

I was stunned. Who had given Sullivan the true story? Dr. Channin certainly hadn't. Channin was the one person I was sure we could trust. Had Sullivan just put two and two together or had someone actually wised him up?

Sullivan continued, becoming more agitated. "And now, I ask you all, what am I to do? I can't trust any of you with my babies at night. I have asked Dr. Jennings to replace you with more trustworthy interns, but he tells me that's impossible at the present time, so, as far as I can see, the only solution is that, until your rotation here is through at the end of next week, I will have to remain in the hospital at all times to supervise your work. That's the only way I can assure myself that the babies will get adequate care."

I felt sick to my stomach; the Pit was bad enough, dealing with Sullivan during the day. Now it was going to be like we were married to him.

Ray was the most upset, and he started in. "You say that nothing like this ever happened to you before. Well, nothing like this has ever happened to any of us either. I've gotten along with everybody I've ever worked with, regardless of their position. I've always felt I've cooperated with attendings, doing what was best for the patient. But with you," Ray, standing since the beginning of this speech, his face red, pointing his index finger at Sullivan's belly, "with you, I feel like I'm doing what's worst for the patient. I'm always having to apologize for your mistakes, and I'm sick and tired of doing that. Don't you have any idea why we had to transfer those twins? It's because, in spite of what two cardiologists and one surgeon had to say, in spite of the advice given by every specialist consulted, you had to have your own way. And did you go to the parents and discuss your opinion with them and win them over to your way of thinking? No. In fact, it was more important to you to get your ugly face on TV than it was to sit down with the family. Do you know the Srnivasans hate your guts? They hate us too because of the way you choose to conduct your damned business. So, when we got someone to sit down with them and discuss the situation in a calm, friendly, supportive way, someone from another hospital who offered them something they never got here, courtesy and respect, they jumped at the opportunity to get their babies out of here and out of your clutches. It was you, Sullivan, not us, who was responsible for the damned transfer of those twins. We were just playing our little roles in the drama." Ray, his face now dark red, standing eye to eye with Sullivan, stopped and took a breath.

I picked up. I was almost as excited as Ray. "We don't question for one second your skill as a technician. You know more damned neonatology than we ever will, but you're not a good neonatologist. You're not even an adequate neonatologist. You're lousy at this job because you always fail to supply one key element that's necessary to make a doctor a good physician: you have no compassion. You ignore what's happening to the families of these kids. What good is there in saving a baby's life if he's going to go home and catch pneumonia because the family can't afford to pay the heating bill? When was the last time you checked to see whether a family had adequate housing, or even a place to put the baby after he was discharged? When was the last time, in fact, you talked to a family for even five minutes without insulting them? When was the last time you were honest with a father and told him what his child's prognosis really was? When was . . ." My speech was interrupted by the sound of a loud, raspy buzzer.

"Code!" Frohman shouted and we all ran for the Pit.

It was the Dead Kid. Kathy O'Connell and Gloria Higgins, the child's primary nurse on days, were on top of the baby, with Gloria pumping on his chest. Dr. Smith, who had appeared for a rare visit near the end of work rounds, was being led out of the Pit by Maureen, the red-haired nurse, when we came barreling through the doors.

When we saw it was the Dead Kid whose heart had stopped beating, Ray, Terry, and I weren't sure exactly what to do. But Dan knew; he threw his arms up and the three of us stopped. We stood, frozen, about five feet from the bedside but, Sullivan, leading the way, and the ever-present Frohman following close behind, continued running and began resuscitation.

Sullivan ordered Frohman to relieve Gloria Higgins and Frohman took her place without questioning, without missing a beat. Frohman, though, had a queer look on his face. Sullivan pushed the first round of meds, just like in the DR, through the baby's UA line—bicarb, epi, calcium, glucose. After the drugs had gone in, he ordered Frohman to stop pumping, and we all looked to the EKG readout mounted on the control panel above the baby's warming table. It was flat-line.

Sullivan then ordered Frohman to continue pumping. The attending pushed the second round of meds. Again, after Frohman stopped compressing the baby's breastbone, the EKG registered flat-line. A third round of meds was given. Again flat-line. Then a fourth, and a fifth. Each time, the result was the same: the EKG was flat.

Frohman continued pumping while Sullivan prepared to give the next round of meds directly into the Dead Kid's dead heart. "Shouldn't we stop?" Simon finally asked, so meekly and quietly that it was difficult to hear over the alarm emitted by the respirator.

"No way!" Sullivan said as he pushed Simon off the baby. Then as Dan had done the day before in the delivery room, Sullivan plunged the cardiac needle under the skin below the left rib cage and thrust it upward and deeper toward the left shoulder. When he saw dark, brown blood enter the syringe, he pushed a complete round of meds. Without pulling out the needle, he looked to the EKG readout. Still flat-line. One more round through the cardiac needle and still nothing on EKG. He pulled the needle out. "Pump the chest, Simon!" he ordered. Simon, still not able to disobey a direct order from an attending, even though he knew the attending was wrong, went back to pumping the chest about a hundred and twenty times per minute.

Sullivan ordered Kathy to get a sterile surgical tray. These were trays containing sterile instruments, used for minor surgical procedures around the Pit. While Kathy was getting it, Sullivan poured antiseptic solution over Simon's hands, the Dead Kid's chest and abdomen. Soon the whole area was soaked with the reddish brown, thick solution. He put on a pair of sterile gloves and, with the tray open in front of him, pulled out a scalpel handle and attached a new blade to it. He ordered Simon to stop pumping and found the soft intercostal muscle located between the two ribs just below the nipple and, with a single, clean cut of the scalpel blade, opened the baby's chest from the breastbone to the back. He pushed his hands through the gaping incision, felt the small, lifeless heart, much smaller than his own fist, and began to pump it manually. He pumped the heart for three . . . four . . . five minutes. When he stopped, the heart returned to its silent, peaceful state. He began manual massage again and continued it for another five minutes, but when he stopped, the heart again died. Again he reached in and again he pumped for five minutes and again, when he stopped, the muscle died. One final time, but again, after the manual pumping ceased, the heart refused to work on its own.

By this point most everyone other than us doctors still in the Pit had long lost interest in the case. Simon, who had been relieved when Sullivan had cracked the baby's chest, had run from the nursery, his hands dripping with brown antiseptic solution, a green, sick look on his face. We four maintained our position, now about ten feet from Dr. Sullivan, not fully believing what we had just seen. Dr. Smith, who had returned to the nurses' station, had been watching the proceedings through the glass window. All of the nurses except Kathy had returned to their work.

When Sullivan finally gave up, he was standing alone. He had been working on the Dead Kid for over an hour. With his gloved hands dripping with gore and blood, he looked at the Dead Kid's waxy, bluish white face and slowly shook his head back and forth. He remained like this, transfixed, for a few minutes.

When the spell was finally broken, he turned and, seeing us standing nearby, approached us. I could see his eyes were moist and redder than they had been during attending rounds. In a calm voice, occasionally breaking, trying to hold back the flow of tears, he looked each of us in the eye and said, "I don't know how, I don't know why, but I know you four are responsible for this. You killed this baby. You wanted him dead, and you killed him. And you'll pay for this. Believe me, you'll pay for this!" And he turned and, keeping his eyes which were welling up with tears, riveted on the floor, he walked out of the Pit.

XXX

Afternoon

Ray, Terry, and I were sick to our stomachs and had no desire to join Dan when he suggested we go to the cafeteria for lunch. Instead we decided to head back to the on-call room. As Dan headed for the cafeteria, he told us, "Sullivan's obviously just flipped out, so don't let him near you. When I get back, we'll have a talk about what to do next."

Dr. Smith was still in the nurses' station when we came out of the Pit. "I'm sorry," I said to him, my head slightly bowed.

"Sorry about what?" he asked as we walked together into the hall. He and I headed for the elevator while Ray and Terry entered the on-call room.

"About the baby dying, and about the way the whole thing was handled."

"Don't feel sorry about the baby dying. It's the best thing that could have happened. And, Dr. Sharon, I want to apologize to you for my request yesterday. I know I put you in a very compromising position. I shouldn't have asked someone else to do something like that if I was not prepared to do it myself."

"It's okay." I shook his hand as the elevator door opened.

"And by the way, Dr. Sharon."

"Yes?" I answered.

"Don't get a postmortem potassium level." He smiled as the elevator doors closed.

I had been too upset to figure out the sequence of events up until that point, but now it suddenly all made sense. I ran into the on-call room and found Ray and Terry in the midst of a conversation. This time I remembered to lock the door behind me.

"I just thought he was irrational and stubborn, with a little alcohol problem. Up until this point, I guess I've been giving him the benefit of the doubt," Terry said, "but now I agree with you; he is crazy."

"He's a paranoid schizophrenic," Ray added.

"Well, what can we do?" I asked. "We're working in real life-and-death situations, and we don't know enough to save our own lives. Our senior resident is a wimp, our attending is a paranoid schizophrenic and an alcoholic and, apparently, we've had a second formal complaint lodged by him against us, which may mean we're going to be fired automatically. You guys know why the Dead Kid died?"

"Cracking his chest didn't help much," Ray said.

"Nah, he was dead way before that," I responded. "His father killed him. His father shot him up with KCl. He just told me."

"Oh, Bob," Terry exclaimed. "That's awful! That's about the most disgusting thing I ever heard. What are we going to do?"

"Maybe Dan will have an idea," Ray said. "Maybe he'll know what to do." And we sat quietly after that for a while, each reflecting on the events of the last two hours.

It was then that I remembered that I had promised Rachel that I'd call Dr. Cozza. "I've got to make a phone call," I said, breaking the silence. "I'm going down to the front lobby."

"Why the front lobby?" Ray asked. "What's wrong with this phone?"

"I guess I'm getting a little paranoid, too," I said. "If you have a private conversation around here, Sullivan somehow seems to find out about it. How is it that he knew it was us who called Channin? Channin told Jennings that he was responsible for the transfer. The walls around here seem to have ears, and those ears have pretty good hearing. So I'll use the pay phone, if it's all the same with you guys."

"Be careful out there," Terry said as I was leaving. "Remember what Dan said."

"I'm not afraid of Sullivan. What's he going to do, crack my chest?" I asked.

"I wouldn't rule that out," Terry answered.

As I walked down the stairs to the lobby, I thought over how strange it was that Sullivan had found out we had called Channin. I was standing on the landing between the first and second floors when the answer hit me: it must have been the nurses. How stupid of us; it was just like interns to overlook the obvious, trying to find something more subtle and mysterious. The Pit had been filled with nurses while I was having my conversation with Channin. Any one of them, as a spy for Sullivan, could have overheard and related the story to Kathy, or to the boss himself.

Angry at myself, feeling betrayed and nauseated and tired, I reached the seedy, run-down lobby and stepped into one of the phone booths. I called Dr. Cozza's office number and got his secretary. Within two minutes, Dr. Cozza's calm and friendly voice was at the other end of the receiver.

"Bob?" he asked, "I've just been thinking about you. How're you doing up there?"

"I'm okay, I guess. It's great to hear your voice. How are you?"

"I'm fine, but you sound terrible. What's wrong, Bob?"

"Things aren't so good here and I need some advice. You're the only person I could think of to bother with this."

"It's never a bother, Bob, and I'm happy you thought of me. What's wrong?"

"Well, I started my year in the neonatal ICU at a hospital called St. Anne's. Ever hear of it?"

"St. Anne's? Isn't that a big regional perinatal center? I remember hearing something awful about that place, but I can't remember . . ."

"If it's awful, it's probably our attending, a guy named Sullivan. He's a . . ."

"Sullivan," he interrupted me, "that's it. John Sullivan, right? He's the raving maniac who's always busting up the ethics conferences at the Academy of Pediatrics meetings. Oh, Bob, he's your attending? He's a real horse's ass."

"That's the one. I just watched him spend a whole hour trying to resuscitate a baby who's been brain-dead for over a week. The kid finally died because his father managed to give him a bolus of KCl."

"The father had to kill the kid?" Dr. Cozza asked. "That's horrible; that's one of the most gruesome things I've heard in a long time. Sullivan's really getting to you, is he?"

"He's getting to all of us interns who started here. He's threatened us, he's reported us as being incompetent, he's . . ."

"Incompetent?" he interrupted again. "Dr. Robert Sharon incompetent? I don't know about those other interns, but I do know some things about you, and one of those things is that you could never be incompetent. Are you doing anything about this? Have you spoken with Dr. Jennings?"

"I don't think Dr. Jennings will be very sympathetic," I responded sadly. "Sullivan's reported us to him twice and, from what I understand, that might mean that we're automatically fired. So I don't think . . ."

"Automatically fired?" Dr. Cozza responded. "Who told you something like that? You think medicine is the military or something, where there are specified rules and regulations? All of us who run residency programs, we know that occasionally an attending and a resident don't exactly hit it off too well, and that's okay. We're not going to penalize ourselves by making silly, inflexible rules that will leave us in a position where we have to sacrifice a good house officer just because he's in conflict with someone."

"We're not going to get fired?"

"Of course not, Bob. But if you do, let me tell you there'll always be a job waiting for you back here at Jonas Bronck, anytime and under any conditions. There's always room in the inn for a guy like you."

"Thanks, Dr. Cozza," I said, blushing in the phone booth. "I should have never left the Bronx."

"No, Bob, I think leaving was a good idea. You know how things are done here at Einstein; you're getting to see how business is conducted at other places."

"Well, so far, I haven't liked what I've seen. I've come into this nursery not knowing anything about how to take care of these babies. I guess I'm supposed to be learning that stuff while I'm here, but I'm not. Sullivan never teaches us anything, and I feel pretty inadequate."

"Ah, don't worry about that, nobody knows what they're doing when they start in the intensive care nursery. But everybody eventually learns, usually through osmosis. I'm sure if you think about it, you'll realize you've already really learned a lot."

"I don't know. . . ."

"Well, I'll tell you, Bob, do some reading, do as many procedures as you can and, most important, stay as far away from John Sullivan as is humanly possible. Now, I'm worried about your state of mind. I would go to talk to Jennings. He's always seemed like a fair man to me, and everyone's always talking about what a great pediatrician he is. He's only human, Bob, he won't bite. Have you tried to do anything else to protest what Sullivan's doing?"

"We went to the last hospital board meeting and tried to point out how dangerous he can be when he has to make life-and-death decisions."

"I've always found that complaining to the hospital board is a big waste of time, and I've served on the board here at Jonas Bronck. Did you have any luck up there?"

"Are you kidding? I mean, there we were, protesting about Sullivan's decisions to keep alive babies with very poor prognoses in a Catholic hospital. The board supports his decisions. They must have looked all over for someone like Sullivan."

"Yeah, I can see how they wouldn't thank you people for bringing up this matter, and go out and immediately fire Sullivan. Have you done anything else?"

"Not really. We've talked about calling a newspaper reporter to try to get a story written about what's been happening here, and we've even thought about chaining ourselves to the delivery suite's entrance to close down all deliveries."

Dr. Cozza laughed and said, "How long do you have left at St. Anne's, Bob?"

"We finish the rotation the weekend after next."

"Well, I don't think there's much else you can do. Frankly, I don't think going to the newspapers is going to help, and I'm pretty sure you aren't taking that chain-in idea too seriously. I understand you, Bob, and I know it probably is bothering you a lot that you can't do anything to make Sullivan be a better human being, but I think you have to think in terms of just surviving this rotation. You may be able to find a way to protest against Sullivan sometime in the future, but I think for now you're going to have to be satisfied with just living through the month."

"Yeah," I sighed, "I guess you're right, but I feel so angry about all this. I feel like I'm being used."

"Bob, I know it might sound unsympathetic, but I'm glad you're feeling this way. If you were feeling any other way, I'd have to say I'd be disappointed with you."

My beeper went off then, paging me to the on-call room. "I've got to go, Dr. Cozza," I said, "duty calls. Thanks for the time and the kind words."

"Good luck, Bob. Stay calm and remember what I told you about a job. Anytime and under any circumstances." We hung up, with me feeling much better than I had when I placed the call. I returned to the on-call room where Ray and Terry were still talking. I had to knock on the door; they had kept it locked.

"You rang?" I said upon entering the room.

"Where were you?" Terry asked. "We were getting worried about you. You were gone a long time."

"I was on the phone . . . with a friend of mine from New York."

"You didn't call somebody from Einstein did you?" Terry asked.

"I did," I responded, surprised. "How did you know?"

"I just figured. I've been thinking about calling my adviser in Seattle. I feel so bad right now, I could really use someone to tell me everything is going to be all right."

"Well, I think you ought to make the call," I said. "My talk with Dr. Cozza made me feel a hundred times better. Also while I was down there, I figured out how Sullivan found out we were responsible for transferring the twins. It's really stupid. . . ."

"If it happened here and Sullivan was involved," Ray responded, "I'd sort of expect it to be stupid. What happened, did the twins send him a telegram from the Medical Center?"

"No, it was my fault. There were a lot of nurses around when I talked with Channin that evening and . . ."

"You mean you didn't talk to him in private?" Ray asked. "With all Sullivan's double-agent nurses around? You're right, Bob, that was stupid."

"It doesn't matter," Terry said, patting me on the shoulder, "his finding out was just another straw on the camel's back. If it hadn't been this that set Sullivan off, it would have been something else."

At this point Dan returned from the cafeteria. "You're all still here, right?" he asked. "Sullivan didn't swallow any of you while I was eating?"

"No, we're all still here," I responded, "and we're waiting for you to tell us what to do next."

"I've been giving this some thought," Dan began, "and I think it's time I tell you how I've learned to cope with Sullivan. I discovered this by accident when I was an intern, and it really became my secret weapon. It works pretty well and it drives him nuts. As far as I know, no one before me ever tried it, but it's so simple, you guys are not going to believe it."

"Yeah," Terry and Ray asked simultaneously, "what is it?"

"I ignored him."

"What?" I asked.

"I ignored him. I did what I felt needed to be done for the benefit of the baby and the family; I essentially became my babies' attending. It was a little rough at first because I didn't know exactly what I was doing, but I learned a lot pretty fast, and from then on it seemed to work pretty well."

"I don't understand what you're talking about," Ray said. "How could you ignore him? He's always after us, looking over our shoulders. And then there's Simon and the nurses, who are like his spies. How could you make your own decisions and ignore what he tells you to do?"

"Well, this is how it worked: I was pretty sweet to him, I went to attending rounds every day, I said, 'Yes, sir' after he gave me an order, and I even wrote everything down on paper, the way Frohman does. Then after rounds were over, I went and did whatever it was I thought was right and the next day at rounds, I told Sullivan I had done everything he had wanted, that the lab tests had shown this or that result, and that the baby was much better. Then he'd say, 'That's very good, now today do this and that,' so I'd write that stuff down and then go about doing whatever I wanted."

"So your patients were really living two lives," I said, "one real and one fictional."

"That's about right," Dan answered.

"How'd you get away with it?" Terry asked. "Didn't he find out what you were doing?"

"Sure he found out," Dan answered calmly, "and when he did, he went apeshit. He called Jennings and told him what I was doing, he tried to get me transferred out of here, the whole works. But by the time he did find out, I had already shown everybody here, the other house officers, the nurses, even Kathy, that listening to Sullivan and following his orders was not only not crucial in the management of these babies but, in some cases, was actually bad for the patients. And I was just a dumb-shit intern at the time. Sullivan went crazy; it really blew his cover, because he always made himself out to be the big-shot expert. Turns out, I showed he was nothing but a bag of shit. He sure had trouble controlling the place for months after I finished."

"You think we could get away with something like that?" I asked.

"Bob, you guys already have. I'm surprised you didn't figure this out for yourselves with the twins. Think about it. You three got away with transferring out a prized patient without Sullivan knowing anything about it, and you did it for the same reason I did what I was doing: it was for the good of the patient. Actually, you guys have a better chance of succeeding than I did. After all, I didn't have anybody like me around. If I had had a senior resident I could trust around then, we probably could have had Sullivan convinced that the hospital had been turned into an old-age nursing home by the end of the month."

"You really think we could get away with it?" Ray asked.

"Definitely," Dan answered, "and you'd teach yourselves a lot more neonatology than you've learned so far."

"Well, let's try it," Ray said, and Terry and I nodded. "What do we have to do?"

"Simple. Look over your patients, decide what you want to do for them, ignore what Sullivan told you to do, and then proceed from there."

Just then my beeper went off, summoning me to the Pit. When I walked next door, the clerk said, "The O'Haras are here to take their baby home. They want to speak with you."

I walked over to Sharon Frederica's warming table and found Mr. and Mrs. O'Hara dressing the baby. "Hi," I said, "so this is the big day."

"Yes it is, Dr. Sharon," Mr. O'Hara said. The baby was being zippered into a little pink dress. "We just wanted to say goodbye and to thank you again for all your help. It has been a hard couple of weeks for us."

"I know," I responded, "it's been hard for me as well. But we all survived."

"Yes, sir, thank God," Mr. O'Hara said. Mrs. O'Hara had finished dressing the baby and was holding her in her left arm. She extended her right arm to me and I took it. "We'll see you next month at the Medical Center, Dr. Sharon," Mrs. O'Hara said. "I made the appointment for your clinic this morning."

I walked them to the door, having some doubts that I would ever see Mrs. O'Hara or the baby again; I was sure I would be out of a job by the time the clinic appointment date came around. But I said, "Okay, I'll be looking forward to seeing you." In another minute the O'Hara family was gone.

I returned sadly to the on-call room. That day I had successfully ridded my service of two chronic patients. I felt sad about losing both of them.

Terry was sitting alone in the on-call room when I entered. "Are you okay, Bob?" she asked when she saw me.

"Yeah, I guess so. The O'Hara family just left."

"Well that's good. I have to tell you, Bob, every time I saw that baby in the Pit, I thought about my own situation and . . . it made me pretty uncomfortable."

Realizing that this was the opportunity I had been waiting for, I started in. "Terry, ever since we had dinner with you guys the other night, I've been wondering . . ."

"You want to know if I told Rachel that we spent the night together last week?" she asked, interrupting me.

"Normally, I wouldn't even ask, but Rachel said some pretty strange things to me after we had left you guys."

"I didn't tell her anything, Bob," Terry said, "but I didn't have to. We mostly talked about the stresses of being an intern and what it can do to you. She's very nice, Bob."

"I know," I replied.

"And she's very perceptive. I had the feeling, while I was talking to her, that she knew about that night. In fact, I was going to ask you today, if I got the chance, if you had spoken to her about it."

"Of course I didn't, Terry. What happened that night, like we said the next morning, was just two friends helping each other through a rough time, in an unconventional way. I didn't think it was necessary to say anything to Rachel about it."

"And I didn't think I needed to mention it to Cliff. But Rachel knew, and I think she has the same opinion of it as we did. She's a good woman, Bob, you should know that."

Just then Terry's beeper went off: "Dr. Costa, 3434 stat!" Because Simon had not been seen for hours, Terry asked me to come with her, just in case a second pair of hands was needed and Frohman didn't show up. I followed Terry down the stairs to the delivery suite, where the clerk, looking up from July's *Family Circle*, announced, "Stat section in DR 3."

I ran into the locker room while Terry went into the nurses' lounge. I changed and ran into the DR, where Terry joined me seconds later. Fredericks and Parris had scrubbed and were beginning to operate. They weren't talking and Parris was working at his usual slow pace while Tom was trying to speed up the pace of the operation. Finally, after getting no response from his nonverbal cues, Tom said, "C'mon, Parris, it's an emergency."

"Don't you tell me what to do," Parris yelled back. "It's bad enough I have to scrub with you. I'll get that Sheila Simpson for disappearing in the middle of the day."

"Look, she had a doctor's appointment, so you got me. You better move it. The blood's pouring out, just pouring out."

"Don't you tell me to hurry up," Parris said again. "I don't have to take this shit from you, you incompetent asshole."

"Me, incompetent?" Tom shouted back. "I'm not the idiot who did a digital exam on a woman who had a placenta previa."

So that was it; this woman had a placenta previa, a condition in which the afterbirth covers the opening leading to the birth canal. If the afterbirth tears, it bleeds profusely; the mother may go quickly into shock because of the rapid loss of a large amount of blood, and the fetus may die or suffer brain damage due to lack of oxygen. These babies must be delivered by emergency section for the sake of both mother and baby.

If placenta previa is present, the obstetrician must be careful not to rupture it when examining the woman. If it does tear, then it becomes a race against time; if a section can be performed fast enough and enough blood can be pumped into the mother, both the baby will survive and the mother will recover; if the section is delayed, the baby will be born dead and the mother will lapse into shock. So Tom was pushing Parris while the anesthesiologist was pushing on the bag of blood from the blood bank, trying to get it into the mother at the fastest rate possible.

But Parris didn't speed up, he took his time, as if he were performing one of his routine sections. Terry and I tensely got set up to resuscitate the baby, and Terry went to the operating table, preparing to take the baby from Tom, while I ran out to call the blood bank to order a bag of emergency-release blood for the newborn.

Tom, knowing that every moment that passed meant more trouble for both mother and child, yelled, "C'mon, Parris, get the lead out," again. Parris, who hated this kind of pressure, was getting angrier and angrier, and the angrier he became, the slower he worked. He also was taking time out to look up and yell at Tom, "Shut up, you asshole, either shut up or get the fuck out of this DR."

After fifteen minutes of battling, the baby was finally handed to Terry, who ran the female infant over to the warming table. Wiping the fresh blood off the baby's skin, we found she was very pale and limp. I was sure her blood pressure was dangerously low and, since she was not breathing on her own, I began to try to intubate her while Terry attempted to put a catheter into her umbilical vein. Terry got the catheter in quickly and began pushing medications and fluids. I put the laryngoscope into the baby's mouth, just as I had done with the very tiny baby who had not survived the last Thursday night. I saw the vocal cords and tried to pass the ET tube through them, but it would not go in. I took the tube out and examined it; it looked fine so I tried to pass it again. And again it stopped about two centimeters below the cords. I tried using a different tube but again met with the same resistance at the same point. The baby's pale white color was rapidly being replaced by deep blue.

The heart was beating slowly. "I can't get the tube in," I said to Terry. The anesthesiologist overheard me and left his position at the mother's head. He was the same man who had taught me how to "deparrisize a parrisized baby." Although he was an expert at intubating anything with a windpipe, he too had a great deal of trouble passing the tube; he tried it three times, but every time he met with the same result. "There's something wrong with this kid," he muttered after the third failure. He put the ambu bag over the baby's face and pushed 100-percent oxygen in under pressure, and within seconds she became less blue.

Although she had never successfully intubated a baby, Terry wanted to try. I took over her job, managing the fluid resuscitation, and pushed very rapidly about two and one half ounces of a solution called plasmanate in an attempt to increase the baby's blood pressure. Terry attempted to pass the tube three times but the tube simply would go no farther than two centimeters below the vocal cords. Each time she tried to intubate the baby turned blue; after she removed the tube and blew some oxygen through the ambu bag, the baby would pink up again.

To add to the panic and confusion in our end of the DR, Parris, having left Tom to finish the operation on his own, now came over to the warming table and began yelling at us. "You incompetent jerks," he carried on, "I handed you a perfectly healthy baby and you can't even do something as simple as intubate it. Which of you is the senior resident?"

"We're both interns," I answered meekly.

"What?" Parris shouted. "Two interns at a stat section without a senior resident? That's irresponsible. I'm going up to report your incompetence to Sullivan right now. I'm not going to let this happen again. I want a neonatologist who knows what he's doing."

At that moment Dan, who had been stat paged by the circulating nurse after it became clear that Frohman was not going to show up, came running into the DR. "What's going on?" he asked, slightly excited.

"We can't intubate this baby," I said, "I tried, Terry tried, the anesthesiologist even tried. We just can't get the tube in."

"Let me in," he said, pushing Terry away. He tried to intubate, but he too could not get the tube to pass into the windpipe. "This is weird," he said after his second failure. "I know I'm in, but it won't go through; this kid must have some weird malformations of the trachea. Let's get her upstairs."

Terry, still bagging through the ambu bag and face mask, and I quickly loaded the child into the warm transport incubator. Feeling like shit, like we had through our incompetence just ruined this little girl's life, I helped Terry and Dan push the incubator out of DR 3 into a waiting elevator and then into the Pit to the waiting warming table that had previously been occupied by the Dead Kid. When the baby was settled in, I asked Terry to stop bagging and tried, one last time, to intubate; but I was no more successful in the Pit than I had been in the delivery room. "Don't bother," Dan said as I was trying, "there's something wrong down there. Keep up the bagging, we need to do a trach."

Dan asked Maureen, the red-haired nurse who had been assigned to this new baby, to get set up for a tracheostomy. Dan then went off to scrub.

Just then Sullivan came running like a madman into the Pit. He had just finished being yelled at by Parris and had built up a good head of steam. Sullivan quickly assessed the situation: not seeing Dan and realizing that Simon was nowhere to be found, he had come upon a critically ill newborn and two very vulnerable interns who apparently could not perform the simple task of intubation. Seizing the opportunity, he started in, "Can't even intubate a full-term baby, huh? What a laugh. You two criticize me for what I do, and you can't even intubate a full-term kid!"

I felt like shit but, once again, Dan came to my rescue. He came flying over from the sink yelling, "You bastard! You leave them alone. This isn't an ordinary full-term kid. You try intubating, big shot!"

Sullivan and Dan stood eye to eye, glaring. Without saying a word, Sullivan shoved Terry, who was still bagging the baby, out of the way, grabbed the laryngoscope and ET tube I had used moments before, and attempted to intubate. He tried and tried until the sweat started to drip down his face. He shoved harder and harder, but he could not pass the tube through the impenetrable vocal cords.

Now it was Dan's turn. "What's wrong, big shot?" he asked sarcastically. Dan had gowned and gloved while Sullivan was trying to pass the tube. "You can't do it? A famous, important neonatologist like yourself can't even intubate a full-term baby? Maybe you should think before you open your fucking mouth!" Dan, sterile, with scalpel in hand, nudged Sullivan, who seemed dumbfounded, away. "Bag the kid, Terry," Dan said. "Let's get her pink again," and Terry went to it.

The baby was now about fifteen minutes old.

"What you doing?" Sullivan asked, regaining some of his composure.

"A tracheostomy," Dan responded. "Do you have any idea why?"

"Shut up, you little shit," Sullivan said, not as sure of himself as he had been a few minutes before. "This baby needs ENT stat! Kathy, go call them and tell them we have a baby with a laryngeal web and a probable tracheoesophageal fistula. Tell them to get their asses over here stat." And Kathy, who had entered the Pit soon after Sullivan had come running in, went off to the nurses' station to do her boss's bidding.

"Great, Sullivan," Dan said sarcastically. "If we wait for them to get here, they'll probably be able to find out the problem during the child's autopsy. The only chance we have for saving this baby is to do an emergency trach. And I'm doing it."

Sullivan didn't object.

Terry and I were back to managing the fluids. On admission to the Pit, the blood pressure had been low and the baby had been in shock. We had given some more of the plasmanate, a solution that is essentially reconstructed blood plasma, and the emergency-release blood I had ordered while we waited for the baby to be born arrived at this point. Terry and I loaded the blood into a syringe and pushed it through the UV line, and the baby's blood pressure increased to 50/30, not great but at least she was out of shock.

Dan performed the tracheostomy. With Maureen extending the neck, he washed down the area with antiseptic solution, made an incision low down, and inserted a large-bored tube into the hole he had created. The skin around the tube seemed to attach around it and it formed a tight seal. Dan taped the tube in place with a tough, sticky wad of tape so there was no chance the tube would slip out. Dan then attached the end of the tracheostomy tube to the ventilator and the baby's chest began to move up and down, up and down with the "siss-pump, siss-pump" of the ventilator. The baby's skin color, which had turned deep blue during the tracheostomy, pinked up nicely.

While Dan was putting the finishing touches on his masterpiece, Terry and I went to gown and glove. We had to remove the UV line and replace it with a more permanent UA line. We performed this job without complication, with Dan, who did not say a word, carefully watching over us. At the completion of our task, Dan said, "That was great, you two do nice work together." It was the first time Terry or I had put in a UA line without help from a senior resident.

The baby, now about thirty-five minutes old, breathed by a ventilator through a tracheostomy tube that bipassed the apparent obstruction; the blood pressure was now 60/40, normal for a newborn; the first blood gas drawn from the UA line Terry and I had put in revealed that the baby was being well oxygenated and wasn't acidotic. In short, although the baby was not breathing on her own and had an as-yet unknown abnormality of her upper airway, she was stable. Within another hour, she began to breathe on her own. She was, by far, not out of the woods yet, but she was not dead.

Although incompetent, although not exactly sure what we were doing, Terry and I had actually contributed to saving this baby's life, and we had done it without any help from Sullivan. He looked on while the three of us worked, not speaking. He had been shaken by what had happened and he didn't know exactly how to deal with it.

I have never again seen anyone perform an emergency tracheostomy on a newborn baby. Of course, in all the years that have passed since that summer at St. A's, I have never seen a baby with so complex a malformation as that little girl turned out to have. At the time of operation, which was performed later that Monday, she was found to have a bony block just below the vocal cords, which could not possibly have been penetrated by the soft plastic of the endotracheal tube or by oxygen. The surgeons also found a tracheoesophageal fistula, a communication between the esophagus, or food pipe, and the trachea, or windpipe. It had been this TE fistula that had kept the baby alive until Dan could perform his tracheostomy, because it allowed oxygen that was placed in the baby's esophagus to pass through the trachea to the lungs.

Although the TE fistula had saved the baby's early neonatal life, its presence following the tracheostomy caused nothing but concern. In addition to oxygen getting to the trachea from the esophagus, food, saliva, and stomach acid could also take this route to the lungs, and their presence in the lungs would cause severe pneumonia and destruction of the lung tissue. For this reason, early surgery was necessary.

Ray returned to the Pit in time for Dan to tell him about the baby and that Terry and I had saved her life in the early minutes in the DR. Although I realized it was really Dan who had saved the baby, I did feel good about the whole affair. It wasn't clear yet whether the month would be salvageable, but at least I was feeling better about myself.

Since everything had settled down, Ray and I signed out to Terry, who was not very happy about the prospect of spending the night on call with Sullivan around. I was getting ready to leave when Ray asked me a favor. "Bob, will you go out with me for a drink?"

"Sure," I answered. "Why ask me so seriously? I love getting drunk with you."

"Well, it's not going to be just you and me. I'm supposed to meet Laurie at a bar near the Medical Center."

"So why do you want me there?"

"Well, I want to tell her tonight about me . . . about me not being a famous nephrologist, so I want you there, just in case. . . ."

"Just in case what?" I asked after Ray hesitated.

"Just in case she walks out on me. I really like her, Bob, I don't know, maybe I'm even in love with her. And if she calls me an asshole and walks out, I don't know what I'll do. I can't take being walked out on twice in the same month."

I felt bad for Ray. "Sure I'll come," I responded, and I put my hand on his shoulder.

We left the hospital in silence. I knew what was going to happen. I just hoped Ray would be able to hold himself together.

XXXI
After Hours

We met Lauren at the Recovery Room, a bar down the street from the Medical Center that was decorated to look like the inside of an operating room. The walls were covered with framed photographs of doctors at work cutting up people.

Lauren, who had gotten there before us, was sitting at one of the bar's booths. She seemed a little troubled by my presence and, after Ray gave her a little kiss on the cheek, she asked, "What are you doing here, Bob?"

"Bob's sort of down," Ray answered before I had a chance to. "He had a rough night and a pretty busy day today, so I thought it would be a good idea if he tagged along with us tonight. If it's okay with you."

"Oh, it's okay," Lauren answered. "Anything happen I should know?"

"Well, Bob and Terry single-handedly saved a kid in the DR today," Ray responded again before I had a chance to say anything.

"Really?" Lauren asked. "That's great. What did you do?"

"Well, we didn't exactly save her life," I finally said. "Actually, we went down to the DR together because Terry was called for a stat section and Frohman wasn't around. We couldn't intubate the baby, so we just kept her going until Dan showed up; he couldn't intubate her either, and we decided the baby had some strange malformation of the trachea. When we got her up to the Pit, Dan did a tracheostomy, and then the kid became stable. So I wouldn't give Terry and me too much credit."

"No, that's silly," Lauren said, "you stayed cool in a crisis, and that's very important. I bet that really impressed Sullivan. You should make sure he puts a note about this in your permanent file."

"It didn't impress Sullivan," I responded with a questioning look. "In fact, he took the opportunity to yell at us because we weren't experienced enough to even intubate a full-term baby, and then when he found that he couldn't pass the tube either, he got angry at us. But even if Sullivan was impressed by what we did, I wouldn't want a note from him in my file, because Sullivan's a schmuck."

Now it was Lauren's turn to look puzzled. "Yeah, sure he's a schmuck, but he is the attending, and he's the guy who writes your evaluation. So if you want to get anything out of this rotation, you better be nice to him."

I didn't respond to her. I was tired and I felt nauseated, it was a hot and humid day and the air-conditioning in the Recovery Room wasn't working too well. Our beers had arrived and I took a long pull on mine as Lauren, just trying to make conversation, asked, "Anything else happen today?"

"The Dead Kid finally died," Ray responded.

"Really?" she asked, concerned. "How?"

"His father knocked him off," I answered, "with a bolus of KCl."

"Oh, good," she replied brightly. "I mean, it's not good that the father had to kill his own baby; I'm just glad the baby didn't die of an infection because I stuck that peritoneal catheter into the wrong place. That would have made me look really bad."

I was so stunned by this reaction, I knocked the remainder of my beer onto the floor, but Ray didn't seem surprised or upset by it. "Come on, Laurie," he said, "it was a normal mistake. It was the first time you ever put one of those things in, and you're sort of supposed to hit bowel the first time you do it."

"No, Ray, that's not the way it's supposed to happen," Lauren responded. "I really blew it, and I bet that ruined any chance I had of getting a fellowship here next year. But going to Ann Arbor with you will be just as wonderful, really."

I didn't know exactly how much of this I was going to be able to take before puking. Here I had just told Lauren about the relieving death of the sickest baby in the Pit, and her reaction was completely self-centered, revolving around how this death might affect her career. I stared at Ray, a little angry at him for actually defending her, but figuring that since she had mentioned Ann Arbor, this would be his opportunity to tell Lauren the truth. When he hesitated, and the conversation lagged, I gladly stepped in. "Haven't you told her yet, Ray?" I asked.

Ray, looking very uncomfortable, opened his mouth, but nothing came out. "Told me what?" Lauren asked, still smiling and relaxed.

A look of panic came to Ray's face as he stammered, "Well . . . well . . . I sort of have to tell you . . . I . . . er," and that's when he looked toward me, pathetically, silently asking for help.

"What are you trying to say, honey?" Lauren asked, her smile vanishing.

"What he's trying to say," I answered, "is that he's not really a renal physiologist."

"I don't understand," she responded, panicking, "you're pulling my leg, aren't you, Bob? Of course you are; this really isn't very funny."

"No," Ray said, "Bob's telling the truth, Laurie. I've never really even been in a renal lab. I can barely do a urinalysis."

"Ray, come on," she said, more panicky, "you wouldn't do anything like this to me."

"It's pretty much my fault," I responded firmly. "Ray was terrified after spending his first night on call with you and you left him out in the Pit all alone. So Dan told us you were interested in renal and that you were the kind of person who . . ." I was searching for a nice way of saying "prostitute," ". . . who could warm up if you found out that Ray could in some way help you."

"What?" Lauren asked, her face getting hard and looking like she was about to burst into tears.

"So we came up with this story that Ray was a famous nephrologist and we spread it around, and I guess you heard about it, and you reacted just the way we hoped you would."

"How could you do such a thing to me?" Lauren asked, her voice rising. "You . . ."

"I didn't mean to hurt you, honey," Ray said in a quiet voice. "I just wanted you to be there if I needed you."

"You used me!" she shouted, loud enough for the people at the bar to hear. All eyes turned momentarily to this woman, her face bright red, her eyes near tears. "You used me," she repeated in a slightly softer voice. "I cleaned your fucking apartment, I did your damned laundry, and I screwed you, and all that time you were stringing me on, you were using me. How could you do it? How could you do such a thing?" And Lauren began crying.

"He didn't mean for it to happen like this," I said, answering for Ray who had dissolved into tears. "In the beginning, we really only did it to get you to stay with Ray when he was on at night. But somewhere along the way, he seems to have fallen in love with you." Ray, still crying, nodded.

"Love?" Lauren repeated, tears and mascara running down her cheeks. But then she snickered and said, "You interns, I swear, you guys are hopeless. You got Sullivan gunning for you, your only friend is that jerk Berkowitz, and then you go fucking falling in love with me. You guys'll never amount to anything unless you get your damned selves straightened out!"

"Us?" I responded, still speaking for Ray. "How about you? You think you'll amount to anything? You don't care about medicine, you don't care about patients, you don't care about being a good doctor, all you care about is getting ahead. What pride can you take in yourself? You aren't a real person, you're just a shell, a candy coating with nothing inside. Personally, I don't understand how Ray could fall in love with you. Sure, you're beautiful on the outside, but you're ugly on the inside."

I guess I touched a raw nerve because she became quiet and could not respond. She had the look of a little girl being scolded.

"Laurie," Ray said, regaining his composure enough to talk, "you are a good doctor. I know you don't think so, but I've seen you in real emergency situations and you know what to do. I've felt sort of comfortable when I've been on and you've been with me. You don't need to use me or anybody else to get a job, you could get one on your own."

"What do you know about it?" Lauren asked angrily. "What do you know about getting a job in nephrology?"

"I don't know much," Ray responded quietly, looking into her red eyes, "but I do know you're a good doctor from a good residency program, and that should be enough."

"I'm a woman," she said in a whisper.

"We know that," I answered.

"There's not a doubt about it," Ray added.

"You guys," she snickered again. "You are so dumb. You think it's easy for a woman to get a good fellowship?"

"Sure," Ray responded, "why not?"

"Because medicine's a man's world. Sure, if you guys are competent, if you stay in line and finish in a program like this, you'll have no problems getting a good fellowship. But that won't happen for me or for any other woman in this program. I've had to sell myself every time I wanted something. In college, in medical school, to get this residency, every time."

"Do you like doing it?" I asked.

"Of course not."

"So why do you do it?" I asked.

"I have to."

"You have to?" I repeated. "You don't have to. Terry's never sold herself, she's competed with men as an equal, and she's succeeded. And besides, you didn't have to even become a doctor in the first place. Where is it written that you had to become a doctor?"

"It was my father," she said, sighing, after a short hesitation. "My father was a nephrologist in private practice. I was an only child and from the time I was a little girl, my father always told me I had to become a doctor, that I had to carry on for him. And because I was a girl, he always told me I had to be extra good at everything I did, I had to be extra smart, and extra pretty, because it was going to be extra hard for me. I never really thought about it much until after he died, when I was in college. At that time, I knew I had to do it, and so I started . . . making some sacrifices."

"Do you like being a doctor?" I asked.

"No . . . not really . . . I don't know. I haven't thought about it much. It's like breathing; it's a part of my life that doesn't require any thought."

"You don't like what you're doing, yet you make sacrifices to get to do it." Lauren's story had changed her from a comical clown into a pathetic creature. "Sacrifices like sleeping with people like Ray in order to get ahead?" She nodded yes. "Jesus, Lauren, how do you do that? How can you live with yourself afterward?"

She started crying and Ray cradled her in his arms. He stroked her beautiful long, golden hair and said, "Laurie, I'll help you, I really do love you," but she didn't react. She kept on crying and put her arms around Ray's shoulders.

"Ray, I'm leaving," I announced, figuring they didn't need me around anymore. I left them locked in embrace, crying their eyes out.

It was hard to believe; I had gotten to know three pediatric senior residents during my stay at St. A's. All three of them had been challenged with the pain, the anguish, the stress of the internship I had just started, and all three had developed different ways of coping with it: Simon Frohman had turned into a sniveling wimp, unable to make an independent decision and unable to question one that had been made; Lauren, who had had a head start down the path, so unsure of her ability, her skill, and her knowledge, had become little more than a prostitute, selling herself for a good recommendation or a promise of one; only Dan Berkowitz had been able to develop a constructive way of dealing with the stress. By ignoring the bad advice of Sullivan and the others of his kind, and by teaching himself what he needed to know, Dan had made himself into a competent physician. And it was because of this that Ray, Terry, and I followed Dan's lead. And it is because we followed him that Dan is the hero of this story.

BOOK III

It was getting late. I had wanted to make it all the way to Boston to have dinner with Ray and Terry at the hotel in which we were staying, but it was already eight-thirty, I still had about an hour of solid driving left, and I was tired and starving. So after I got onto the Mass Pike in Sturbridge, I stopped at the first Howard Johnson's for something to eat.

In most things during life, we tend to remember the good times and forget the bad, but it was just the opposite during my internship. During that month in the Pit, when things were going badly during the first two weeks, I remember even now what I ate at every meal, what clothes I wore every day. But when things started to improve, as they did during those last two weeks, my memory fades and, as a result, time during those last two weeks seems to have passed very rapidly. The good times were due mostly to Dan, who became our main focus. Sure, we continued to fight with Sullivan, and he continued to threaten us with reporting us to Jennings and replacing us with other interns but, by following Dan's suggestion, we ignored him. And with Dan's help, we started doing what we wanted to do. Some of the babies got better, others didn't.

At HoJo's, I had a cup of coffee and an English muffin, and then I headed back to the highway, eager to get to Boston. While I drove down the Pike, I tried to recall those final two weeks. Although I can't remember all the specifics, the feelings and the spirit of that time remain with me. How importantly those last two weeks would bear on the rest of my life. For it was then that I started to enjoy neonatology.

XXXII

Tuesday, July 13

Morning Rounds

I entered the Pit at seven-fifty and was met by a hostile, frazzled Terry.

"Hi," I said innocently, "how was it?"

"I'm glad you're finally here," she said with a sneer, "because I'm leaving now. I've had enough of this place! I've been pushed around for the last time by that jerk!"

"What happened?"

"I didn't get any sleep. Every time I lay down in the on-call room, Sullivan banged on the door and ordered me to do something. He wandered around the unit all night, having me do CBCs on all the stable kids in the growers row! He said they looked anemic. Anemic, my ass! One of the lights down there was out, that's all. All the blood work was normal. And he was all over me about that new kid with the trachea and esophagus you need blueprints to figure out. She was pretty stable all night, but the ENT guy showed up, and he and Sullivan came up with about a hundred tests they thought needed to be done by this morning. And who had to do them? Me. I spent the whole damned night doing pointless scut and being told how incompetent I was by that asshole!"

"What did Simon have to say about all this?" I asked. "Did he at least help you out?"

"Frohman," Terry screamed, pulling at her hair, "that other pillar of the Boston medical community! That schmuck never even showed up!

No one's even seen him since the Dead Kid bit the bullet, and he hasn't even called. Sullivan's definitely going to have him beheaded."

"That wouldn't be so bad," Ray said. He had joined us during Terry's tirade. "Simon would do pretty well without a head. And he'd probably be less confused about things." Terry smiled.

"Ray, how did everything go last night," I asked, "after I left?"

"Oh, sort of like I expected," he answered, not looking terribly sad. "She called me an asshole a few times and told me she never wanted to see me again."

"Sorry to hear that," I responded, not sorry at all.

"Well, it's not so bad," Ray said, "she is a real jerk. She is pretty, but did you hear some of those things she said?"

"Yeah," I answered. "Oh well, it's probably for the best."

At this point Dan entered the Pit and asked, "Where's Frohman?"

"Not here," Terry answered. "The worm never showed his face last night."

"He didn't show up to be on call?" Dan asked, his eyes opening wide.

"No, he never came," Terry said, smiling in response to what she thought was Dan's look of mock terror. "It's a great loss, isn't it?"

Dan did not smile. "Something's wrong," he said tensely, "something must really be wrong. Frohman's never missed a night on call. You can call the guy a jerk, you can call him a wimp, but he is at least dependable. If he wasn't here last night, something terrible must have happened. We're going to have to go look for him, but we'd better make quick work rounds first."

That was the first morning Dan led us on rounds and it was a real experience. As we arrived at each baby's warming table, Dan had us present a capsulized summary of the child's course and, at the end of each presentation, he asked, "What is this baby's biggest problem?" We had to think it out for ourselves. Then Dan, using the Socratic method, taught us what caused the problem and asked us what we wanted to do about it. And we gave him our recommendations. He concluded by saying, "Fine, just don't let Sullivan know what you're doing." That morning we got more teaching about neonatology than we had gotten during the rest of the month. Our patients, rather than being unfocused objects surrounded by wads of uninterpretable data, with multiple serious problems that were beyond the realm of manageability, became children with finite, graspable disorders. For the first time during that month, Ray, Terry, and I could figure out which end was up. And although all this occurred on rounds that morning, the time spent was no more than had been spent on work rounds every morning with Simon.

When it was nearly ten, we realized we had to do something. None of us wanted to confront Sullivan yet, we needed time to plan exactly how we were going to approach the man. We knew that if we were to hide in our on-call room, the boss would surely find us. Dan, who was going to begin to check around the hospital for Simon, suggested we use the resident's room on the third floor. Thinking that was a great idea, I led Ray and Terry down to the abandoned part of the old St. A's where the room was located.

"You guys aren't going to believe this place," I said as I opened the door and walked inside with Ray and Terry right behind. It was then that we saw Simon. He was lying on the comfortable double bed, staring up at the ceiling, totally oblivious to us.

I thought he was dead. He moved not at all when we entered the room; he moved not a muscle to the sound of our voices calling to him, or to the feel of our hands slapping his face. But his chest moved up and down, almost imperceptively as he breathed. His heart was beating inside his chest, and his pulses felt strong in his arms and legs.

"He's catatonic," Terry diagnosed.

"He's flipped out," Ray simplified.

"Jesus Christ," I exclaimed, "so this is what happens to you when you start your senior year at St. A's."

"God," Terry said, "who would have ever thought something like this could have happened?"

"It was the Dead Kid dying," I said. "Simon must have realized what Sullivan was doing was wrong, but he couldn't yell at Sullivan to get him to stop. So he just slipped off the edge."

"His hands are still covered with the antiseptic stuff," Ray observed. "We're partly responsible for this. We should have seen what was happening to him and done something about it."

"Calm down, Ray," Terry ordered, "let's not go overboard. I feel sorry for Simon too, but let's not forget he brought on almost all his own problems and added a lot to ours. We could've seen what was happening to him, but he could've seen what he was doing to us, too."

"Let's not argue," I said. "We have to figure out what to do."

We tried to arouse him again, but he retained his stony, fixed stare. We even tried dumping cold water over his head, as they used to do in the movies, but he remained the same. "We'd better get some help," Terry finally suggested.

"Let's get him to the Medical Center," I said. "We'd better call an ambulance." I dialed 911 and had to repeat a few times that we needed an ambulance for an emergency in St. Anne's Hospital, Room 324. I guess they weren't used to getting calls to pick up patients who were having emergencies within the walls of a hospital.

After I got off the phone, we sat on the worn easy chairs, reflecting on all this and waiting for the ambulance. Simon remained lying in bed, not moving. "You know," Ray finally said, "this could have happened to any of us. Simon wasn't that different from us."

"Well, the difference between us," I said, "is that Simon couldn't stand up for what he thought was right. After a while, he had trouble even knowing what he thought was right and then finally, he had trouble just thinking."

"What protects us," Terry added, "is that we know exactly what's wrong with this place and we're trying to do something about it."

"That's right," I said, "this whole thing just reaffirms that we must follow Dan's advice."

Our musings were interrupted by a knock on the door. When Ray opened it, two paramedics pushing a gurney entered. "What happened?" the first paramedic asked. He was about my age, had red hair, a red moustache, and a ruddy face.

"This is Dr. Frohman," I said, pointing to the body. "He's a senior resident at the Medical Center. He seems to have lapsed into a catatonic coma and is totally incapable of being roused."

"How'd you guys get in here?" the red-haired guy asked, obviously not believing a word of the story. "You're pulling my leg, right?"

Our faces told him we weren't. "No," Ray said, "we're not pulling your leg. He really needs help."

The paramedics poked and prodded Simon until they had convinced themselves that he truly was catatonic. And then they loaded Simon onto the gurney and took him out of the room. We followed them until they disappeared behind the closed door of the elevator.

We headed back to the Pit silently, each of us thinking about Simon during the trip, thinking about what had happened to him, and thinking how close we were to the same fate.

Sullivan was waiting for us, and furious, when we entered the Pit. It was bad enough that no one, not even Frohman, had shown up for his attending rounds, but the fact that there was no doctor in or around the Pit was just too much for him. As we entered, Ray's beeper went off, and he was saved from catching a prime piece of Sullivan's wrath by a well-timed Parris section.

When he saw us enter, Sullivan approached, like a lion ready to attack. Looking tired and very angry, he said facetiously, "Oh, good morning, Doctors. How nice of you to come to the nursery. We've missed you."

Terry, dog-tired after dealing with this man's ranting and raving all through the night, and still very upset about Simon, started to go for him, but I put a hand out and, remembering Dan's advice, responded very sweetly, "Oh, we're sorry, Dr. Sullivan. We had an emergency."

Sullivan seemed a little put off by my tone, but he had been rehearsing this chewing out in advance and wasn't going to be stopped because of a little friendliness in the victim's tone. "Oh, an emergency? An emergency in the delivery suite? No, I looked for you there. An emergency in the well-baby nursery? No, Berkowitz was down there and he said you weren't around. And you certainly weren't up here. Those are the only three places in this hospital where emergencies occur, Doctor. Do you want to add lying to the growing list of offenses you've committed since coming to St. A's?"

"No, Dr. Sullivan," Terry answered, now under control and realizing what I was doing, "we really were at an emergency. Honest." She sounded like an angel, but Sullivan still continued his rehearsed speech.

"You know, I'm embarrassed. I'm embarrassed because in the greater Boston area, in Massachusetts, in all of New England, in fact, in the whole Northeast, my nursery, year after year, has the lowest rate of newborn mortality. I'm proud of that fact; it's a reflection on me. Because I'm so committed to this nursery, because I care so much, putting this place above my family and social life, I've been able to achieve these statistics. But over the past two weeks, in fact, since June twenty-eighth, the day you interns arrived here, our mortality rate has soared. I haven't changed the way I do things; the nurses haven't changed the way they do things; the babies haven't changed. The only thing that has changed has been the interns. So I have to conclude that it is you interns who have caused the mortality rate to rise.

"And what is it about you three that made the death rate go up? Is it incompetence? Well, I've seen better than you, but I've also seen worse, and even with the worst, this hasn't happened; so, it probably isn't your technical incompetence that's caused it. But what am I to think when I come into the nursery and find no one here? What would have happened if there had been a code? There would have been no doctors around to resuscitate the baby, the baby would have died, and the mortality rate would have gone up. So I have to conclude that it is your attitude that's the problem; you three just don't give a damn. You don't care about my babies, you are all selfish, and you don't care about anything but yourselves."

He had by this point gotten the whole speech out. We didn't interrupt him once. I'm sure he expected us to yell back, and for there to be a terrific scene which would have ended with him telling us to clear out of the Pit and to never come back. But, using our new philosophy, that didn't happen; instead, we agreed with him.

"You're right, Dr. Sullivan," I said sweetly, "we've let you down. Ray, Terry, and I, we've had some trouble adjusting to life as interns. I know that's not a great excuse, but it's the only excuse we have. We've just had a meeting and discussed everything and we've decided that you're right about a lot of things. If you can forgive us now, we promise we'll shape up. Please, just give us another chance."

"What?" Sullivan asked, seeing my mouth move and hearing words come out, but not believing what he was hearing. "What's going on?"

"It's the truth," Terry responded. "We're sorry and we want you to forgive us."

"I don't believe you," Sullivan said. "You've lied to me before. Why should I think you're telling the truth now?"

"We're not lying," I said solemnly. "It's because of Frohman that we've changed our attitude. You have to believe us."

"What do you mean?" he asked, confused. "Where's Frohman? What have you done with him?"

"I'm sorry to tell you this," I said very dramatically. "Simon has just been taken to the Medical Center by ambulance. He appears to have suffered an acute psychotic breakdown."

"We were with him," Terry added. "That was the emergency. That's why we weren't around."

Sullivan stared at me and Terry, clearly frightened and upset. "A breakdown?" he asked.

"Yes, sir," Terry answered. "We found him in the resident's room, catatonic. He'd been there since yesterday. We called the ambulance. We think it happened when he wanted to disobey your orders when you were resuscitating the Dead Kid."

"My God," Sullivan uttered as he started to leave the Pit.

"Dr. Sullivan?" Terry shouted after him. "Are we forgiven?"

He turned to look at Terry but didn't say a word. He soon turned back again and walked out through the door in the nurses' station.

Terry and I, happy about our performance, soon followed him out and couldn't stop laughing as we entered the on-call room. "I think he bought it," I said. I thought, for the first time at that point, that I was going to make it through. I thought the last two weeks were going to be a breeze.

XXXIII
Wednesday, July 14
On Call

No, a breeze wasn't exactly what it was, but the last week and a half of the month did pass a lot more smoothly than the first two and a half weeks had. This was due almost entirely to Dan's help, but it was also partly due to our new, seemingly friendly relationship with Sullivan. He had won us over to his way of thinking, he thought, and therefore we had become worthwhile creatures.

Simon Frohman was lost to us for the rest of the month, having been admitted to the psychiatric ward at the Medical Center with a diagnosis of acute schizophrenia. He remained catatonic for nearly a month, despite doses of psychotropic medications so large they would alter the mental status of a schizophrenic elephant. In Simon's absence Dan unofficially filled in, and on work rounds every morning we formulated two separate plans of action for each patient. The Plan A was what we wanted to do, what we thought actually needed to be done for the baby. The Plan B, the plan upon which we were not going to act, was the order that Sullivan had given for the baby's care for that day. As it turned out, our A Plan only rarely coincided with the B Plan.

Dan's leadership was unofficial because Sullivan simply forbade Dan to enter the Pit, so Dan had to sneak around in order to supervise us. As soon as work rounds ended, he headed for the well-baby nursery. If we had questions or needed help, we called him down there. I guess Sullivan assumed we were making work rounds in the early morning alone; he never questioned us about it. He didn't even seem interested.

Attending rounds continued to be pretty much a waste of time with Sullivan going on and on, spouting nonsensical opinions, but rounds became more exciting that third week, because Ray, Terry, and I felt as if we were playing parts in a drama. We wrote down everything the man told us to do, even though we had no intention of doing it. We invented phony lab values when he asked us about tests he had ordered to be performed the day before. And we fabricated information about each patient's condition, and the inputs and outputs for the day before. In short, we talked a good game.

And Sullivan appeared to love it. He told us that he was proud of us and that he'd misjudged us. But most importantly, he recanted on his threat to never leave the nursery.

On the evening of the first day of playing this game, I took the sign-out from Ray and Terry, and Dan and I sat alone in the nurses' station, waiting for something to happen. We didn't have to wait long.

Baby Girl Donovan soon returned from the Medical Center, now stable after the operation that repaired her coarctation, but still in need of close monitoring. She came by ambulance and was accompanied by Dr. Channin. "Hi, Dan, hi, Bob," the cardiologist said as he entered the Pit, pushing the back of the gurney, "glad to see you boys. I thought you'd both be dead by now, with Sullivan in prison for the double murder."

"Nope, Dr. Channin," Dan responded. "We've survived. We're coping."

"Coping?" Channin repeated suspiciously. He and the ambulance attendant had stopped the gurney by an empty bed space. Maureen was picking the baby up, trying not to disturb her right arm in which an IV was precariously stuck, and transferred her to the warming table. "What do you mean by coping? That doesn't sound kosher."

"Well, they've adopted me as their attending," Dan said.

"That's what I thought it meant," Channin responded with a smile. "Have you told your real attending about this? Or are you lying to him?"

"It's not exactly lying," I said. "We're just giving Sullivan the impression that we think what he's doing is great. And then we just do what we think is best for the patients. It's more like . . ."

"Like lying," Channin said, completing the sentence.

"I guess," I conceded.

"Census must be pretty low here by now," Channin said, smiling. "I took two patients, or was it three?, out of here last week, and that was before you decided to do whatever you wanted. How many other attendings have you guys conned into taking a patient or two back with them?"

"Oh, you're the only one, Dr. Channin," I said.

"Great!" he answered. "It's always great to know that when the members of the house staff are thinking of lying to and deceiving their attendings, the first name that comes into their little heads is Channin. Oh well," he sighed, "I guess it's just my lot in life!"

"You should be proud," Dan said. "It just shows how much we love you. Well, how is this child? Great, I bet."

"Baby Girl Donovan is excellent, no matter how you look at her. Her aorta's working just fine, thanks to Dr. Dover's magic knife and about ten centimeters of plastic graft. And since you're interested, the Genetics boys have checked her out, and they found she has a normal number of chromosomes. You know why that's important, Dr. Sharon, sir?"

"Normal chromosomes?" I asked, trying to think it through and come up with an explanation of why this might be important. My brain's memory bank finally reached the genetics section and I hesitantly said, "Turner's syndrome?" reciting the name of a disorder that I thought was associated with coarctation of the aorta.

"Bingo," Channin said, impressed. "Dan, let this boy go home tonight without having to take call and put it on my tab. Seriously though, the chromosomes were normal, so there aren't any other abnormalities we have to look for. The kid should be a star from now on. Dan, that was really some pickup! You saved this kid's life!"

"I'll say," I said.

"It was nothing," Dan responded modestly, "nothing, that is, for a brilliant diagnostician like myself."

I laughed. "How are the Srnivasan twins?" I asked Channin.

"I'm glad you brought them up, Bob, because, after only one round of testing, it appears that we have a winner in our Siamese twin survival Olympics. The cath data shows that the one on the left is the winner. She has the largest part of the heart on her side of the chest."

"That's good, I guess," I responded tentatively. "When do you think the surgery might get done?"

"They're scheduled to go in early tomorrow morning. We had to set it up as an emergency because the studies showed that the heart has been deteriorating under all the strain. I just hope it isn't too late. The surgery will probably last all day. Would you like to come and see it? It promises to be really bloody."

"No thanks," I answered. "I get sick at the sight of blood."

"Well, you sure picked the right profession! It's a good thing you didn't become a butcher. Dan, where did they get this guy?"

"He's not so bad, Dr. Channin, really. He's just been made weird by being so close to Sullivan for so long."

"Yeah, I guess I can understand that," the cardiologist answered. "I guess being around that guy would turn even Joyce Brothers into a quivering mass of jelly. Well, I must be leaving now. Do you two have any questions?"

"No," Dan answered. "Do you have any answers?"

"I guess not," Channin answered, laughing. "All you have to do with this Donovan baby is check the blood pressure. If it goes up, give me a call. I'm open twenty-four hours a day. And we deliver!"

"Okay," I answered. The ambulance driver was ready to leave.

"I'll call tomorrow to give you a blow-by-blow description of what happens at the Srnivasan operation," he said as he headed for the door.

"Great," I said, feigning a gag reflex. "I'll look forward to that."

"And I'll be sure to send you an emesis basin, Bob," he said as he headed out the door.

Dan and I then examined Baby Girl Donovan. I saw the large scar which was healing well that went across the baby's chest. Other than this imperfection, the baby looked pretty good.

Our examination was cut short by a page to the DR. My beeper went off first. Dan got beeped moments later. They were stat pages, so we ran downstairs and, as we entered the delivery suite, found Fredericks and Schwartz pushing a stretcher toward DR 3. "Crash section!" Fredericks yelled. "Thick mec! Move it!"

My heart sank; I guess Dan's did too, for this was almost a duplication of the scene that had greeted us when we arrived for the delivery of the baby who became the Dead Kid. As we ran for the locker room, the face of the Dead Kid appeared in my mind, and the prospect of having to face the struggle I faced during the Dead Kid's life was just about too much to bear.

We dressed and ran into DR 3 and prepared for the baby. We

turned on the warmer, we unwrapped the endotracheal tube and the umbilical artery catheter, we lined up the syringes containing the medications we would need if resuscitation was necessary. And I again took my place next to Tom. The surgeons worked lightning fast, their instruments moving in perfect harmony, and while they worked, Tom told me the story: "two weeks overdue; membranes just ruptured out in the labor room; it was a sea of meconium, just a sea of the stuff! It looked like pea soup. The last contraction brought bad decelerations but the heart rate did come up a little after we turned her on her side. It's still only about a hundred now." It really was the Dead Kid's story all over again.

In what seemed like seconds, I was holding the baby. Although I expected a dead kid, this child wasn't dead at all—this child was alive. He was moving and even let out a little cry.

I ran the baby over to the warming table and laid him down and Dan jumped on him. He suctioned the mouth, getting out a good amount of thick, greenish meconium. I counted the heart rate; the heart was pumping about a hundred times a minute. Dan was beginning to insert an endotracheal tube into the baby's windpipe when a nurse leaned into the DR and asked, "Can I borrow one of you pediatricians? We need you for another delivery."

Since Dan was busy, I followed the nurse who, running ahead, led me into one of the labor rooms, calling out to me, "This woman just walked in off the street and blew the baby out. We barely got her pants off."

Entering the room, I saw lying on the portable warming table what looked like the smallest baby ever born; it was gasping through its nose. My first impulse was to simply turn and run from the room, but I fought that off. "Is there any portable oxygen in here?" I asked, as my second impulse took hold. The nurse, without answering, handed me an oxygen bag with a premie ambu bag attached and I began pumping oxygen from the bag into the baby's lungs. She pinked up a little around the face, so I had the nurse continue the bagging while I listened for the heart rate. It was low, only about sixty beats per minute; I decided the baby needed to be resuscitated. I had to put a UV line in. Although I had done this before with assistance, I had never put a line in by myself.

With my whole body shaking, I poured the antiseptic solution over the baby's entire lower abdomen. From the portable red code cart that the nurse had wheeled into the labor room, I removed the package labeled "umbilical tape," opened it, pulled the thin ribbonlike cloth out, and tied it around the freshly cut umbilical cord stump, just above where the cord rises from the abdominal wall. I cut above the tape with a sterile razor blade, but suddenly blood spurted out from the cut surface. I hadn't tightened the tape enough. So I pulled the tape tighter, until the bleeding stopped. At this point I again listened for the baby's heart rate; it had dropped to fifty. And I panicked even more.

I grabbed the sterile bag that contained the sterile UA catheter and tore it open. I injected some saline through the tubing and set to work trying to find the umbilical vein within the mess that now made up the umbilical cord. The vessel wasn't hard to find, and I threaded the plastic catheter into the thin-walled, wide-bored vein. It passed easily; I stopped advancing it when the catheter was in about six centimeters and pulled back on the plunger of the syringe I had attached to the end of the plastic tubing. Dark blood returned. I was in!

With my hands shaking even more, I reached for the medications. I remembered the order—bicarb, epinephrine, calcium, then glucose. Before giving the first medication, I listened again for the heart. The beat had dropped to forty. My nightmare of the baby dying in my hands was again coming true!

I had to act. I pushed the first med: bicarb, 1 cc; I switched syringes. Epinephrine, 1 cc; another switch. Calcium, 1 cc; then with another switch, some glucose solution. I listened for the heart rate again; it was up to a hundred and ten. I listened, transfixed, for a while longer. It went up to a hundred and thirty. I had resuscitated the baby!

With the heart rate now stable, I took over the ventilation from the nurse. Bagging the baby seemed to be succeeding in keeping the blood well oxygenated, but this was only a short-term solution. This baby had respiratory distress syndrome and she needed to be intubated. And I had to do it!

With some hesitation, I took the premie endotracheal tube and laryngoscope from the code cart. Using the laryngoscope to guide the way, I pushed the baby's tongue aside and saw, thanks to the bright light, what looked like the pearly white strings of the vocal cords. With my right hand I pushed the endotracheal tube along the path created by the laryngoscope and tried to push it between the vocal cords. But the tube slipped away and passed into the esophagus. So I pulled it out and tried again, and this time, with a little pressure, the tube passed into the baby's windpipe. Holding the ET tube steady with my left hand, I attached the ambu bag directly to the end of the ET tube and began pushing oxygen through it. The baby's chest moved up and down, up and down, in time with the bagging.

I taped the ET tube in place while the nurse again took over the bagging. As I was taping the UV line in place, Dan came in.

"What is going on here?" he shouted, having no idea that this little baby had even been born.

"It's okay," I said, relieved that he had come to rescue me. "The baby's stable."

He inspected the situation. "Bob," he asked with a smile, "did you do all this yourself?"

"Yeah," I said, nodding and returning his smile.

Without saying another word, Dan came over to me, gave me a bear hug and a big kiss on the cheek. "That's my boy!" he said, now smiling from ear to ear. "I knew you had it in you!"

Together we lifted the infant from the portable warming table and put her into the transport incubator next to the meconium baby Dan had been working on. That child was now doing fine, and Dan felt we had to watch him only overnight before sending him down to the well-baby nursery, where he belonged.

We reattached my premie's ambu bag to the portable oxygen tank and, with me forcing oxygen into her lungs and with Dan pushing the transport incubator, we brought both babies up to the fifth floor. When we arrived in the Pit, the night nurses, who had arrived while Dan and I were in the delivery room, were surprised to find two babies in the transporter rather than the one they had expected. Angela took charge of my premie. She weighed in at 825 grams, about one and three quarter pounds. Although she wasn't, as I had originally thought, the smallest baby ever born, she still was the smallest baby I had ever resuscitated! And she was showing us she was a real fighter: she was moving around, trying to pull the tube out of her mouth, and wiggling like a worm.

The other baby was admitted by Kathy O'Connell. She was working a night shift in place of, she said, a nurse who had called in sick. I didn't give this much thought, except to realize that my chances for getting much sleep that night were ruined.

While Angela was getting the premie settled in, Dan and I set to work again. Gowned and gloved, we removed the temporary UV catheter and replaced it with a more permanent UA line. "Bob, you saved this baby's life," Dan told me as we were changing the lines. "If this baby amounts to anything, she owes it all to you for being so good to her in that labor room, when she really needed it. And she's going to amount to something, you wait and see! She's going to be a star!"

In fact, I was soon to find that she actually was a star. Her name was Baby Stellar and I was to find, by reading what Tom Fredericks could piece together about her history, that Ms. Stellar, the child's mother, was fifteen years old, was unmarried, and had just finished her freshman year in high school. She had tried to conceal the pregnancy from everyone, including her own parents, and had received no prenatal care. On the morning before the baby had been delivered, she had begun to have labor pains; when she could bear the pain no longer, she had presented herself, alone, to the delivery suite at St. A's. She had been ready to deliver and had barely made it into the labor room before Baby Girl Stellar had made her world premiere.

Dan and I got the two admissions squared away, the meconium baby sleeping comfortably in the second row and Baby Stellar thrashing around, trying to cry, though the position of the endotracheal tube through her vocal cords made this absolutely impossible, in the first bed space of the first row. In keeping with our new plan of functioning in the Pit, I felt it was time to call our attending at home to discuss these new admissions with him. Dan agreed that this was an excellent idea and told me that we would discuss what actually needed to be done, that is, Plan A, after I was done listening to Sullivan's version of action, Plan B.

I called the number listed for Sullivan on the three-by-five card taped over the clerk's desk, and Dr. Sullivan himself answered. "Hello?" his voice said, sounding relaxed.

"Dr. Sullivan? This is Bob Sharon at the hospital. I'm calling to tell you about the three admissions I just got."

"Three admissions?" he repeated. "Sounds like you're having a busy night. Okay, who's the sickest?"

"I guess it's the twenty-seven weeker. . . ." I then launched into the story of the Star, but I didn't mention that I had done the resuscitation alone.

"Sounds like a good case," he said after I had finished the presentation. "Good job, Dr. Sharon. What would you like to do for this baby now?"

I was surprised that he even asked; he seemed too nice over the phone. In my paranoid mind, I figured that maybe this wasn't Sullivan; maybe I had gotten the attending at another nursery. "Support ventilation," I said, "monitor blood gases, and provide maintenance fluids through the UA line."

"And?" Sullivan asked, after waiting through a long pause.

"And what?" I asked, having finished telling what I wanted to do.

"Well, why was this baby born so early?" he asked.

"Prematurity's very common among teenaged mothers," I responded.

"Well, that might be the reason, but how about infection?"

"There was no sign of infection," I answered quickly. "The mother didn't have a fever, her white blood count was low, and the baby's been very vigorous."

"Doesn't matter, Dr. Sharon. You have to consider infection in any child born prematurely. So you have to get a blood culture and a urine culture, do a spinal tap, and start the baby on antibiotics. Okay?"

"Okay," I answered without hesitation. I had no intention of doing any of these things but, as far as Sullivan was concerned, they were already done. "Anything else?"

"No, that's all for that baby. Who's next?"

"At the same time this premie was born, we had a baby with a touch of meconium aspiration." I quickly told him the story of this baby.

"What do you want to do for this child?" Sullivan asked.

"Nothing," I answered. "He's fine!"

"Fine?" Sullivan answered, a little annoyed. "You sucked meconium out of the trachea and you say the baby's fine? Meconium's pretty dangerous stuff. This baby could get into a lot of trouble!"

I looked through the glass that separated the nurses' station from the Pit at the infant in question. He was sleeping like a baby (as they say). He certainly didn't look like he was in trouble. But I just said, "Yes, sir," and sighed quietly.

"Okay. Does he have an ET tube in place?"

"No," I answered. "We pulled it out."

"Well, reintubate him. Suction out his trachea with a small amount of sterile saline every hour. This child also needs a sepsis workup and needs to be started on antibiotics as well."

Again I said, "Yes, sir," with no intention of doing any of this.

"Okay. What else?" Sullivan asked.

I told him the story of Baby Girl Donovan, how Dan had diagnosed coarctation of the aorta, how she had been transferred to the Medical Center for surgery, and how she had returned now for post-op care. Needless to say, Sullivan was shocked that he had not heard a word about this baby before this point, and he was angry. "Why wasn't I told about this case last week?"

"Oh, I'm sorry, Dr. Sullivan," I said trying to sound sincere, "but that was before Ray and Terry and I turned over our new leaf."

"Well, don't you find this to be working out better?" he asked. "You three will get a lot out of the rest of this month, you wait and see. You'll have a great time."

A great time!

I didn't answer. He didn't have any suggestions for worthless workups that needed to be done for Donovan. I was soon wishing him a good-night and hanging up the phone. I joined Dan, who was sitting on a stool in the Pit, talking to Angela.

"You done with that?" he asked as I approached.

"Yeah," I answered, "and wait'll you hear what he wants. . . ."

"Come with me," Dan said, interrupting me in midsentence and leading me into the on-call room. "Don't you learn? I figured you would have figured out after Sullivan found out about the Srnivasan twins that you can't talk about what Sullivan wants to do in a nursery full of nurses, one of whom is Kathy O'Connell, if we're not going to do it. As you may have found out by now, the walls around here seem to have perfect audiograms. Now, what idiocy does he have for us to ignore tonight?"

"Sepsis workups for Baby Stellar and the Meconium Kid," I said, "sepsis workups and antibiotics for everybody."

"Bullshit," Dan responded, "there's absolutely no reason to start either of these kids on antibiotics, let alone to stick a needle into their backs. I've seen a lot of infected newborns, and neither of these kids looks infected."

"I agree," I said, "so what should I do?"

"What do you think?" Dan asked.

"Don't do it," I answered.

"Right. Tell him you're doing it, but don't. They'll do fine. Anything else the master wanted done?"

"Yeah," I answered. "He wants the Meconium Kid reintubated and suctioned every hour."

"Typical," Dan said. "That kid's trachea was clean as a whistle when I got through sucking that shit out. I washed through enough sterile saline to drown the kid! There's no chance there's any more of that stuff down there!"

"I agree," I said. "So we don't reintubate?"

"Correct. It'll be a little more difficult though, since Kathy's taking care of that kid. I wish to hell she wasn't here tonight. She really makes me nervous. I always feel like she's gonna stab me in the back with a chest tube when I'm not looking."

"So what'll I do?"

"Don't do it. Just don't tell her he wants it done. Maybe you'll get away with it."

"Sounds good," I answered.

I set about doing my work. I had a lot of paperwork to do, including writing up three admissions. I wrote long detailed notes on Baby Stellar, my star, and Baby Jones, the Meconium Kid, but only a short transfer note on Baby Donovan. And during the time I was working, the results of the first blood gas we had drawn from Baby Stellar's UA line came back, showing that she was being perfectly ventilated, with just enough oxygen and not too much carbon dioxide in the blood. The baby remained stable through the night and, in fact, during the early morning hours it became possible to begin to lower the oxygen concentration we were supplying her with. This was a sure sign the baby was improving and that, barring any disasters, she would do pretty well.

I finished all my work at eleven-fifteen. I got under the sheet on the on-call room cot at around midnight. I didn't expect to get much sleep, what with the double hex of three fresh admissions coupled with the presence in the Pit of Kathy O'Connell. But surprisingly, I fell into a deep, sound sleep and was allowed to remain in dreamland for nearly three hours. And through the rest of the night, I was called only occasionally to react to blood gas results on the Star. This was a second clue

I failed to take during that night that everything was not exactly right in the Pit.

When morning came, I brushed my teeth, changed my clothes, and headed into the nurses' station. And I realized that, with this night over, I had only three more on-call duties in the Pit. Three nights would be easy. I was going to make it! I was going to survive!

XXXIV

Thursday, July 15 After Hours

Thursday was another beautiful, hot summer day. Boston had had a week of phenomenal weather, the temperature reaching a high in the low nineties in the late afternoon, and never getting below eighty the rest of the day. To us interns, however, the weather most days was always the same. The Pit was always seventy-two degrees and the sun, represented by the neon lights, was always shining. Nothing ever changed in the Pit.

But on Thursday at around 5 P.M., I finally was able to get out of this artificial hell. I had spent thirty-three hours in the Pit, and I was sick of it.

Thursday had passed pretty well. On work rounds Dan had told Ray and Terry, in vivid detail, about what a good job I had done in the DR with the Star. Ray and Terry were really happy and excited for me. I told the team what the A Plan for this baby was and what Sullivan's B Plan was supposed to be. I repeated this for Baby Jones, the Mec Kid, who was looking and acting the way a newborn should and, by all rights, should have been transferred to the well-baby nursery that morning, but wasn't going to be because Sullivan wanted to watch for infection and late respiratory distress. Ray and Terry were also happy to meet Baby Donovan, the baby with the repaired coarctation of the aorta, who was doing fine, and glad to see that Baby Rose, the child with the complex tracheoesophageal malformation, had made it through the night.

Our new system seemed to hold up well through attending rounds that morning. Kathy, tired after her twelve-hour nursing shift, had gone home to sleep before rounds started. "Thank goodness," I thought, because with her gone I could lie to Sullivan until I was blue in the face, telling him I had done everything expected of me during the preceding night.

Sullivan was satisfied with the way things were working out. He took the opportunity to point out how much better cooperating than fighting with him was, and the three of us nodded our heads like automatons. If this was what he wanted, then this was what he was going to get.

The most difficult part of that Thursday was my first visit with Ms. Stellar, the Star's mother. I knocked on the door of her private room on the third floor and after hearing, "Come in," I entered.

She was a kid! She was fifteen years old, but she looked younger. It was clear that she had been crying; her face was tear-streaked and her eyes were red.

"Hi, Ms. Stellar," I said from the doorway. "I'm Dr. Sharon. I'm the baby's doctor." I entered and walked to the bed.

"Hi," she said with a sad expression.

"I just came by to tell you that the baby's doing pretty well, considering how small she is. How are you feeling?"

"Okay," she responded with the same expression on her face.

"Mind if I sit down?" I asked, sitting in a chair. She didn't answer.

"Are you having any pain?" I asked after a long pause.

"No," she answered in a monotone.

I wasn't getting very far so I tried probing a little deeper. "Since I'm taking care of the baby, I need to know some things about you. Mind if I ask you some questions?"

"No," she answered.

"How old are you?"

"Fifteen," she said quietly, after some hesitation.

"And the baby's father?"

More hesitation. Then, finally, "The baby don't have a father!"

"Everyone has a father," I said. "And remember, I'm the doctor. I won't tell anyone if you don't want me to."

Again some hesitation. Then, "He's sixteen."

"Do you know him from school?"

"Yeah. We go to the same school. Only I can't go there anymore."

"Why not?" I asked.

"Because I had a baby. They don't let kids back in once they have babies."

"How do you know that?" I asked.

"My friend Cheryl, she had a baby last year and they didn't let her back in. They said it'd set a bad example for the other kids."

At last I was getting somewhere. This girl was feeling a lot of guilt. "Well, what school will you be going to then?"

"Well, there's this special school they have that Cheryl goes to, where only girls with babies go. Only I can't go there either. I can't go back to school."

"Why not?"

"Well, I'm gonna have to get a job and make some money for me and the baby. I gotta find us a place to live."

I was a little surprised by this. "Where were you living until now?"

"At my parents' house."

"Can't you go back there?"

"No." She started to cry. "My parents don't want me anymore."

"That's silly," I said. "Of course they want you. Have you spoken with them about this?"

"Yes," she answered, her crying intensifying. "They were here this morning. They told me I'm a disgrace to them, that I'm a whore and a tramp. They said they can't face their friends anymore with a daughter like me." Her words faded into heavy sobs.

I didn't say anything for a while. I let her cry and held her hand. Finally when her tears had slowed down, I said calmly, "Your parents are reacting this way now only because they're so upset and surprised. In a little while they'll realize that you and the baby need them, and then they won't let anything bad happen to you. I'm sure they still love you and that they'll want you and the baby to stay at home. Give them a few days to work through the bad feelings. You just stay calm and try to get yourself strong again. We'll work on fattening up that baby a little. Everything'll work out. Trust me!"

She clutched tightly at my hand and we sat like that for a while. Finally I rose and said I had to go. I told her I'd see her again the following day. When I left, she didn't say goodbye.

It was also on Thursday that the ENT surgeons took Baby Girl Rose, the baby with the tracheoesophageal malformation, to the operating room on the second floor of St. A's to try to figure out what the hell was going on in this baby's neck. The surgeons did some bizarre, creative procedure, putting tubes in here and drains in there. The net result of all this was that the baby, who had gone into the OR breathing on her own, requiring just a little supplemental oxygen blown her way, came out sick as a dog, respirator-dependent, and looking (because of all the plastic tubing) like she was eating spaghetti through her neck. Baby Rose became the sickest patient in the Pit.

But otherwise the day passed uneventfully. After signing out to Terry, Ray and I went off to the bar down the street for a beer. I was dying to find out the latest installment of Ray and Lauren's ongoing soap opera relationship, and Ray was eager to talk.

Kelly's was pretty empty when we arrived. We had, during the course of the month, become the bar's steadiest customers; I knew things had to be getting serious when the bartender greeted us by name. As our first beers arrived, Ray filled me in on the gory details since I had last left them, locked in an embrace, in the Recovery Room.

"She cried for a while after you left, I guess," he said as I took a pull on my beer, "and that sort of wasn't so bad. We held on to each other and I thought everything was going to be okay, but then she suddenly sat up and said, 'You fucking shit! You deceived me because you wanted to use me, and now you're telling me you think I'm good and that I can get a job on my own. How do I know you're not lying to me now, just to get me back into the sack?' I didn't have a very good response for that."

"I bet," I agreed as I drank more beer.

"Well, anyway, she said she never wanted to talk to me again."

"So you're upset?" I asked.

"I don't know, Bob. I mean, when all is said and done, she really is sort of a schmuck. When you told her how the Dead Kid died, her first reaction was relief that he didn't die of the infection she had caused; now that's sick! But she is really pretty and she was good in bed, and I sort of needed that since my wife threw me out. It's kind of hard to take being rejected by two women in the same month."

"What happened when you were on with her on Tuesday? Did she talk to you at all?"

"Nope, she didn't even tell me she was going to the on-call room because she had a headache. I haven't seen her or talked to her. Nothing."

"Well it's not so bad," I said, trying to imitate Ray's response to all the bad news we had gotten during the month.

"Yeah?" he asked.

I hesitated, and finally said, "I can't think of anything to say."

Ray laughed and said, "Thanks for trying to cheer me up, Bob."

We worked on our beers for a while in silence and finally Ray said, "I'm not feeling very good about this Plan A and Plan B business."

"Why not?" I asked.

"Well, for a couple of reasons. First, it seems to work pretty well on kids who have straightforward problems, like the kids you brought up last night, but what happens if there's a kid who's not so straightforward? What happens if Sullivan tells us to do something and we don't do it, and the patient dies?"

"Yeah," I responded, "I've been thinking about that too. Even with the Star; what happens if she turns out to have an infection? I don't think she does, she has no signs of one, but what do I know? If she is infected, and we don't start the antibiotics, she's going to die, and it'll be our fault."

"And another thing," Ray continued, "we're physicians. We're trained to be honest, and here we are, in the first month of our internships, lying left and right. It doesn't feel right."

"Yeah, and besides we're bound to get caught sooner or later," I added. "And when we do, the shit's bound to hit the fan."

"I've been thinking about these things but, on the other hand, I've been thinking back over the month: the Dead Kid, Baby Torres, and all the others. They wouldn't have suffered so much if we had done what we wanted and ignored what Sullivan had to say."

"I guess it comes down to this: we have to start feeling confident in what we're doing. We have to start feeling that the decisions we make are as good or better than the decisions Sullivan makes."

"I don't think I'm ready for that yet," Ray responded as he finished his beer, "I don't think I know as much as Sullivan and, even though I know my heart's in the right place, it's scary making decisions based only on emotion."

I finished my beer. "Ray, I've got to go home. I have to get some sleep."

Ray, wanting to drown his sorrows some more, stayed behind. I gave him a couple of bucks to pay for my beers, then drove home to Watertown. I didn't feel hungry; by this point I had lost five pounds, mostly because I never felt like eating—I was never hungry. My clothes were starting to hang on me.

I sat out on the terrace outside our living room and watched the sky darken and the night develop. It became a beautiful night.

And then I fell asleep.

I dreamed that night a new dream. It was similar to the old one, but it was in one way very different: I am in the delivery room; I am handed a baby by Dr. Parris; the baby is normal in every way; and then it stops breathing.

But in this dream, I don't panic; and I resuscitate the baby.

XXXV
Friday, July 16

Up until Friday morning, I had thought that I could predict Sullivan's reaction to the admission of any baby; no matter who the kid was, I had thought, no matter what was wrong with him, Sullivan would order that everything possible be done at all times, regardless of the child's condition. I had thought that this was a given, that at least this attitude was unchanging from patient to patient. But I found out on Friday morning that this was not the case.

I was feeling pretty good when I arrived in the Pit on Friday morning. Things seemed to be going well; all of my patients were improving, we were getting along with Sullivan, I had successfully resuscitated a tiny baby single-handedly and, most importantly, I wasn't scheduled to be on call until the next day. The only negative things on my mind were the facts that, because of my schedule, Rachel wouldn't be coming up from New York for the weekend, and that I wasn't exactly feeling comfortable with our ongoing deception of Sullivan. But all this considered, I entered the nurses' station that morning feeling calmer and more at ease than I had felt all month.

Terry, on the other hand, was a nervous wreck. She had had her second bad night in a row, another night without sleep, caused not by the presence of sick patients, but rather by the presence of a sick attending and a bizarre senior resident.

Jennings had apparently had a pretty rough time finding someone to cover for the psychotically incapacitated Simon Frohman. None of the remaining senior residents would voluntarily spend a night in the Pit, so Jennings had to sweeten the deal a little. He offered anyone who would work one night in place of Simon an extra weekend day off at any time during the year he or she desired. And even with this inducement, only one person stepped forward: this person was Kooper.

Kooper, who as far as I could tell didn't have a first name, was, according to Dan, the worst senior resident in the pediatric program, and perhaps in the whole Medical Center. Kooper was an obese (in excess of three hundred pounds), short (about five feet five) cherub who made no bones of the fact that he cared for two things, and two things only: sleeping and feeding his belly. He was lazy and couldn't care less about the problems of our patients.

"So there I was, sitting in the nurses' station at about six-thirty, when this big, fat, dirty, smelly guy walks in." Terry was relating the story to Ray and me as we sat in the on-call room, drinking coffee. "And he says to me, 'I'm Kooper. You Costa?' "

"It sounds like a Tarzan movie," I said.

"Yeah, well he didn't look like Tarzan," Terry continued. "Anyway, I said, 'Yes,' and he said, 'I'm your senior resident tonight.' I nearly vomited. He sat down next to me and asked me what was happening, and I told him things were pretty quiet except for Baby Rose, and he said, 'Good,' 'cause he hated working in the Pit and he was only doing it to get a weekend day of his choice off, and he didn't intend to even lay eyes on any babies, let alone be any help. It would have been okay if he had just left at that point and gone and been depraved in his own on-call room but, no, he decided to sit there and flirt with me for a while. The only way I managed to get rid of him was by going and examining a few of the babies; as soon as he saw me heading into the Pit, he cleared out."

"Sounds great," Ray said, "sounds like perfect St. A's material."

"So you were alone the rest of the night?" I asked. "That doesn't sound so bad."

"If only I had been alone for the rest of the night!" Terry sighed. "First there was Kathy; she was working last night for one of the other nurses whose father had died. . . ."

"Yeah, she worked Wednesday night, too," I added, "but she didn't bother me all night long."

"Well she bothered me all night," Terry responded angrily. "She kept checking everything I did. Was I sure I really wanted this child to get such and such a dose of ampicillin? Shouldn't I have started that child on antibiotics? She was always looking over my shoulder; it was worse than when I was on with Simon."

"I sort of hope that other nurse is back tonight," Ray said. "Which nurse was it?"

"I don't know," Terry said, "no one would tell me and, from what I could tell, everyone who's usually here was here."

"That's funny," I added, "the same thing happened the night before."

"But still, it doesn't sound so bad," I said. "You can answer Kathy's questions from the on-call room cot."

"Stay with me, Bob, you're getting ahead of the story. The fun started at about one-thirty, when I got a call from Sheila Simpson, who was covering OB last night. Sheila said the daughter-in-law of some big-shit benefactor who had contributed like a billion dollars to the Medical Center had just been admitted in labor and 'Daddy Warbucks' wanted to inspect the neonatal team that was on call. It was a perfect night for us to be inspected. I went down to the DR on my own steam, but the security guards just about had to use a crane to get Kooper out of his bed. When he finally did hit the DR, Kooper was cursing and he looked messier and fatter than he had before. He smelled a little worse too. Well, guess who Daddy Warbucks turned out to be."

Neither Ray nor I could even try to guess, so Terry told us. "It was that guy Stone, who came around with Monsignor Vitale at the beginning of the month and who was so happy to see us at the hospital board meeting."

"The guy who didn't understand why he had to listen to the interns complain?" I asked.

"One and the same," Terry responded.

"Great," Ray said, "I was hoping he'd come back. He's just about the only person I've ever come across who's more obnoxious than Sullivan."

"That's right," Terry continued. "So anyway, this guy took one look at Kooper and he told his daughter-in-law to get herself dressed, they were going over to Women's Hospital. But Adams, who is the daughter-in-law's doctor and who was there all through this, said, 'Nonsense, this guy doesn't have to be in the delivery room. I'll give Sullivan a call and Sullivan will be there personally.' "

"So they decided to stay?" I asked.

"Of course," Terry answered.

"And Sullivan came in?" Ray asked.

"Also correct," Terry responded.

"I'm starting to see how this could have been a bad night," I said.

"A bad night indeed," Terry continued. "Well, Sullivan got here about two-thirty and he was also cursing and looked horrible. He went down to the labor room and personally insulted both Daddy Warbucks and his daughter-in-law, calling the guy the same kind of things he had called him the last time he'd seen him. The guy was just about to leave again, but Adams convinced them to stay. Then Sullivan came up here, and he beeped Kooper, who had snuck off and gone back to bed. Kooper refused to come at first, but when Sullivan told him he was going to call Jennings right then to tell him Kooper hadn't shown up and should be forced to work two extra weekend days to make up for it, Kooper was up and in the Pit in about thirty seconds. Sullivan chewed him out, told him he was a disgrace not only to the medical profession, but to the human race as well, and that Sullivan would get back at him for getting him out of bed at two in the morning. And he did get back at him, too."

"What did he do?" I asked.

"He kept Kooper up, in the Pit, all night, doing crazy things, like cleaning out the wheels on the transport incubator with tweezers. Sullivan said the wheels get clogged up with hair and stuff, and they need to be cleaned out periodically. When Kooper was finished with that, he had him rearranging the supply bins. The guy was sorting out butterfly needles at four in the morning, ridiculous stuff like that. I had to help him at first, but after a while Sullivan made me a supervisor because, after all, I wasn't responsible for him having to get up; but I still couldn't go to sleep."

"Great," Ray said, "so you'll be in terrific shape for the rest of the day."

"Well, did the baby at least come out okay?" I asked.

Terry gave me a dirty look and said, "The baby hasn't even been born yet. This is the woman's first pregnancy and she came in in very early labor. She should have been sent home but, because her father-in-law owns the Medical Center, Adams was afraid that she'd deliver on the Fitzgerald Expressway and her father-in-law would have St. A's turned into a used-car dealership, so she stayed, and we all waited. She probably won't deliver until this afternoon."

It was eight o'clock and we decided to go into the Pit to see if Sullivan had showed up for rounds. Since it was Friday, and Sullivan would be making rounds with us, Dan decided to stay away. A wise choice.

Sullivan was there, waiting. It was obvious that he hadn't slept all night. Everyone reacts differently to sleep deprivation; some people become paranoid, others get very cranky. Sullivan apparently became ridiculously giddy. "Hi, guys!" he said when he saw us. "Dr. Costa, I'm awfully sorry about putting you through those exercises last night, but I had to do something to that fat pig and I certainly couldn't let him do all those silly things without having you do some of them. Goodness, it sure was funny watching him clean out those little wheels with that tiny pair of forceps in his fat little fingers."

I looked at Ray and he looked back at me; was this really John Sullivan talking? Terry didn't answer, and we went on into the Pit.

The nursery that morning comprised of six sickies, including the Star, whose respiratory picture was still improving although she was still respirator-dependent; Baby Donovan, who really wasn't all that sick; Baby Jones, the Meconium Kid who was still in the first row only because of Sullivan's stubbornness, but who was entirely well and entirely normal; a thirty-two weeker whom Ray had brought up the previous Saturday, who had been extubated and now just needed a little supplemental oxygen blown past her; the thirty weeker Terry had brought up the previous Friday night, who was still respirator-dependent and may have suffered an intracranial hemorrhage; and the sickest baby in the hospital, still respirator-dependent, still looking like she was eating plastic spaghetti through a hole in her neck, following her ENT surgery the day before.

In addition to all these sickies, there was the usual assortment of chronics and growers. In the past week no patient had been discharged, only Baby Singer had been transferred to the growers row and Baby Summlitz had become a member of the chronics row, but things had changed during our time in the Pit. Two thirds of the patients had "turned over." Ray, Terry, and I had been involved in the acute phase of two out of every three babies present that morning. It was becoming "our nursery."

Sullivan, hysterical all through rounds, made little jokes about everything. If he hadn't been so punchy, he would have been almost pleasant to be around that morning.

The clerk called to Sullivan just as we started the growers row; Adams wanted him down in the delivery suite. "We'll finish rounds later," he called to us as he left the Pit.

Ray, Terry, and I went to our on-call room. "He's sure acting weird," Ray said as we all settled in.

"Yeah," I added, "he's acting . . . well . . . almost friendly."

"You think it's because we're showing him some respect?" Terry asked. "Is that all he needed to become our friend?"

"I don't know," Ray responded, "something tells me not to trust him. I sort of get the feeling we're going to get screwed if something goes wrong."

"It's like Channin said," Terry added. "If something goes wrong, blame it on the intern."

"Channin!" I yelled. "Holy cow, I forgot. The twins were supposed to have their operation yesterday. He was supposed to call."

"Let's call him," Terry suggested, and Ray agreed. I called Channin's office, and his secretary told me he was in the cardiac ICU. She gave me the number, I called it, and he was on the line, sounding tired, in less than a minute.

"Hi, Bob," he said slowly, "sorry I haven't gotten back to you, but things have been kind of hectic here."

"I'm sorry to bother you," I responded apologetically, "I'm just trying to find out what happened."

The cheerful peppiness was missing from Channin's voice as he said, "Things didn't go as well as we had hoped. Dr. Dover ran into some complications. The heart muscle looked a lot more damaged than we had expected. The procedure took about sixteen hours and, when it was over, we couldn't get the surviving twin to come off the cardiac bypass pump we had been using. We tried for about two hours, but we just couldn't get the heart beating again."

"She's dead?" I asked, feeling a tightening in the pit of my stomach.

"No," Channin said, "not dead. After some more manipulations, we finally got the heart beating on its own, and we got her off the pump, but she's suffered a lot of hypoxia. So far she hasn't put out any urine and I don't know what we did to her brain. We'll have to wait."

"Oh no!" I said. Ray and Terry, just seeing my face tighten up and hearing my little bit of conversation, knew that things were bad.

"Dr. Dover and I have been with the baby since she got out of the OR. I feel like an intern!" He half laughed.

"Jesus," I said with that horrible feeling still in my gut, "this is all our fault. If we hadn't transferred the twins out of here behind Sullivan's back, none of this would have happened."

"Don't be a schmuck, Bob," Channin said, "this procedure had to be done; one of the reasons the heart muscle was so damaged was that we waited too long. If you want to blame yourselves for anything, and I know you do because that's what interns are supposed to do, blame yourselves for not getting me to move them out earlier. You guys did exactly the right thing."

"You sure?" I asked.

"Would I lie to you?" Channin answered.

"Well, I still don't feel good about this."

"Bob, I'm not asking you to feel good about it, I'm just telling you it's not your fault. This isn't a phone-in radio show with a psychologist. I've got to go. I'll talk to you later," and he hung up.

"What happened?" Terry asked.

"The heart was already damaged at the time of operation," I answered, "and he thinks the surviving twin may have suffered brain damage because they had trouble getting her off the pump."

"At least she's still alive," Terry said.

"Damn," Ray said, "this is all my fault."

"Channin said it definitely isn't our fault. He said the heart was damaged because the babies were transferred too late."

"I guess they really would've both died if they hadn't done the operation," Terry responded.

"Doesn't matter," Ray said sadly, "doesn't matter if they would have died or not. I feel terrible; I feel responsible."

"Those poor parents," Terry said. "Haven't they gone through enough?"

"Well look," I responded, "there's a chance the baby will survive."

"Survive for what?" Ray asked. "So she can become a GORK in GORK clinic?" We were all quiet for a long time.

Our silent meditation was broken by the telephone's ring. The clerk said Sullivan was back and wanted us in the Pit. When we entered, Sullivan was angry and cursing. He kicked the door between the nurses' station and the Pit open. Behind him came a nurse who was pushing the transport incubator, which now had spotless wheels. In the incubator was a good-sized, crying, active baby.

"Shit!" yelled Sullivan, who had hurt his toe kicking the door. He said nothing further to us but walked into the Pit, the nurse with the incubator following him. He stopped at the first empty bed space in the growers row and pointed, saying something to the nurse pushing the incubator and to Maureen, the red-haired nurse, who had come to meet them. They set to work transferring the baby to the warming table. Then Sullivan, his face very red, came back to the nurses' station. "You three listen to me," he ordered. "None of you are to do anything for Baby Stone. Do not get a history. Do not examine him. Do not write anything in the chart. That baby is fine and does not need to be in an intensive care nursery and I'll be damned if I am going to expend nursing and house staff energy on a well child." Before we could respond, he stormed out of the nursery.

"What the hell was that about?" I asked.

"He's sort of flipped out again," Ray said.

"It was the night without sleep," Terry added. "It's okay for us to do that shit every third night, but the one night Sullivan takes call, his glue comes unstuck and he starts falling apart at the seams."

Dan soon came running into the nurses' station, just about doubled over with laughter. "Did he get here yet?" Dan asked.

"Who? Sullivan?" I asked.

"Who else?" Dan answered. "Did he bring that baby up yet?"

"Yeah," Terry responded. "What the hell is going on?"

"It was great," Dan said. "I'm down there in the nursery, minding my own business, reading the paper, when suddenly in comes Sullivan, wearing scrubs and pushing a transport incubator with a nurse. He drops the kid off and starts to leave, when in comes this older guy, and he says, 'What are you doing with my grandson?' "

"That's our friend Daddy Warbucks," Terry said.

"Yeah, whatever," Dan responded, not paying attention to Terry. "Anyway, Sullivan says, 'He's going to the regular nursery, and that's that,' and this guy says, 'Oh no he ain't, he's going to the intensive care unit,' and Sullivan says, 'Eat shit,' and the guy says, 'Oh yeah, well I'm going to give the monsignor a call and see what he thinks about you telling me to eat shit,' and then Adams runs in and takes Sullivan aside and they have a nice private talk, and the next thing I know, Sullivan gets the transport incubator and starts pushing it out of the nursery, and the guy says, 'That's better,' and then they all left. So I assumed they came up here."

"That's exactly what they did," I said.

"Who the hell is that guy?" Dan asked. "He looks familiar, but I can't remember where I've seen him before."

"He's some rich guy who contributed a ton of money to the Medical Center," Terry said. "He came around with the monsignor earlier in the month and Sullivan gave him an earful that day. His name is Stone."

"Of course," Dan said, a look of recognition coming to his face. "It's James Casperson Stone himself! The surgical pavilion at the Medical Center's named after him. That kid's his grandson?"

"Yeah," Terry answered, "and Sullivan's been here all night waiting for him to get born."

"Where'd Sullivan put the kid?" Dan asked.

"In the growers row," Ray answered.

"The heir to the James Casperson Stone Foundation is only in the growers row?" Dan asked with mock scorn. "That will never do! I'm sure the James Casperson Stone Foundation will demand that the child be placed at least in the sickies row, if not in Sullivan's office."

And sure enough, as we watched, James Casperson Stone himself, his son, James Casperson Stone, Jr., and Dr. Adams all entered the Pit and when they found that the baby had been placed in the growers row, James Casperson Stone himself yelled at Adams, and Adams demanded that Maureen, the red-haired nurse, transfer James Casperson Stone III into the sickies row. And then the two older James Casperson Stones, along with Dr. Adams, filed out of the Pit. And just a few minutes later, James Casperson Stone III became the seventh patient in that sickies row.

And that seemed to be the end of it.

Because of these events, grand rounds and the combined perinatal/

neonatal conference were not held that Friday; Sullivan was just too angry and Adams too busy, because he had to calm down the James Casperson Stone family. So Terry and I took the opportunity to get our work done and managed to get out of the madhouse early.

XXXVI

Saturday, July 17
On Call

Saturday looked like it was going to be another scorcher. The newspapers were filled with stories about how hot it was in Boston and how, with so little rain over the first month of summer, the Boston metropolitan area was facing a water shortage. But none of this bothered me: I was spending the day in the Pit and I had enough to worry about.

Ms. Stellar was dressed in blue jeans and a T-shirt when I went to visit her after lunch. She really looked like an average, although somewhat overweight, teenager. When she saw me, she said, " 'Lo."

"Hi," I answered. "How are things?"

"Okay. I'm going home soon."

"To your parents' house?"

"Yeah, Dr. Sharon. You were right about them. They do want us to come home. My mom said she'd take care of the baby, so I can even go back to school!"

"That sounds great! How do you feel about it?"

"Pretty good. 'Cept they're grounding me for a full year! I gotta come home from school every day and help take care of the baby. I can't go out at night or nothing! It's gonna be pretty dull!"

"It won't be so bad. At least you'll have the baby to play with." I felt like Ray saying this.

"Yeah, I guess so," she said sadly. "But I'm sure gonna miss goin' out at night and stuff. Oh well!"

"Oh well!" I repeated.

"When do you think Rainbow will be ready to come home?"

"Rainbow?" I asked.

"Yeah. The baby. That's what I named her. Isn't it a neat name?"

"I guess," I said noncommittally.

"Well, when do you think she'll be ready?"

"Not for a while. She's not too sick, but she has to gain a lot of weight before we can let her go. She probably won't be ready for another month or so."

"That's okay," she answered. "My mom says it's okay for me to come and visit her, so I promise to come every day. At least every day that I don't have too much homework to do! And I'm gonna give her her bottles, if that's okay with you, Dr. Sharon."

"Oh, it'll be okay for you to give her her bottles," I said, "but she can't drink from a bottle yet. She's too small."

"She's so small, she can't drink from a bottle? How do you feed her?"

"Through a tube."

"Yecchh" was all she said.

"But she'll be big enough to suck in a few weeks and then you can feed her."

"Okay. I gotta go now, Dr. Sharon. My dad went to get the car a few minutes ago. He should be waiting for me downstairs by now. I guess I'll see you when I come to visit Rainbow tomorrow." She walked to the door.

"I guess," I said, following her out. And she walked down the hall to the nurses' station and then, accompanied by a nurse, to the elevator. Within a minute they were gone.

I walked back toward the Pit slowly, thinking what a disaster this was for this little girl and for the little girl's little girl. And for her parents, who would now be saddled with the responsibility of bringing up and caring for their own grandchild who, although the prognosis at that time was excellent, still might well end up with one of the many handicaps that occur so commonly in the babies who are born too soon.

It was when I reached the Pit that the day, that the month, in fact, that my whole career took an unexpected turn; because it was on that Saturday afternoon, while making rounds in the sickies row, that I noticed a subtle abnormality in one of the babies. And that subtle abnormality led to an important discovery.

James Casperson Stone III was in the sickies row, but he wasn't supposed to be sick. He was lying on his warming table, kicking around, crying, active, and vigorous, the way a normal newborn should be. There was only one problem: he was as orange as a pumpkin.

At first I thought it was the lighting in the Pit. But the Star was lying next to James Casperson III, and the Star was pink. "It must be a little jaundice," I thought.

I mentioned this thought to Gloria Higgins, who was taking care of both James Casperson III and the Star that day. "Does this baby look a little yellow to you, Gloria?"

"A little yellow?" she asked. "Bob, this baby looks like a Checker cab. I sent off a bilirubin on him this morning; I guess I forgot to tell you about it."

"Did the level come back yet?" I asked.

"No," she answered, "the labs work pretty slow on the weekends around here, but it better be low! I don't know how old James Casperson, Sr., would take to his first grandson having to have an exchange transfusion done by an intern."

"I better call the lab," I said. "In the meantime, turn on the bililights."

"I'm way ahead of you, Bob. I already set them up." And with that, she turned a switch and the bright blue-white fluorescents started up.

I called the lab from the nurses' station and was told the bilirubin level was 14.2, not yet in the danger zone but very high for the first day of life. And then those words hit me: first day of life! And I suddenly saw little Freddie Endicott being carried out of the Pit for the last time to begin his new life at the Waltham Home. And then one word appeared in capital letters across my mind; and that word was GALACTOSEMIA.

Now, there are maybe a hundred causes of high bilirubin levels, and many of these disorders actually manifest during the first day of life. Galactosemia is just one of these and, in fact, one of the rarer ones. But at that time, during that afternoon, while I was alone in the Pit, it was the only one I had ever heard of, and therefore I naturally assumed it was the disease James Casperson III had.

Having diagnosed James Casperson III's medical problem, I ran excitedly from the nurses' station out to the baby's bedside. "What have you been feeding this baby?" I asked Gloria in a frenzy.

"House special," Gloria answered, "Similac. The little guy was lapping the stuff up yesterday, but he's a little slow today."

"Bag him for a urine," I ordered, still excited.

Just then James Casperson, Sr. and Jr., came waltzing into the Pit. James Sr. was acting as if he owned the place which, in fact, he did. When he saw that his grandson was under these funny fluorescent lights, had a urine bag strapped to his genital region, and had a bruise on his left elbow, the site from which Gloria had drawn blood, he went apeshit. "What's all this?" he screamed.

I was standing there, waiting for James Casperson III to urinate, so I couldn't duck the issue. James Sr. was addressing the question to me. "The baby's a little jaundiced," I answered tentatively. "The lights are to bring the bilirubin level down in the blood. Bilirubin is the chemical that causes jaundice."

"I know bilirubin causes jaundice," James Sr. sneered. "I built the damned liver research center at Boston General! What I want to know is why the hell is my grandson jaundiced?"

"I'm not sure," I answered. "It's not unusual for babies to be a little yellow in the newborn period."

"That baby's not jaundiced," he said, pointing to the Star. "That baby over there isn't jaundiced either," he said, pointing to Baby James. "What's your name?"

"Dr. Sharon," I answered meekly.

"Well, Dr. Sharon, those babies aren't jaundiced, and I want to know why my grandson is. Is Dr. Sullivan here?"

"No, Mr. Stone. He doesn't come in on Saturdays."

"Does he know about this? About my grandson being jaundiced?"

"No," I answered. "I just found out myself."

"Well call him, damn it!" James Sr. ordered in a strong voice. "Let's hear what the hell he has to say about this!"

"If you don't mind, Mr. Stone, I'd like to do some tests first before we call him. Dr. Sullivan will have a better idea of what's going on then."

"Didn't you hear me, Sharon? Call Dr. Sullivan now!"

"Okay," I answered. "I don't think it'll help. But if you want. . . ."

And I walked to the nurses' station and, for the third time during the month, called Dr. Sullivan at home.

After a couple of rings, Sullivan's voice said, "Hello?"

"Hi, Dr. Sullivan. This is Bob Sharon. I'm sorry to bother you. . . ."

"This better not be about Baby Stone," Sullivan said angrily.

"It is," I responded, "I'm sorry. . . ."

"I thought I told you you are not to have anything to do with that baby, and I don't want to be bothered with him either. We all have more important things to do than worry about some well child."

"Well, I tried not to get involved, but the baby looked jaundiced this afternoon, and Gloria sent off a bili and . . ."

"Did you order the bili?" Sullivan interrupted.

"No," I said, initially not realizing how important this question was.

"She sent off a blood test without an order from a doctor?" Sullivan asked, still angry. "That bitch. Who does she think she is, making a decision like that on her own? I'll kick her ass but good."

"Well, it turns out she did the right thing, because the bili level was 14.2. On the first day of life, 14.2!" I was trying to impress Sullivan with the degree of hyperbilirubinemia.

But he was not impressed. "So what? The baby's normal. Probably just a little blood group incompatibility between him and his mother. That's what usually causes these cases of high bilirubin."

"I think the baby has galactosemia," I said, stepping out on my limb.

"Bullshit!" he roared. "That baby does not have galactosemia. That baby is totally normal and you are full of shit. I forbid you to do any further lab tests." Sullivan usually did every lab test in the book in cases in which the baby may have some exotic disease, but in this case, because the baby's grandfather had ordered Sullivan to do something Sullivan didn't want to do, he was ignoring a real problem in a baby who really needed help.

"Can I keep him under bili-lights?" I asked.

"Absolutely not," Sullivan answered.

"Okay," I said, not really caring what Sullivan wanted or didn't want me to do. "I only called because James Casperson Stone, Sr., ordered me to."

"Oh, he ordered you to, did he?" Sullivan asked. "Well give him a message for me, will you, Dr. Sharon?"

"Sure," I said.

"Tell him to go fuck himself!" And with that, Sullivan hung up.

Gloria was standing next to me when I hung up the phone. She held a test tube filled with urine in her hand. "Fresh from the oven," she said as she handed it to me. I started for the makeshift lab setup we had in the back of the chronics row, but as soon as I hit the Pit, James Sr. came at me like a bull. "Well, Sharon? What'd Sullivan have to say?"

"Do you really want me to tell you?" I asked.

"Sure," James Sr. said. "What'd he tell you?"

"He said you should go fuck yourself!"

James Casperson Stone, Sr.,'s eyes nearly popped out of his head. "Why, that fucking son of a bitch! I'm calling the monsignor right now!" He started to walk away. But then he realized that he still didn't know what Sullivan had to say about the baby. "Did the bastard have anything to say about the jaundice?" he asked, coming back toward me.

"Yeah," I answered. "He said nothing's wrong."

"Nothing's wrong? Then why is my grandson bright yellow?"

While we were talking, I was doing the test that would make the diagnosis. I had put five drops of James III's urine plus five drops of tap water into a test tube. Then I had added a white pill, called a Clinitest tablet. The solution began to foam up, and in five seconds the liquid was green; in fifteen seconds it was dark brown.

James Sr. and I watched silently as the color change took place. "What does that mean?" he asked, becoming a little panicky, probably realizing from the expression on my face that something was wrong. "What does it mean, when it turns brown?"

"It means your grandson has galactosemia."

"Galactos . . . what's that?"

"You own a liver research center at Boston General, don't you? Why don't you ask them what it means?" I asked and started to walk away.

"No, really," he said, now more panicked, as he followed me toward the baby's bedside. "What is it?"

We were by the baby's side at this point. "Mr. Stone, look," I began in a conciliatory tone, "you've been busting everyone's chops around here since you and your grandson arrived. If you want people to cooperate with you, you have to cooperate with them. Are you willing to do that?"

James Casperson Stone, Sr., was panicked enough to say yes.

"You're not going to make any unreasonable demands from here on? You're going to let us treat your grandson like a normal baby?"

Even though he answered yes, I didn't really expect him to keep these promises, but if he would be just a bit more cooperative, things would be easier to manage from here on.

I explained the condition to James Sr. and James Jr., and Gloria also listened in. "I just did a test to measure reducing sugar in the urine. Normally, the test is negative, but in this baby it was extremely positive, meaning the baby is spilling a sugar in his urine."

"Sugar in his urine?" James Sr. asked, surprised. "You mean my grandson's got diabetes?"

"No," I answered. "Although diabetics spill sugar in their urine, when newborn babies do it, it usually is caused by a sugar called galactose. Galactose is a breakdown product of the sugar found in milk, lactose. Babies with galactosemia lack an enzyme in their bodies that breaks down galactose."

"How do you get this disease," James Sr. asked. "Is it catching?"

"Well, it usually runs in families."

James Sr. shook his head. "No one in our family ever had anything like this."

"Are you and the baby's mother related in any way?" I asked, looking to James Jr.

"Well, we're married!" James Jr. answered, and I could see why his father did most of the talking: James Jr. seemed like a dullard.

"I mean, are you distant cousins or anything like that?"

"No," James Jr. said quickly.

"Yes they are," James Sr. said, sighing. "Son, we have to be straight with this doctor. He's trying to help us. My son and my daughter-in-law are related."

"My grandfather and my father-in-law's mother were brother and sister," James Jr. said. "Is that important?"

"Yes, it is," I said. "This consanguinity just about clinches the diagnosis."

"What . . . what'll happen to the baby?" James Sr. asked.

"Well, hopefully we caught it in time. All we have to do is keep the baby off of foods containing milk sugar. If we do that, the baby should do fine."

"And if we don't do that?" James Sr. asked.

"Well, when untreated, most babies die of infections in the first two weeks of life. And most of those that survive are brain-damaged."

"Oh my God!" James Sr. groaned.

"How sure are you the baby's got this galac . . . galact . . . this disease?" James Jr. asked. "You're just an intern, aren't you?"

"Yeah," I answered. "I'm just an intern. . . ."

"Keep your mouth shut, son!" James Sr. ordered. "I saw that urine turn brown. He knows what he's talking about!"

"Actually, we won't be positive until we get a blood test done that'll confirm it. That test is done by the state lab and usually takes a couple of weeks to get results."

"Couple of weeks, huh?" James Sr. repeated. "That's bullshit! I'll get those tests done this weekend. Anything else we have to do now? Any way I can help you?"

"No," I answered. "We have to do some tests to make sure the baby doesn't have an infection right now and we'll have to start him on antibiotics and change his feeding but, other than that, nothing else needs to be done."

Just then Dan came walking into the Pit. He saw James Sr. talking to me and figured I needed help. "What's going on here, Bob?" he asked. "Is everything all right?"

"Yeah," I said. "I think the baby has galactosemia."

"What?" Dan asked, his eyes opening wide. "You told Mr. Stone that?"

"Yes, he did," James Sr. said.

"Excuse us a minute," Dan said, leading me by the collar, away from the Stones. "Bob, do you know what you're saying?" he asked when we were far enough away to be sure we wouldn't be overheard. "You know how rare galactosemia is? You know what Stone'll do to you when he finds out you're wrong? You can't say something like that without proof!"

"I have proof!" I said.

"What proof?" Dan asked.

"Well, the clinical history is compatible. The baby's got a bilirubin of 14.2 on the first day of life."

"Well that's worrisome," Dan said, "but that's hardly proof that the baby has galactosemia."

"And the family history's compatible," I said. "The parents are second cousins."

"So what? Lots of people marry their cousins and have normal kids with high bilirubins."

I was taking Dan as far as he would go. With every piece of evidence I gave him, he became a little more worried that Stone was going to have me dismantled and shipped back to New York in a packing crate. But then I finally let him have it: "And the Clinitest gave a four-plus reaction for reducing sugar."

"What?" Dan asked, his eyes opening wide.

"Yeah. It turned dark brown. James Sr. was watching me do it. That's why he believes me. I think it made him into a new man. He's not belligerent anymore!"

"You sure about this?" Dan asked.

"Yep," I said, sure of myself.

"Did you run a control? Did you run the test on a urine from a baby who doesn't have galactosemia?"

"No," I said, suddenly a little shaken. "Why should I have done that?"

"Bob, this is a very nonspecific test. If the tablets have been lying around for a long time, if the kid's on any medications, you can get a false positive reaction. You gotta check these things out!"

"Oh shit!" I said, feeling a sinking sensation in the pit of my stomach. "If the kid doesn't have galactosemia . . . oh shit, I scared these people for nothing . . . and . . . oh shit!" I was speechless.

"Get hold of yourself, Bob. Let's repeat the test." Dan led the way. We stopped first in the growers row and drained some urine from the diaper that was around the bottom of one of the healthiest babies in the unit. Then we went back to James Casperson III and picked up the urine specimen I had originally tested.

"Well?" James Sr. asked as we approached the bed space.

"We're going to repeat the test," Dan said. "We'll be right back," and we continued walking to the lab in the back of the Pit.

Dan performed the test. He knew some tricks I didn't know, like you're not supposed to touch the tablet with your fingers, and that the tubes were not supposed to be shaken at all during the fifteen seconds it takes for the reaction to occur. He added five drops of urine from each specimen to separate test tubes, then he added five drops of water, then using the cap of the bottle, he added one Clinitest tablet to each tube. I held my breath and he held his.

Within five seconds there was an obvious difference between the tubes. In fifteen seconds the difference was more obvious. Again James Casperson III's urine turned dark brown while the healthy baby's urine remained clear.

"I'll be damned!" Dan said. "Bob, this baby on any antibiotics?"

"Not yet," I answered.

"I'll be damned!" Dan repeated again. "I've been doing this test for two and a half years! I've never seen one this positive before. Bob, this kid's got galactosemia!"

I was tremendously relieved! I've thought about this emotion a great deal since that time. I was actually pulling for this kid to have a potentially devastating metabolic disease! "What's happening to me?" I asked myself later that day, "Why do I want this kid to have this disease?" I didn't have an answer at that time. But I did later in the month.

Dan and I went back to James Casperson III's warming table. "Mr. Stone," Dan said to James Sr., "Dr. Sharon here seems to be correct: the baby does seem to have galactosemia. Bob, have you mentioned what needs to be done?"

"I think so," I said. "I told the Stones that the baby needs a sepsis workup, needs to be started on antibiotics, and needs to be changed to a nonlactose-containing formula." James Sr. nodded as I mentioned each item to confirm that I had told him about it.

Dan looked at me and smiled. "How'd you know all that?" he asked.

"Freddie Endicott," I said. "I did a little reading."

Dan continued smiling. "Dr. Sharon is right. We need to do all of that, and we need to do it right now. Would you mind waiting outside while we work?"

"Shouldn't Dr. Sullivan be called?" James Sr. asked.

"Mr. Stone, I'm gonna let you in on a secret," I said, "Sullivan is totally worthless! He may be an attending, but he's going to be of no help to you or to your grandson during this hospital stay."

"Okay," he answered. "I think I understand. We'll wait outside."

Dan and I set to work. With Gloria's assistance, we performed what Dan referred to as the four-needle approach to preventive care: one needle in the back to get the spinal fluid to test for meningitis, one needle in the bladder to test for a urinary tract infection, and two needles in the arm, one to get blood for blood count and to rule out sepsis, and one to start an IV so that antibiotics can be given. But since I was doing the procedures, it was more like the ten-needle approach.

I got the blood work on the first stick. I drew 10 cc of blood and shot appropriate amounts into different tubes for the tests required. But when I tried the spinal tap, I missed four times to get the needle into the proper space. The baby kept squirming out of Gloria's hold.

"Amazing," Dan said as he watched me, "you can diagnose galactosemia and you can't even do a spinal tap. Just amazing!" He nudged me away and took over. With one thrust of the needle, he was in and crystal clear spinal fluid came dripping out. "Well, he sure doesn't have meningitis," Dan said upon seeing the clear fluid, because spinal fluid in meningitis is cloudy, not clear.

The bladder tap was also done by Dan. I had never seen one done before, and the one I saw that day looked so barbaric that I hoped I never would be called upon to do one myself. In doing a tap, a needle is inserted in the midline, just below the belly button, and is advanced farther down until urine appears in the syringe. The procedure looks and feels as if the baby is being run through with a sword.

Finally Dan started an IV and we gave the baby some antibiotics. While Gloria hooked up the IV tubing, Dan and I went to see the family.

"How is everything?" James Sr. asked, approaching us as soon as we entered the nurses' lounge.

"Fine," Dan said. "We do this stuff for a living. You get good at it after a while."

"All the tests are done," I added, "and we're giving the baby some antibiotics now."

"There were some samples you wanted me to get run?" James Sr. asked.

"Yes," I said, handing him a tube filled with blood that would be used to measure the level of the enzyme that is deficient in children with galactosemia. He put the tube in his shirt pocket.

"You both know," Dan said, "that Bob here probably saved your baby's life."

"Please," I protested, my face turning red.

"No, Dr. Sharon," James Sr. replied, "I realize what you did in there. And I won't forget it, you can be sure of that."

And James Sr. never did forget it.

XXXVII

Monday, July 19
Attending Rounds

The level of bilirubin in the blood of a newborn is generally low on the first day of life, higher on the second day, and highest on the third. If the highest level of bilirubin reached is less than twenty, there is little chance, in a full-term baby, that brain damage will result. But after twenty is reached and surpassed, the risk of the baby developing kernicterus, or "yellow brain" disease, increases greatly.

On Saturday night when James III was about thirty-six hours old, a repeat blood sample was taken from the infant's arm and sent to the lab. It revealed that, despite the use of phototherapy, the bilirubin level had risen, although only slightly, to 14.8. On Sunday morning when the baby was two days old, the bilirubin level was 15.6, and by that evening it was 16.9. Since Monday was the child's third day of life, it was on this day that we had to be careful; it would be expected that the level would peak on this day, and reaching a level of 20 seemed definitely possible. If this occurred, we weren't sure whether Sullivan would order the exchange transfusion that was necessary in order to guard against the possibility of brain damage.

Terry on Sunday and Ray, when he arrived on Monday morning, were both impressed that I had diagnosed James Casperson III's galactosemia. "I was lucky," I told them both, "it was the one disease I knew about that causes high bilirubin in the first day of life. If either of you had seen how yellow that kid was, you would have diagnosed it too."

"Doesn't matter, Bob," Ray said, "you did it yourself. Doesn't matter whether you were lucky or if you had advance warning, or anything. You saved the kid's life."

"Well, we don't know that for sure yet," I said. "We don't even know for sure if the baby's really got galactosemia."

"Oh he's got it," Terry responded, "and you picked it up."

Dan, taking us on work rounds that morning, was happy to find that James Casperson III was still alive and that he seemed to be thriving, sucking down his lactose-free formula. No results from either the sepsis workup or the enzyme levels that James Sr. was going to get run were back yet, so for the time being we were continuing the infant on the lactose-free feeds, the antibiotics, and the phototherapy.

The only other baby who was still a concern to us that morning during rounds was Baby Girl Rose, who was still respirator-dependent and, although no worse than she had been at the end of the preceding week, just slightly improved in her struggle for life. Otherwise, all the other players in the Pit that morning were in good shape. The Star, whose respiratory problems were almost all but a memory, was breathing on her own and requiring only a little supplementary oxygen. Although she was still intubated, Dan told us we could yank out the tube later in the day, after she had been off the ventilator for a full twelve hours. We knew that Sullivan would want the tube kept in for at least another day or two, however.

At ten o'clock, Ray, Terry, and I filed into Sullivan's office for attending rounds. We were surprised to see that Kathy was there. She was still working the night shift, supposedly still filling in for the nurse whose father had died. During the past week, after working all night, she had gone home to get some sleep, but this morning for some reason she was hanging around for rounds.

"Let's start," Sullivan said after we had settled ourselves. "Who's sick?"

"I guess the only big change that's occurred since Friday was in Baby Stone," Terry said. "Bob picked up that the baby has galactosemia." She smiled broadly.

Sullivan, however, looked angry. He stared first at Terry and then at me. "I thought I told you three you were to have nothing to do with the Stone baby! And I expressly ordered you, Dr. Sharon, not to do any further lab tests and not to institute any therapy. That baby is fine and he is not in need of a neonatal ICU!"

"But he's not fine," I said as calmly as I could. "He really does have galactosemia. He's got a bili . . ."

"Bullshit!" Sullivan yelled, interrupting me. "You disobeyed my orders! I don't want to hear anything else from you!"

"I think we should hear more about this, John," Kathy said. I opened my eyes wide when I heard her say this; it was strange enough that we were arguing with Sullivan because he wasn't being aggressive enough in his management of a patient, but it was downright bizarre to find Kathy taking our side in any confrontation with Sullivan. "I was here on both Saturday and Sunday nights, and it does sound like the baby has galactosemia."

"We'll find out about galactosemia when we get the report back from the state lab in two weeks," Sullivan shouted back to Kathy. "You keep your mouth shut in the meantime." And then, to no one in particular, Sullivan whispered, "Bitch!"

I thought Kathy was going to slug him. She rose and walked toward Sullivan, but when she reached his desk, instead of physically assaulting him, she launched into a verbal barrage against our attending. "It's going to be just like it was with Endicott, isn't it? You're going to ignore it and ignore it until it's too late. Well, I'm not going to stand for it this time! I've gone along with you in everything, even when I knew what you wanted to do might harm the babies, because you are the boss, and I've been taught in my schooling to respect you. Well, this is the last straw; I am finished! I'm finished following your ridiculous orders, and I'm finished spying on these interns! You are a menace to these babies and I am just not going to be a party to it anymore!" And with that, she stormed out of the office.

"Stupid bitch," Sullivan sneered as she left. "You unreliable, untrustworthy, stupid bitch!"

"What's that she said about spying on us interns?" Terry asked.

"Never mind what she said," Sullivan ordered, "she's irrational. You three listen to me. I don't want . . ."

"Never mind what you want," Terry returned, interrupting Sullivan, "what did she mean by that? Has she been spying on us? Is that why she's been working nights this past week?"

Sullivan shot Terry an angry glance. "Why? Do you three think that you're so trustworthy you don't need to be spied upon twenty-four hours a day? You three must think I'm a real idiot; you think, just because you start acting nice to me, because you start coming to attending rounds and say, 'Yes, sir,' once in a while, that I suddenly forgot what you did to me during the first half of this month? I know you've been lying to me. I know you haven't been doing, and in fact never had any intention of doing, the things I've told you to do. I know you've been trying to get away with doing what you want to do, what you three think is right, which is usually exactly opposite of what I tell you to do. But that's what I expected from you. You're all liars and fools. But it's okay; I've taken care of it."

"What do you mean, you've taken care of it?" I asked.

"I've taken care of it," he answered with a sneer. "You told me you started antibiotics on that baby with meconium aspiration and on the premie you brought up last week, Sharon? I know you didn't. But I did."

"You what?" I asked, not believing him.

"I started the meds. I had Kathy do an LP and draw blood cultures and then I ordered the nurse to start antibiotics on both of them. I'm not going to leave my babies open to infection, just because you think you're smart enough to disobey my orders."

"But we interns are the only ones who are supposed to write orders for the nurses," Terry shouted. "They're not supposed to accept orders from anyone else."

"Bullshit!" Sullivan shouted back. "You naïve idiot! You actually think the nurses take any orders from you three? They know that every order you write, no matter how trivial, has to be checked with me. And after I review them, I tell them whether they can carry them out or not." And then he laughed to himself and muttered, "To think I'd let them write orders! What a laugh."

As the weight of Sullivan's betrayal began to sink in, my beeper sounded. "Dr. Sharon," it squawked, "two calls. First call 3199, bacteriology lab, 3199. Then outside call, please call 99." And then it shut off.

I rose, approached Sullivan's desk, and staring into his eyes, picked up the phone on his desk and dialed 3199. He didn't try to stop me. I continued staring into his eyes as I said, "This is Dr. Sharon answering my page," after the technician picked up the phone in the bacteriology lab.

"Dr. Sharon," the voice said, "I have a report of positive blood and urine cultures on one of your patients."

"Is it Baby Stone?" I asked.

"Yes it is," the voice responded. "We have growth of *E. coli,* sensitive to ampicillin, in all specimens received."

"Okay," I replied, still staring into Sullivan's eyes. "*E. coli* in Baby Stone's blood and urine cultures. All organisms sensitive to ampicillin. Is that right?"

"That's it, Doctor."

Sullivan's jaw dropped as I hung up the phone. Ray and Terry both grinned broadly when they saw that.

Next, I dialed 99 for my outside call and said, "Hello? This is Bob Sharon."

"Dr. Sharon?" the voice repeated, "this is Phil Landau at the Liver Research Center at Boston General. Mr. Stone left a sample of blood with me for testing. He told me to call you with the results."

"Yes, Dr. Landau?" I said. "Do you have them?"

"Yes I do. Analysis shows a total absence of transferase activity in the red blood cells, which is consistent with the diagnosis of classic galactosemia."

My eyes lit up as I said, "Let me write this down. 'Total absence of transferase activity, consistent with a diagnosis of galactosemia.' " Ray and Terry cheered in the background. Sullivan's jaw dropped even lower and his eyes opened as wide as saucers.

"How's the baby doing?" Dr. Landau asked.

"Pretty well, considering," I answered. "We just found out he's growing *E. coli* from his blood and urine, but so far he's been asymptomatic."

"You started him on antibiotics early?" Landau asked.

"Yeah," I answered, "we started them prophylactically when we found reducing sugar in the urine."

"Pretty good pickup," Dr. Landau said.

"Have you told Mr. Stone yet?" I asked.

"Not yet" was the reply. "Is the kid a friend of his family?"

"No," I replied, "he's James Casperson Stone III."

"Jesus!" Landau responded, "I didn't know. I'll give Mr. Stone a call immediately."

"Well thank you, Dr. Landau," I said, and we hung up.

Sullivan still hadn't recovered by the time I hung up the phone. "Well, Dr. Sullivan," I sneered, "you're right again."

"Get out of my office!" he ordered in response to my remark. "You three bastards, just get the hell out of my office and leave me alone."

"We'll be glad to leave, you cretin," Terry said as we walked out.

"I feel pretty weird," I said as we headed for the nurses' station.

"Weird?" Ray asked. "You shouldn't feel weird, you should feel great. Bob, you actually saved that baby's life!"

"Aren't you happy you made the diagnosis, Bob?" Terry asked.

"That's just it," I replied, "I feel weird about making the diagnosis. I mean, although there are a lot of benign causes of jaundice, over the past two days I've been rooting for this baby to have something not so benign, galactosemia. And when I found out he had galactosemia, it actually made me happy. Isn't it a little weird to be happy about the fact that one of your patients has a bad, rare disease?"

"I don't know, Bob," Terry said, "I wasn't happy because the kid had galactosemia so much as I was happy that you were right and that shit head was wrong."

"Yeah, me too, Bob," Ray added, "but I see what you mean; I was happy you made the diagnosis, but I hadn't even thought about the baby or his future."

"What's happening to us?" I asked. "A month ago, when we came here for the first time, all we knew how to do was to feel sorry for these poor babies and their families, but suddenly there's this ego thing involved. It was more important for me to be right in my diagnosis than it is for the kid to be healthy."

"I don't know, Bob," Terry responded. "I hear what you're saying, and it sounds right, but there's something wrong with the logic."

"Will you guys do me a favor?" I asked.

"Sure," Ray answered.

"Tell Gloria about the diagnosis, and tell her to keep doing what we've been doing for the baby, regardless of what Sullivan says."

"What are you going to do?" Terry asked.

"I've got to have an emergency talk with Dan." I left them and ran down the stairs to the third floor and then through the run-down, sweltering corridor until, slightly out of breath, I reached the well-baby nursery. I found Dan in the usual place, with his feet up on the clerk's desk in the nurses' station, reading the *Globe.*

"Bob," Dan said when he saw me, "Mr. Galactosemia! Boy, I think you really hit the jackpot this time. Saving the life of the heir of the . . . hey, what's wrong with you? Why are you so . . . glum?"

"I'm depressed, Dan."

"Depressed? Why?"

"I'm not exactly sure. I just got a call from the guy at Boston General, confirming that James Casperson III had galactosemia, and I felt happy about it. Dan, I felt happy that the baby had this terrible disease!"

"That's it?" he asked when he noticed I had stopped talking. "You are depressed because you felt happy that the kid had a bad disease?"

"Yeah," I said sadly. "Dan, at the beginning of this month, I didn't know shit about taking care of these babies; all I knew how to do was empathize with them and their families. But now I know a little bit, and I suddenly find myself having to feed my ego. Why's this happening to me, Dan?"

"You're kidding about this, aren't you, Bob?" Dan demanded.

"No," I answered.

"You really can't figure this out for yourself?"

"No, I can't. Why am I acting this way?"

"Bob, you're concentrating on ego, but ego has very little to do with this. Look, when you came into this place, it's true you didn't know anything, but now you know a lot. You know how to do technical things, like start IVs and UA lines, and how to intubate babies and even run codes. You've even learned a new language; when you came here, I'm pretty sure you didn't understand what anyone was saying on rounds, am I right?" I nodded yes. "And you've learned a lot about the natural history of some diseases. Bob, I know it may sound corny, but you've become a doctor this month. Your thinking is the thinking of a doctor, and one of the things that doctors do is help people. Now in reality, there are only a few diseases we can do anything about, but galactosemia is one of them. My God, we know that babies with galactosemia are usually dead of infection in the first two weeks of life, or are left severely brain-damaged, like Freddie Endicott, if the problem isn't picked up in time. But you picked it up in time in the Stone baby, you caught it so early that he never became more symptomatic than being jaundiced! If you had waited a few more hours, he might have become septic and died right then. . . ."

"He was septic," I interrupted. "The lab called to say he was growing *E. coli* in his blood and urine."

"Even better," Dan said. "Bob, as a doctor, you wanted to be right about the diagnosis because you had done everything right, and you wanted the baby to have a disease you could treat, so he'd get better."

"But it's not like I was happy the kid had galactosemia rather than cancer," I replied, "I was happy the kid had galactosemia rather than being normal."

Dan thought about this for a minute and said, "I don't know, Bob, I guess you're right, to a certain point. But hoping the child has a problem that when treated will leave him normal is what being a doctor is all about. The only reason you reacted differently this month from how you would have last month is that you made that transition."

"Well, I'm not sure I like it."

"You don't like making a diagnosis, treating the patient, and having everything turn out okay?"

I thought about this for a minute. "Well, when you put it that way," I answered, "I guess . . . sure I like that. That's why I became a doctor."

"Of course that's why you became a doctor," Dan said. "And if you play your cards right, Bob, you are going to make a damned good doctor. Just don't let them get you down!"

I smiled. "I feel better," I said.

"Of course you feel better. Now get back to work."

"Thanks, Dan," I said, still smiling.

"Think nothing of it, Bob," Dan concluded.

From my meeting with Dan I returned to the Pit, where I was met in the nurses' station by Ray and Terry. From the look on their faces, I knew something terrible had just happened.

"You okay, Bob?" Terry asked.

"Yeah," I responded, "Dan really put things into perspective. But what's wrong with you two? You look like you've seen a ghost."

"We just got some bad news," Ray said. "Dr. Channin called and . . ."

"The twin?" I asked, again feeling the tightening in the pit of my stomach.

"Yeah," Terry replied sadly. "She died about an hour ago."

"No" was all I could say.

They led me into the on-call room, where we sat silently for a long time. Finally Terry spoke, "Dr. Channin said she died because her heart was too far gone by the time they got the surgery done. He said both of the twins would have been dead by now anyway if they hadn't been separated."

"This is such a hard job," I said. "This medicine is hard to take."

XXXVIII

Tuesday, July 20

I arrived Tuesday morning to find Terry well rested but pissed off. "How was the night?" I asked.

"Oh splendid," Terry answered. "It was wonderful to be on call for another night with Kooper! I never thought I'd miss Simon Frohman."

"He was here again last night?" I asked.

"Yeah, at least that's what I was told. I never did see him though, which wouldn't have been so bad, except that I got called down to the DR for the birth of a premie. I wound up doing everything myself."

"You resuscitated the baby yourself?"

"Yeah, you learn to be pretty self-sufficient when you're on with Kooper. That *putz.*"

"How's the baby doing?" I asked.

"Well, she's a twenty-nine weeker and it's been touch and go with her. I wasn't sure what respirator settings to put her on and I guess I used too much pressure because she blew out her left lung. But I put in a chest tube and she's much better now."

"You put in a chest tube without a senior resident telling you what to do?"

"Yeah, but a senior resident wasn't necessary because Angela Meroni was with me. She told me exactly what to do; I guess she's seen hundreds of them put in."

Pretty soon Ray and Dan arrived and we started to make rounds. The problems of three babies concerned us most that morning. James

Casperson Stone III, although he was still active and alert and was guzzling down the lactose-free formula, had had a maximum bilirubin level of 18.9 at seventy-two hours of life and, although a rise of bilirubin on the fourth day of life was rare, if it were to occur in this baby, we would have to do an exchange transfusion. Terry's premie from the night before, Baby Dunbar, was also a concern. She was doing well, with an adequately functioning chest tube and mild respiratory distress that required very low pressure assistance from the ventilator. But the final, and biggest, problem patient that morning was Baby Rose. On rounds Dan asked, "Do you guys think this baby is a little blue?" We all did, so we got a blood gas on her and found that she had severe acidosis, a lack of oxygen and an excess of carbon dioxide in her blood. While we discussed what the possible causes of this sudden change might be, the baby's heart stopped beating, setting off alarms and buzzers. Ray, Terry, Dan, and I, with the help of the nurses, then resuscitated the baby. When we got a chest X ray after the resuscitation, we found that the baby's left lung field was filled up with what Dan called "gunk." There was pus, or something like it, down in that left lung, and this had probably led to the baby's deterioration. We all agreed that the accumulation of this stuff was probably mechanical, that there was probably an obstruction of one of the tubes either going into or coming out of this baby's neck, and we decided that either the ENT surgeon who had performed the procedure in the first place or a plumbing contractor had to be called stat, that the baby had to be returned to the OR, and that another exploratory operation needed to be performed.

The ENT surgeon was called, and he left his office and came to St. A's immediately. He agreed with our impression and plan, and he had the child in the operating room in less than thirty minutes. Sullivan, not speaking to us, showed his face in the Pit just minutes before the surgeon appeared. He accompanied the child to the OR, where he would supervise the care of the baby during the operation.

Because the procedure took over six and a half hours, with Sullivan in the OR that whole time, our day was rendered much more palatable. We did our work, and by four-thirty Ray and Terry had signed out to me. Knowing that if Baby Rose were to survive the operation, I would get no sleep that night, I tried to get some rest while things were still quiet in the late afternoon.

It was about four o'clock when James Casperson III's bilirubin level came back from the lab and, mercifully, it had dropped to 17.5. No exchange transfusion would be needed; the child had made it over this hurdle.

At about five o'clock Dan appeared in the nurses' station, bringing with him a half gallon bottle of Coke. We sat in the nurses' station, drinking the Coke and talking. "How are you feeling, Bob?" Dan asked, pouring some of the Coke into two urine specimen cups.

"Okay, I guess," I said.

"You upset about the Srnivasan twins dying?"

"Yeah," I answered, taking a sip of the Coke.

"But you're feeling better about the Stone baby and his galactosemia?"

"Yeah," I answered again.

"You sure are talkative today," Dan remarked.

"Well, Dan, this being a doctor business isn't easy. There's always death around, and all this depression it leaves. It's hard."

"Yeah?" he answered, draining the Coke from his cup and pouring us both some more. "What did you think it was going to be like?"

"I knew it was going to be hard, but I thought the hard part was all going to be physical. I figured the stress was going to come from working long days and the long nights on call. But the physical stuff is nothing compared to all the work you have to do emotionally; all these ups and downs are murder!"

"I know what you're going through," Dan said. "We all get to this realization sometime during our internships: the physical work just keeps us busy; it's the mental work that destroys us."

"It takes so much out of you!" I sighed. "What I don't understand, Dan, is once we realize how much work there is to be done, why don't we all either quit medicine and get jobs in car washes, or commit suicide?"

"Well, some of us do get jobs in car washes or go into radiology or pathology where we don't have to get involved with warm bodies and the problems that those warm bodies cause, and some of us do destroy ourselves, either right away by committing suicide or slowly, by getting into drugs or alcohol, like Sullivan's doing; but for the most part, most of us go on, either because we find we like doing this or for the reason I didn't leave to do my senior year elsewhere."

"Because the deadline's passed?" I asked.

"Yeah," he replied, "because the deadline's passed. We stay where we are because it's easier to stay than it is to go. Changing fields is a lot of work, and most of the work is emotional; you have to admit to yourself that you made a mistake and that maybe you wasted five or six years of your life preparing for something you just don't want to do."

"So why did you really stay?"

"It wasn't because I didn't want to admit a mistake. Bob, I like doing this; I like the feeling I got when I diagnosed Baby Donovan's coarctation, and the feeling I'll get when I see her parents take her home at the end of this week. It's true, although the depressing times are bad, when you get one of those highs that comes along once a month or so, there's just nothing in the world like it."

"So you think it's worthwhile staying in medicine?"

"Sure, Bob. And besides, you're overqualified to work in a car wash."

Once again Dan had rescued me.

Soon after my conversation with Dan had ended, after the half gallon of Coke had bitten the dust, I walked into the Pit to check on Baby Dunbar. But before I could get to the child, I was intercepted by James Casperson Stone, Sr., who was visiting his grandson. He said he wanted to speak with me. In private. So I led him into our on-call room.

"You guys sleep in here?" he asked upon seeing the room.

"When we get to sleep," I answered.

"Phewww," he said, expelling air through his pursed lips, "this is awful! You interns deserve better than this."

"We don't have much choice," I said, smiling.

"Well, I'll see what I can do about it," he said. "Dr. Sharon, I'll get right to the point. My man at the Liver Research Center at Boston General told me the results of the test he did, and he also confirmed that you had saved my grandson's life with your quick thinking."

"Well, I didn't exactly save his life," I said, my face turning red.

"No, I know who I can trust, and Landau over at the center is one guy who wouldn't bullshit me. So because you did what you did, I want you to know I'm grateful to you, and that I must find a way to repay you."

"Well, that's not necessary," I said, my face still red. "I was only doing my job." The last time I had a conversation like this with the parents of one of my patients, the baby wound up being named after me. I knew that wasn't going to happen this time!

"Yes it is, Dr. Sharon. Believe me, it is. Now here's what I'm going to do. First, I'm having my lawyer write a letter to Jennings, commending you for your skill and knowledge. This letter will go into your permanent file and believe me, with all the money I've given to hospitals in and around Boston, it will carry a lot of weight when you're looking for a job after you're done with your training."

"Thanks," I uttered quietly.

"Next, now that I see this room," he said, looking around once again, confirming that he was really seeing what he was seeing, "I'm going to give some money to this damned crazy hospital, expressly for the purpose of building a reasonable on-call room for the interns. Yeah, I think about ten grand ought to cover it. I'll have them call it the 'Bob Sharon Intern On-Call Room.' How about that?"

"It sounds great," I answered without much enthusiasm.

"Now, is there anything I can do for you? Is there anything I can help you with?"

I thought about this offer for a while before saying no. "Thank you for offering, but there really isn't anything I can think of."

"I know it must be hard," he said, "working with certain attending physicians who tend to . . . abuse those under their command. And I know that somebody in your position might try to take some steps to correct the situation. I just want to tell you, I'm aware of some of the things you've done during this month here at this hospital and, well, let me say I'll try to help sway certain high-ranking hospital officials to see things . . . should I say, your way?"

And that was the end of our conversation.

I went about my work, checking out Baby Dunbar as I had originally intended to do before being intercepted by James Sr., and I looked over the other babies in the first row. And then Baby Rose returned from the operating room.

She returned on a portable warming table, surrounded by medical personnel: Dr. Sullivan was at the head of the warming table; Dr. Robbins, the surgeon, was to the baby's right; a respiratory therapist working the ambu bag connected to the baby's tracheostomy tube was off to the left; and Maureen, the red-haired nurse who had assisted Dr.

Sullivan in the OR, was at the foot of the table. "We better go have a look," Dan said as they entered, and I followed him into the Pit.

The baby looked like a pithed frog: she was lying flat on her back on the mattress, her arms and legs tied down and spread apart; there were now at least nine spaghetti-like tubes emerging from the region of her anatomy corresponding to the neck. "It's going to be a long night!" was all Dan uttered.

We soon found out that just about everything was wrong with the baby. Most patients who are in good health would have some difficulty coping with six and a half hours of surgery. But this baby had been critically ill when she had gone into the OR, and she came out dehydrated, hypotensive, severely anemic due to surgery-induced blood loss, in renal shutdown due to the low blood pressure, and with an erratic heart rhythm, caused by the fact that her blood electrolytes had been thrown out of whack by a combination of all the above factors. In addition, the baby remained respirator-dependent. And Dan was certainly correct; it sure was going to be a long night.

Some of the baby's problems were easy to correct, and we corrected these as rapidly as possible; we gave her a transfusion of blood and a rapid infusion of normal saline solution, and soon, her anemia and dehydration improved, and with these, her blood pressure normalized. We adjusted her ventilator settings while carefully monitoring her blood gases and corrected imbalances in her blood oxygen, carbon dioxide, and pH. Within a few hours her blood electrolytes and her heart rhythm had returned to normal. But then, after all this was done, we sat back and waited.

We all sat at the warming table. Dan and I were on one side, Sullivan and Robbins on the other. We sat on high stools, waiting for something to happen. Sullivan did not speak to us, nor did we speak to him. We waited for a sign that she was responding to all that we had done; we waited for her to pass urine, for her to breathe once on her own, for her to open an eye and to look at us, anything, anything at all. And, in silence, we all hoped. We hoped that, if no sign of response, of improvement were to come, at least the baby would not die.

But outside of hoping and waiting, there was nothing any of us could do. Among the four of us, years and years of medical expertise had been accumulated, yet even Sullivan and Robbins could do nothing to make this baby better. There was nothing that was taught, nothing that could be learned, that could help this baby. It was out of our hands. We, as doctors, were helpless, impotent, overwhelmed.

So Dan, Sullivan, Robbins, and I kept our vigils in silence all through that night. And when the morning sun appeared through the picture windows of the Pit, Baby Rose was still alive.

EPILOGUE

Technology had brought us together at St. A's that summer; a computer had linked Ray, Terry, and me with the pediatric program at the Boston Medical Center as part of the National Intern and Resident Matching Program. Another computer, the one programmed to prepare the master intern on-call schedule for that academic year had placed Drs. Costa, Brewster, and Sharon in the Pit for the first rotation.

Technology had also given Dr. John Sullivan the tools he needed to keep alive anything with a heart and lungs. The ventilators and the plastic tubes and lines that had been developed following the invention of neonatology had made it possible for him to become a godlike figure and to torment all the dead kids and their families who had the misfortune of passing through St. Anne's intensive care nursery.

But it was human emotion that caused the change that developed in us during that month. It was our outrage with the methods Dr. Sullivan used, our concern about the harm that he was causing the patients, and our inability to allow this to go on that initially raised our consciousness enough to complain to the hospital board and, when no action on that front was taken, to try to come up with other options. But it was the realization that it would do no good and that protecting our patients from this crazed man might be the only positive thing we could accomplish that led us down another road. And finally, it was the fact that all our efforts had been useless, that Sullivan had seen right through us, that led to the realization that fighting this man on his home turf was hopeless.

We returned to our rightful place, the Boston Medical Center, after the final full weekend in July, disheartened and dispirited but aware of the fact that we had made a transition. Ray, Terry, and I went our separate ways: Ray to a rotation in the Outpatient department, Terry to the General Pediatrics floor, and I to the Infectious Disease ward. Although we kept in contact, we were never again as close as we had been during that first month. But we each knew that we had shared something during that first month, and that created a permanent bond between us.

During that internship year none of us lived up to the expectations that had been set for us before we ever came to Boston. At the Medical Center we did adequate jobs, just enough work to get by, but nothing outstanding, nothing spectacular. We had lost something, something very important, during that first month at St. A's. We were jaded by the experience; we didn't trust anybody. We had been hurt very badly.

Ray, Terry, and I terminated our affiliations with the pediatric program of the Boston Medical Center on June 30 of the next year, the final day of our internships. None of us has ever regretted that decision.

Saturday, June 16, 1984

After spending the night sitting on the floor of Terry's hotel room, drinking scotch and catching up on eight years of each other's lives, Ray, Terry, and I stumbled into my Volvo for the short ride to the scene of the crime, St. Anne's, where the symposium was to be held. A lot had happened to each of us since we had last been together at that hallowed institution and, interestingly, our experiences at St. A's had influenced each of us in the career choices we had made.

Terry, following her internship year, happily caved in to Cliff's urging that she take a year off and have a baby. From her reaction following the birth of Baby Girl O'Hara, this didn't surprise me in the least. The baby, a boy, had been born in November, nearly a year and a half after we had first set foot into St. A's. Throughout her pregnancy, Terry had threatened to name the baby Sharon had it been a girl. "Just think," she had told me during that time, "someday there may be nurseries full of babies named Sharon after you. Not to mention all those 'Bob Sharon Intern On-Call Rooms' of the future." But mercifully the child was a boy, and she named him Steven. After Cliff finished his first year of residency at Beth Israel, the Costas moved back to Seattle, and Terry entered a developmental medicine fellowship. "It's amazing, Bob," she had said sometime during the preceding night, "you remember how I was after that first follow-up clinic?"

"Do I ever," I replied, winking my eye.

She laughed. "Well, that's pretty much what I do for a living now. Most of my practice is made up of children with bad brains caused by prematurity. And you know what? I like it."

"You like it?" I asked.

"Yeah, I really do; there's not much I can do for them, but there are some things, like controlling their seizures a little better or making them more alert. And whenever I accomplish anything, even the tiniest change, the parents think I'm working miracles. It's nice."

Terry had had a second child, this one a girl, two years before the symposium, and she did not name that child Sharon, but Amanda. Both children were thriving, and Cliff and Terry both had their practices in Seattle.

Ray had returned to Ann Arbor the day after our internships ended and had been offered a job as a resident at the University of Michigan, his alma mater. Ray had not spoken to Lauren since the day we left St. A's, nor had he ever reached a reconciliation with his wife. He had lived alone until three years before the symposium, when he met a woman who was a physical therapist at the university hospital, and they were married within six months. Ray told us that he really loved her and that, for the first time in his life, he seemed to be having a mature relationship with a woman. "I don't know," he said, smiling, while pouring some Chivas Regal from the bottle into his glass, "I sort of miss the shouting I used to do with my first wife sometimes." But over all, Ray sounded pretty contented.

Amazingly, Ray had actually chosen to pursue a career in pediatric nephrology; after his residency he had done a fellowship in renal disease and, following that, had become a staff nephrologist at the University of Michigan. And he was eventually to become a world famous renal physiologist.

We could see St. A's rising in the distance, from a block or so away. "Look," Ray said as we made our approach, "it's just an old building."

"Alcatraz was just a building, too," Terry responded.

I parked the car and we went in. The whole place looked exactly as it had the day we had left. We walked through the lobby, the lobby Ray had been sitting in when Terry and I returned from follow-up clinic the day of our meeting with the hospital board; the same chairs were set in the same positions, the newspaper machines were dispensing the *Globe* and the *Herald American* in their same locations, it even seemed like, behind the information desk at the rear of the lobby, the same nun was there who had been there eight years before: I felt once again as if Alfred Hitchcock would step out at any moment.

We had arrived late, and when we reached the auditorium, the room in which combined neonatal/perinatal rounds had been held every Friday, was packed, with no seats to be had. We stood at the back of the room, listening to the speaker and searching the room. It had not been remodeled; it still resembled the masterpiece of a crazed and color-blind interior decorator. Here and there I spotted a person I knew: a guy from our internship group here, a nurse who had worked nights in the Pit there, but nobody I had any interest in talking to.

But then Ray nudged me and he pointed to a person seated way in the front. There in the third row was Simon Frohman. A little while later I saw who I thought was Kathy O'Connell, and I nudged Ray and pointed. He responded by nodding. But these were not the people I had come to see; and Dan Berkowitz was no where to be found.

We listened to the first talk on the program, a program which promised to be exceedingly boring. This first presentation was given by Dr. Manly, the current director of neonatology, who had replaced Sullivan the July we left Boston. She spoke in facts and figures, of mortality rates and admission rates, and about the changing epidemiological profile of hospital-acquired infections and . . . and on and on. If we hadn't been standing, I'm sure the three of us would have each fallen asleep, but instead we stood and listened. "Notice anything about her?" Ray asked.

"No," I replied, "unless you mean that she's cuter than Sullivan."

"Well, that goes without saying, but that's not it. She hasn't mentioned yet that in all of New England, along the entire eastern seaboard . . ."

". . . in fact, in the entire world . . ." I added.

"That the Pit's mortality rate is consistently the lowest."

"Right," I said.

"She must be sort of normal," Ray added.

The next speaker was Dr. Jennings, chairman emeritus of the Department of Pediatrics at the Boston Medical Center, a man who had scared us shitless during our stay at St. A's but with whom we had ultimately become friends, a man we had found we could trust. Jennings spoke about the history of St. A's, from the time of its founding through the reconstruction and then up to the present. But while Jennings was speaking, people began to exit from the auditorium to stand around in the hall outside and talk. At first people walked out singly, but steadily, larger and larger groups began to exit until there were just as many people outside as there were inside. People were beginning to realize that the symposium was not going to be so hot, but that it provided a chance to meet and become reacquainted with colleagues they had not seen for years.

Through direct conversation and/or rumor, we gleaned information about a number of people who had contributed to making our month at St. A's all that it was. Simon Frohman had spent five months as an inpatient at MacLean's Hospital in Belmont, Massachusetts, following his psychotic breakdown during the death of the Dead Kid. I had heard that upon completion of his hospitalization Simon had become a different person; he had become more assertive and, although still not one of the most creative people to ever carry a stethoscope, much more of a leader. He had taken the rest of that year off to recover and then had repeated his senior year. I had had no contact with Simon since the morning we had found him in a catatonic coma on the bed in his on-call room, and I did not speak with him at the reunion either, nor do I ever intend to try to find him again.

It seemed obvious that Tom Fredericks was headed for big trouble. Already on probation by the middle of July, Tom was canned in the second week of August after becoming involved in a fistfight outside DR 3 with, of course, Dr. Parris. Although I never got the whole story straight, I do know that he knocked Parris cold, and the elective section they had been scrubbing for had to be canceled. Tom, like Simon, took the rest of that year off and finally settled in Texas, where disillusioned with obstetrics, at least the way it was practiced in Boston, he left the field and became an anesthesiologist. Now working in Houston, Tom did not attend the symposium.

Kathy O'Connell, following her fight with Dr. Sullivan concerning James Casperson Stone III, was fired from the staff of St. A's in the middle of August. But before she left the Pit, Kathy had made a very important friend. At the conclusion of our month, Kathy had taken over the care of James Casperson III, much the same way as she had done with Freddie Endicott, and James Sr. loved her for it. Upon her release, he got her a job as director of pediatric nursing at the Boston General Hospital, which was one terrific job. It was as the director that she became a powerful administrator and, within a couple of years, rose to national prominence in nursing administration and education.

The sponsors of this reunion had, for whatever reason, failed to formally invite the many nurses who had worked in the Perinatal Center through the years since its inception. Whether this was intentional or accidental, it was a serious error; the nurses were the people who, day in and day out, made the nursery work, who were on the front lines, and who really saved our babies. And so through the symposium, I would get no news of what had become of Angela Meroni or Gloria Higgins or Maureen, or any of the other nurses who shared our nights on call and our days of stress.

Three people, highly important and influential to us during our month in the Pit, were nowhere to be found on that Saturday morning. The first was Parris. Three years before, during the height of the winter, Parris had been trying to shovel snow from his driveway so that he could get his Mercedes out of the garage and go to the hospital for one of his scheduled sections. In the middle of a big shovelful, he felt crushing chest pain and collapsed into the snow. His myocardial infarction had been massive, and he was pronounced dead on arrival at the Medical Center. In the months following his death, there was a dramatic decline in the rate of cesarean sections performed at the St. Anne Perinatal Center. The man was generating nearly 50 percent of the total figure himself.

John Sullivan had not shown up for the Saturday conference, but he was not dead. Dr. Sullivan had continued working at St. Anne's until the December after our rotation. At that time his contract was terminated; the official reason cited by the hospital board was that Dr. Sullivan had been involved in too many legal cases and that premiums on his malpractice insurance had skyrocketed, making it far too expensive for the hospital to retain his services any longer. He was replaced by an interim director, who served as neonatologist until July, when Dr. Manly took over.

Although this was the official reason for his firing, many rumors circulated about why Dr. Sullivan really was fired. The most popular theory suggested that an extremely large contribution had been offered to St. A's by an anonymous donor. The money was directed to be used at the discretion of the hospital board, the only stipulation being that the director of the Neonatal Intensive Care Unit must be someone other than John Sullivan.

Sullivan, despondent over being fired, searched the New England region for months but could not land another job in neonatology. His reputation, as they say, preceded him. Finally because he needed to support a wife and children, he settled for a job as a research physician for a Boston-based drug company. I was greatly relieved to hear that this man was no longer involved in making life-and-death decisions.

The third person missing during that first day of the symposium was Dan Berkowitz. Like the story surrounding Sullivan's dismissal, many rumors were circulating that day as to the whereabouts of Dan: some people said that they had heard he was a successful private practitioner in Long Island; others had him working as an academic gastroenterologist in California; more than one other story had him dead, from different means—a gunshot wound suffered while he was an innocent bystander in a supermarket holdup, a knife wound, gotten during a mugging, or, interestingly enough, a ruptured aorta following unsuccessful surgery for repair of a coarctation. But no one knew anything for sure. It made me kind of sad to realize that Dan, my senior resident during my first night on call, who had meant so much to me during a very important time in my training, had voluntarily or involuntarily vanished from my life.

After standing out in the hallway, listening to stories like these for a while, Ray, Terry, and I decided it might be fun to pay a visit to the Pit. We went up at around eleven. But fun was not exactly what it was.

When the elevator door opened, it was just like being an intern again. Walking into the nurses' station, looking through the window at the babies in the Pit, I was enveloped in the buzz of activity. It all started coming back to me, all at once, and I suddenly felt the urge to run from the room and blow lunch. Terry felt just like I did, but Ray didn't. He wanted to make rounds! He wanted to touch the sickies, he wanted to pass a UA line, to intubate. Ray wanted another chance.

On our way out, I lead Ray and Terry toward the on-call room. I had not seen it since it had been redone, thanks to the generosity of the Stone Foundation. It was in the same place it had been before. A sign on the door read "Bob Sharon Intern On-Call Room." Inside, it was much different from the room we used to sleep in. It had been expanded in two directions, using space previously allotted to the Pit. The cot we had slept on was replaced by a real bed with a firm mattress. There was a bookcase filled with texts pertinent to neonatology. There was a desk, light blue carpeting on the floor, and framed prints on the blue wall. Lying on the bed when we entered was, apparently, an intern. "Can I do something for you?" he asked.

"No," Ray answered, "we're just sort of looking."

"This place is restricted to interns," he said indignantly. "We don't allow the families of the babies in here."

"Families of babies?" Terry repeated. "Heaven forbid. Do you know who this guy is?" she asked, pointing to me.

"No," the guy answered. "Who is he?"

"He's Bob Sharon!" Terry said proudly.

The intern thought about this for a minute or so. "Bob Sharon? The name sounds familiar. Do I know you from somewhere? You sell me insurance about a year ago?"

"Insurance?" Terry yelled. "This is the Bob Sharon Intern On-Call Room! Didn't you ever read the sign on the door?"

Giving her a nasty look, the guy rose from the bed, walked to the door, looking at us the whole time, opened the door, and looked at the sign. "Yep," he said, "it is the Bob Sharon On-Call Room. Well congratulations, Bob. You have a wonderful name!" He went back to the bed.

Ray, Terry, and I broke up into hysterics. "These interns," Terry said. "What a barrel of laughs they are." And we left.

We decided to get the hell out of St. A's at that point. The rest of the symposium was going to be a real bore. We just wanted to talk and have some lunch, so we went back to the hotel and decided to eat in a restaurant there.

We had just ordered when a slightly familiar looking woman approached our table. I knew I had seen her somewhere before, but I just couldn't place her. She was attractive, was about our age, had short, dark brown hair, and a pleasant face. "Ray?" she asked as she reached us.

"Yes?" Ray asked, turning to look at her.

"Ray, don't you know me?"

Ray looked at her for a minute, his face turning redder with embarrassment at not recognizing her as every second passed, until finally he realized who it was. "Lauren?" he asked, his voice reaching a very high pitch.

"I thought you guys might be here for this!" Lauren said. "I was hoping I'd run into you. It's been a long time."

"It sure has," Ray said, still slightly confused. "Scuse me for not recognizing you right away. You look so . . . different."

"Different?" she asked. "Oh, you haven't seen me since I let my hair go natural. It really has been a long time. I've had dark hair for five or six years now."

"What are you doing, Lauren?" I asked, astounded that this was really Lauren.

"I'm working in Boston," she said. "I'm working as a pediatrician for the National Health Service. I have an office in Roxbury."

"No kidding?" I said. "How long have you been doing that?"

"Oh, since . . . what . . . a year and a half since I finished my residency."

"You ever do a renal fellowship?" Terry asked.

"No. I realized a lot of things near the end of my residency. I never really wanted to be a nephrologist. I didn't even want to be a doctor. I just wanted to make my father happy. It's a lucky thing I found out that if I relaxed about the whole thing, being a doctor was a lot of fun. I mean, I follow a lot of families, I like seeing the kids grow up and seeing how they cope with the world. It gives me a good feeling. And I feel pretty good about myself. What are you doing, Ray?"

Ray laughed to himself. "I've been waiting to say this to you for a long time, Lauren. I'm a nephrologist at the University of Michigan." He said this last line with a straight face.

Lauren broke out laughing. "You are kidding this time, aren't you? You're not really a nephrologist are you?"

"Not only is Ray a nephrologist," I answered, "but he's a world famous renal physiologist." We all broke out laughing.

"You just trying to get me into bed, Ray? Because it's not going to work this time!" Lauren smiled. After speaking with us for a few minutes more, she went off to rejoin the people with whom she was having lunch.

"Amazing!" Ray said after she was gone. "Eight years ago I loved that woman!"

"No you didn't, Ray," I said. "That Lauren and the one you loved are two separate people. Personally, I like this one a lot better!"

Sunday, June 17, 1984

The picnic was scheduled to begin at noon. Ray, Terry, and I decided to have breakfast in the hotel, check out of our rooms, and leave for the picnic at about twelve-fifteen. The weekend had flown by.

When I was checking out of my room, the hotel clerk asked, "Are you Dr. Sharon?"

I told him that I was.

"We have a message for you. A phone call. It came this morning." He handed me a folded slip of paper. The message written on the paper said:

> Dear Bob, Terry, and Ray,
> Sorry I can't be with you today.
> Have a nice time at the picnic.
> I'm proud of you all.

And the name attached to it was Dan Berkowitz.

"When did this come?" I asked excitedly. "Did he leave a number where he could be reached? Did he say where he was?"

"Hold on, hold on," the clerk said. "The time should be written at the top of the page. And if it ain't on that paper, the guy didn't say it!"

"Is there any way of tracing the call?" I asked anxiously.

The clerk looked at me as if I were crazy. "Doc, are you kidding?" he asked. "You know how many calls we got since that one came in? There ain't a snowball's chance in hell we could trace that one!"

"But can't we . . ."

"Take it easy, Bob," Terry interrupted, trying to calm me down. "Maybe he'll call back. If he does, maybe he'll leave a number the next time."

"And besides," Ray added, "at least we know he's all right!"

"Yeah," I said more calmly. "You guys are probably right. Maybe he wants to stay hidden. Maybe this was his way of letting us know everything's okay with him."

The picnic was held at a park across the street and about a block away from St. A's. At the entrance to the park, a nun was handing out blank name tags. She gave us one each. As instructed, Ray, Terry, and I wrote in our names and the month and year in which we served as slaves in the Pit.

It was a beautiful summer day. The park was filled with children, some of them normal, many of them with noticeable handicaps, all of them patients at one time or another in the Pit. At one end of the park, a large barbecue pit had been constructed. A cook from the hospital's cafeteria was serving up hamburgers and hot dogs. Throughout the rest of the park, around cardboard signs on which a year had been written, nests of picnic tables were arranged. Ray, Terry, and I naturally migrated immediately to the sign that read "1976."

We were surrounded by a group of eight-year-old children and their parents. I was approached immediately by a little girl, who walked with a mild limp, but who looked otherwise totally normal. I looked at her name tag. It read "Danielle Summlitz."

This was Baby Summlitz, the first patient I was assigned when I entered the Pit on that Monday morning in late June. The baby had been suspected of having an intracranial hemorrhage, but she showed no signs now of having suffered a neurologic catastrophe.

Danielle was holding her mother's hand. I introduced myself to Mrs. Summlitz, who had aged considerably since I had last seen her. My introduction, however, was unnecessary.

"I know who you are, Dr. Sharon," she said. "How do you like my little girl?"

"She's beautiful!" I said. "It's amazing!"

"This is your first picnic, isn't it, Dr. Sharon?"

"Yes it is," I answered.

"Well, you're in for a lot of amazing sights! Danielle and I would like to thank you again, Dr. Sharon. Thank you for helping my little girl be so good!"

I was touched. Danielle was certainly a beautiful sight. "I can't get over it," I said to myself, as the Summlitzes and I parted. I walked to Ray and Terry and said, "You guys see that kid over there? That's Baby Summlitz!"

"That's nothing, Bob!" Terry answered. "Look at this little one!" Terry was kneeling and talking to a child who had multiple scars on her neck. "Dr. Sharon," she said formally, "I'd like you to meet Jennifer Rose."

"Baby Rose?" I asked.

"One and the same!" Terry answered with delight. "Listen! Jennifer, tell this other doctor what you just told me!"

The child spoke in a raspy, hoarse voice, the result of many, many surgical manipulations of the airway and larynx, but what she said came out clearly understandably, and it was a more beautiful sound than if it had been sung by Beverly Sills. "My mommy, my daddy, and I want to thank you very much!" Baby Rose said.

"Oh God!" I uttered, putting my arms around Terry and this little girl. "I think I'm going to cry."

"Jennifer, do you know this doctor sat up with you one night when you were a little baby, when you were very, very sick?"

"My mommy, my daddy, and I want to thank you very, very much!" Baby Rose repeated again, this time with a little more feeling. Ray, Terry, and I laughed.

I gave Jennifer a hug again and then felt a tapping on my shoulder. I turned and there stood Mr. and Mrs. O'Hara and Sharon Frederica. "You finally showed up at one of these things!" Mrs. O'Hara said.

"I'm so glad to see you!" I said, gushing with emotion. This was all getting ridiculously mushy, but we were eating it up!

Sharon Frederica now had the typical stigmata of a child with Down syndrome. She was clearly developmentally delayed, but she had grown well and probably was functioning at the level of a normal five or six year old. "How's my girl doing?" I asked.

"She's doing pretty well, Dr. Sharon," Mrs. O'Hara said. "We got her toilet trained, she can count to fifty, she knows the alphabet, she can spell her name . . . Sharon, how do you spell your name?"

"S . . . H . . . A . . . R . . . O . . . N," came the reply, slowly, tediously, but correctly.

"Great!" I said.

"Sharon, do you know who this man is?" Mr. O'Hara asked his daughter.

"No," came her reply.

"This is Dr. Sharon. You're named after him!"

"I am?" she asked.

"Dr. Sharon, we haven't found a doctor who's as good with little Sharon here as you were," Mrs. O'Hara said. "We're sorry you moved out of Boston. You doing okay?"

"Yeah," I answered, "I'm doing fine."

"You have any children yet?" Mrs. O'Hara asked.

"Yes I do," I answered. "We have a little girl."

"Oh that's fine," Mrs. O'Hara said, "that's just fine."

We spoke for a few more minutes, and then got separated in the crush of children. That afternoon we saw just about all the children who survived, intact or just about intact, the month we spent at St. A's. Ray, Terry, and I were riding high on this wave of emotion. This was really what being a doctor was all about! Only Ray presented anything resembling a sobering thought.

"You know, this sort of is a skewed picture of what really happened that month," he said at around three-thirty.

"What do you mean?" I asked.

"Well, these kids, these are the ones who made it. This is the best we do. The dead kids and the kids who live at the Waltham Home, they don't show up at these picnics."

"Yeah, Ray," I answered him. "But look at these guys. If we didn't do what we did, all of these kids would be living in the Waltham Home or worse. These kids legitimize us!"

"I guess you're right," Ray said. "That sounds pretty good." And he repeated that line, "they legitimize us!"

The party was beginning to break up around four o'clock. But two events were still to occur. At four, a large, black limousine pulled up to the front of the park and, out of the back doors, came all three James Casperson Stones, along with the child's mother. Upon entering the park, this parade immediately approached the sign reading "1976" and, upon reaching the group of 1976 graduates, Mr. James Casperson Stone, Sr., headed directly for me.

"Dr. Sharon," he said, tapping me on the shoulder. I turned around to look at him.

"Mr. Stone," I said with some surprise. He offered me his hand and I shook it. "Dr. Sharon, I'd like you to meet my grandson."

James Casperson Stone III came forward in a blue blazer, a white shirt and blue striped tie, blue shorts, and knee socks. He already looked like a member of the junior chamber of commerce. "Pleased to meet you, Dr. Sharon," he said clearly and distinctly.

"It's an honor to see you," I responded, "but I'm a little surprised to see all of you here."

"Dr. Sharon, we came here today expressly for the purpose of seeing you again," James Sr. said. "It's been eight years since my grandson was born. You can see, he's grown into a fine young man."

"That's for sure," I replied.

"And he owes it all to you. We want to thank you again."

"Mr. Stone, as I told you at that time, I was only doing my job."

"Well, as I told you at that time, that's not the way I see it. Eight years ago I offered to be of any help to you I could, but you've never taken me up on my offer. The statute of limitations on that offer is nearly up; for the last time, is there anything I can do for you?"

As I had done eight years before, I thought about this offer, and just as I had done at that time, I said no.

"All right then. Dr. Sharon, it has been a pleasure seeing you again. Don't be such a stranger to Boston. As you know, you have an open invitation to come and visit our family anytime you like." He turned to leave and his entourage followed.

"Oh, Mr. Stone?" I called after them, remembering the one question I wanted to ask. Simultaneously, to the sound of my voice, the heads of James Casperson Stone, Sr., Jr., and III turned. "Yes?" James Sr. asked, reapproaching me.

"There is one question I wanted to ask you."

"Yes?" he asked.

"Dr. Sullivan's firing. Did you . . . . ?" I didn't have to finish the sentence.

With a smile on his face, James Sr. asked, "What do you think?"

"I think yes," I answered.

He smiled again. "Think of it as a little present to you and the other guys who were there that month! The guy had it coming!"

"He sure did!" I said.

The crowd was beginning to thin out when Dr. Sullivan finally made his appearance. He stood alone, under a tree. He had not aged gracefully. His hair was all white now, and he was much fatter than he had been during the summer of our internship. He had deep lines around his eyes and across his forehead. I figured I'd say hello.

"Dr. Sullivan?" I said as I put out my hand. "How are you doing?"

He looked at my face and couldn't quite place it. "Fine," he said. "I'm sorry. I know I know you, but I can't remember your name."

"I'm Sharon," I said. "Bob Sharon."

A smile came to Sullivan's lips. "Oh yeah!" he said. "You're Sharon. You were one of those troublemakers! You're one of the guys who went to the hospital board, aren't you?"

I nodded yes.

"Do you know I came that close," he held the index finger of his left hand very close to his left thumb, "to having you three fired? But I guess I didn't have to. You three got yourselves kicked out of the Medical Center by the end of your internships anyway, didn't you?"

He left time for me to answer, but I didn't. There was no need to correct his facts.

"Tell me, Dr. Sharon," he finally continued, "did you ever find another job?" He said this with bitter sarcasm in his voice.

I had waited for this opportunity for a long time. I had practiced it, rehearsed it out loud when I was alone in my car or in the shower. The revenge, I had thought, would be sweet when it would come, but now, standing in front of this pathetic old man who had lost everything that was important to him, I just felt pity. "Yes, I did," I finally answered. "I'm working at Einstein Medical School now. I'm a neonatologist. I'm director of the nursery at the Jonas Bronck Hospital."

Sullivan blanched and lost his smile. "Well, I guess we taught you something about neonatology that month," he said after a moment's hesitation, and he turned away, with tears forming in his eyes, not giving me a chance to respond.

I've thought about what I would have said to Sullivan had he stayed in his place. "Yes," I would have said, "yes, I did learn a great deal about neonatology that month. I learned the most important lesson: I learned to trust my own instincts, and those who earn trust, but to trust very little else."